CHOKEPOINT

A NOVEL

John P. Morse

IDLEKNOT PRESS

This is a work of fiction taking place in the near future. Names, characters, places and incidents are the product of the author's imagination or are used fictionally. Any resemblance to actual events, locales or persons, living or dead is entirely coincidental.

www.johnpmorse.com
Idleknot Press
Morse, John P.

Chokepoint

ISBN 978-0-9976450-2-6 (paperback)

ISBN 978-0-9976450-3-3 (eBook)

Cover Design/Artwork by Eric VanGronigen

Formatting Design by Madeline Silva

ALSO BY JOHN P. MORSE

Half Staff 2018

To Carole,

My wife, my North Star, and my best friend

I Corinthians 13

PART I

CHAPTER ONE

Antalya, Turkey

Dan Steele had difficulty blending into a crowd. On the sleepy waterfront in Antalya, his presence was obvious since it was late fall, and the tourists had left. His six-foot three-inch frame dwarfed the people walking along the ancient harbor. Wearing blue jeans and a pullover sweatshirt emblazoned with the crest of UPPA, the University of Pau and Pays de l'Adour, he didn't have that carefree look of a sightseer. A cool sea breeze flattened the fabric against his body, outlining broad shoulders and a narrow waist, not the physique of a sedentary office worker on low season holiday. As he walked, all his senses were tuned to his surroundings: the smoothed cobble stones under his feet, idle talk between deck hands, fishy smell of seawater, the rainbow sheen of oil roiling between the boats moored stern first against the stone-walled quay and the people passing by, working, relaxing, and restless.

Spotting *Iklim* painted in large gold-leafed letters across a raised wooden planked stern built with a row of windows, he continued past the boat. He fished a bottle of water from a vendor's washtub, checked its plastic seal, and selected a round, seed-covered pretzel from a circular stack piled on a disk balanced on a young man's head. Sitting on the faded blue wooden slats of a wrought iron bench about 100 feet away from the ketch, he watched people. Stretching his legs out straight, he ran his hand through a head of thick dark hair and rubbed the stubble which had sprouted on his face during the overnight international flight to Ankara and the domestic connection to Antalya.

Hundreds of fishing boats converted for tourist cruising on the Aegean and Mediterranean Seas were available for charter, with a captain, cook and a single deckhand doubling as waiter, bartender, and storyteller every evening after anchoring in one of the quiet, secluded coves that lined the azure sea along Turkey's coastlines. Most of the boats appeared to have used the same designer. Formally known as a Gulet, the two-masted sailing vessel was eighty feet long and almost twenty-four feet across the beam.

Iklim boasted a number of hidden modifications, decidedly not added to attract tourists. A team of US Navy engineers had upgraded the ketch with a gas turbine engine, deck-mounted tripods to support large caliber machine guns, an armory, and three iron-barred cells the size of oversized dog cages. A modern communications suite was disguised into the topside structure. The after deck could accommodate a sixteen-foot Zodiac rubber boat built to military specifications. Though it flew the flag of Turkey, the captain and crew were Turkish-born US citizens paid in local currency converted from a check drawn from the United States Treasury.

After another round of stretching, Steele added the remainder of the pretzel and empty plastic bottle to an overflowing trashcan before meandering along the edge of the quay wall to *Iklim*. Walking up the steep, narrow metal gangway hanging from its stern, he ducked under a bleached canvas awning rigged to cover the after part of the deck. Steele strode on the solid planks and disappeared through a midships wooden door that opened to a different world.

The darkened main cabin featured a bank of full color screens depicting the eastern Mediterranean Sea and the countries abutting its shores. Two data terminals flanking the screens processed surveillance information from ships, aircraft, submarines and satellites operating in the region. All-source intelligence reports overlaid the symbols and kept two console operators busy maintaining a coherent operational picture.

Steele studied one of the displays and saw the familiar symbols for US Navy and Allied ships and submarines. One unknown surface track near the coast of Syria attracted his attention.

"Do you have anything on track S42?"

"No, we think it's a Russian destroyer operating in support of the Coastal Defense missile system they are putting into Aleppo. The carrier has a surveillance asset headed that way, and we should have a positive ID within the hour. The chatter is mostly Russian with some alternating Arabic thrown in from time to time. Probably a translation."

"Thanks. Is Rami aboard?"

"Right here, Dan," said a burly man with a lustrous black beard emerging from behind a blackout curtain that shielded the rest of the cabin's lights.

"Rami, it's been a long time. How are you, my friend?"

"Still vertical and breathing. Life is good. No complaints. And how about you?"

"Anxious to get underway."

"Always the way. Follow me, and I'll show you to your cabin."

Rami opened the polished mahogany door identified by a simple oval brass disk displaying the numeral 1. The cabin had a built-in berth with a small sink and mirror, a stand-up locker and a porthole open to the sea. Rami put his hand on Dan's shoulder.

"I was very sorry to hear about the tragedy in Virginia that took your wife and two sons. My family was looking forward to your visit last year. I heard nothing from you and thought something must be wrong. One of your colleagues told me the story.

"The worst day of my life," he choked out the words, suddenly looking away, his eyes glistening with tears.

Knowing that he'd inflamed a raw nerve lying just beneath the surface of Steele's confident exterior, Rami moved quickly from the subject.

"Maybe after the mission you can spend a few days in Antalya. You're always welcome."

"I'd like that." said Steele.

"Good. How would you like a cup of my Turkish coffee?"

"Yes, as long as you promise not to read the grounds," Steele forced a laugh.

Rami's face beamed. He ardently practiced this ancient tradition but had a widely-known reputation for his predictions being consistently wrong.

"I'll put on the kettle," Rami said.

"Thanks. It will help me with the jet lag. Give me three minutes, and I'll see you in the galley."

Steele gripped the sides of the small stainless-steel basin and looked at his face in the small mirror. His face was sad, drawn and forlorn. His red-rimmed eyes wouldn't fool anyone. He should have been here in Turkey with Jill. As he studied his reflection, his mouth contorted in grim determination. Now was not the time for self-pity. However painful, he had to wall off those emotions deep inside his soul and hidden from view.

Others arrived throughout the day. Once aboard, they remained below decks. By late afternoon, Rami and the young mate appeared topside. The diesel engines growled to life, and they cast off the lines and maneuvered the ketch from between two of its cousins. After clearing the harbor, the passengers emerged for some fresh air. The mood was relaxed and friendly, and the men swapped stories about their circuitous travel to Antalya.

After a meal of grilled lamb kabobs and fresh fish, they watched the sun drop into the western horizon over the stern and then gathered below decks around a large blueprint of the objective area. All were accustomed to special operations missions. Several were active duty SEALs that had temporarily discarded their identities. Four supporting communications and intelligence experts rounded out the team.

What they had conceived after weeks of planning and refined during practice raids on a mock-up in the Arizona desert was ready to be executed. Along the way, Steele solicited the team's ideas on how best to accomplish the mission, and none were reluctant to provide unvarnished input. He knew each of them well. They were ready. For what seemed like the hundredth time, he reviewed the approach, timeline, assignments and discussed several contingency questions with confidence. Steele had a reputation for being over-prepared and that included having thought through all the things that could possibly go wrong.

Though no longer wearing a Navy uniform, his exploits as an active duty SEAL elevated the level of trust between the team-members. The details of most special operations were highly classified, but the cadre of men and women fighting the United States' other wars knew the service reputations of the brave souls who fought them.

The team's mission was to capture a bomb-maker who instructed eager students at an international terrorist training camp sited on the Mediterranean Sea in eastern Turkey near the border with Syria. It was an ideal location, since those studying the craft were able to put their learning into practice just a few miles away from the classroom. Sponsored by Hezbollah, the school opened its doors to screened students from any country where Shia terrorists were actively spreading fear through explosives. Forty apprentices were enrolled to learn the deadly craft from an expert.

As the sun rose, the men assembled topside, limbering muscles that would be tested later that day. The cook prepared a breakfast of fresh fruit, yogurt, smoked fish, skewered beef, eggs, white cheese and oblong flatbread. Small bowls filled with roasted hazelnuts and brined olives lined one side of the table.

After breakfast, they selected weapons according to their individual tastes from the armory. Steele chose a Heckler & Koch MP5K machine gun and disassembled it on a small square of canvas spotted with oil. He inspected the moving parts, cleaning and lubricating the gun as he reassembled it.

He opened an envelope which contained two throwing knives made of Brazilian walnut, known as Ipe, a dense tightly grained hardwood more than three times stronger than American Black Walnut. The knives were hand-crafted by a retired Army Ranger who found Ipe's strength, balance and accuracy rivaled the titanium blades favored by those wanting something lightweight and extremely strong. Steele found the center-balanced knives the most versatile, able to be thrown by the blade or the grip. The eight-ounce weight carried enough force to stop any target with a quiet lethality that made them perfect for this type of mission.

The coastal traffic had lightened after the high summer season, and just a few other boats were sighted during the 30-hour diesel transit that followed the uneven coastline staying well to the north of Cyprus. *Iklim* drifted several miles northwest of the objective area just off the old Turkish city of Samandag. As expected, a dark, moonless night fell over the coastal waters. Within an hour, the men launched the rubber boat into the dead calm water, while *Iklim* headed off-shore towards the finger-like projection of Northern Cyprus' easternmost landmass. Lying atop the inflated gunwales and clad in black, eight commandos landed and carried the inflatable up the wide beach to the base of a date palm rustling gently in a light breeze.

The coxswain remained with the boat and two of the men carried an assortment of explosives to defend the flanks. The other five followed the high-water mark to a stand of palm trees fifty yards from their objective: a low Bedouin tent staked into the sand. Until now, they'd only seen it from satellite imagery. Air-conditioned, it was thought to be the local equivalent of a Western man-cave, likely outfitted with large screen TVs, a refrigerator and perhaps a microwave. A generator behind a nearby cinder-block building housing the resident students and armed security staff fed power to the retreat.

Intelligence estimated that ten to twelve of the instructors and staff usually spent evenings together, and the target should be among them. After taking several minutes to observe the surroundings using night vision goggles, Steele was ready.

Through a lip microphone, he whispered to his team, "OK, guys, here we go. We get the package and haul ass out of here." He raised the short, lightweight, silenced machine gun to the firing position, hoping surprise would be sufficient to complete the mission without using it, recalling the oft-quoted warning of a famous field marshal in Prussian army: "No battle plan ever survives first contact with the enemy." The only contact he wanted was to snatch the bomb-maker and immobilize the others with plastic handcuffs and duct tape. A small knot grew in Steele's throat as it usually did before showtime.

Two men advanced to positions on either side of the tent. One sliced a small hole in the thick woven fabric and slowly pushed a tiny wire-mounted camera inside. He turned a Vernier dial with his fingers, panning the room and zooming in on the people and the interior layout. The interior surveillance seemed like it took hours, but no one liked surprises. If nothing else, it was thorough. They all waited patiently.

The cameraman finally spoke into his microphone, "Nine guys on the south and east side. Weapons stacked near entry point at the north and a couple of pistol belts hanging on a clothes tree just to the left. Just laughing and scratching and smoking hubbly-bubbly. Local news is on one TV, and a soccer match is playing on the other."

"OK. We're on the move," said Steele as the three men moved to their positions.

After a quiet approach from the north, Steele pulled back one side of the tent's entry flap and stepped through, flanked by two of the team, weapons leveled at the group.

"Show me your hands, now!" His words were translated into Arabic by the man on his right. As their eyes panned the room, the two other team-members entered from the southern side, weapons ready. Lounging on low overstuffed couches and bolsters, with their sandals scattered on a thick floor of hand-woven carpets, five wore tactical uniforms and the others wore the traditional thobe, a neck to ankle robe. Window air conditioners mounted on frames built into the canvas walls hummed in the background, swirling the sweet-smelling smoke from two hookahs.

Steele took a step forward and asked, "Where is Abu Sayed?" He looked at the eyes of the men as no one answered the question. The Intelligence Community had only a name and no photo. Steele was playing a potentially dangerous game of "Will the real Abu Sayed please stand up?" The eyes of one robe and one uniform unconsciously identified the man seated in the middle of the group, somewhat younger than the others and clean-shaven. Wearing a white long-sleeved robe, sitting cross-legged and leaning against a floral bolster, he knew that he'd been fingered. The younger man shifted his body and responded, "Here's Abu Sayed," as he pulled the pin on a grenade and pitched it towards the trio.

The operator to Steele's right pulled a hefty uniformed man to his feet and drove him to the ground on top of the grenade as it exploded, spattering everything with a warm red froth. Bolting for a side entrance, the grenade thrower was spun around and floored as two 9mm rounds from Steele's MP5K hit his upper right shoulder. The others held their hands high in the air and watched in stunned silence, glued to their seats as an alarm sounded in the distance. Lights winked on in the barracks, and a warning came through Steele's earpiece: "looks like someone just sounded reveille."

Steele strode across the room and roughly grabbed the grenade thrower and brought him to his feet. The loungers were pushed to one corner of the tent by two of the team.

"Yalla," he yelled to the team, pushing the man ahead of him.

A watchkeeper shaped charge was set in front of the group to guard them: any movement or sound would be detected in the sensor's 45-degree beam and detonate the device. A green lamp flashed with a steady beat. Huddled together, they looked like they were posing for a graduation photo.

"Remember, don't move," cautioned the last commando as he turned to leave. The team doubled-timed back towards the beach with their captive.

Five seconds later, an explosion rocked the night as the electronic sentry did its job. Truck headlights pierced the darkness and headed towards the tent. Steele's earpiece crackled, "Looks like the hornets are swarming." Four hundred yards to go, and they ran hard in the loose sand. Light pick-up trucks fitted with fifty caliber machine guns and armed trainees drove to intercept the intruders on the beach. A trip wire rigged 200 yards to one side of the landing point triggered a string of explosives, and the trucks' tires detonated anti-personnel mines seeded to protect the path to the sea. The three men assigned to secure the escape route fired a barrage of tube launched grenades. Though fitted with a lightweight engine and a small fuel bladder, carrying a 500-pound inflatable in the sand and simultaneously firing at a pursuing enemy had not been part of the plan.

While the explosive devices halted the major assault, one truck got through the perimeter unscathed and continued to pursue the uninvited visitors. The raiders fired more grenades to slow the hornet's progress. Steele shoved the captive into the boat and jumped over its inflated walls into the forward section, and the engine whined as the team launched and propelled to sea. A single heavy machine gun pumped rounds at the waterborne raiders with a deadly cadence. With a maximum range of three miles for the fifty caliber machine guns, they would remain in its killing zone for several long minutes. One round ripped through the mid-ships' inflation chamber, lodging in the aluminum deck plate. After running at full throttle for ten minutes, Steele motioned the coxswain to slow down.

"Roll call," said Steele. The men responded in order. Everyone was OK except for the Chief who pushed the uniformed man onto the grenade. He described the several deep shrapnel lacerations to his legs as cuts from shaving his legs. Steele shook his head with the dark humor.

"Doc, take care of the Chief first and then see what kind of damage our prisoner has to his shoulder. Just keep him alive."

They continued in complete darkness. Standing well offshore,

Iklim's gas turbine engine pushed the ketch at 30 knots closing to recover the raiders.

"Hey boss," said the corpsman. "The Chief will need a few stitches when we get back to the ranch. I've applied a compression bandage and stopped the bleeding. Our passenger is in shock but stable. Don't think you hit anything critical."

"OK, good."

"Just one more thing. Did you know this big bad terrorist is really a she?"

CHAPTER TWO

Moscow, Russia

"This situation in Kerch is starting to annoy me," said the man seated at the end of a small conference table. He picked up his coffee cup, studied the dark surface of the contents and stared at the men lining the table's sides. "Perhaps the people of the city need to be reminded we annexed Crimea years ago in response to a popular referendum and control much of the Ukraine today. We have bent over backwards to mollify these simple, misguided farmers, and now they have set up camp in the center of town and intend to stay there until independence can be restored. How naïve can some people be? So, how do we quickly persuade them to abandon this hopeless protest and get back in line?"

"Yes comrade, we could send some of our destroyers to the port as a show of force."

The man at the end of the conference room knew that the only recommendation from the thick-skulled Admiral would be a naval option. Saltwater must have addled the man's brains. Reluctant to dictate the next steps to this group of so-called advisers, he hoped at least one of them would offer a more creative solution. He responded to the Admiral, whose uniform was dripping with gold braid with a large section of the dark blue cloth dedicated to a vast array of colorful medals awarded for lasting 38 years in the service of the Soviet Navy.

"That's a good option, Admiral, but I fear that the time to prepare the naval force will permit the protests to continue. Things will become more complicated with time, and the press will get interested in the story. I'm certain you agree with this reasoning. So, I believe that we need a quick response with boots on the ground. Other ideas, gentlemen?"

After a further forty-five minutes of unproductive chatter, the man at the end of the table delicately summed up the meeting.

"Given the broad range of creative ideas on how to respond to our countrymen in Kerch, I will recommend to the State Secretary the immediate dispatch of a small Alpha Group team to restore order. Thank you very kindly for your thoughts and suggestions. Our meeting is adjourned."

Days later, the Alpha Group directorate met to discuss the operation.

"Gentlemen," said General Yuri Urodov. "You've all read the State Secretary's directive to Alpha Group to quell the disturbance in Kerch. I have some initial thoughts but would like to hear your ideas on how to best approach this situation."

A massive uniformed man sitting on the right of the table between two colleagues offered a quick response, "Tell the Navy to carry a company of our crack Army regulars down there to implore the people to end their protest."

The small group roared with laughter until some of the men at the table were actually brought to tears. Unamused, General Urodov sat patiently at the head of the table and offered an indulgent smile waiting for order to be restored. He took several long drags on the unfiltered cigarette that stained his fingers yellow. Constant exposure to tobacco smoke cast his face with a waxen, jaundiced appearance.

"Thank you, General Zlodeyev, for that less than helpful suggestion. As you already know, that option is off the table. Are there other ideas?" His voice signaled that the time for frivolity was over, and he expected everyone to get down to the serious business at hand. He stabbed out his cigarette to underscore his unhappiness with the general's sarcastic response.

"General," said Zlodeyev, "I apologize for my outburst and silly suggestion to send the Navy and Army. The situation in Kerch is clearly a mission for this team, as the Minister so rightly decided. If I may offer a more thoughtful suggestion, I propose the following." The lights dimmed, and the large screen came alive with a detailed presentation of an operation planned with meticulous care.

"Very impressive work, General," Urodov said, dismissing the plan and its creator by asking, "are there any other ideas from the group?"

There were none.

"Very well. I will study General Zlodeyev's recommendation along with some courses of action I have developed. Please let me know if there is any reason why you and your teams could not execute this plan or something similar in the next three weeks. That is all."

Urodov closed his thick leather planner and waited for his commanders to leave before returning to his large desk. Lighting another cigarette, he began thinking how he could make this minor military operation an embarrassment for Nikolai Zlodeyev, the man who suggested the plan and the man Urodov would assign to carry it out.

CHAPTER THREE

Mediterranean Sea

While the crew retrieved the boat using a portable davit on *Iklim's* afterdeck, the Chief and prisoner were carried down to the galley where tables were rotated on their bases and joined into a makeshift trauma ward. The corpsman scrubbed and pulled on a pair of surgical gloves, irrigating the Chief's legs with sterile water and then scrubbing the wounds with a sponge packaged with germ-killing hexachlorophene. He deftly administered a tetanus booster shot and used a disposable syringe to inject a local anesthetic into the three deep wounds requiring sutures. The Chief joked that he had a future as a leg model before the raid and now his chances were slim to none.

With the preps completed, the corpsman turned to the prisoner, who was strapped to the table with four plastic tie wraps. He cut away the blood-stained thobe at her waist and the cotton undershirt covering her torso, removing the compression bandages impregnated with silver nitrate applied during the transit from the beach. The bleeding had stopped. Her eyes were still fluttering with shock as he examined the gunshot wounds on her right shoulder, cutting the plastic tie wrap so that he could examine both sides. Because the bullets entered from her upper back, there were clean holes through her shoulder blade, and the exit wounds indicated that the bullets passed through without being deflected by other bones. The collarbone seemed intact as the bullets passed through her body between the collarbone and her small right breast. Holding her on her left side, he irrigated the wounds then injected anesthetic on both sides before probing as deep as he could to find any metal fragments that might have been left along the bullets' path, finding none. Finally, he hung an IV bag over the patient. Her eyes opened.

"I'm going to open a vein to give you some fluids for the shock and an antibiotic."

She stared at the corpsman and asked in well-spoken English with a faint British accent, "Aren't you going to rape me first?"

"No, that is not part of the procedure. I am here to treat you medically. How bad is your pain?"

"The pain of being captured by infidels is intense. The bullet wounds are an annoyance."

"Are you injured any other place?"

"No."

"Good, please hold your arm in this position so I can start the IV."

Iklim paralleled the Turkish coast on its diesels in a darkened ship condition without the customary navigation lights. Rami expected little traffic for the rest of the night. One of the intelligence officers came on deck while the team was stowing gear with the aid of muted red lights.

"Hey, Steele, what were you thinking? The objective of this raid was to capture Abu Sayed, not his mistress."

"Look, you sent us in to find the tango without a mugshot or even a description. And because none of these guys was wearing a name tag or party hat, I guessed the one who attacked us had something more to lose or gain by not being captured. I don't have ESP. We didn't find out he was really a she until we were on the boat headed back. Let's hope she knows more than you think."

"Yeah, maybe she does, something significant like the size of Abu Sayed's crank. It's not going to be easy explaining this operation up the chain. Our overseas facilities are not equipped to handle women, so this is going to be a major problem. Seems to me that this operation was a complete bust."

Steele turned and stopped in front of the man. "I've heard enough of your initial assessment. I recommend that you strike below before a freak wave washes you overboard."

"Are you threatening me, Steele?"

"No, I wouldn't do that. I was just telling you a sea story. Strange, unexpected things sometime happen up here on the weather deck." The man returned below-decks without another word.

Energized by their investigative success with the journalist killed in the Saudi consulate in Istanbul, the Turkish authorities responded quickly to an emergency call and descended on the bomb-maker's training camp before Dan Steele finished stripping off his all-black nylon stretch pajamas. They cordoned off the crime scene and called for more resources to examine the area for clues.

Steele pulled on a pair of jeans and a t-shirt and walked to the trauma ward. With three new stitch lines on his legs, the Chief lay on his back sleeping on the table. The corpsman was packing the prisoner's gunshot wounds. Her dark eyes were open and staring at a distant object somewhere in space. The IV needle was taped to her lower left arm. Steele noticed her arm below the elbow was badly burned, the leathery, mottled flesh twisted after being cooked by fire. He wondered if this burn had been caused by scalding liquid or perhaps an accident with a bomb.

"How did it go?" Steele asked.

"No problem. The Chief will be fine. He can walk out of here when he wakes up." Steele noticed that the Chief and the corpsman were still wearing the long black pajamas from the operation. "The woman is out of the woods. She needs to have these drains advanced daily as the hole fills in. She's been pumped full of antibiotics but will require regular care for proper healing. Maybe we can find a rack somewhere on the boat for her to rest instead of moving her to one of the cells. She speaks English fluently."

"Thanks Doc, great work. I'll ask Rami about a berth where she can rest and be secured at the same time."

Steele went to the operations center and slid into a swivel chair bolted to the deck at a communications terminal. There were two digital clocks over the console reflecting local time and one for the current time — 7:45 a.m. — in Washington, DC. He jotted down a few bullet points on a sheet of paper and dialed the secure telephone that would ring on Admiral Wright's desk.

"Morning Admiral," said Steele after the handset was picked up. "I hope I'm not calling too early."

"No, I've been in the office for over an hour. Everyone's got his hair on fire about what happened over in Turkey, and the morning news is all over it."

"News travels fast. Here's a quick summary: First, the team is in one piece with some minor injuries. Second, we have a prisoner aboard with non-life-threatening gunshot wounds. Third, the clandestine raid we planned went off the rails when the prisoner rolled out a grenade. Fourth, the remaining group didn't believe what they were told about the watchkeeper. Fifth, several trucks tested our perimeter defense and it worked. Sixth, once underway, we discovered that the prisoner is a woman. Over."

"A woman? You're kidding, right?"

"No, I just saw the corpsman finish patching her up. It's definitely a woman."

"OK, got it. No fingerprints left at the scene?"

"None I'm aware of."

"Listen, Dan. The extraction plan for you and the team will likely change. You were motoring over to Marmaris and then splitting up to return separately, right?"

"Right," Steele replied.

The Admiral continued, "The Turks know the raid came from the water and will be trying to figure out what type of boat was used for transport. In the next few hours, they will be combing through the immigration photos trying to see if a team came in. Even though you were traveling under different names, they can match up the photos from your ports of entry with any departure location."

"I understand. Also, Plan B was to drop the team off individually, and have them swim ashore, adding time and distance to a staggered departure from different airports. With the prisoner, I was also thinking we might continue up the Bosporus into the Black Sea to Romania where we still have a small facility. We will make modifications to the boat so it cannot be easily identified if the Turks decide to study the recent departures from Antalya."

"Good. I'll get Cass to work return logistics. I'm certain the Turks will piece things together in time. Sandy is keeping tabs on State. I'll call you back in two hours."

All the major television stations and their local affiliates breaking news teams glommed on to the story from Turkey. Though they were just fragmentary reports, it was clearly the major story of the day. The anchors pitched it as an international whodunit, and the intriguing possibilities would be endlessly talked out in front of a nation glued to another international crisis. Pandemonium reigned inside the Administration as one overseas media outlet suggested that the US might be involved, a claim the White House flatly denied.

Steele found Rami on *Iklim's* darkened bridge.

"Good to see you back in one piece. I was a little worried."

"We all made it back OK. We have a guest with a couple of gunshot wounds. Is there another berth aboard where she can be secured?"

"She?"

"Yes. She... I'll tell you the whole story over a cup of your coffee. I think our departure plan will be modified because of the mess we left behind in the camp and on the beach. Where are we now?"

"Take a look at the radar repeater. We are not radiating, but the electronic chart shows us abreast of Cyprus about 30 miles from where we picked you up."

Just before sunrise, *Ertan*, the boat's new identity, spelled out on the name board now covering the gold-leaf letters, stopped engines at a point ten miles west of Cyprus. An acoustic pinger had been active for an hour after it was lowered over the side to the depth specified. On deck, the team swung the davit into position and lowered the rubber boat tying off a line forward from its bow to position it along the hull. Two hundred feet away, a submarine surfaced, its black hull almost invisible against the dark sea. A Los Angeles attack submarine, USS *Newport*, interrupted its routine patrol to retrieve the special operations team. Passengers usually were transferred from a submarine to a surface vessel or helicopter for medical conditions which couldn't be treated aboard. In this case, the submarine was taking passengers. The submarine's Commanding Officer remained in the conning tower and observed the transfer, raising her binoculars to get a better look at the activity on *Ertan's* deck, gently rolling with the sea close to the submarine's starboard beam. A tall man with dark hair seemed to be in charge. He was wearing a pair of jeans and a pull-over shirt that covered a well-proportioned strong body. I wish he'd come aboard with the others she mused.

Wearing civilian clothes, the passengers paddled the boat to the sub and used a rope ladder with rigid plastic steps conforming to the curve of the pressure hull to reach crewmembers on the flat deck. Once the passengers were aboard, the submarine returned to the depths, and the only trace that remained was the rigid-hulled inflatable swirling where the submarine submerged. The transfer had taken all of four minutes. Rami maneuvered *Ertan* close to the inflatable, and Steele jumped down into it. He slashed the inflation chambers and removed the drain plug near the engine. The boat filled with sea water and started its trip to the bottom in less than a minute — one less link to the bloody raid.

Continuing up the narrow Bosporus was too risky, even with a new identity. Through the US Embassy in Ankara, Cass Thomas chartered a flashy, high speed off-shore racing boat from a Turkish businessman who kept the boat moored in Izmir, a port midway up the Aegean Sea. In sixteen hours, the boat would rendezvous with *Ertan* near an island off Bodrum, a popular seaside vacation city. The charter would come with a trusted pilot and a retired Turkish Naval officer who worked occasionally in support of the US Consulate in Istanbul. Rami and Steele laid out the track, and Rami touched up the diesels to a higher rpm to ensure *Ertan* would arrive on time.

***

It was 10:00 p.m. on a night black as pitch. *Ertan* drifted at the rendezvous point in the lee of an island. Half a dozen rubber fenders that looked like inflated rigatoni were positioned along the ketch's starboard side to protect the polished fiberglass hull of the sleek forty-three-foot luxury cruiser which throbbed out of the darkness and maneuvered alongside. Equipped with twin high performance six-cylinder engines, the vessel could fly forty-two knots on the open water. Its narrow hull cut through seas with ease, ensuring a comfortable and exhilarating ride. Though ten years old, the boat was meticulously maintained and had been leased for several big screen movies shot in Istanbul.

Steele climbed down an accommodation ladder to the after deck and the prisoner was lowered feet first. Dressed in a man's loose-fitting shirt and cotton pants, her hands were secured with a makeshift belt and plastic tie wraps to prevent escape. Steele led her forward, waving at Rami as the two boats separated. There were two cabins below, one with a double bed and adjoining bathroom and the other with a single bed. Steele steered the woman into the smaller bedroom and told her to lie down on the bed. He retrieved a hank of nylon parachute cord from his pocket and secured her legs to the corners of the frame and then fashioned a loop and placed it around her neck like a choking leash to restrict any upper body movement. Her hands remained tie-wrapped to the belt.

Up on deck, he met the Captain sitting in a high-backed bucket seat strapped into a harness on the pilot's left.

"Captain, I'm Dan Steele."

"Demir," replied the man. Of medium build with a shock of sandy hair, he had a trimmed mustache and a firm handshake. He got right down to business. "The difficult part of this transit is through the Bosporus where there will be considerable traffic in both directions. My recommendation is to maintain a fourteen-knot speed in the Aegean and Sea of Marmara so we can enter the Bosporus the morning after tomorrow. We'll transit into the Black Sea by mid-day and reach Constanta, Romania the following morning. By sea, the entire trip is close to 650 nautical miles. The pilot agrees."

"That sounds like a good plan. Do you know the pilot?"

"I've worked with him before. He knows these waters well and controls this racing machine with great skill. I plan to stay here for the night while you are busy babysitting our passenger."

Steele went below and knocked on the cabin door before entering. The woman locked on to him with her dark eyes.

"I need to use the bathroom."

Steele left and checked out the small bathroom and shower in the other cabin and then untied the paracord and cut the plastic tie wraps binding her hands.

"OK. What is your name?"

"My name is Sahar. What is yours?"

"Dan Steele."

The woman got off the bed, and Steele walked her to the small head.

"You have two minutes alone."

"A woman needs more than two minutes. Are you married? If you were, you would be more sensitive to our needs. Give me three minutes or you'll be cleaning up after me."

"Three minutes."

After four minutes, Steele banged on the door just as she opened it. They went back to the smaller cabin where he used the paracord to secure the woman to the bed as before. He opened the adjacent cabin, splashed water on his face and lay on the large bed, tuning his senses to the background noise before falling asleep. He awoke with a start. It was 4:00 a.m. and the background noise continued with a familiar hum. He got up and opened the other cabin door and found the bed empty. The woman was gone.

CHAPTER FOUR

Washington, DC

Months before the trip to Turkey, Steele had been invited to Washington for a meeting. Because he was called by his old boss, Admiral James Wright, Steele assumed that someone knowing Wright might have some light consulting work which could be tackled by a former SEAL. While not ready for a full-time job, Steele had no source of steady income and needed work, even if on a per diem basis. He walked into the impressive Headquarters of the Department of Transportation located on M Street in the Southeast quadrant of the District of Columbia. The building accelerated the revitalization of the District formerly known as the "Combat Zone." Now bustling with office buildings housing contractors working for the Naval Sea Systems Command headquartered at the refurbished Navy Yard, hotels, trendy restaurants, and the modern-day equivalent of brownstones with manicured yards and on street parking replaced vacant lots and abandoned walk-ups.

Chrome and blue-tinted glass framed the large lobby windows and repeated the modern industrial motif in smaller dimensions on the building's façade, at least eight stories high. After a routine identification check, Steele successfully passed through the lobby metal detector, collected his cell phone, wallet and money clip from the little plastic tray and followed a uniformed escort to a key-operated unmarked elevator in the back of the building. The escort entered a code into the elevator keypad, and Steele waited for the Washington Nationals Stadium, built a few hundred yards to the southwest, to come into view as he was whooshed to an upper floor in the glass enclosure. Instead, he felt the elevator descend. Its doors opened into a large open room with a vaulted ceiling chiseled from the bedrock.

"Welcome to the cavern, Dan."

"Sandy! It's great to see you," he said throwing his arms around the short, stocky man wearing rumpled khakis and an open- neck shirt.

He leaned back and saw the friendly gap between Sandy's two front teeth.

"You look terrific," he said. "I thought you'd be back on the Appalachian Trail this fall."

"And I thought you'd still be wearing a hospital johnnie instead of a suit and spending most of your time doing physical therapy," said Sandy. "We can catch up later. Right now, we've got a group waiting for us." Sandy extended his arm to the right towards a door cut into the sloping ceiling of the bedrock. He placed his palm on a biometric reader, and Steele heard the whoosh of compressed air as the heavy armored door swung open.

Steele's field of view expanded as familiar faces from the recent past greeted him. He smiled when he saw Admiral James Wright, his former boss at the Domestic Terrorism Cell of the Department of Homeland Security.

"Morning Admiral," he said as Wright gave him a familiar bearhug after shaking his hand. The Admiral stepped aside for Cass Thomas.

"Good morning, Lieutenant, I'm glad to see that you are traveling on your own power." She smiled broadly and hugged Dan in a politically-incorrect embrace that signaled how close they'd become during their time together at DHS. She was a diminutive powerhouse both mentally and physically, and Steele recalled the fact that she'd saved his hide twice, once as the Operations Officer on a US Navy destroyer and more recently, as a Defense Department security policeman.

"OK," announced the Admiral, "I know we are all anxious to find out what's transpired over the last 60 days, and why we find ourselves together again. There will be time for that. But we've got a lot of ground to cover this morning so let's get started."

Steele helped himself to a mug of steaming black coffee and joined Sandy and Cass at a long V-shaped conference table. The Admiral stood at the open mouth of the V in front of a large screen. He was trim and relaxed, wearing an open-neck plaid shirt with gray flannel trousers and polished loafers. Steele first saw him in stereo with the other image wearing a summer white Navy uniform with a single row of ribbons below his gold aviator wings. The double view collapsed as the man started speaking.

"I'm sure that you are wondering why you have been invited here to this odd place with a few of your old teammates from DHS. I'll fill in some of those squares this morning with a classified overview, and then you'll have to decide how to proceed, OK? Captain Owens planned to be here this morning but was called into a meeting. He's a key sponsor of this initiative."

"Thanks, Admiral. It all feels very familiar."

"About a month ago, the President's National Security Advisor asked me to end my short-lived retirement to create a small cell to conduct operations that will be off the government books. In other words, this cell does not officially exist. We are an extra-governmental impossible mission force reporting directly to the National Security Advisor. Any operations we undertake will be approved by a triumvirate that includes her, the Deputy Attorney General and the Vice Chairman of the Joint Chiefs of Staff. Day to day oversight will be exercised by the NSA herself.

The reason for the decision-making triumvirate is to ensure that the operations we will be taking on have some level of oversight. You'll recall some of the recent actions of the FBI that went unchecked. The Bureau is still reeling from the charges that their actions were politically motivated. None of that kind of behavior will be tolerated by this Administration, and I believe that the checks and balances put in place for this organization will keep us on the straight and narrow. While we will operate outside the law and, in most cases without the protection of the US Government, we will comply with the spirit of our statutes."

"Admiral, you said will. Does this mean that the cell has not yet been activated?"

"No. We are up and running but have not yet been assigned any missions."

"OK. Will you borrow the operators from the service branches or Special Warfare Command?"

"Yes, that's the concept. We are just getting organized and need some operator talent to establish a real capability before we are thrown into action. That's why you were invited here, Dan. The vision is that we will take on sensitive tasks without any US Government fingerprints on the people or outcome. Plausible deniability is still very important to the White House and the three letter agencies. Like I said before, we can't be found on any organization charts. We are off the books. The very existence of this cell is classified, and only a handful of people even know about it. The initiative is code-named Pisces."

"I wonder how many agencies control their own little cells doing exactly what this group is supposed to do without the same level of oversight or ability to deconflict their actions?"

"Good question, Dan. I've often wondered that myself. Frankly, I feel better about the triumvirate with the type of work that I think we'll be assigned. I don't mind having a boss who's talking to President Bowles on a daily basis."

The briefing continued for another hour. The Admiral leaned with his palms on the table and looked at Steele. "So, that's the pitch I can give you today. There will be more if you decide you'd like to join our little group. I'm sure you've got a thousand questions and may want some time to think about it. There's no job security with this offer. This is not the Department of Homeland Security. I can tell you that the compensation is high with no W-2, and the job comes without any benefits except the opportunity to do something for your country that will never be revealed or acknowledged. Sound familiar? Any questions?"

"Thanks, Admiral. Is there any plumbing down here in the cavern?"

"Sure, I'll show you the way." The Admiral looked at the group and said, "We've got some lunch coming in 20 minutes so let's all reassemble then."

As they were walking to the bathroom, Steele asked, "I thought you'd be up in Rhode Island digging clams and going for long walks with Carole along the Sakonnet River. Must have taken a team of horses to drag you back here. Is she still up there?"

"I know it's hard to believe, but she and I are back here in Northern Virginia living in our old house on Arlington Ridge. She missed her friends and couldn't stand to have me underfoot every day, shooting off in a dozen different directions with nothing getting done. She diagnosed me with a case of adult onset Attention Deficit Disorder. I felt like a caged animal. We've put our retirement on hold for another few years. I rented our new house to a Captain assigned to the Naval War College. He'll be there for a three-year tour, and Carole and I will have another decision to make at that point. By the way, there's not much challenge to catching quahogs once you learn how." Both men laughed as they re-traced their steps and joined the group behind armored doors.

A casual lunch provided the opportunity to catch up. The team replayed many of the events of the recent past as each relived parts of the operation that had brought them together and almost ended the lives of both Sandy Matthews and Dan Steele. It seemed like only yesterday. These were good people and close friends. With his physical therapy sessions ending in the next two weeks, Steele was eager to get back to work.

On medical leave since he left the Department of Homeland Security's Domestic Terrorism Unit in early August, Steele had been on a rigorous rehabilitation regime that included strength and agility training as his injuries from an underwater explosion healed. The bones in his fractured forearm had knitted together and his arm strength returned to levels higher than before the break. The chunk ripped out of his thigh left a large scarred depression in his leg, but his swimming routine proved he had regained his aquatic skills and endurance.

He desperately needed to get back in the loop. Without access to the stream of all-source intelligence reports, there would be little hope of locating the man who'd masterminded the terrorist attack on the Chesapeake Bay Bridge and Tunnel two years ago that took the lives of his wife, Jill, and their two young sons. That day still burned with white hot intensity inside him. While he could travel to Albania as a private citizen and hunt down the man known only as Spence, Steele wanted him brought to justice and to pay the long price for his deeds. Merely killing Spence would not be sufficient. The man needed to spend the rest of his years exposed to the raw, undisciplined life as just another number in a population behind bars.

After the briefing, he had a few questions, but all were minor details. When the Admiral excused himself after lunch to make a telephone call, Steele walked with him.

"Admiral, I don't need to think about this at all. How do I join your Pisces team?"

"Great. I thought you might be interested and have the process already started. There's a large manila envelope on the desk in your office on the other side of the conference room. Welcome aboard!"

Steele spent the rest of the day completing non-disclosure forms, setting up a polygraph for the next morning and ending the day with an extended session with a psychiatrist trying to find any personality defect that might be disqualifying. She found none. His official start date would be the following week.

Before traveling to DC from his home in Virginia Beach, Virginia, Steele booked a flight to Providence, Rhode Island to visit Jill's parents. The loss of the couple's only child had all but killed their spirit and clearly shortened their life expectancy. He stayed in close contact with them and visited whenever he could. It was painful for him to witness what the death of their daughter and young grandsons had wrought. Steele was affected in a different way, strengthened by the resolve and determination to bring their murderer to justice and have him rot behind bars.

He left the Department of Transportation Headquarters and headed for Dulles International Airport on the Metro — the only way to travel inside the Beltway during the peak travel periods that included most of the morning and from mid-afternoon. From Vienna, he took a cab to Dulles and, after security checks, boarded a large bus that connected the main terminal to the mid-field gates.

Following the overhead signs to his departure gate, he recognized a SEAL teammate while passing an open restaurant in the concourse. The two hadn't seen each other for years. As he approached the table, another familiar face appeared.

"Well, well, well, if it isn't steely Dan Steele."

"Richie, how are you?" said Dan, extending his hand.

He ignored the hand and looked across the table at the other SEAL. "Do you know this guy?"

"Sure, we served together on Team Two a few years back."

"Well, this is the jerk that sent me to Captain's Mast and is responsible for me getting bounced off the team and out of the Navy." Richie's overseas flight was likely hours away, and he'd filled the waiting time guzzling draft beer. His speech seemed slurred, and he was obviously feeling no pain as Steele tried to shift the conversation.

"What are you up to these days?"

"I guess you could call me a soldier of fortune, ready to sell myself to the highest bidder when there's a need for my skills." Richie's voice was loud and attracted the attention of several patrons sitting at the bar. "You know, I still can't believe that you ran me out of the Navy."

Fully aware that he was making an unpleasant scene, he took to the stage. According to Richie, his thin frame and scraggly facial hair made him babe magnet. A vertical line of white from an old scar across his left eyebrow arched his brow in a v-shaped tent. He claimed that it added significantly to his attractiveness to women. His brown puppy-dog eyes were the final attribute that made him so desirable. With his body's perpetual tilt to the left, he presented himself as an edgy, cocksure man looking for trouble. Since Steele had seen him last, he'd had a colorful serpent needled around his neck with its head extending onto his exposed right cheek.

"Folks, let me introduce the choir boy, Dan Steele," he said, getting the attention of patrons on both sides of the bar and adjacent tables. "Here is a former Navy SEAL with two stellar accomplishments. Number one was getting me thrown out of the Navy on some trumped-up charges that he created with the other brass; and number two, and probably most important to understanding what kind of slime he is, this is the boy scout who abandoned his wife and two children on the bottom of the Chesapeake Bay to save his own hide. They drowned. What do you think of that?"

Richie refueled with another gulp of beer, paused to make sure that he still had a rapt audience and continued, "The old lady I can understand but those boys? How could you let them drown like that? I'm thinking that maybe there was a question of paternity that you wanted to have die with them. Anyway, I'm tired of looking at your face. Get the hell out of here, Lieutenant." Richie punctuated his final dismissal by throwing the remaining beer in Steele's face. Slamming the empty mug down on the table, he took a stance that screamed his desire to fight.

Steele slowly pulled a paper napkin from the table's holder and wiped the froth off his face keeping his dark eyes locked to Richie's, folding the wet paper and placing it on the table top. His response was deliberate and cautious. Richie may have been drunk and obnoxious, but he was also a fearless fighter skilled in hand to hand combat. Steele took a measured step in his direction and spoke in a gentle voice.

"I just can't believe that you're still in denial, Richie. You've developed some very poor manners too."

Infuriated that he was unable to bait Steele into a fight, Richie lunged, swinging his right hand in a savage roundhouse designed to knock Steele's head off his shoulders. All he got was air. Steele deftly side-stepped the punch and brought the punching arm behind Richie's back in a smooth motion.

"Richie, you really need to work on your anger management and improve your interpersonal skills, especially in public where people can get the wrong impression." He calmly seated Richie back into his chair, still holding his arm in a lock. Even with his dulled senses, Richie grew sullen with the sharp pain of the submission hold, knowing that any sudden movement might result in a broken wrist or worse. Steele's left hand moved to Richie's neck where he found a little-known pressure point that he agitated with his index finger like an acupuncture needle, leaving Richie silent and staring into space from a rigid, catatonic body. He released the wrist lock on his right arm and sat down at the table.

"How did you do that?" asked the other SEAL, astounded that Steele had neutralized Richie so quickly.

"I'm been doing physical therapy over at the Naval Hospital in Portsmouth for the last couple of months, and one of the therapists is a retired Japanese guy whose father commanded a submarine in the Pacific during the war. He really accelerated my recovery. I saw him training in the gym one day and learned he'd been a martial arts instructor teaching self-defense and the use of submission holds. He's volunteered at the hospital for years, and I luckily ran into him. We started talking, and he was curious about my injuries. He showed me a few variations on the floor exercises that I was doing to rebuild my legs. After a week doing those, my recovery really ramped up. I saw him again and talked about improving my fighting skills, and he agreed to teach me. You know what kind of hand-to-hand training we got during training. More brute force than technique. Well, this guy brought me to another level. Frankly, my formal physical therapy was over weeks ago, but I keep going back to learn more. I work with him for 90 minutes three times a week, and I've never felt more confident about my ability. It's amazing stuff." Steele stood and clapped Richie on the shoulder.

"He'll be like that for the next ten minutes or so," he said to the other SEAL. "Look, this guy is bad news. Try to stay away from him at all costs. I've got to head down to the commuter terminal to catch my flight. Good to see you again. Take care and safe travels."

Richie Bouffard had deployed to Colombia years before with a team that included Steele for a joint training operation. On the last night, the Colombian special forces hosted a farewell party for their American counterparts in the old city of Cartagena. Some of the host team brought their wives to the event. After being fortified with alcohol, Richie began charming one of them. He maneuvered the woman out to the open portico overlooking the harbor and forced a kiss on her and then roughly reached under her skirt. Her scream brought her husband and others outside to the porch.

Richie cold-cocked her husband with a heavy wine bottle serving as a candle holder and continued his advances, oblivious that there were several SEALs, both US and Colombian watching him. One of his US Navy team-members separated the two and was thanked with a vicious punch to the face. Richie left the party and stormed off into the night, missing the return muster the following morning and delaying the team's flight back to the United States. The incident escalated through both countries' military chains of command, and the Americans departed the country with a successful training operation clouded by the actions of Petty Officer Richie Bouffard.

Steele was appointed to investigate the matter. His finding of facts led to formal charges. A subsequent court-martial resulted in an eighteen month stay in a military prison, a reduction in rate, and a punitive separation from the Navy. After his sentence was formally read to the court by the military judge, Richie swore aloud at his appointed military lawyer and addressed Steele as he departed the proceedings.

"You and I are not finished. Watch your back."

Steele hadn't seen Richie since but took the threat seriously at the time and more seriously now. As a weapons expert, Richie was a virtuoso in designing explosive packages of any size or strength which could never be traced. Steele arrived at his gate while partitioning a portion of his brain to keep tabs on Richie Bouffard.

CHAPTER FIVE

Moscow, Russia

Years before, then-Colonel Nikolai Zlodeyev traveled to Moscow to visit his previous commander and mentor. He walked down a long corridor until he found General Dmitri's room, a large single reserved for ailing Russian military commanders. A look of excitement came over the General's face from the hospital bed when Zlodeyev's large frame darkened his open door, but his body didn't move.

"Niko, thank you for coming. It's so good to see you."

"General, I am so happy to be here to visit with my commander, mentor and best friend. How are you feeling?" Zlodeyev pulled a folding metal chair close to the patient.

"I'm not well Niko. The doctors try to sugarcoat the situation and keep running endless tests, but the fact is that I am dying and perhaps have a month to live. But to live like this?" he gestured to his body that was covered by a white starched sheet that had been tucked in tightly on three corners so that he couldn't move. A single morphine drip from an intravenous bag hanging from a metal pole next to the bed kept the pain at bay. The catheter bag was filled with dark orange fluid, a mixture of concentrated urine and the spillover of bile. His kidneys were failing.

"Are you sure? Have you gotten another opinion? Do you have the best doctors available? This can't be true. You were as strong as a horse at the Officers' Ball."

"Yes, I've been through all of that, but the answers come back with great consistency. I'm on my way out, Niko. But, let's talk of other things. I understand that your unit performed remarkably in Georgia. Did you travel to Tbilisi?"

"Not officially. We were stationed in Abkhazia for most of the time but did conduct several weeks of covert surveillance of Tbilisi."

"How about the women there, Niko? I'm told that they look like Swedish models."

"Our surveillance did include time to get a pulse on the city, and we found the girls to be attractive and good sources of information. Much better than being in a camp with 10,000 soldiers!"

The bedridden General convulsed with laughter ending with a raspy cough that sounded like his lungs were filling with fluid.

"The times we had my friend. The best of my life." The man coughed again and continued. "Since I will die soon, I want to tell you a secret that can make you very rich."

The Colonel slid the chair closer to the bed.

"I will tell you the secret if you promise to grant me a wish. Agreed?

"What, that you want 55%?" the colonel laughed.

"No, that's not my wish. I have no family except for our Spetsnaz comrades. No. I have lived a good and very comfortable life. I don't need any money."

"What then, do you want me to bring you a woman?" The question set off another round of laughing and coughing which finally quieted.

"No, Niko. First, I want to tell you a story. Think back to the days of Czar Alexander I. That little French queer, Napoléon Bonaparte, was taking over Europe and despite the polite exchanges between the two, Russia was the next country that Napoléon planned to conquer. Worried about the Frenchman's real motives and their consequences, the Czar called a meeting of his counselors. Once blinded by the ambitious and large thinking of the Emperor, he now understood that Napoléon's expansionist ideas knew no bounds. The previous offer of a ruling partnership for the entire European landmass had been nothing more than a clever ploy to reduce the battle front until it was time to force the Russian's hand, either through capitulation or attack. Alexander stood firm, and it looked now as if the young French upstart would unleash his Grand Armée on the homeland."

The General paused for effect. He was a well-known storyteller and took on the role of the characters to transport his listeners to the setting and immerse them in a dialog that felt as real as if they were in the room when it took place. A sheen of moisture appeared on his pale forehead as the General warmed up to the heart of the story.

"So, when will he collect his armies together to begin the march?" the Czar asked his assembled military and political advisers. Alexander would often ask these questions to stir debate among the group and to ferret out who really had the pulse on the situation. He could later use this information during his long sessions with the Court mystic who sat behind him in an outer row of chairs positioned for the lower ranking advisers.

"According to dispatches we have intercepted and information passed to our agents in Paris and other European capitals, I believe the Grand Armée will mass for an assault on Moscow in six months' time," replied the Czar's senior military adviser. "I assume Bonaparte discounted the Russian winter in formulating his strategy. There is much hopeful discussion among his generals about whether our country might simply yield to his threats of invasion."

Political, economic, religious factors, the readiness of Russia's army and defense of the city were also discussed. Alexander tried to find something useful in the meeting, but there were no new revelations. It was yesterday's goulash put back in the oven and presented with some fresh garnish.

Later in the day, Alexander met with his Court mystic who summarized the meeting with a dismissive tone.

"The advisers tell you what you want to hear, my Czar. Their brains are pickled with vodka. It's the same information that you were given at the last Council meeting. A waste of time."

"Petr, this time I agree with you. So now, I look to your assessment of the situation to understand how things with the Frenchman will unfold. Tell me what you see."

"Yes, my Czar. The Frenchman is angry with your rebuff of his request for your younger sister's hand in marriage to unite the two kingdoms of Europe. I read the dispatches and listen to others within your court and believe that the die is already cast. Napoléon will form the Grand Armée and will march through his most recent conquest, Poland, and then continue to our fair city of Moscow. Timing is uncertain, but there is no question that he will march to Moscow and demand your sword and your crown. He intends to expand his empire three-fold with the addition of the lands that you rule. Can he do it? By all accounts, he has the means, and I believe he also possesses the will to proceed with the plan."

"What measures should be taken now?"

"I agree with the Generals about increasing our fortifications along his most likely route and would urge you to begin that work immediately. We also need to prepare Moscow. If Napoléon arrives in our city in the dead of winter, his army will be looking for shelter, warmth, and fresh food. I believe we should take steps to make Moscow a town devoid of all of these necessities."

"What are you suggesting?" said the Czar, a mask of shock on his face.

"The city itself must be burned, freshwater wells poisoned, livestock dispersed, firewood removed, root cellars emptied. Napoléon must find Moscow a city with no means to sustain life."

"This is a very bold plan. We can discuss it, but I want no mention of it to the others. Yes, I understand what you mean. What's left of the Grand Armée after our soldiers resist their march will find nothing in Moscow to sustain them, and no Czar to surrender his sword. It's a brilliant way to bring the Frenchman to his knees without his army pillaging our city."

"Thank you, my Czar. One thing further. Our city is blessed with treasures that please the eye and carry great historical significance. I'm referring to the vast treasures of your court. The paintings and icons, the ancient statuary and carvings, the gifts of gold, crowns and jewels that capture the majesty of Russia and reflect its greatness. These cannot feed an army, but they are part of our culture and must be preserved when the Frenchman's army is finally decimated by Mother Nature herself."

"I agree. How can this be done?"

"Because the Grand Armée will likely take the route through Poland, their foragers will move up to 100 miles astride the line of advance. Thus, we must hide the treasures well beyond his grasp. I will study the maps and will bring you a complete plan next week if that is acceptable?" The mystic's voice rose slightly at the end of the question to signal he was seeking the Czar's approval to begin planning.

"Yes, I will look forward to it. You've given me much to consider, and I value your wise counsel."

A knock on the door interrupted the story, and a uniformed nurse came into the room and handed the bedridden man a small paper cup with several pills and a glass of rusty tap water. The General took the pills without talking to the nurse who turned and left the room, closing the door behind her.

His voice was hoarse, and his energetic recitation added to his labored breathing.

"So, the plan was approved by Czar Alexander. As the city's citizens prepared to re-locate, the Palace and Museums were emptied of their treasures. Dozens of horse-drawn wagons left for Crimea with a company of the Czar's own soldiers under a papal writ to ensure nothing could interrupt the caravan."

"A papal writ? I understood that Napoléon did not get along with the Pope and made no effort to mend the rift with Czar

Alexander."

"Yes, many of the churches were also emptied of their treasure, and the Pope was seeking an ally against Napoléon. Rome was promised half of the value in exchange for the writ and a secure location to prevent the treasure from falling into the hands of the Grand Armée. The writ also safeguarded those making the 900-mile trip."

"Such a trip would have taken months. And now you are going to tell me that the treasure still exists and was never returned to Moscow?"

"Exactly. That treasure hasn't seen the light of day in 200 years. A force of 120 Russian Army soldiers protected the caravan during the journey that took almost five months. Sixty wagons were needed to transport the cargo. A vault was dug in the Port City of Kerch in Crimea behind the site of the Saint John the Baptist Church, first built almost 1300 years ago. I've seen pictures of it. The exterior is candy-striped, fashioned by alternating rows of local limestone masonry with red clay bricks. Still a magnificent structure. You can see many fine photos of it on your computer. The soldiers vanished. No one knows whether they were murdered to keep the secret or met their fate another way."

"How did you learn of the treasure?"

"My father was a biblical scholar who discovered the plan buried in the Papal archives in Rome and, to my knowledge, I was the only one that he told. I have dreamed of retrieving the treasure for years and now, could not possibly last for even a visit there. Quite a story. Don't you agree Niko?"

"Yes, if true, the treasure would be priceless today."

"You are right. Now, I've shared the secret with you and hope that you will find a way to recover the treasure and keep a Czar's fortune for yourself."

"Thank you, comrade. Now, what is your wish?"

The two men sat and talked for another two hours, laughing and crying and reliving two lifetimes of military service that were woven so closely together.

"It's time Niko."

"Goodbye my friend," said the Colonel as he rose and held the pillow over the patient's face. After a few weak twitches, the pillow was removed and propped under the General's head. Colonel Nicolai Zlodeyev walked from the room, left the hospital and found his way to the Officers' Club. He gulped down a tumbler of vodka and felt it burn all the way down his throat and into his stomach.

CHAPTER SIX

Aegean Sea

Steele's heart pounded as he looked around the cabin. He found pieces of the paracord neatly cut through. So, she had a blade of some sort that she must have stolen from the medical tray the corpsman used to dress her wounds. Why wasn't he more thorough in searching her body before tying her to the bed? He respected women and treated them gently, perhaps too gently in this case, forgetting that the woman tried to kill him and escape. He might be dealing with a dangerous bomb-maker who just happened to be a woman. She didn't impress Steele as someone who would jump off the back of a boat, but he was ready to be surprised.

Inspecting the galley that featured a single burner alcohol stove and a small fridge with a dining table pulled down from the bulkhead, Steele reasoned that she must be still aboard, hiding in a small compartment covered by the bone-colored leather or exotic paneling fitted over the boat's fiberglass structure. He stepped on something that confirmed his suspicions, a small stainless-steel screw an inch long stood proud of the carpet outside the berth where he left her.

Steele took a few seconds to set the hum of the boat's engines and the sound of water rushing past the boat's narrow beam and tuned his hearing for changes from that sound. He began to search the cabin, running his hand down every joint, where adjacent sections of paneling were joined together by H-shaped channels of stainless steel that provided structural strength where it was affixed to the fiberglass ribs. A built-in settee held life jackets and nothing else. Ditto the small bench facing the dining table. The only entrance to the propulsion compartment was from topside near the steering station so the chances of her hiding there were remote.

Steele checked the most obvious place to hide...the bed itself. The mattress was set onto a raised platform fabricated of sheet metal and covered with a paper or cloth matching the rest of the room's paneling.

Testing his theory, Steele jumped up on the bed and, bracing himself with his palms against the false overhead, began walking towards the middle of the bed and then shifted all his weight along its edge before stepping into its center. If the woman had sliced and wedged herself into the foam mattress, he would surely provoke a reaction. He did.

The woman rolled out of the bed on the opposite side waving a razor blade between two fingers in her right hand. Steele could see some seepage of blood past the packing on the right shoulder of her shirt. Steele jumped down from the bed facing the woman.

"What's your next move, Abu Sayed?" Steele asked.

"To cut your neck and then carve out your heart."

"I think you should save your strength. I need to redress your wounds and advance the packing. The corpsman gave me explicit instructions so you will heal without any complications or infection. If you don't want me to escort you everywhere, including the bathroom, I suggest you put the razor down and stop this nonsense while you have a chance."

"Nonsense? You think that your insincere kindness will change me? If I don't kill you, one of my students will. Allah is on our side, not yours." The woman threw the blade at Steele, and it fluttered to the middle of the bed where he retrieved it and placed it on a shelf.

"Thanks. Now lay down on the bed so I can dress your wounds."

To his amazement, she complied. Steele tied her legs to the two corners of the bed and left wrist to the top corner, leaving her right arm free. He grabbed the medical kit the corpsman had put together and returned. Though it had been just over eight hours since her initial treatment, the seepage indicated that she had compromised the wound with her effort to escape.

He washed his hands with an antiseptic scrub and pulled on latex gloves before re-dressing the wounds. The woman was surprised with his gentle touch. Here was a man who had shot her twice less than twelve hours ago and now he was dressing the holes in her shoulder with the skilled hands of a doctor.

"Where are you taking me?" she said, wincing as he advanced the dressing inserted into the holes.

"To Romania. We are about to enter the Bosporus strait separating the European and Asian sides of Turkey and should reach Constanta tomorrow morning."

"And what will happen there?"

"You will be transferred to a facility ashore for questioning."

"I answer the questions, then the men kill me. Is that the plan?"

"I think you've been watching too much television," said Steele but also wondering what did happen in the facility to the rare female prisoners turned over. He finished the external bandaging and peeled off the gloves.

"Thank you," the woman said as Steele secured her right arm and left without a reply.

Steele emerged on deck and sucked in a deep breath of the salt air as the boat cut through the water near the Golden Horn, the oldest part of the city and the location of the Turkish Navy's first naval base in the heart of Istanbul. Though small, the base took up precious real estate that could be used far more efficiently, and there were plans afoot to migrate the base across the Bosporus to a commercial shipyard on the Asian side of the country.

The remainder of the transit went smoothly as did the transfer of the woman to a team of civilians. Steele walked her off the boat, guiding her to a car where a man in a lab coat met them. She was flanked on both sides by hard men who were likely local security guards for the facility. Before ducking into the car, the woman looked back at Steele and smiled. Steele was handed a set of new clothes. A car was waiting to take him to the airport for the flight back to the United States.

CHAPTER SEVEN

Port Kavkaz, Russia

Brigadier General Nikolai Zlodcyev studied the video screen being fed by a datalink from a bird-sized drone flying at a thousand feet over the Crimean city of Kerch, etching the images in his mind. He glanced at his watch--04:45 a.m. The first rays of the sun would soon be bending over the horizon in the brief period between night and day. Leaving the small trailer that served as a mobile command center, he walked to join his little green men preparing for the day's mission. They wore uniforms just like those of the Russian Army but devoid of any insignia.

He met with his lieutenants to review the timing and assignments planned in the previous weeks — a straightforward mission. They would embark in five high speed boats at Port Kavkaz located in the Kerch Strait, where the Sea of Azov separates Russia from Crimea on its way to the Black Sea. To the south, construction of the twelve-mile bridge to Kerch would permanently bind Crimea to mother Russia and consolidate another piece of the plan to rebuild the Soviet Union.

The drone's infrared camera had revealed a group of about eighty townspeople from a population numbering 145,000 who had barricaded themselves in front of the municipal hall in the center of town to protest the clumsy annexation of the large peninsula from Ukraine. In 2014, a questionable referendum confirmed that an overwhelming percentage of the populace had voted to secede from Ukraine, to rejoin the Russian Federation and to invite the Russian military to push back the insurgents. The brave souls resisting the Russian bear knew their feeble protest would prove meaningless in the end but believed in their cause, to a point.

The General and his lieutenants toasted to the success of the mission, first with over-sized glasses of cold vodka and then with chilled glasses of kvass, the blood of the earth, a salty fortified drink concocted from fermented scraps of rye bread mixed with water, a bread culture like sourdough and shredded beets. The vodka was clean, almost medicinal, its distillation scientific. Drinking kvass was like poking a straw down through the rich soil of Belgorod and finding a vein of complex primal fluid fermented by nature and full of life itself.

"Let the only blood shed today be from those we must disperse," said General Zlodeyev. "Be safe and protect yourselves, comrades. Now let's go see how serious our countrymen are about resisting the will of the Mother."

Black, the water ran to the south with a strong current. Powered by inboard engines, the darkened boats cut through the sea with their engines muffled through underwater exhausts. The thirteen-mile transit took just thirty-five minutes with the squads landing in the harbor that had been surveilled by the drone during their approach. Timed to reach different wharfs in the port simultaneously, they fanned out and moved into the heart of Kerch. Armed like a modern infantry, the sixty little green men walked unopposed through the sleeping streets and rendezvoused in the town square 30 minutes later with their weapons slung...a cake walk.

It was just dawn when the group stopped twenty yards from the barricade. The protesters were removing their blankets and a fire had just been kindled to prepare coffee and to warm a pot of soup. After weeks of sleeping outside exposed to the cold air coming off the sea, they were tired, their commitment lethargic. The exhausted men and women carried a few shotguns and several bolt action hunting rifles in addition to sickles and other workaday implements. They were facing a nearly equal-sized force of crack Russian soldiers armed with modern weaponry capable of turning them into bleeding corpses in a minute's time. Zlodeyev could see the fear in their faces and the strain of knowing that their protest was about to end.

The General strode another ten paces and addressed the crowd of proud and simple people assembled to protest what they believed was a political takeover of their homeland that would be violently executed if the past were any predictor of the present. There were no illusions about the way that democracy really worked in Russia's former states and no question that the Federation's hierarchy was committed to restore the grandeur of the Soviet Union as it tightened its iron grip.

"We do not intend to harm you. We are here on the orders of the Russian Federation to ensure that the wishes of those wanting to rejoin Russia are protected," the General said in a clear confident voice. He paused and was interrupted by another determined voice coming from behind the barricade.

"Anyone trying to control this town will have to come through me," said a bearded colossus swinging a heavy double-bladed ax. He marched through a movable break in the barricade strung with simple barbed wire used to pen livestock. "We are people of a free Crimea."

"Comrade, we respect the people of Crimea. We've come to restore order and security," declared the General in a soothing tone. "Please do not make this more difficult."

The General studied the man in front of him. The firm set of his jaw and solid stance were telling, and the tattoo on his right forearm identified him as a former Spetsnaz paratrooper. These men were tough as nails. The puckered scar on the man's left arm confirmed that he was not new to combat. That he emerged as the citizens' leader was clear, and he was not backing down. The General weighed the tactical options, concluding that this standoff would only be resolved by Plan B.

"So, we have our orders, and you are refusing to disperse peacefully. As you can see, my men are heavily armed. We could easily force you to disband, but there would be blood spilled without reason. You are either brave or foolish. I hope you will reconsider your challenge."

As the man took several steps forward, there was no doubt that he was ready to settle the matter by a fight between the two. The

General slowly removed his green blouse, handed it to one of his men and prepared mentally for a man to man fight. He relished a no holds barred encounter and never backed down from them. It was not as stark as David versus Goliath. Both were large men, but the giant would clearly win a tape measure comparison in all categories.

The General's large chiseled frame faced the towering giant whose face showed no signs of fear.

"So, I see that we are brothers in arms," he said nodding at the tattoo. "Hand to hand?" he asked. The other man defiantly nodded and tossed the ax behind him. The town's cobbled square swelled with onlookers. The two combatants circled on the hard stones. Neither had ever lost a fight.

The giant took a traditional boxing stance to begin, but the General was not fooled. The Spetsnaz were highly trained killing machines, experts in close quarters combat, and this man would be no different. They knew all the tricks to get an enemy on the ground and beat him to death. His quickness in trying the first take-down surprised everyone. He tested the General's reactions with a series of feints before trying a high take-down. He bear-hugged Zlodeyev off the ground, holding him in a crushing vise-like grip. The General's legs were useless and one of his arms was pinned to his body as the giant's hydraulic grip continued to squeeze Zlodeyev who looked like a man with no good options. The giant shrugged off the rapid punches to his head and neck and continued to tighten his grip. Zlodeyev felt the air being pushed from his lungs and gulped in a quick breath that could be his last. When the giant lifted his head, the General was given an opening. Three vicious head-butts forced him to release his death grip.

Separated, Zlodeyev took in some deep breaths to oxygenate his lungs and regain his composure. He again sized up his opponent. The giant's labored breathing signaled he was not in top combat condition, and his broken, bleeding nose didn't help the flow of fresh air needed by his lungs. But there was no doubt plenty of fight left in him. Most onlookers thought that the match could go either way. The two closed once again with the General delivering a twisting punch to the giant's solar plexus followed with an open cupped hand blow to each of his ears. The man staggered backwards. A quick succession of body blows to his kidneys and kicks to the groin dropped the man to his knees. Now on all fours, his quick, shallow breaths sounded like a dog's after running after a rabbit.

The General thought that he'd had enough. He extended his hand to the man and pulled him up from the ground. It had been a good fight. An animal grunt followed as the ax-man pulled a knife from his boot and raised his arm to slash the victor. The General expected the former Spetsnaz fighter would carry a knife. Old habits are hard to change. He dropped to the ground and rolled away from the deadly arc and once again faced the winded combatant, nimbly avoiding a series of feeble thrusts.

The giant mustered all his remaining strength and charged with the knife extended like a spear. The General used the momentum to turn into the giant, disarming him and twisting his arm until he heard the popping of ligaments tearing away from adjacent bones. Now breathing heavily and leaning against Zlodeyev like a boxer who had fought through the punishment of a twelve-round match, the giant looked surprised as the General retrieved the knife from the ground, buried it into the man's lower belly and then pulled the blade upward, opening him up to his rib cage. The hiss of a collapsing lung signaled the end of the fight. The defiant eyes rolled back into his bearded head.

"Comrade, I am glad that you've kept your knife very sharp but sorry you forced me to use it against you. As I said before, you are brave but not very smart."

The man's body slumped to the ground leaving the General's white T-Shirt and arms stained with fresh blood. With the bloody knife in his right hand, he licked its edge and addressed the shocked townspeople with a steady, authoritative voice.

"You will dismantle this barricade and disperse in the next thirty minutes, understood?"

The General glanced at the Byzantine façade of Saint John the Baptist church a few blocks from the town center and smiled. While his mission was to secure Kerch and tamp down any organized resistance, he had volunteered his unit for another reason. He had requisitioned several large trucks and digging equipment that were being barged over from the mainland and would arrive later in the morning.

"There's nothing like starting the day with a good fight, especially when you walk away as the victor," he laughed to one of his lieutenants.

CHAPTER EIGHT

Kerch, Crimea

To pinpoint the exact location of the vault, the General sent one of his young disciples to Kerch posing as a graduate student in archeology. Sergei left a week before the forces arrived in Port Kavkaz. He convinced the groundskeeper to permit him to survey the grassy, open field behind the church for a research project he was doing as part of his graduate studies. Sergei charmed the groundskeeper by buying him a large roast, a basket full of fresh vegetables and several growlers of beer from the local brewery.

After fifteen minutes of walking with a hand-held sensor that he swept from side to side, Sergei found the sealed space. He carefully measured the location of the corners and edges of the vault, marking those with iron pins shoved just under the roots of the thick grass. His careful measurements would enable the dig to begin immediately after some simple triangulation.

With the protesters dispersed, the General and the rest of the little green men established their headquarters right off the town square, taking over two hotels. The more important work in Kerch was about to begin. Still dressed as a student, Sergei met with the General after a celebratory luncheon that the General hosted for all the fighters who had joined him for the mission. The two walked in the quiet town square and found a bench in the shade of a large tree.

"Did you find the vault?"

Sergei answered with a question. "How did the operation this morning go?"

"No problem. There was an old Spetsnaz fighter who tried to argue with our orders, but I persuaded him to disperse with the others."

"I thought it best that I maintain a low profile so had an early breakfast and headed to the Library on the other side of town."

"OK, Sergei, enough of this chatter, did you find the vault?"

"Yes, I found it the day I arrived on the ferry from Port Kavkaz."

"So quickly? I thought it might take you several days and perhaps involve some excavation."

"No. I used a miniaturized gravitometer developed by the Israelis to detect tunneling of the Arabs from the Gaza. The device uses gravity to determine where open cavities exist. The oil companies first used the technology to locate seams and pockets in an existing well field to maximize the recovery from a single drilling site. It's a long story involving a Russian émigré living in Tel Aviv who liberated one of the sensors in for repair. What a capability. It reminds me of the foliage penetrating radar that our ground forces used in Africa. Easy to use without raising any suspicion. I have a very detailed map of the underground structure and a digging plan. After that, I turned my attention to the selection of wharfs for off-loading our equipment."

"Tell me more." As he leaned back on the bench, relaxed after a raucous meal with many toasts, the General divided his brain with one part looking intently at Sergei and listening to every detail of his analysis of the dig site while the other part focused on the event that brought them together. Sergei's thin, wiry body was topped with a flawless, smooth face ringed with curly, jet-black hair. Besides his classic features, his voice was soft and sweet. He would have been an ancient Greek singer accompanied by a lyre to entertain a King's court. People misread his thin frame and soft voice as effeminate. Those delicate features belied a man with a nimble, computer-like mind and fierce loyalty, traits not always valued in the ranks of Russian soldiers.

Sergei joined the Army to please his father who had told him that the discipline and physical training would make a man out of him. What actually happened is that Sergei was not strong enough to endure the rigors of forced marches with heavy packs. He tried, but his slender frame and lack of core strength just couldn't be molded into an infantryman. Transferred to a clerk's position in supply, he thrived. Within a few weeks he knew both sides of the logistics business — the formal method of requisitioning everything from bullets to boots and the informal one that enabled him to deliver whatever was needed quickly without going through all the channels. After he successfully turned around a readiness review by obtaining parts that had been missing for weeks, the General commended him and learned that he was being abused mentally and physically by a brutal masochist who took all the credit for the young man's hard work.

Impressed with his knowledge and resourcefulness, the General rescued Sergei and made him an operations analyst. An unusually gifted young man, a brilliant tactician and military planner with the ability to forge a detailed plan based on a concept or a big blue arrow strategy outlined by the General, he joined the Alpha Group team without the rigorous physical training, weapons proficiency or knowledge of explosives. Well-respected in the unit, all the fighters counted on his meticulous planning and also recognized his special relationship with the General. He had never let the team down.

"The actual vault is about eight feet under the grade and is covered with some protective material like leather or carpets. I assume its walls are probably lined with the local limestone, the same blocks that were used to build the church. Because it's an active church, I recommend that we establish our operations center next to the site and erect a perimeter to keep people at a distance. The church can remain open, and the services should continue as scheduled. The digging can be shielded from view by ten-foot plastic mesh construction barrier which will arrive with the digging equipment. There will likely be some of the faithful complaining about the noise, and I recommend we stop excavation during services. Based on my readings, a couple of medium diesel-powered backhoes with lifting bars should be able to get us down to the vault with a few hours of digging."

"Excellent job, Sergei. I knew you were the right person to send on this mission." The General hugged the junior Lieutenant like a son.

After two backhoes lumbered through the town square on rubber treads to minimize any impact on the cobble-stoned roads, the construction supervisor started the excavation within hours of Zlodeyev's landing in the port. Lights were strung around the site as the digging began. The General expected a twenty-four-hour operation with most of the daylight being used to inventory, photograph and curate his new collection. A team of three professional curators would arrive in Kerch that day. They would be well-compensated for their services and pledges of secrecy.

The General's first report came within six hours.

"We have uncovered what appears to be the roof of a forty-five-foot square carved ten-feet into the ground and covered with two layers of heavy timbers eighteen inches thick. The heavy hand-hewn timbers were covered with animal hides and copper plates. The wood looks dry, and there is no evidence of any water penetration. It looks like a sealed crypt. We have drilled lifting eyes into the timbers and have removed ten of them from the first course. The second course runs in the opposite direction so we will shift the equipment and wait for your order to remove the final row of timbers."

"Very good. I will come over about midnight to observe the opening."

The General tried to stay focused on his paperwork and knew that his presence at the site might cause some nervousness within the digging crews and slow down the effort. Excitement coursed through his body as if he were facing an animal in the arena. He paced back and forth in the hotel suite, looking at his watch every few seconds.

Finally, he strode to the site five-hundred feet away, consciously stopping himself from running. Arriving just as the rigging crew removed the last timber of the first course, he watched two men wielding gasoline-powered blowers raising large dust clouds as they walked, blowing off two centuries of dust accumulated on top of the timbers. The General looked at the cleaned timbers and pointed to one in the center of the lower course. Not only was it visibly narrower than the others, but it also had an "X" carved in its face.

"Lift the center beam first and then the ones on either side," he ordered. The fasteners were drilled into the first timber. Once a second timber was similarly raised, he signaled the foreman to stop. He scrambled down the mountain of excavated dirt with a long black flashlight and peered into the vault on his hands and knees, not believing his eyes. On the vault's floor some twelve feet below was a pedestal with a large wooden box. The bright red wax of the papal seal was visible on its top as if it were sealed the day before.

"Lift another three beams on either side so we have a twelve foot access. Wake the curators and tell them that they will begin in an hour's time. I will direct the placement of the ladders and lift from down below." He jumped through the three- foot gap in the beams and disappeared into the ground. The engineers were shocked that he would enter a vault sealed for two hundred years with no concern that the oxygen had long been used up. There was an imminent danger of death by asphyxiation. The engineers positioned a low-pressure ventilator in the gap and began pumping fresh air into the void below.

Astounded as he looked around the vault, the General saw a trove that he could never imagine. He remembered the American movie where an eccentric father and son team discovered an underground cavern filled with priceless antiquities from around the world. That cache paled by comparison. The wooden box contained an extensive numbered inventory citing the location of each item and annotations regarding its source. Paintings were crated and sealed with wax to protect them from moisture during transport and for the few years they were expected to remain in the vault. Jeweled samovars, crowns, swords and early artifacts from the Bronze Age were all here. Priceless was an inadequate word to describe the collection.

The General stood on the wooden box and grasped the beam overhead, pulling himself up and out of the vault in a single fluid motion. He motioned for the supervisor.

"Thank you for the fresh air. I suspect there is no oxygen in the vault at all. Proceed as I directed. We need to use the remainder of this timbered area for our curators to examine, catalog and photograph the collection before it is transported to the harbor."

After seeing the curators setting up to begin the process of emptying the vault using the handwritten inventory list, the General returned to his temporary quarters in the hotel and withdrew a small painting framed by an array of dazzling gemstones from his uniform pocket. Though cut with the crude implements of the time, the artifact was stunning in its beauty. The General marveled at the craftsmanship and wondered how long individual gem cutters would work on each of the facets to produce a gemstone of sufficient quality to present to a Czar.

He tucked the painting under his pillow and fell into a deep sleep.

CHAPTER NINE

Sana'a, Yemen

The debacle in Turkey had disappeared from the front pages of the newspapers, supplanted by another story re-energizing the #metoo movement. The evening talk shows were once again electrified by accounts involving the President's Treasury Secretary, a tall, lean, big drawl Texan with a known penchant for beautiful women.

A widower thought to have driven his wife to an early grave because of his frequent infidelity, he'd been accused of using his position and power to test drive women in the department at every opportunity. While he claimed that he never forced himself on any of the women, jealousies between his consorts added fuel to the outrage that he had the audacity to engage in these activities in his Headquarters office.

It had been fitted with a small bedroom that he used to rest before the many evening events on his calendar. Those late afternoon naps were generally accompanied events and rarely restful. One reporter discovered that he'd arranged a daily maid service to change the linen on his bed and replace the towels cascading above a hot tub installed after he expanded his office. People stayed glued to their televisions while the stories of his conquests came into homes across America each evening. The channels were accused of offering tidbits that had the rating organizations nervous about what was appropriate for children under thirteen to watch.

While the mainstream media covered the Treasury Secretary, the back-channel communications circuits between embassies and cooperating intelligence agencies were running hot in an attempt to get one of the potential countries involved in the bloody raid inside Turkey to blink. The US tried to tie the raid to a new special operations cell of Sunni fighters funded by Saudi Arabia, the Israelis claimed it was a Russian operation, and of course, Syria blamed the CIA. Cautious, the Turks were slower to point fingers, but the lack of any corroborating evidence made it impossible to blame the Americans. Only time would resolve the matter. For now, it would be consigned to the cold case intelligence files that every country had locked away for the next incident for which no one claimed responsibility.

The Pisces team was kept on life support and directed to keep their heads down. An unexpected request came in to provide a civilian with a military background to accompany a United Nations mission to Yemen, and the Admiral nominated Steele, thinking that he could use a few days away from the office. Despite his protests, he was badged as a State Department analyst and issued a diplomatic passport, with his piece of the mission funded by an unidentified component of the Department of Defense. Redeeming himself on this mission was a long shot, but Steele accepted the assignment to do some thinking. Maybe the idea of joining a top-secret organization executing special operations was not the right choice. It clearly had some perks, but the work was dangerous and unpredictable. Pisces could be shut down in a heartbeat, then what? There must be a better application of his skills. He joined the US-based UN contingent traveling from New York in a chartered commercial plane flying to Yemen via Frankfurt, Germany where the European delegation would join them.

They touched down in Sana'a early in the afternoon. Leaving the international airport in an old tourist bus freshly painted United Nations blue and bearing a large UN on its sides, Steele felt vulnerable. He was traveling in a war zone with no weapons, no clear intelligence and no friendly firepower to protect his back. A complicated civil war raged in Yemen. The Iranian-backed Houthi rebels were fighting for Allah, and the pro-government forces were trying to prop up a regime that they only half-heartedly supported. Al-Qaeda in the Arabian Peninsula also joined the fight.

He consciously amped up his situational awareness,

disconnecting all the unnecessary sensory feeds to focus on the ten-mile ride into town. Sitting three rows back from the front of the bus, he watched the blue flashing lights of the security car leading the bus suddenly veer left off the roadway. The bus screeched to a sudden stop. A pickup truck blocked the highway about 100 feet ahead. A machine gun was mounted in the truck's bed, and a gunner leveled the barrel at the bus's windshield.

Three men entered the bus, each with a Kalashnikov rifle slung over their backs. Also wearing pistol belts but still clinging to the traditional jambiya curved dagger in their belts, Steele recognized them as Houthi rebels. These were not nice people.

"Good afternoon," said the burly leader, his fatty jowls covered with a thick stubble of beard. He spoke with an accent pointing to both formal language education and extended exposure to Americans. "We are here to collect your money, jewelry, phones, and passports. You are contributing to a good cause supported by the people of Yemen who have been oppressed by the regime in exile, Saudi Arabia and its infidel puppet, the United States. The UN is another puppet supporting the West and the status quo. Anyone resisting this voluntary donation to the needy will be shot."

An official rose from the middle of the bus and spoke with a refined British accent. "This is a UN contingent traveling to Sana'a with the agreement of your government. We are protected by international law."

"I will show you what your international law means to me," said the burly man, striding quickly down the aisle and cracking the spokesman's head with the butt of his rifle. "I do not care to hear your objections. Now, get your valuables ready so we can collect them. The sooner you comply with this demand, the sooner you will be on your way to our majestic capital city."

The collection was proceeding slowly as the men stopped at every row, glanced at passports and relieved each of the passengers of their valuables. Everyone had been advised about the scourge of petty theft in Yemen, but armed robbery of this sort had not been mentioned in the country summaries that all the passengers were given before the trip.

"Ahmed," one of the collectors called to the leader in Arabic, "guess what I found?"

"What?"

"A Saudi princess."

Ahmed strode down the aisle and grabbed the passport. He studied the photograph and looked intently at the woman's uncovered face. She wore the traditional balto, a black one-piece head to toe dress appropriate for a Muslim woman venturing into public places. He pulled her roughly from the seat and threw her over his shoulder, carrying her off the bus. The woman screamed in English and Arabic, kicking and pounding the man's back with all her strength.

A dirty blanket materialized from the back of the pick-up truck, and the man spread it on the hot roadway as the woman, still flung over his shoulder, struggled to free herself. Positioned just thirty feet from the side of the bus, the occupants would have a front row seat for what would happen next. He initially choked her, using his body weight to make her lose consciousness. Then he slapped her limp form across the face several times cutting her lips. The savage blows created rivulets of blood that streamed down her cheeks, disappearing in the dark scarf covering her hair. The man threw his rifle to the side, glanced a warning at the passengers and screamed at the body in front of him, "Your warplanes killed my family — my wives, my sons and my daughter. Now you will return home with a survivor's seed growing inside you."

Steele's eyes met those of a Marine from the Embassy who had met the contingent at the airport to serve as a local escort to see them safely to the hotel. Nothing needed to be said. Both men sprang into action at the same time. The two collectors on the bus were mesmerized by the scene outside, and their rifles were difficult to maneuver in the narrow walkway separating the rows of bus seats. Both men were tackled and taken down to the floor and relieved of their rifles and knives.

Steele grabbed the rifle of the man he had subdued and chambered a round. Standing behind the glass of the open side door, he took a bead on the machine gun operator standing in the truck watching the leader ready to rape the young woman. The gun did not fire.

With the machine gun operator still captivated by the activity on the side of the bus, Steele crouched and ran towards the truck with his rifle leveled at the man. Seeing the gun barrel caused the machine gun operator to raise his hands and back away. Steele used the rifle to steer him off the back of the truck and then delivered a knockout blow to his bearded chin.

Steele crouched along the side of the truck and got a good look at the burly leader who now had the Saudi woman exposed with her balto and skirt pushed up past her hips, her panties ripped aside. He removed the pistol belt and dagger and stepped out of the long cotton pants worn under his ankle length, stained white thobe, kneeling between her legs, ready to mount her limp body like an animal.

Steele walked clear of the truck towards the man, stopping just short of the edge of the blanket. The man roared with anger grabbing the jambiya and jumping to his feet. Steele threw the useless Kalashnikov rifle to the ground and took a fighting stance.

The burly man walked away from the woman and took the time to enumerate the consequences of Steele's actions, "Infidel, you will die by my hand, slowly after watching me and my brothers savage this girl. We will then kill everyone on the bus one by one and kick their severed heads down into the valley. You will die last."

"No. I will kill you and bury you and your brothers with a pig." Steele knew there were no pigs within a thousand miles, but it was the thought that counted. He wanted to throw the man off-balance mentally. Without focus, the leader would be much easier to defeat.

The man produced a deep-throated and chilling roar as he lunged. Steele parried the blow but got nicked under his extended elbow by the assailant's razor-sharp blade. The two men closed, and Steele found that the Houthi was wiry and strong as well as light on his feet despite his paunch.   Steele tried to gain some mechanical advantage with a powerful stomp on the top of the man's sandaled foot. He yelped in pain and backed away but held the curved dagger with a firm grip. The two circled on the tarmac seeking an opening in the other's defenses. Steele felt confident about besting his opponent, but the knife was a deadly equalizer. The Saudi woman regained consciousness and ran for the temporary safety afforded by the bus.

Steele landed a solid blow on the man's jaw before the bladed scythe arced towards his chest, missing the mark. The burly one deftly reversed the arc making a lateral slice through the air just an inch from Steele's chest. Separated, the man wiped blood from his mouth and chin with the back of his hand and then again charged. He would bury the curved blade in the Westerner's belly and open him up like a spring lamb. Steele dodged the outstretched knife but was knocked off his feet by the man's shoulder. Steele rolled away and jumped to his feet just before another charge. This time, Steele deflected the arm, landing a sharp blow to the man's kidney and tripping him to the ground. But he still gripped the knife. Winded, the man rolled over and sat upright on the same blanket he spread on the roadway to defile the Saudi woman. Speaking to Steele between gasps as he sucked in deep lungfuls of air, he said,

"Infidel, I know I'll lose this fight, but I will never again be imprisoned by the old government here. You have won, but now that victory will be meaningless. May Allah forgive me of this great sin." He plunged the jambiya into his torso and opened himself up, eviscerating his internal organs that spilled out onto his white thobe, glistening with the fresh oxygenated blood in the hot afternoon sun. He worked the blade of the knife under his rib cage probing for his heart, before toppling on his side with his last breath. Steele had watched men die before but none like this.

He turned and walked to the bus where the passengers were too shocked to say anything or able to comprehend what they'd just witnessed. The Saudi woman was sobbing uncontrollably while being comforted in the embrace of another woman who looked at Steele with a thousand-mile stare.

He'd found an ally in the Embassy Marine who moved to the front of the bus, still holding the rifle.

The Marine said, "We need to get out of here pronto. We are about halfway into the city. I think we need to continue there and hope to get some help along the way."

"I agree. I think we can leave our friends where they are. We can take these two collectors with us. What happened to the driver?"

"He took off."

"Can you drive a bus?"

"Sure. I drove five-ton trucks in the war so I think I can handle this." The Marine punched some numbers into his cell phone, cradled it between his neck and shoulder as he shifted expertly through the gears.

"OK," said Steele as he raised his voice and addressed the others. "We are heading on to Sana'a." He saw the bleeding spokesperson momentarily rise to cast the deciding vote in the matter, but he sat down again nursing the oozing laceration on his forehead.

Three minutes after the bus got up to speed, Steele looked ahead and saw a white pickup truck parked on the shoulder and then spotted a white-robed figure kneeling in the middle of the road. The angle of his arms and the metallic glint of the tube he carried on his shoulder confirmed a Rocket Propelled Grenade was being aimed at the bus.

"Get down," he commanded as he stood, startling the Marine staring at the man in the road but not recognizing that he was directly in the line of fire. Steele saw the smoke trail as he hit the floor. The RPG flew high, hitting the metal frame of the bus just above the driver's head. The explosion was deafening as shrapnel penetrated the bus's thin sheet metal skin and found soft flesh.

The blast dislodged the driver from his seat. Steele looked through the shattered windshield at a bearded man in the middle of the road calmly loading another round. This would be an easy shot with no mistakes. He quickly stepped over bodies on the floor and jumped into the blood-covered driver's seat, grabbing the wheel and yanking it hard to the right. With its accelerator floored, the bus bridged the open shoulder and veered down a gravelly hillside washboarded by the last rainstorm. The bus was not designed for off-roading. Steele knew that every yard traveled reduced the probability of kill for the shooter and that a crossing target at increasing range would be almost impossible to engage. He glanced in the rear-view mirror and saw the white pickup on the main highway now pacing the bus.

Seconds later, he saw that the steep hillside ended with a sheer drop-off. Turning to the left would take the bus back up the hill, making it a large, slow moving target. Turning to the right would move them closer to the white truck following them on the main road.

He yelled over the panicked screams of the passengers, "I will stop the bus. Leave as fast as you can and take cover along the cliff. Use the emergency door in the back. Stopping NOW." He slammed on the brakes and pulled the emergency brake simultaneously. The bus skidded sideways, almost turning over after going up on its left side wheels before finally settling upright. Steele looked up the hill and saw the white truck stopping. The shooter jumped out to get a clear shot at the bus that was once again facing him directly.

"Go, go, go," Steele yelled as he picked up a woman draped in a black balto lying on the floor of the bus. He bolted out of the side door, running towards the cliff. Within seconds, another RPG round went through the center of the open windshield frame and exploded with a brilliant flash. Red hot shrapnel penetrated the gasoline tank and engulfed the bus's skeletal remains in an explosive fireball coughing heavy black smoke.

Steele wondered "How many made it out?" Minutes passed.

Finally, flashing lights converged along the highway. Sirens blaring, several ambulances threaded their way down the hillside to a nearby clearing where a pair of skinny goats was staked.

"Thanks for saving me," cried a weak voice. The woman Steele carried off the bus had pulled her headscarf off her head, releasing short length, tightly curled blonde hair.

"Are you injured?" he asked.

"My left leg," she said, pulling up the thin black fabric. A jagged piece of sheet metal was poking through a hole in the blood-soaked jeans.

"Don't try to move," he said, "You've got a nasty piece of the bus buried in your upper leg and have lost a lot of blood. Just lay back. I'll flag down one of the medics." He ripped the jean's seams from her ankle and then pulled the stretchy denim fabric away from the laceration just above her knee, knotting the ends above it. Her hazel eyes were fluttering with shock. Steele helped an EMT move her onto a stretcher and then picked up the other end and headed for an ambulance.

After he pushed the stretcher into the vehicle, the woman mustered enough strength to grab his arm and look him in the eyes. "I'm Isabel," she said. "Thank you...?" pausing at the end for him to fill in the blank. Her accent sounded Scandinavian.

"Dan Steele," he said. "Good luck."

He made a quick survey of the scene and found the UN liaison officer on the radio.

"That was one hell of a piece of driving you did back there. If you hadn't taken over the wheel, I think all of us would have been dead right now."

"I know the driver and several others were left on the bus. Have you got a fix on the rest?"

"Not really, most of the people got as far away as they could. They are spread out all over the hillside. I've seen a lot of lacerations from the shrapnel. One man may have broken his ankle jumping out of the back of the bus, but other than that, we've just got a bunch of people suffering from severe shock and confused as hell about what just happened."

"What's the immediate plan from here?"

"Not sure. The team leader is the Brit over there in the white linen suit who is still dazed from that rifle butt to his head. My guess is that we'll probably head back to the airport and wait for further direction. This was certainly not part of the plan!"

Steele returned to the bus and the smell of burned flesh filled his nostrils. He found the Embassy Marine's burned body in the doorway. The first shot drove a sharp piece of window frame into his neck like a spear. A shot of bitter bile filled his throat as he turned away from the body and walked towards the rocky cliff, looking aimlessly at the barren landscape below.

CHAPTER TEN

Sana'a, Yemen

The setting sun brought a winter chill to the international airport located at an elevation of over 7,000 feet. What was left of the UN team assembled in the terminal after reversing their earlier course and returning to the airport protected by a phalanx of military vehicles and police cars. The final tally: three dead, five seriously injured, several severe lacerations, assorted contusions and a fractured ankle.

Finally, as the long day approached midnight, a motorcade of three tourist buses surrounded by Yemeni policeman and military vehicles safely made the transit into town. The UN contingent was assigned rooms in the same three-star hotel planned as their base for the ten-day mission. Luggage was transported in a separate van and piled onto carts in the lobby. Now sporting a bandaged head, the British man in the soiled linen suit announced that the team would meet the next morning at 10:00 a.m., giving everyone free time to recover from the recent ordeal and to regain their bearings. He promised to have some answers about the future of the mission by that time, although several people had already made up their minds to leave Yemen on the first available flight, even if they had to pay for the ticket on their own.

Steele got to his room, peeled off his blood-stained clothes, knotted them in a plastic laundry bag and threw them in the trash. He showered and settled down in the front of the 19- inch color TV. Stretching out on the bed, he immediately passed out and slept soundly until 05:30 a.m. when he heard the call to morning prayer.

The mullah was in the middle of the Muslim wake-up call when his recorded A Capella was interrupted by the bedside phone ringing in Steele's ear.

"Good morning, Dan, it's time to rise and shine!"

"I just heard reveille sounded from the top of the minaret just outside my window. Is this a back-up call?"

"No, this is your local Defense Attaché."

Steele responded, "I'm thinking of a song."

"Wasted Days and Wasted Nights," came the correct response.

"Thanks for connecting with me, but Lord Fauntleroy has called a meeting for ten o'clock this morning when we'll find out what will happen next. As I'm sure you know, we got off to a rough start yesterday. Major Turner was killed. If it weren't for him, we might have all ended up dead. Semper Fi."

"He was a good man. We are all sick about it. Turner was on a one-year unaccompanied tour and left his wife and daughter back in Camp Lejeune. They'll get the formal notification sometime later today. Look, I just found out the UN has decided to pull the plug on the assessment. A plane will be coming in late tonight to return the group to Europe and then on to CONUS, so I thought you'd might like to get the lay of the land over here so you can prepare a useful report for your sponsor. If you are up to it, I'll be over about 0700 for breakfast at the hotel, and we'll go for a drive."

"Sounds good. After yesterday, I hope I'm not pushing my luck. See you soon." The Defense Attaché, Colonel Terry Bullard, had been identified as a local point of contact. Maybe something of value could be salvaged from this trip after all. Feeling like he'd just completed a five-mile run in soft sand, Steele stood under the tepid shower for twenty minutes before getting dressed, stretching three adhesive strips over the slice on his arm and heading to the lobby.

Colonel Bullard wore a variation of the many desert camouflaged uniforms. His thick neck rose from a blocky body and supported a large round head with close-cropped salt and pepper hair.

He had a friendly, broad smile. Shorter than Steele, his handshake was bone-crushing. A very tough guy, Steele concluded as the two were led into the empty dining room and took a table in the corner.

They wolfed down a breakfast of pita bread with strained yogurt and warm beans served from a bulbous brass pot with a narrow neck and some sweet Yemeni tea with milk and seasoned with cardamom. When crushed, the tiny black cardamom seeds added both flavor and an exotic aroma to the tea. Feeling like a new man, Steele briefly replayed the Houthi attack from the previous day, and the Colonel agreed that it fit the pattern of previous rebel attacks but with an uptick in the aggressiveness. Nothing was off limits for these Iranian-backed crusaders. Steele took additional time to recount the selfless actions of the dead Major and hoped that his family would understand that he saved many people by his actions.

"How long have you been over here?" asked Steele.

"Too long," said the Colonel, "The Army sent me to Monterey to learn Arabic, and this is the reward. Truth is that my wife bailed on me after meeting an original California surfer boy down in Carmel. It didn't much matter. This is an unaccompanied tour, and we would be separated anyway. So, I'm coming up on three years in the job and have already got my twenty in, so I'll probably retire from here. How about you?"

"I left the Navy after six years and just finished up a stint at the Domestic Terrorism Unit of DHS in DC. My farewell gift was a big chunk of flesh ripped out of the back of my thigh and a broken arm. That's a story for another time. Now I'm a DOD contractor of sorts and got volunteered for this job by my boss. This assignment looked like a milk run. Seemed like I zigged when I should have zagged."

The two walked outside and climbed into an SUV. The Colonel checked-in using the dash-mounted radio before turning onto an unpaved, dusty side road. Driving in silence, Steele got his first views of a place that he'd never visited before. He recalled a briefing where someone had described a trip to Yemen as entering a time machine where you stepped back 300 years. The traditional Bedouin heritage was on display everywhere: the baked mud structures, men carrying the traditional curved daggers on belts cinched around their flowing white robes, and women protected by the long black balto sometimes paired with brightly-colored headscarves revealing only their dark eyes, the fleeting suspicious looks of merchants who stood outside shops and watched everything. Steele felt that they were under constant surveillance.

A Saudi-led coalition of eight Arab states began an air campaign in 2015 against the rebels and had killed thousands of people in airstrikes, inflaming the population by taking the lives of so many innocent families. Some of the precision-guided munitions landed on schools and hospitals. The United States, as well as France and Britain supported the Saudis from behind the scenes, and reports from the field revealed the indiscriminate killing in heavily populated areas.

Things had to be very serious for the Saudis to get involved and their objective, as well as the other Gulf States joining them, was Sunni dominance, to throw a bulwark up against the radical Iranian regime that would use any means to expand their influence in the region. Yemen was merely another playing field. A deposed president with a large loyalist following squaring off against all the varieties of regional extremists.

"Did you hear about the Houthis launching those missile attacks aimed at US warships operating near Bab-el-Mandeb?" asked the Colonel who seemed to know every back road of the city.

"Yeah, they missed or fell short. I know that the ships fired interceptors in defense but never heard much more about it."

"That's right. Our analysts assessed they were coastal defense cruise missiles donated by our friends in Iran. Before then, our relationship with Yemen couldn't find a middle ground. We moved between supporting the regime and trying to distance ourselves as if the country never existed. The National Security team is constantly wrestling with where to place the bets going forward. State protected a Foreign Aid line item in the President's budget for Yemen, usually earmarked for an invitation to a military officer to join their American colleagues at one of the service schools. Anyway, what you see here is partially the result of those policies colliding with the ongoing fundamentalist fervor that shows no signs of weakening. This place is a mess. And because Yemen sits along a strategic waterway where the Red Sea's width narrows to a river-sized channel entering the Gulf of Aden before joining the Arabian Sea, the political situation is problematic. No approach seems to work."

"What do you see in your crystal ball? What's this place going to look like in five years?"

"My guess is that civil war will ebb and flow until a leader emerges to lead the majority, whether fundamentalist or modernist. Yemen will respond to a strong man, not a propped-up democracy. The free world just doesn't understand the concept. The Arab spring got everyone's attention and has pushed a superficial reform where the governments become more benevolent and provide for the larger population. But at the end of the day, the Middle East will not get any more civilized by western standards than being headed by a benevolent dictator with royal blood running through his veins."

Colonel Bullard drove under the hotel's front portico, a simple frame topped with a faded green mesh garden cloth to shade guests from the sun which just after 2:00 p.m. was baking. Three smaller buses crowded the parking area, and Steele could see some of the UN team ready to board for the 3:00 p.m. departure for the airport.

"Thanks, Terry. Great tour. I have a better idea of what's going on here and came back in one piece. Don't know if our paths will cross again, but I hope so."

"I'm sure they will. Safe travels and let me know if you ever need anything from this side."

The two shook hands, and Steele watched the dusty swirl as the SUV left the hotel. He had an uneasy feeling that he and Colonel Bullard would see each other again sooner than either one of them could imagine.

CHAPTER ELEVEN

Washington, DC

Steele's routine visit to Yemen with the UN gave the Pisces team and its short chain of command a chance to recover from the bloody operation in Turkey which still plagued them. It had the opposite effect. Since his return from capturing a woman instead of the bombmaker, the attitude of the team at home had changed. Demoralized by the results of the first mission assigned to Pisces, their confidence was shaken. Outsiders had labeled it a complete bust. Supportive and unwilling to lend credence to the critics, Captain Hank Owens remained a strong champion. Lesser men would have cut and run. Admiral Wright felt the pressure when he started down a familiar road at the end of an office conversation. Here comes the zinger, Steele thought.

"Come on, Dan, just look at the facts. This was supposed to be a clandestine operation. Instead you blended a tentful of bad guys into marinara sauce, littered the beach with bodies and captured a woman who still refuses to cooperate. This was a disaster. State is trying hard to disavow any US involvement. The Secretary compares this operation with the Saudi hit squad killing the Post journalist in their own consulate. The Turks are relentless, still probing for answers, and I don't know how long we can hide from the press. They are all over this story. The only people happy about this state of affairs is the FBI who are enjoying an organizational breather from the focus on their internal issues. Fortunately, the interrogation piece is being handled overseas. I've been called up to speak with the National Security Advisor several times, and she's thinking about shutting us down. Maybe I should have stayed in Rhode Island battling quahogs.

And maybe it was too early after your injuries for this kind of assignment, I don't know, but things are getting uglier every day."

"Admiral, we've been over this before. What can I say? The plan was solid, and we executed it. I agree that taking the woman seems like a bad call on my part, but we can't put the toothpaste back in the tube. I was totally ready for this op. The Monday morning quarterbacks would grouse about this no matter what the outcome. It wasn't pretty, and there's been a lot of damage control required to put this behind us. But all this post mortem second-guessing has become a major distraction to the group, and it's not helping us plan for the next mission, assuming we'll get another assignment."

"Ok, fine," said the Admiral in an unfamiliar cold voice and putting his hands in the air in an exasperated show of surrender. "Let's get back to work."

"Yes, sir."

Dan left the Admiral's office caught up in a torrent of emotions.

"Hch, Dan, have you seen the report from Syria in this morning's traffic?" asked Cass Thomas who intercepted him in the hallway.

"No, I'm not sure that I'm interested."

Cass followed him into his office and closed the door. "Look, Dan, I know things have been tough for you since the mission to Turkey. I hear all the talk. Just wanted you to know that I'm in your corner, so if you need someone to talk or cry or drink some whiskey with, you can count on me."

Steele slumped into his chair. "Thanks, Cass, I appreciate that. I feel like the 'Man in the Arena', pointing to a framed poster of the famous excerpt from Theodore Roosevelt's 1910 speech at the Sorbonne hanging on his office wall. But I'm not ready to throw in the towel by any means. It's a beautiful day outside, and I think I need a long walk to clear my head. I'll see you later."

Steele's inner voice ruminated in a dark space: If a mission does not go smoothly, OK. But to send a team into harm's way and then criticize the results was the meanest form of support. A classic case of psychological displacement, he was feeling the heat generated by the bureaucracy in Washington. The city just couldn't help itself and looked for the opportunity to turn any victory into defeat. The town was cold. Plenty of emotional outbursts, but they were right out of a script.

Walking west along M Street towards the former USCG Headquarters at Buzzard Point, Steele remembered the times he'd visited the base in the past and how it still had that combat zone feeling to it. Years ago, no one would ever leave the Navy Yard on foot. The renovation of Southeast continued at an incredible clip, and the incentives offered by the District were successful in securing development funds and luring all sorts of retail outlets into the area. Buzzard Point seemed to be located just outside the development boundaries.

He paralleled South Capitol street and just past the Nationals Stadium, while he replayed the tape from Turkey in his mind for the millionth time, he was jolted back to reality when he saw four young men on the sidewalk apparently shaking down an elderly couple. Steele saw a trim, well-dressed man hand over his wallet while one of the younger men was rifling through the woman's handbag. Steele kept walking towards the group and their attention shifted to him.

"Hey, pretty boy, are you lost or something? Just empty your pockets, and you'll be able to continue your walk. Put up a fight and you may find yourself and these old folks hurt real bad." One of the punks raised the bottom of his hoodie enough for Steele to see a 9mm pistol butt in his belt. Another had a set of nunchucks that he removed from the small of his back and began a rhythmic exercise to show their lethality in his practiced hands. Steele was out-gunned. The sensible thing to do was to comply with the demands and add his cash, cards, phone and watch to the goods the men had already collected. But today, after the earlier discussion with the Admiral, he didn't feel particularly sensible or cautious. He reached for his wallet and came up empty-handed.

"It's a beautiful day, and I am enjoying my walk. Now you guys can return the lady's handbag and the gentleman's wallet and walk away, no harm no foul or you can try to take whatever you want from me and suffer the consequences." One of the four responded with a nervous laugh while the others just stood there with gaping mouths.

"You are not just pretty, you are stupid too," said a tall gangly black man sporting multiple gold chains around his tattooed neck as he stepped towards Steele. Steele replied,

"And you are very brave."

Except for the brief encounter with Richie Bouffard, he'd not used the fighting skills he'd learned during his convalescence, so here was another opportunity to test the techniques outside the gym. He knew he was being reckless but felt that a little street fight might relieve some of his pent-up frustration. Sure, the smart response was to hand over his stuff and walk away. But Steele felt restless and unsettled and confident enough to fight back against these punks. These guys picked the wrong time to attempt a two-fer by robbing Steele.

The guy with a basketball player's build threw a hard punch at Steele's head which he easily avoided while kicking the attacker's knee sideways, forcing it in an unnatural direction, stretching and popping as tendons and ligaments were torn from the upper and lower knee joint. Writhing in pain, the man grasped his leg with an agonizing scream. One tough down.

Two others came at him together. Steele blocked the punches from one and caught one of the nunchucks and twisted it from the attacker's grip. Using their combined weight and momentum, he ducked and wedged himself between them to force a face to face collision that broke the nose of one assailant and left the other in dire need of dental work. Disoriented and seeing only stars, the broken nose was on his knees applying pressure to the gusher spouting from his nostrils.

The bleeding mouth still had some fight left in him, and Steele dropped him with a blow to his chest and a swift kick to his groin. Number four, the one with the gun, decided to cut his losses. He abandoned his injured posse and ran from the scene. Steele retrieved the couple's belongings and watched the toughs hobble away, leaving a trail of blood on the sidewalk.

"Are you folks OK?" asked Steele.

"We are now. I don't know what we would have done if those thugs had stolen our things," said the woman.

"Can I help you get somewhere? This is not really a safe place. Where are you going?"

The man responded, "We are headed to the Navy Yard to meet our son-in-law for lunch."

"The Navy Yard is that way," said Steele pointing in the opposite direction. "I'll walk with you to the front gate if you are able to continue."

"That would be wonderful. I'm Admiral George Timms and this is my wife, Abby."

"It's an honor to meet you both. I'm Dan Steele, former US Navy Lieutenant."

Twenty minutes later, he watched them head through the gate at the Navy Yard and waved goodbye. As he walked away, he felt a new spurt of energy and a renewed confidence.

When he returned to the cavern, Cass approached him with a telltale frown on her face.

"How was your walk?"

"Invigorating. My head is clear, and I'm 100% back in the game. Where are the cables that you mentioned earlier?"

"In the middle of your desk. But first, you may want to stop by the little boy's room and clean up the strawberry stains all over your face and shirt."

CHAPTER TWELVE

Moscow, Russia

Having just returned from his assignment in the Ukraine, Brigadier General Nikolai Zlodeyev walked the familiar halls. There were many nods and even slight bows from the other uniformed and civilian workers walking between offices and meeting rooms. The building reminded him of a scaled down version of the Pentagon he once visited with a military delegation from Russia.

In Moscow, a new National Military Command Center was under construction and would offer all the conveniences of modern war-making, including a centralized command and control structure which would doom most special operations missions to failure. The future generals and admirals in the field would be mere automatons manipulated by electronic strings controlled by the political puppet masters. The Alpha Group still retained its independence, but the writing was on the wall. Soon, all operations would be micro-managed from Moscow. The man he was about to see was one of the architects of that future.

He entered the large office on the third floor that overlooked the courtyard through floor to ceiling windows. Though the windows were made of single pane glass and the metal frames were poorly fitted to the casing, they let in lots of light but also water that leaked in with the frequent rain and snow. But to his administrative commander, General Yuri Urodov, the trade-off seemed worthwhile. Urodov navigated around the side of the massive wooden desk and greeted the General with a firm handshake. The two sat in armchairs facing the glass windows separated by a small table covered with boxes of cigarettes and cigars. Urodov shook a cigarette from an open package and lit it, inhaling deeply and expelling a cloud of acrid smoke. On rare occasions, Zlodeyev would smoke a cigar but didn't plan to stay with Urodov long enough to enjoy one.

Zlodeyev shifted in the worn leather chair and leaned forward. Despite the cloud of smoke filling the air, Zlodeyev immediately smelled Urodov's signature cologne. Considered masculine in its day, he applied the scent liberally every morning whether he showered or not. It was marketed in Europe as an equestrian scent, worn by racehorse owners and polo players. The brand that Urodov purchased made him smell like a horse that had been ridden hard and put away wet. Everyone joked about it in the Headquarters, and several colleagues suggested that he'd purchased the remaining inventory of the discontinued fragrance in liter jugs at a knock-down price.

Each man despised the other, but the façade of good humor and comradeship persisted even behind closed doors.

"So, General, welcome home. Once again you have served our mother Russia with great honor and courage. I understand that your unit efficiently disbanded the protesters and restored order in Kerch."

"Yes, the operation in Kerch went very smoothly, thanks to your brilliant plan. We broke the will of the resistance on day one and maintained a presence in the town for one week. Once again, things are peaceful in the city. We made many new friends, particularly with the attractive and lonely women of the city."

Both Generals laughed heartily, recalling similar campaigns when they were in the field together.

"It's a tough job but someone has to do it, right?"

"We are just increasing the pool of potential candidates for the future Alpha Group. Is this not part of our responsibility?" The laughing continued.

"Nikolai, I am hopeful that you might explain one part of the many reports that came across my desk related to the mission. You requisitioned some heavy earth moving equipment from the mainland. I got a query from the General Staff about the cost of expedited shipment and return. Why did you need such equipment?"

"As you can imagine, the insurgents in Kerch did not greet us with open arms. They seemed ready to resist us by any means possible. I used the equipment to clear an open area for a command post and defensible perimeter. I'm sure that the transport proved costly but know that you share my concern about having my men exposed to imminent danger. That would have been reckless. I am happy to report that all my men came home safely except for a few cases of venereal disease which as you well know is a hazard of conducting operations overseas."

Both men again laughed at the remark and the visual image it provoked. However, Zlodeyev noted that Urodov's laugh seemed a bit forced after his response and prepared for more questions related to the details of the operation.

"I see. I will inform the bookkeepers about your need to build defenses. I heard a somewhat different report but now understand your need for the equipment." Urodov stubbed out his cigarette and tried to suppress his rising anger with the stories that he was being fed.

"Were there any other events that happened in Kerch that I should be aware of?" The level of tension between the two men rose. The bureaucrat versus the warrior. Urodov was a perpetual headquarters fixture with a vast network of internal spies, informal communications channels and a box full of markers from people he had "pardoned" for their indiscretions. He was trying to get more leverage on Zlodeyev. However, the warrior was well-prepared and expected this type of exchange. Zlodeyev was in total control of his emotional balance and further infuriated his boss as he shifted the conversation and tried to lighten the mounting level of suspicion between the two.

"No, nothing out of the ordinary. It turned out to be a routine mission, just the right assignment for an Alpha Group cadre. I hope the Minister is pleased with the outcome. I apologize for being so short today, but I have another appointment over at the training center. Before I go, Yuri, I brought you a small memento from Kerch that I hope you can find a place for in your display case." The display case extended down an open wall in Urodov's office. Glass-topped, it held an impressive collection of battlefield souvenirs collected and given as gifts from warriors over the years. Urodov was very proud of its contents and lived vicariously as the one who collected the artifacts on the battlefield. It brought him closer to the self-image he longed for. Though the case could be filled with genuine battlefield relics by Nikolai alone, he had never contributed anything for the case. One of Urodov's aides had mentioned this shortcoming to Zlodeyev during his last visit to the office.

The General brought out a small, crudely made plastic thermometer with a bikini clad woman in the foreground of a seaside scene. The base was bannered Kerch. Zlodeyev handed it to the general with great ceremony as if the gift were presented after a drum roll to signal its significance.

Yuri Urodov's sallow face flushed with Nikolai's obvious disrespect. He resisted the urge to summarily dismiss Zlodeyev. Instead, he faked a laugh and said, "Made in China too. What a surprise! I expected that you'd bring me an antique jeweled icon. But thank you for this thoughtful gift. I think I'll place it here in the rubbish bin."

General Urodov stood and faced his seated subordinate with a cold sneer. "Please stop by my aide's desk and schedule a meeting before the end of the month. By that time, perhaps your recollection of events in Kerch will have improved. And I want a detailed report of your activities on my desk within one week's time. Do you understand me?" Not expecting a response, he continued, "You know, Niko, you should not toy with me. You should recognize where your bread is buttered. Your protectors are dying off, and your day is coming. I will bust you down, and you'll end up cleaning urinals at the Officers' Club."

Nikolai merely smiled as he rose from his chair, towering over Urodov. He turned and left the office without a word. He had saved Yuri's hide enough times and knew the tough talk was just that. There was nothing that his boss could really do other than to write a meaningless report. Nikolai had his friends and markers as well which he would use to protect himself. Still, the balance was changing with time, and Urodov's idle threats could become real in the future.

CHAPTER THIRTEEN

Outside Moscow, Russia

Bright lights ringed the dirt arena. A low white-washed wooden fence defined the circular field about one hundred feet in diameter and protected the onlookers from the action. Heavy hats and coats protected them from the penetrating cold. Metal bleachers banked up from four sides in the makeshift colosseum. It was a Saturday night, and the spectators were betting on their favorites in this modern-day cock fight taking place a stone's throw from Moscow. With limited seating, Cowtown offered an intimate setting and thrived on bizarre excursions from its usual no-holds-barred fights. The cage fights popularized in the Western world seemed very civilized by comparison. No rules. No referee. The promise of a series of bloody contests stirred the bettors to a fever pitch.

There were ten events on the night's playbill, and the crowd had already been treated to several bloody encounters between men willing to participate in a contest that ended only when one of the contestants was knocked unconscious, pleaded for the end, or dead. Here, there was no emperor being entertained, just a mix of spectators and bettors ranging from farmers to the Russian mob. If you had the money to pay a modest entry fee entitling you to an unreserved seat and a glass of vodka, you were treated just like everyone else. There were no box seats at the arena.

The main event on a Saturday night was the big draw. Some brave brawler would face an animal in the ring. Blood sport. Contestants squared off against bulls, wild dogs, and even exotic animals like tigers. The announcer walked to the center of the blood-soaked sawdust covering the soil and spoke into a wireless lip microphone.

"Ladies and Gentlemen, tonight's Main Event features a contest you will not see anywhere else. In the arena Nikolai Zlodeyev, originally from Belgorod, will face a wild boar from Ussuriland tipping the scales at 750 pounds."

As he strode into the ring, wearing long leather shorts and canvas boxing boots, his skin glistening from a combination of sweat and oil applied to his frame, there were cheers from the stands, and the frenzied pace of the betting quickened. Zlodeyev stood six feet nine inches in height and tipped the scales at 330 pounds. He looked like one of the contestants in the World's Strongest Man competition except that his skills were not limited to picking up cars and throwing large wooden poles over fences. There was no doubt that he could do that too, but his real skill was the unadorned fight, one-on-one without the aid of weapons — a modern-day gladiator who had proved his skills in the same ring many times before against men and animals.

Zlodeyev considered these fights the truest form of sport with an obvious winner and loser. Team sports were nuanced. A coaches' bad game plan, the loss of a key player, a disputed call by the referee could all lead to defeat. No excuses existed in a contest like this one. Just two combatants trying to best the other in any way they could. It was raw, unscripted, live, and always bloody. For Zlodeyev, being here in the arena was the pinnacle of personal pleasure. Sex, alcohol, drugs, money, and power in a single mind-blowing dose. He waved to the crowd and took his place in a white circle like a batter's on deck circle and got ready to face his opponent.

The monster was released from a cage at the opposite side of the arena and seemed frozen by the bright flood lights. His coarse hair, snout, and sharp curved tusks complemented the large set of testicles that swung between his hind legs. The vicious feral pig was the product of a large domestic swine and a large boar. They had been spotted all over the world, including a huge boar rummaging through a dumpster in Hong Kong. This particular swine had the personality of a mean junkyard dog and had killed one of the men who had captured it.

The wild beast's flat nose smelled and then spotted the man

standing fifty feet away. The boar took stock of the man walking in his direction before he charged. Zlodeyev faced a small freight train running for a collision when the thick skull and tusks would drive into his legs and rip through the major blood vessels before opening his belly and chest to feast on his internal organs. Zlodeyev crouched and moved to the balls of his feet. He knew he was more agile and smarter, but at a certain point, the sheer weight and killer instincts of the pig zeroed out any advantage intelligence might bring. After all, he thought, what human being would be in the ring with this animal in the first place? Most people would never even consider it.

Zlodeyev sidestepped the charge and landed a blow to the boar's midsection as he ran past him, but was not quick enough to avoid one of the tusks that tore through the thick belting leather of his shorts and opened up a gash above his knee. The crowd roared as the odds shifted in the animal's favor, and the betting increased at a frenetic pace. Zlodeyev shifted his approach, now becoming the hunter as he closed the distance within the small arena. The boar stood as if he were thinking about the next attack, his exhalations sparkling as clouds in the cool night. There were no outward signs of Zlodeyev's punch causing any damage.

Zlodeyev approached the animal, thinking that he must break one of the animal's legs to gain an advantage. He swept in low around the animal's hind legs before the pig turned and squealed as he butted the general into the air. Zlodeyev got to his feet quickly and took a fighting stance, now with two tusk wounds in his chest that were pumping blood and staining his shorts before dripping to the soil.

Inflamed by the taste of the blood, the boar quickly charged to finish his prey. Zlodeyev feinted to the right and then moved to the left, wrapped his arms around the beast's neck and rode him to the ground. With his legs flailing, the pig's neck was stretched backwards. The veins in Zlodeyev's arms stood out like thick cords as the blood refreshed his muscles. His thick legs were planted in the ground to gain the mechanical advantage. Sharp fore hooves raked his lower back as the boar tried to maneuver out of the head lock being applied by his human foe. Covered with coarse hair, his short, thick neck was pulled back as the grip tightened. Massive yellow teeth in front of the tusks chomped the air, and the animal's thick saliva ran down onto Zlodeyev's arms, threatening to slacken his grip. The tusks scraped Zlodeyev's chest as the boar tried to move his head from side to side. With any change in position, the razor-sharp flutes of the tusks could open a man's chest in an instant.

Using the large muscles in his massive legs, Zlodeyev suddenly pivoted, violently twisting the boar's neck as the two fell to the bloody ground. The sound of tearing flesh and muscles was drowned out by the excited screams from the crowd. The thrashing ended abruptly. The pig was dead, and Zlodeyev rose and raised his fist to the crowd in the universal victory sign. The match had taken less than two minutes, and the crowd went wild with the fervor of the fight, the betting and most of all, the blood.

Zlodeyev's share of the purse would pay for the doctor to stitch up his wounds and to buy a few rounds of vodka for his friends, but it was worth so much more than a few rubles. He tasted the animal's dried blood on his hands and smelled the wild scent of the pig. He felt an undeniable pulse of pleasure all over his body. This was real sport — blood sport.

CHAPTER FOURTEEN

Durres, Albania

After being carefully wrapped in clear plastic sheets covered with air-filled bubbles and placed into crates or heavy cardboard boxes, the Kerch artifacts were loaded, filling thirty containers. A ship accustomed to transporting military hardware for the Russia Federation craned the containers from the wharf into its hold where they were secured to the interior cargo deck for the transit. Three days later, the ship berthed in the old port of Durres, Albania and off-loaded the containers onto intermodal tractor trailers.

The cargo was consigned to Double Eagle Industries, an international transportation and security firm recommended to Zlodeyev by his mentor. Escorted by armed security guards, the trucks were led to the capital city of Tirana, where the shipment would be stored in a high security warehouse owned by the company. Cargo theft and pilfering were serious issues in the port and also in the capital, with most merchants assuming a ten percent loss of goods that would find their way into the country's thriving black market. But this warehouse operation was off-limits. Double Eagle's Chief Executive, a powerful man known only as Spence, was very security conscious, and no one would cross his path. These goods were 100 per cent secure.

CHAPTER FIFTEEN

Aberdeen, Hong Kong

With just a loin cloth covering the sinewy body baked by the sun to the color of drying tobacco, the Merchant panned the harbor which used to be home to thousands of people living in the floating city. Sitting on the afterdeck of his junk-rigged wooden boat that had just returned to offload its cargo of fresh fish, he missed the intimate community which lived on their boats and made their living from the sea. Most had been relocated to high-rise flats. Hundreds of floating restaurants were replaced with a few massive eateries catering to thousands at a time. Sampans used to ply the waters and bring the tourists in twos and threes, but they were few and far between these days. Once a thriving fishing port, the waterborne part of the city had been thrust into modern-day commercialism. A few permanent boats remained in Aberdeen, and the Merchant's floating home was one of them. He paid handsomely to cling to the past.

He communicated via cable and face to face. Still suspicious of electronics, he understood their convenience. The Merchant presided over a large network of both suppliers and buyers interested in the unique. His trade matched eager buyers with one-of-a-kind pieces of art or sculpture any museum would have paid top dollar to acquire for their own collection. The clients were very wealthy people who could afford to buy an irreplaceable piece of history. As an added measure of security, new clients had to be recommended by someone who had done business with the Merchant in the past.

A steady stream of ancient artifacts entered the market from the war-torn sites in Syria, Iraq and Afghanistan and continued unabated from Egypt. The flow from Europe had been reduced to a trickle but made up for the lack of quantity by the quality and name recognition that lured buyers and drove prices higher. Business was booming. The Merchant had become a rich man. He enjoyed the buying and selling and the position of being a single middle-man between a limited supply of antiquities and anxious customers with unlimited desires to possess them. Yet he preferred the simple life of a fisherman and liked getting out on the water every day, never appearing on anyone's most wealthy list because his dealings were not made public nor were they reported.

He opened one of the cables in his morning stack, holding it very close to his face as he slowly read the English words aloud, "I HAVE A LARGE QUANTITY OF RUSSIAN ANTIQUITIES FROM THE REIGN OF CZAR ALEXANDER I. WOULD YOU BE INTERESTED? The cable originated in Moscow and was signed with coded entries of D23 and M42. The Merchant knew D23 as a Russian General, a long-time supplier of goods. He had introduced and vouched for a potential client years before and advised the Merchant to expect a future communication. Though he'd not done any business with M42, the opportunity to handle a large quantity of antiquities from that era was intriguing.

The Merchant turned to his assistant and said, "Respond that I will look forward to seeing the collection. Give M42 the details on how to post photos on our secure server. After I review the holdings, perhaps we'll put the portfolio up for 24 hours with a one-time coded access for our top buyers." He looked forward to seeing the photographs of the collection on the large screen below decks.

CHAPTER SIXTEEN

Belgorod, Russia

As a child, Nikolai Zlodeyev's memories narrowed to a single period of a painful experience with a man introduced as his uncle. At nine years of age, Nikolai stood taller than many adults and had a naturally strong frame from the work around the farm, situated in the black soil region just north of the Ukraine. Following a long afternoon and evening of drinking with the boy's father, the uncle approached him in the barn after supper. He seemed like a friendly man who had brought some candy from the city.

"Ah, Niko, your father told me that I would probably find you here. I saved a piece of candy for you. Would you like it?"

"Yes, Uncle Joe." The boy took the candy bar and unwrapped it.

The man roughly grabbed the boy between his legs exclaiming, "Niko, you are built like a horse. Take off your pants and Uncle Joe will show you some things."

"No, I don't want to do that."

Inflamed with the vodka, the man slapped Nikolai across the face and then unbuttoned his pants.

"You are to obey your elders, Niko. Didn't your father teach you that?" asked the uncle. Niko was molested that night and every night that the uncle visited the home. Uncle Joe enjoyed beating the child too, sometimes before and sometimes after their encounters. Niko never spoke a word of the abuse to his parents who thought the uncle was friendly and very generous with the food and vodka he would often bring.

The agricultural collective took most of the revenue generated by the small farm for the State's needs. It was a constant daily grind, and these unexpected visits from Uncle Joe with presents of food and drink were always welcome. Because he always had some time alone with Niko, his parents may have had a sense of what was going on with their son, but times were tough and survival was the key. They would do anything to improve their meager existence in the farming communities of the former USSR.

At school, Nikolai's massive frame and willingness to fight older boys preying on the younger boys earned him quite a reputation. Likewise, his mind had developed faster than his peers, and his thirst for knowledge about everything made him a standout student. There were no opportunities to play on any teams or engage in sports in the small town so he began exercising and lifting farm equipment to build up his body.

When he was twelve, a visit from his Uncle Joe changed everything. The man confronted the boy in the barn where he was lifting a stack of heavy iron harrow blades that he'd bolted together. His rippled torso glistened with sweat. Uncle Joe was beside himself with excitement and ordered Nikolai to perform.

"No, you are not going to use me again."

"Do I have to remind you again to respect your elders?" the man said as he swung an open hand towards Nikolai's face. Niko caught the swinging arm, immobilizing it. Uncle Joe's eyes widened with shock as the boy struck back with a fist to the man's chest that sent him to the straw that lined the stall converted to a makeshift gym.

"I guess I need to teach you a lesson. You need to learn some respect," said the man as he picked up a rough pine board and walked towards the boy. He swung the board at the boy's head, and it shattered over Niko's forearm as he blocked the blow. The boy calmly lifted a pitchfork off the wall and faced Uncle Joe.

"You will never take advantage of anyone else." He pushed a five-tined pitchfork into Uncle Joe's abdomen and raised him up until he was six inches away from his own face, looking intently at the shock and fear beaming through the man's eyes. His rapid breathing smelled of alcohol. The boy carried the squirming, suspended body to a rough-hewn post supporting the second floor of the barn and its roof and thrust the pitchfork deep into the wood. The man struggled frantically to remove the pitchfork that had punctured his bowels, bladder and pancreas. A mixture of blood, bile, urine, and stomach acid began seeping from the holes, the liquid finding its way past the tines and flowing steadily onto the whitewashed floor of the barn. Niko continued his workout, occasionally glancing at the dying man, satisfied that his death would be slow and painful.

The next morning, Uncle Joe's body was stiff and cold to the touch. The boy emptied the man's pockets, and unzipped his pants. Uncle Joe's penis was engorged with collected body fluids. Niko used his pocket knife to remove the organ and stuff it in the man's gaping mouth. Then, he dug a hole four feet deep in the rich loose soil and folded the body into it. Uncle Joe's grave was sited at the base of a pile of rotting brush that had been cleared from the field. Niko told his parents that Uncle Joe had never come to the barn the previous evening. Strange, thought his parents. He left his car and never came back for a visit. No one heard from him again.

Well-liked by his classmates as well as the school's administration which gave him credit for keeping order among the students and setting an example of rare citizenship, the boy graduated at the top of his class. Because he saw no future in the broken-down farm which had deteriorated with his father's drinking, he joined the Army at age 17. He enjoyed the rigor of training as well as the discipline. Even though all the recruits wore the same olive drab uniforms, Nikolai Zlodeyev took additional care with his clothing and boots and personal grooming. He became a stand-out recruit by every measure. Order was important to him and helped block out the years of physical torture from Uncle Joe. Nikolai excelled at all the basics required of a combat soldier and was identified as a natural leader.

After basic training, he was sent to a tough educational finishing school that would prepare him to join the officer ranks. Here too, he excelled and became the youngest officer to join the Spetsnaz. Hand to hand combat became an obsession. Mastering the fighting skills from different cultures and disciplines coupled with his physical size and strength made him a poster child for the military. He had a well-developed sixth sense that enabled him to anticipate an opponent's next move and find a chink in any man's fighting armor immediately and take the best approach to defeating him. A one-man killing machine. Zlodeyev's sharp intellect was matched to his imposing physique and fighting ability. Tough-minded, he learned to outwit an opponent on the field of battle as well as work the bureaucracy to his own advantage.

When the super-elite group of fighters was selected for the newly formed Alpha Group, Nikolai Zlodeyev was on everyone's short list. The pinnacle of Special Operations, a small group of these fighters could limit an enemy's military options, change the outcome on the battlefield, and shift the tide of a campaign. Uncle Joe would have been very proud of him.

CHAPTER SEVENTEEN

Washington, DC

To Steele, it seemed that the Pisces team was always standing by. On the SEAL teams, they waited too, but there was little idle time. Exercises, inspections and training filled the calendar. The uniformed operators were a step closer to the action and to the ultimate decision-makers that ordered go or no go. Here, as a team waiting for a call that might never come, the day-to-day work was mostly administrative. Because of the routine, Steele's fitness remained at a very high level, and his energy level soared. But he missed the variety of the challenges that the teams faced in managing a schedule that was structured to maintain a high state of readiness while being ready to deploy on a moment's notice. He still questioned his decision to get sucked into the dark side of the government.

Mid-morning, the Admiral called a staff meeting for the inner circle. Sandy Matthews, Cass Thomas, Dan Steele, and Nate Jones, the team's Intelligence Community liaison, attended. A recent recruit to Pisces, Nate seemed to know everyone in the seventeen agencies making up the Intelligence Community, and the Director called him by his first name. No one could quite describe the relationship that Nate enjoyed within the community, and he had the ability to get immediate responses to any question the Pisces team might have. An invaluable resource who had a sharp sense of humor, he often said that if he left the government, he'd try to be a stand-up comedian. He fueled his plump body with a never-ending supply of super-sized sodas, smoothies and milkshakes, rarely eating solid food in the office.

"Good morning. I brought you together this morning to share some positive news for a change. I just learned that the woman Dan captured over in Turkey three months ago finally started talking. Don't ask me how the interrogators were able to persuade her, but they were. And the good news is that she is indeed Abu Sayed, the bomb-maker that was complicating our mission in Syria."

The small group began clapping with a sincere burst of support.

"I want to apologize to Dan publicly. As you know, the upper echelons in the Pentagon and the Intelligence Community were incensed that we missed the real target. There was even talk of shutting us down. I'll admit that I had doubts about the mission, the target, and the circumstances at the time. But more important, I questioned Dan's ability to lead a team, wondering if the last adventure we had together had somehow affected his judgment. How could I have been so easily swayed by the misguided wisdom of the crowd? We will all make mistakes along the way, but we should never resort to Monday morning quarterbacking within this group. So, I apologize for my behavior. I hope this event will re-calibrate everyone's thinking from here on in."

Steele smiled and looked around the conference table and then at the Admiral. "Thanks, Admiral. I was beginning to doubt myself too. I hope that they can squeeze a lot of information out of her. The fact is that she is off the streets and a number of her colleagues are also gone. Others will take their places, but we made a difference. Now more than ever, we need this cell ready and able to engage the opposition at every level. As the Admiral said, there will be mistakes, and there's no doubt that we'll come up short from time to time. But I believe in this effort and know that it's necessary. I'm ready to keep pressing forward."

"Well said. Before we break up, the National Security Advisor will join us for lunch today here. She'd like to meet all of you. She'll be here at noontime. I'll give her an overview and show her around, and we'll meet in here about 12:30 p.m. for lunch."

The Admiral came around the table and shook Steele's hand and clapped him on the back. "Great news, Dan."

Steele's former SEAL Team Two skipper, Captain Hank

Owens, escorted the National Security Advisor to the Cavern to meet the Pisces team and to congratulate Steele personally. The mood was light and cheerful as she revealed some of the issues that were crossing her desk and assured the team that the successful raid in Turkey would certainly cause her to look to their capabilities more often in the future. Tall and lithe and believing that a woman could never be too rich or too slim, she exuded a polished confidence of someone who could swim through the shark-infested waters of the governmental bureaucracy with style and grace and emerge unscathed.

"Abu Sayed provided details on the students and their home countries as well as the regional supply chain which we have disrupted. We've removed a threat to our forces in the theater and also have leads on her students and where they are practicing the trade. So, I thank all of you for your efforts, especially Dan and the team he led. It's always easier to offer your appreciation with twenty-twenty hindsight, after all the facts are in. But that's a political reality. Thank you, Admiral, for the briefing and tour. Captain Owens and I must return to the real world, but I enjoyed this brief introduction to all of you.

Cass stuck her head in Steele's office later in the afternoon.

"Dan, be careful, the National Security Advisor is currently single and has a reputation as a cougar."

"Cougar?" asked Steele.

"Yes, she preys on young virile men like you, uses them and then spits them out."

"Where did that come from, a supermarket tabloid?"

"No, it's partly a reputation she has with the other women in this town and partly my watching the way she was eying you during lunch."

Steele sat back in his chair and laughed. "I get it, you set the hook and were reeling me in."

Cass smiled broadly. "I almost got you this time. In all

seriousness, though, I'm glad the woman turned out to be the right target. You've really been through hell since you came back. Remember, I'll always be in your corner."

"Thanks, Cass. I appreciate that. You're a great friend. I'm sure I'll need your support again soon."

Chapter Eighteen

The Art World

Before long, the whispers became casual cocktail conversation. Select buyers had the rare opportunity to acquire unique artifacts from the reign of Czar Alexander I. The stunning portfolio of photographs and detailed descriptions of the artifacts confirmed that they had been carefully curated. In addition, there was an ironclad provenance backing each of the thousands of pieces. This enticed buyers from all over the world to acquiesce to the extraordinary valuations. Nothing like this collection had appeared on the market for decades, and the artistic range of the treasure was breathtaking.

The Merchant cleverly divided the lot, initially offering only a third to specific buyers to spur competition and to drive both demand and prices higher. It was a chance in a lifetime for those choosing to invest. Russian buyers were particularly offended that they were not given the first opportunity to acquire Czar Alexander's treasure. The Holy See was also investigating the treasure's ownership and ready to claim their rightful share from the transaction. Several investors willingly parted with the treasures they bought to double or triple their money by selling them to art museums anxious to include some of the items in their own collections.

Photos soon found their way into the Arts section of newspapers where a specific piece was dissected by an expert in antiquities, describing its history, the quality and cut of the gemstones, and the intricacy of the metalworking or craftsmanship of the artist. The stories were not missed by Federation officials who wondered how such a dig could have been orchestrated in Kerch. They also began to pose legal challenges to ownership. Possession might be nine tenths of the law, but the remaining ten percent demanded a serious inquiry. Soon, there were official questions raised, and wild stories began to emerge. Individuals sworn to secrecy came out of the woodwork wearing the mantle of a concerned citizen anxious to right any potential wrong for their government.

At the same time, money flowed like a swollen river into accounts in Albania, Hong Kong, Madagascar, and a secret account in Switzerland. Still wearing a uniform and masquerading as a loyal general serving at the pleasure of the President, Nikolai Zlodeyev became an extraordinarily wealthy man. Smart military officers knew that their time in the sun could be limited by any number of external forces so each designed his own golden parachute to ensure that his lifestyle would not suffer any downturn after leaving the service. The treasure from Kerch would guarantee that lifestyle in spades, even after a portion of the spoils was distributed to others involved. While the General's life did not outwardly change, the money he had safely squirreled away in Switzerland would not merely sustain his current lifestyle but significantly enhance it.

The General was a realist. All good things must come to an end. He needed a simple exit strategy for the time when the stories would implicate him directly. How could he steal a Czar's treasure and believe that he could just take off the uniform and walk away? He had already started working on Plan B.

CHAPTER NINETEEN

Moscow, Russia

The military police came for him in the early morning. Nikolai Zlodeyev wore a freshly pressed uniform. There was no struggle or resistance as the officers led the General from his spacious flat to a waiting car that whisked him through the city traffic to Military Headquarters in the Kremlin.

To the long list of charges brought against him, he responded "not guilty" to every individual infraction read by a military magistrate who saw things differently.

"There is sufficient compelling evidence here to warrant a military trial which I hereby order. In addition, because these charges are so severe, I am placing you under house arrest. You may stay in your apartment where there will be military police to guard you. In addition, your telephone line will be disconnected, and you will surrender any mobile communications devices in your possession. You are permitted to meet only with your legal team. Any violation of the terms of this house arrest order will leave me no alternative than to remand you to the military prison. Do you understand?"

Zlodeyev nodded.

"I am setting a trial date for 30 days from today. If your attorney needs additional time, I will consider it. Do you have any questions?"

The General shook his head. Led from the court room, he spotted Yuri Urodov sitting alone in the gallery. The strong smell of cologne signaled his approach as Urodov intercepted him.

"I warned you not to toy with me, Niko. I'm sorry that it must end this way." His broad smile and yellowed teeth lent a vicious bite to his sarcasm.

"It doesn't end until the fat lady sings, Yuri, and I can assure you that she'll never sing on this set of trumped-up charges. I am disappointed that you were not able to come up with anything that would really stick. This is a joke, but one that I'll not forget, my friend."

"Take him away," ordered Urodov. The timbre of his command revealed the fear that still coursed through his body. There would be no peace until Zlodeyev faced the six long rifles of a firing squad.

CHAPTER TWENTY

Moscow, Russia

The court room resembled an elaborate Hollywood stage set. A large auditorium was gutted for the proceedings, and the ample space allowed the presence of witnesses, spectators, and foreign journalists. Dozens of ranking officers from all the services filled the rows of new plastic chairs that were still off-gassing a pungent chemical smell. There were two large conference tables in front of the ornate fence that separated the formal proceedings from the gallery. To the left of the bench, the State's team of lawyers prepared to bring a strong, well-documented case against the accused, General Nikolai Zlodeyev. To the right, the General's defense team was similarly prepared to defend a Russian hero who had fought for the homeland in legendary operations. There was no jury.

Right on script, General Zlodeyev walked down the center aisle flanked by two colonels. A giant of a man, he wore the uniform of the Alpha Group, a super elite cadre of Russian Special Forces. At six feet nine inches tall and weighing over three hundred pounds, his body looked like a piece of sculptured steel. Before sitting, he stared at the rows of his colleagues and smiled.

The panel of judges, three military and two from the Supreme Court, filed in from a door behind the bench and took their seats. A gavel announced the beginning of what had been termed the trial of the century. Despite the panoply of the grand event and the strident arguments and evidence presented by both the Prosecutors and Defense, the verdict had been dictated weeks before by the President himself. The General would be found guilty of multiple crimes.

The General's mind was a million miles away as he heard the

prosecutors recite the long and repetitive list of charges: assault and battery, murder, theft, misappropriation of government property. Excessive use of force, rape, torture and cruelty to animals. His handpicked team of fighters were the best in the business. Men he trusted with his life. Sometimes they got a little carried away and took care of their personal needs that fell far outside the mission scope. Trained killers compensated in bizarre ways. The General was solely interested in how the men performed in combat. What they did after the fight was their own business. Collateral damage was widespread in the General's unit. The list of charges against him went on and on. He was being tried for his own shortcomings as well as those of his unit. Who had been keeping book over the years?

The State even included a slide show where a dozen artifacts were displayed, asserting that these treasures of Czar Alexander I rightfully belonged to the Federation's citizens. How could this arrogant man in uniform be so callous when he was taking the bread from the mouths of thousands of innocent women and children? The General had considered killing the curators who cataloged the artifacts unearthed in Kerch but thought that his gift of an artifact of their choosing would be sufficient to keep them quiet. Another lesson learned the hard way.

The General relaxed at the table during the course of the week's proceedings. He knew the outcome and had been preparing for it for months, long before the State got around to enumerating the specifics.

Sergei, the brilliant planner who most observers discounted as Zlodeyev's uniformed manservant, attended the proceedings every day, and the General's legal team provided an easy method for the two to communicate by a coded system. Everything the team discussed was monitored and recorded, and a video monitor kept track of things through four cameras mounted in the corners of the room. Urodov personally ordered Zlodeyev's unit to be disbanded before the trial began, with all the fighters assigned to other commanders. There would be no eleventh-hour rescue when he was pronounced guilty.

Zlodeyev estimated that the trial would last two weeks with

the verdict being read just before Victory Day, a fitting time for the President to show the world that he had continued to revere the Great Patriotic War but also to emphasize that no one was above the law, even those wearing the uniform. The President's handlers saw the trial as an opportunity to showcase his achievements in modernizing Russian society and embracing the rule of law. The proceedings should serve to silence the critics of a regime that would restore the glory of the larger Russia by taking back the countries that were still clinging to the silly idea they could become independent nations and turn their backs on the Mother.

They would find a way to weave this story into the Victory Day celebrations as both a triumph and a warning. Zlodeyev represented the past, a dinosaur warrior who needed to be excised from the organization to ensure that no others would dare to cut the same wide, unruly swath that he had over the years. No one would ever again disrespect the Federation's laws or so blatantly trample their spirit. A new day was dawning. The future had arrived.

Just as he anticipated, the trial lasted just over two weeks, and the General was now confined in the military prison adjacent to the Kremlin. Escape was out of the question. He had six days until he returned to the courtroom to hear his fate. Sentencing was scheduled for May 8th which fell on the eve of Victory Day. Zlodeyev met with his legal team several times each day. Those listening to the conversations reported that the endless discussions were a rehash of the charges and the laborious reading of case law. Why would anyone spend hours with a defense team when sentencing was just days away?

Urodov added his own a sense of the dramatic to the proceedings. He worked directly with the President's communications team to fine tune this hearing into a major State event. In fact, Urodov pushed for the release of the photographs of Czar Alexander's treasure to be shown as part of the evidence.

While most buyers had little interest in bringing their recent purchases into open view, a number of wealthy Russians were among the investors who tried to claim something irreplaceable from the country's rich history. In some cases, they were more than ready to come forward and somehow suggest that they were really serving the public good by recovering them. Public sentiment was sufficiently roused to provoke protests in the city and to claim that the military should be reformed. One commentator used the now-famous American presidential slogan of "drain the swamp" to describe a new mandate for Russia.

CHAPTER TWENTY-ONE

Washington, DC

Steele found himself in a slump. He had put his life on hold after his wife and two young sons drowned at the bottom of the Chesapeake Bay, and he longed for the return of something more fulfilling in his life. Not ready to jump into the vibrant ninety miles per hour Washington, DC social scene where there were plenty of beautiful, smart, available women, he was certainly an eligible bachelor, or widower to be precise, but he found no attraction to other women. Maybe it was a matter of time. He found the courage to talk to his primary care physician about his feelings, shedding the tough exterior and seeking a better understanding about himself and his capacity for a real relationship sometime down the road.

"No one can replace Jill."

"I understand your feelings, Dan, but you also have to be realistic. We both know that you still love Jill today, but she is never coming back. It's time for you to move slowly back into the social scene with people other than your office colleagues, and not just women. You cannot become a cloistered monk and live a happy life. And I know that Jill would not have wanted you to walk along the cliff on the edge of a major depression without doing something about it."

"I don't even know where to start. It just doesn't feel right to me. Jill is still with me. I feel that I'd be cheating on her to even date another woman."

"Dan, again back to reality. There's no denying that you suffered a terrible loss. This situation has all the earmarks of a double drowning, and you'll be the next one to drown if you can't pull yourself out of this. I know you don't want to be taking medication, and I respect that. But for your long-term health and to keep your clearance, if you don't move towards a more normal social pattern, I'll have to refer you to a specialist or prescribe something to take the edge off your feelings. I'm worried about you. Something has to change."

"OK. I understand. I don't know how to resolve this, but I'll try to take some baby steps to see if anything changes. I guess I'm just frightened of starting something new when I feel the way I do."

"Fine, I want to see you again in one month. Call me anytime you need to. And keep the faith, Dan. There are more people than you know who've battled similar circumstances and found themselves strong and happy in their lives. You can beat this."

CHAPTER TWENTY-TWO

Moscow, Russia

Orchestrated to the last detail, the courtroom was packed with an overflow crowd. Following his conviction, an adjacent room was gutted to accommodate the wire services and additional press invited to witness and to report on the momentous event. The Chiefs of all military services would attend. Senior leaders of the Alpha Group were seated in combat uniforms and face-shielding black silk balaclavas with pinhole screens to cover their eyes. Members of the cabinet would take the first two rows of seats, arranged so that roaming photographers would have clear shots of the accused as well as a Federation Who's Who which created a colorful backdrop. An electric atmosphere made the room tingle with excitement.

There was even a catered lunch in the nearby press room where the journalists could eat and drink while filing their stories. Free phone and high-speed internet connections would enable rapid reporting, and the communications staff had been augmented with scores of spokespeople to facilitate the stories that would be immediately written. Outside, armed Russian soldiers ringed the venue to ensure that nothing could go wrong after the sentencing. Everything was locked down tight.

The General entered the courtroom from the back of the room at precisely 11:00 a.m., escorted by two soldiers goose-stepping as if they were pacing the bride at a wedding processional instead of a sentencing. Those carnivores wearing press passes around their necks had ample opportunity to take photos, and the deliberate pace added tension to the atmosphere. Taking his seat at a polished table with the price tag still affixed to its Queen Anne leg, the General patiently awaited his fate. The judges were ushered in on cue, and the Chief

Justice rambled on about the violations and summarized the charges against the General. Finally, it was time for the main event. General Nikolai Zlodeyev stood at attention, ramrod straight, as the judge read the conviction writ in a solemn manner.

"Having been found guilty of these charges, you, General Nikolai Zlodeyev, are sentenced to sixty years imprisonment without the possibility of an early parole. Further you will be stripped of your military rank and your military pension will be forfeited."

Two military policemen approached the general and unceremoniously ripped the insignia from his tailored uniform, in a public shaming that was only used for the most heinous offenses committed by those wearing the Federation's military garb. Zlodeyev smirked with the attention, a heavy-handed attempt to break him down emotionally and move him to an outburst as he faced the cameras.

"Do you have anything you wish to say to the Court?" asked the Chief Justice. All the eyes in the room fixed on the General, wondering what type of response he might give. Urodov had visited him the night before and urged him to admit his crimes and seek leniency, to talk about the fog of war and how his judgement had been clouded with so many high intensity operations attended with a constant fear of losing lives, including his own. Everyone knew about the countless American soldiers returning from Iraq and Afghanistan with PTSD. People would understand such a diagnosis to explain the atrocities committed as a result of traumatic combat operations. Urodov pleaded with Zlodeyev.

"Think about your friends and the men that you led. Do the right thing, Niko, and try to take your punishment with honor and some humility. This will be the last opportunity you have to admit your crimes and to establish a more fitting legacy. Don't throw it all away."

Now hours later, addressing the benched panel before him, the General responded, "As a military man in the service of my country, my previous plea of not guilty stands. The Court chose to ignore many facts of this case, and I am going to prison for crimes that I could not possibly have committed. Evidence has been ignored, and not one of my subordinates has been permitted to testify to the veracity of the charges. The script for this proceeding must have been crafted in Hollywood. I believe that the court is acting on the basis of higher level, politically driven instructions and what I say will not make any difference. It's a sham. That is all."

The press was already rushing to file their stories, and Zlodeyev stood with his back to the gallery, waiting to be escorted to prison. Heavy stainless-steel shackles and short chains binding his hands and feet were the final insult. His arms would always be in view as the chain linking the shackles for each of his arms passed through a thick metal ring secured by a wide nylon web belt. A new chapter in his life was beginning, and the General was looking forward to it.

CHAPTER TWENTY-THREE

Moscow, Russia

Four guards carrying stubby machine pistols took positions flanking Zlodeyev as he left the courtroom by a side entrance. He would be escorted down a long narrow corridor and out to a waiting security van on the other side of the building away from the officials making statements to the press or being interviewed on the building's steps, taking advantage of the warm day full of sunshine. Then, a short ride to Moscow's central prison where he would be further humiliated by joining the general population. The big man set the pace with shackles which limited his stride to 18 inches between steps.

After a few hundred feet, the prisoner stopped alongside a bathroom in the corridor.

"I need to puke."

"Our orders are to escort you to the van with no stops," replied the officer leading the parade.

"I understand your orders. I am shackled by my feet and hands and need to puke. I can do that here in the can or will sit down and heave all over myself. Then you can carry me the rest of the way with my vomit all over your uniforms."

The officer ordered one of the guards to check the bathroom which was dirty and was filled with the pungent smell of old urine. A guard used his boot to flush the filthy toilet bowl that was missing its seat. Just a closet-sized, seldom-used single stall and washbasin that had apparently dropped off the janitor's cleaning list. Led into the bathroom by two of the guards, the prisoner entered the stall, and closed the thin metal door, got down on his hands and knees before violently retching into the toilet bowl. The leg shackles clanged loudly against the tiled floor as he heaved what seemed to be days of gourmet prison food into the toilet. A retched odor filled the small bathroom gagging the two guards who moved towards the open door off the corridor. After two more body-wrenching spasms, the prisoner opened the stall door, cupped his hand and rinsed his mouth with the rusty water barely flowing from the basin's spigot, and the procession continued. Less than a minute's delay on the trip to the van.

But a precious minute for Nikolai Zlodeyev who had choreographed that stop a thousand times. As a military man accustomed to acting in scenes that had to be completed in a single take, the prisoner entered the stall, and dropped to his knees with his shackled feet visible to the guards. While they were momentarily distracted by the violent retching and foul smell, Zlodeyev was joined by his double in the stall. He left by the same hidden door that had been constructed in the bathroom weeks before. As his double continued the shackled march down the hallway, Zlodeyev entered an isolated service vault connected to a narrow unlit trunk where water and sewage pipes joined bundled electric distribution, telephone lines and data cabling snaking under the building. The service trunk also hosted a population of well-fed rodents that roamed freely.

By the time the military phalanx and the double reached the van, Zlodeyev's shackles had been cut with hydraulic shears. He zipped himself into disposable white coveralls. A public works construction crew had blocked off a small work site on a side street where they labored on the sewer. Wearing a white plastic helmet, safety glasses and a respirator, Zlodeyev climbed a ladder and squeezed through a manhole before getting into a common white transit van parked at the site. The van moved away from the site at slow speed, heading northeast out of the city while the double continued the trip to Moscow's central prison. The General sat on the floor in the back of the van, estimating that he had a fifteen-minute head start to escape the noose that would soon encircle Moscow in an attempt to find him.

So far, the plan worked flawlessly, but Zlodeyev knew that they were only in the opening minutes of an escape that could fly off the rails at any time. There were many moving parts that had to mesh together like the gears on a mechanical Swiss watch. A thousand things could still go wrong.

CHAPTER TWENTY-FOUR

Moscow, Russia

Urodov sat in the lead car passenger's seat with a driver and two soldiers armed with machine pistols on either side of the back seat. The menial task of taking a prisoner across town seemed like a job far beneath an officer of Urodov's rank, but he did not want to leave anything to chance. He could relax only when the heavy barred doors were closed on his former subordinate. Ignoring the no smoking sign inside the staff car, he lit another cigarette and inhaled the tangy smoke deep into his lungs.

After dropping the prisoner, he planned to return to his office and read the wire reports of the sentencing while he enjoyed a bottle of icy vodka from his office refrigerator along with a Cuban cigar that he'd saved for this celebratory occasion. Because he'd broken up Zlodeyev's unit more than a month ago, he doubted that any of his former charges would try to intercept the motorcade along the way, but he learned long ago to never underestimate a desperate and resourceful man. Behind the first car was the van carrying the prisoner with three armed guards with another car carrying armed soldiers following closely behind. Only another two kilometers to go. Any attempt to disrupt this heavily armed and very public convoy in broad daylight could happen only in the movies.

A trash truck roared out of a side street heading for an impact on the lead car. The driver floored the car and the truck swerved, clipping the bumper on the right rear side of the car and spinning it around. Hearing the sound of automatic gunfire, the two guards bolted from the car, locked and loaded. Urodov drew his pistol ordering the driver to alert headquarters that the convoy was under attack.

The van's driver had been shot, and the van carrying the prisoner careened into a light pole, its warning lights still flashing. The guards took defensive positions and were engaging several men wearing black tactical gear and laying down a heavy barrage of fire at the van and those protecting the prisoner. Urodov saw Zlodeyev sitting upright in the car as if nothing was happening. The van's gas tank erupted into a fireball that momentarily stunned the combatants on both sides. Sirens blared as police cars converged on the scene. Unexpectedly, the combatants stopped firing and withdrew.

Urodov smiled. Yes, these were certainly Zlodeyev loyalists that made a pitiful attempt to rescue him, but they would not give their lives to set him free. There were limits to loyalty these days. He looked at the van but could not see the prisoner. Running past the flames and black smoke that had engulfed it, he looked into the van through the open sliding door and saw that the prisoner had vanished.

At the same time, the reinforcements had arrived, and there was great confusion about what had happened. Urodov finally got everyone's attention by firing his pistol into the air.

"General Zlodeyev has escaped. He is shackled hand and foot and probably went this way. Set up a perimeter now. We will go door to door until we find him." Urodov's afternoon cigar and vodka vanished in the flames of the van. Unless he found the prisoner quickly, he might take his place within the prison walls.

Chapter Twenty-Five

Milos Air Base, Russia

By the time the van arrived at the deserted air base 125 miles northeast of Moscow, the sun was setting. Zlodeyev and his unit used the base for training, filling a spacious hangar with scale models of targets and large topographic sand tables representing objective areas. The tactical table where they planned the operation in Kerch was housed in the building.

On the runway ready to take off stood the familiar Tupelov Tu-154 aircraft painted with the logo and colors of the Aeroflot fleet. Zlodeyev had used a long-standing marker to get an air transport commander to give up one of his aircraft and a crew. The van driver and another passenger ran to the plane while the General hurried behind them, glancing down the runway where a single flare burned in the distance. He boarded the plane, and it began to move.

In the cabin, Zlodeyev joined a party as the men cheered when they saw him. Thirty of his fighters were making the trip. They were now deserters who exchanged their military lives for a generous signing bonus to follow the General. Though nothing beyond the bonus was promised, following him would surely be rewarded. None of the men could return to their country where they would forever be fugitives. Some left families behind, making impossible promises to join them again in a third country. All were lured by the thought of doing their jobs at a high multiple of their current place on the pay scale.

Zlodeyev took his time walking down the center aisle, greeting his comrades in arms as brothers. These were fighting men he could depend on. He was halfway through the cabin when the plane lifted off. The hot yellow sun on the right side of the aircraft flooded the cabin as the aircraft climbed on a southerly course. If challenged, the aircraft would use the call sign of a plane in re-fit. They would leave Russian airspace within an hour. Handshakes and bear hugs and impromptu toasts continued until the General reached the front of the aircraft where he found Sergei with the thick operations plan open on his lap. He embraced the younger man, laughing and smiling as he took the seat next to the Lieutenant, ready for an update.

"General, we have successfully executed the first two phases of the plan with few surprises. Your double escaped, and the door to door search will turn up nothing. A number of sightings had been planted in Moscow, designed to throw the manhunt off the scent. We had one man wounded in the escape, but nothing serious. A friend in the Foreign Ministry processed a routine diplomatic request for our landing in Sana'a, and we have arranged ground transportation for our team and cargo. So far so good."

"Excellent, Sergei," said the General, "none of this could have happened without your plan. The swap in the bathroom worked perfectly, and I'm glad to hear that Dimitri escaped along with our team attacking the convoy. Did the specials arrive?"

"Yes, General. We have 120 tactical nuclear-tipped projectiles and six fifty-five gallon drums filled with liquid chemical agents in the cargo bay. I had to use all your markers and nearly twenty million dollars to get everything organized."

"Good, and a worthwhile investment that will make us very rich. Has everyone been paid?"

"Yes, all have received five million dollars in advance of the trip as you directed. There were a handful on the proposed slate that could not accept the signing terms for family reasons. We planned for that eventuality. They are all trusted fighters and have also been rewarded in advance for their consideration and silence."

"Does anyone else know our destination?"

"No."

"Excellent. Does the PA system have a microphone

somewhere in the forward cabin?" the General asked.

The General rose stiffly. He'd been running on adrenaline for several weeks. There had been no time or space for his daily physical regimen, and he looked forward to getting back into shape in the coming weeks. He stood in the front of the plane and spoke into the microphone.

"Welcome aboard! No, I am not your cabin attendant here to wish all of you a safe and comfortable flight. But I am pleased that you have chosen to join me on this new mission where the objective is to accumulate enough personal wealth so that we can all grow old and fat along some beach or mountain dacha in some new country that you will call home. It may be impossible to establish that retirement location in our homeland, but I think that the compensation will allow you all to swallow that bitter pill."

Loud laughter filled the cabin as the General paused.

"Our destination is south. We'll land in approximately seven hours."

The plane's route actually was southeast, adding about 400 miles to the 1,500 mile flight if the large transport plane were a crow. Sergei designed the route to avoid the new Moscow air traffic control radar that had doubled the size of its airspace with a sophisticated radar and identification system. They would initially fly towards Afghanistan and then continue south and west towards the horn of Africa.

By the time the plane neared the Indian Ocean, General Urodov was frantically following tens of Zlodeyev sightings that covered hundreds of square miles. Urodov smiled, knowing that his former subordinate had orchestrated an escape that included a complex array of false cell-phone calls, pre-planned sightings and abandoned cars. The smile was fleeting. There would be a broad internal investigation, and a high-ranking scapegoat would be identified to take the fall. Urodov had already abandoned the search and was thinking about how to save his own skin. He lit another cigarette and added a lungful of smoke to the noxious atmosphere of his office. If he could avoid being named the scapegoat, Urodov would volunteer to be Zlodeyev's executioner.

Part II

CHAPTER TWENTY-SIX

Moscow, Russia

It was 02:00 a.m. and General Zlodeyev had been missing for nearly 14 hours. Urodov peered at his overflowing ashtray, stubbing out another cigarette, looking through the latest cloud of smoke he exhaled. He thought of the phrase "fog of war." How apt. A dense impenetrable fog bank was the only thing left behind when the General vanished. Urodov didn't know the details of how his managed to escape, but it would all be revealed in the coming days.

The Ministry of Defense panicked, and damage control plans were developing at all levels. Few believed that the General could escape the manhunt underway and expected that he would be flushed out of hiding like a startled rabbit. Urodov knew the fugitive too well to share the sanguine predictions. Pieces of the complex puzzle were falling into place, but every minute that passed convinced him that Zlodeyev had successfully evaded the dragnet. Members of the General's previous unit had been rounded up and questioned, leads followed and sightings run to ground. Offers of rewards were informally made known.

Urodov resigned himself to reality and looked ahead to the witch hunt that would ensue, including the need to find high-level scapegoats. Taking charge of the escape post-mortem and defining the path the investigation would follow could be the key to his own survival. He already had a plan, a short list of vulnerable scapegoats and a plausible explanation for the failure. The effort to hunt down the General wherever he was found and mete out final justice needed to be bull-dogged by someone who could take control of the resources and drive them. The vivid image of Saddam Hussein being discovered hiding in a desert spider hole came to his mind.

Standing in front of the bank of windows, he looked across the Kremlin's darkened buildings, musing. A few lights winked back at him but, for the most part, the buildings were dark. The offices were closed, their inhabitants home sleeping. Urodov fancied himself a soldier statesman and felt the weight of the Federation on his shoulders. Understanding his responsibilities and his destiny, he would give all to the Federation and be rewarded in the future with a much grander office suite, attendants and secretaries to respond to his every whim. This was merely the time of penance he would serve until his meteoric rise to power, first within the military ranks and then as a civilian. His future glowed warmly against the cold, vacant offices. Returning to his desk, he briefly reviewed the lined pad of paper sitting in the middle of the blotter. His plan was simple and straight-forward, designed to keep him on point and have many others involved with chores that needed to be completed but were subordinate to the major thrust of the campaign plan he had conceived. Others might try to challenge his position, but none had lived so closely to the crisis and had spent the time devising a plan that would recapture the escapee. Execution of the plan would springboard its architect onto a fast track to higher positions.

Urodov appropriated a large conference hall and requisitioned support staff as if he'd been given the authority to do so. All the services would respond his requests. A large command center sprang into being within hours of the escape, with tentacles into military and civilian law enforcement agencies and internal security organizations which would process all the leads. Urodov did not ask anyone for permission to set up the machine. First, he knew that it would be far better to ask for forgiveness rather than permission. And second, this effort would naturally have ten-foot pole marks all over it. Few wanted to risk their careers by direct involvement in this matter. However, they were happy to support someone else stepping into the breach of a high risk but losing proposition. Within most organizations, self-preservation had a higher priority.

Urodov smiled. If anyone could turn this disaster into a victory, he could. He began working the phones and directing the effort with a rapacious enthusiasm. In the end, he would win and looked forward to exacting a heavy price from General Zlodeyev.

CHAPTER TWENTY-SEVEN

Sana'a, Yemen

The big plane landed in Sana'a without fanfare. Russian planes were common in Yemen in years past, though their usual destinations had been Aden or Hodeida. The capital's international airport had recently opened with UN oversight, and day to day operations had become a repetitive routine. A parched desert wind carrying microscopic granules of sand blew steadily as the men exited the airplane and loaded several trucks lined up like the buses that shuttle passengers from airplanes at outlying terminals. It looked like a large camping expedition going into the desert. Once the cargo was loaded, the convoy of cavernous SUVs with pick-up trucks and two heavy transport trucks began a long and potentially dangerous transit. Sergei purchased a safe passage writ from a tribal leader outside Sana'a that would provide some level of protection for the six-hour journey to their destination.

The convoy had been on the road for nearly two hours when Sergei glanced down at his watch and nudged the dozing General. The Tupolev transport plane which delivered them to Sana'a should be well out over the Indian Ocean heading on a more direct route back to Russia. Though sworn to secrecy about the mission and paid a cash bonus for keeping their mouths shut, the General wanted more time to prepare for the inevitable assault that the Federation would mount to hunt down the team.

While still on the ground, the aircraft's communication system suffered an undetected fault in its long-haul radios. The plane's crew could still talk to the control tower, and the navigation system would continue to operate normally. What capability was affected would only be discovered after they were airborne. Similar faults had occurred on the aircraft in the past, and the crew would not be concerned about continuing on their return route. They were anxious to forget all the details of this flight. Loss of satellite communications would keep the plane's destination and movements unknown. Another surprise was the explosive device hidden in the midships lavatory. It had been set assuming that the plane would refuel and be somewhere over the Indian Ocean when it would drop out of the sky in a brilliant fireball and disappear in its vast expanse. Dead men tell no tales.

Zlodeyev wondered how long it would be before Moscow discovered that he and his crew had escaped to Yemen. Certain the orders would be to kill the fighters and to capture him so the Federation could stage another public trial and sentencing to keep him locked up for the rest of his life or more likely, face a firing squad, after he'd been tortured enough to name his accomplices and hand over the proceeds from the sale of Alexander's treasure. Until that happened, he would be shackled and guarded around the clock. He anticipated frequent hand overs to the special intelligence units that would use any of the various methods available to them for information extraction. Zlodeyev would be the perfect guinea pig for some of the chemical-based methods still in beta testing.

"You know that they will come after us, Sergei. There is no doubt in my mind. We have a small window to prepare, so keep thinking. Your brilliant planning got us to this point, but we need time to prepare the compound and begin operations."

Sergei said, "I am convinced that the Federation's concentration will remain on Syria for the near term. They will have no appetite for involvement in another campaign with complicating politics. On the balance scale, it just doesn't make sense. But once there is a resolution on Syria, they will begin the hunt in earnest. I think we have some time before we get a whiff of Urodov's cologne."

The transit over Yemen's broken roads had surely shifted vertebrae and loosened teeth from their sockets by the time the convoy passed through a tall perimeter wall where a low, modern stuccoed single story building with a red-tiled roof curved in a gentle arc with a wide overhanging porch. Surrounded by transplanted palm trees, it looked like an oasis in the otherwise barren coastal plain whose landscape was only broken by natural wadis, small washouts along the shoreline where the scarce rain pooled with run off into lower-lying depressions.

At one end of the structure, a fabric cover that resembled a miniature stadium dome covered an area the size of a tennis court. The building and grounds looked like a destination resort out of a travel magazine plunked right in the middle of nowhere. What was missing were the bevy of topless female sun-worshipers reclining on beach-toweled pool chairs. Except for the palm trees, the land between the building and the perimeter wall was cleared and offered an unprotected killing field to defend the compound. After exiting the vehicles, the General led the team to the other side of the building facing the Red Sea.

Even in the early part of May, the combination of heat and humidity coming off the Red Sea was unbearable as dusk pushed the light out of the sky. While walking to the sea side of the building with Sergei, the General said, "This is incredible. Only hearing your description and now seeing the final result is just amazing. This is grander than I ever imagined it would be, Sergei. I know that the furnishings have been selected with great care. Here we'll live in great style and comfort while making money."

"Yes, the construction was costly. We had a narrow window to complete the design and get things moving. A Dutch contractor took on the job, and I selected this design from something they constructed along the south coast of St Maarten, an island in the Caribbean owned jointly by the French and the Dutch. Believe it or not, the hardest part of the job was not buying the property or getting the equipment to the site but buying the cover for the arena. I tried to purchase it from a French company that makes large radomes for protecting radars, but they were not interested in retooling their operation for such a small job. I finally found an American company to weave it to our specifications. I think it will fulfill our needs very well. It's air-conditioned and ringed with bleachers like a Roman amphitheater."

Mocha, Yemen seemed like an odd destination for a group of fighters incentivized to desert the armed forces of the Federation and leave their country with little more than the clothes on their backs and an assortment of weapons of mass destruction. Now home to some 15,000 people and located several miles south of the compound, the city of Mocha itself had seen its share of conflict over the years. The Turks had a stranglehold on the entire Arabian Peninsula for many years. A robust coffee trade flourished as early as the fifteenth and sixteenth centuries and abruptly ended when buyers found that the same product could be purchased for a third of the price in Ethiopia, Yemen's African neighbor.

In the early 1900s, after attacking the forts built to protect its harbor, the British shifted its hub for maritime operations to the port of Aden. Ships flying flags of continental Europe followed the market and made commercial stops in Aden or loaded beans in Djibouti, bypassing Mocha. The Red Sea deposited years of sand and silt in the shallow harbor, making it unfit for any sizable maritime traffic. Mocha was off the map for modern commerce of any kind. The once bustling city just died in place, the victim of a market economy.

What intrigued the General was the fact that when Mocha was at its operating height, trade had been brisk, particularly with the Europeans. Under Turkish Ottoman rule, ships entering the Red Sea were required to stop at Mocha to pay duty on their cargoes regardless of their port of origin. The General intended to revitalize the concept by establishing Mocha as a modern-day virtual toll house, collecting a duty from ships transiting the Red Sea. He would not require a break in a vessel's transit but instead would take advantage of electronic funds transfers for payment. He had dreamed of such a scheme for a long time. Eventually, the toll charges would be passed on to the consumers. No one would notice a modest increase in the cost of goods; it happened all the time.

What was left of the coffee trade had been demolished during construction, and the area around the compound looked like an endless, dusty plain. Years ago, coffee would be carted from the highlands to the port to be washed and sorted before drying on a large open field covered with a dried mud mortar painted white to intensify the sun's rays. The large new building dominated the landscape where the dried beans had been stored in jute bags for loading onto ships arriving at the port. A smaller modern blockhouse had been built on the northern side of the compound near the sea to magazine the special weapons that Zlodeyev would use as a formidable bargaining chip. That building was off-limits to everyone except the General.

He addressed the contingent while standing on the sea wall with the Red Sea and a dilapidated pier as his backdrop.

"Comrades, this is our destination. Three hundred years ago, this site boomed because of coffee. It will now be the center of another type of commerce that we will create. We are in the final stages of making this building our new home. Inside, there are individual air-conditioned bedroom suites, each with a living room overlooking the sea. There is a modern kitchen and dining facility as well as a sports bar with satellite television. There is a media room and, of course, an exercise room with stationary equipment and weights. My office is in the middle of the building along with the operations and communications spaces.

We drilled a deep well for fresh water and have plenty of generator power. You will be very comfortable here. Our urgent first task will be to make this compound and building defensible and to secure the perimeter. The locals you will see here in the compound in the daytime have all been carefully vetted, but each of them poses a potential risk to our operation. Make no mistake, we need to be vigilant and use our skills to make this compound a fortress. Join me for dinner in the dining room in one hour."

The compound itself was rectangular, set on a roughly ten-acre plot of land with its western boundary delineated by the Red Sea. It was surrounded by a mud brick wall over twelve feet high with a motorized metal gate connecting the compound with the outside world. Surveillance cameras bristled along its perimeter and another 200 feet of ground beyond the wall had been cleared of the parched scrub brush and vegetation.

The first morning shocked all the occupants of the new compound as the hot red sun began the impossible task of raising the temperature of the Red Sea to match the air. The humidity created an effect like a steam-injected bread oven. Sure, the accommodations were very comfortable, and the signing bonus still glowed. But here they were, in the middle of no-where in a desolate area of Yemen. Still, they trusted the General, and each of the fighters had made a commitment for a single year at the site in hopes that the fortune that they'd been paid to join the expedition could be multiplied by an operation they knew nothing about. The heat was unbearable and the sandy hills blew small particles of sand into every crack and crevice of the compound. Why would anyone choose to live in this hell hole?

CHAPTER TWENTY-EIGHT

Moscow, Russia

Thirty uniformed and civilian leaders crowded into the President's conference room. Among them was the pool of scapegoats selected by General Urodov and the President's Security Adviser who seized the opportunity to implicate and to discredit some of the administration's more vocal critics. Urodov himself would deliver the briefing. The President, accompanied by the Chief of the General Staff of the Russian Federation of Armed Forces, was greeted with a nervous applause. No one in the room questioned how ruthless their leader could be. Several of the invitees were squirming in their seats before the President arrived. Once settled in his chair with a glass of water, he nodded at the podium. Urodov began the painful recitation of failures at all levels of the government. Urodov's monotone sounded like a medical examiner inspecting a body's organs and describing their appearance into a microphone for later transcription.

"Though we isolated General Zlodeyev from his former colleagues, he managed to communicate with them from his prison cell. Exactly how that occurred we do not know." Urodov paused as several people turned to look directly at the Director General of the prison sitting in the second row. "Here is the bathroom," said Urodov tapping a detailed photographic montage of the courtroom and access points and corridors that connected it to the outside world "where we believe the swap took place."

"Wasn't he being escorted by armed guards?" the President blurted out, his face taking on a reddish color reflecting his anger at the small lapses that, when added together, gave the rogue the chance to escape. He wondered if the General had inside help and who among the people seated before him may have been complicit.

The original thirty-minute briefing prompted heated questions from the President exploring one failure after another. Urodov anticipated the reaction and prepared the briefing to elicit the angry response on display. His strategy seemed to be working. After two hours, the President's face was contorted in an apoplectic stare of disbelief. Everything that could have gone wrong did go wrong. The story sounded like a comedy of errors, but the President was far from amused.

Urodov continued the litany that he felt certain would lead to at least one suicide within the next twenty-four hours.

"The General and a small group of his former fighters were able to fly from Milos Air Base and disappear. We have not been able to determine how they got the plane and crew, but we are looking at our aircraft inventories, crew rosters and reviewing flight plans. Neither he nor the plane have been located. What makes this escape even more problematic are the weapons that he was able to somehow steal and take with him."

The President's Security Adviser approached the President and whispered in his ear. The briefing came to a sudden end as the President took the floor.

"Thank you, General Urodov, for detailing all the shortcomings that led to this embarrassing situation. Disclosing the fact that we have lost control of some of our old tactical nukes will offset important leverage we have built up over the years with the Americans and others. This is a disaster. Let there be no mistake. One or more of you will be held accountable for these terrible lapses of responsibility. I am deeply disappointed with the situation and expect the situation to be reversed. Let me reiterate to all of you. This is also your best opportunity for redemption, so I urge all of you to find Zlodeyev. Bring me a plan to repatriate the General and the weapons quickly. This time there will be no mistakes."

The conference room emptied quickly as the audience rushed to relieve their bladders in the hallway bathroom. Some of the older men rushed to their offices to clean themselves and change their underclothes. Some believed the briefing had the effect of painting a large target on their bodies. Their remaining days alive might be already numbered, and the countdown clock had started to tick.

CHAPTER TWENTY-NINE

Moscow, Russia

As part of the government's communications strategy for Zlodeyev's trial, a British journalist, Emma Bolden, had been granted unprecedented access to the General for an exclusive interview after the sentencing. She saw this interview as a means to land her own international news show in London. Perhaps she'd call it Around the World with Emma Bolden. Her name would be on everyone's lips. There would be wardrobes and make-up assistants to help cover the lines that had been created by the years spent as a foreign correspondent with impossible hours, wearing rough uniforms and body armor instead of the stylish, flattering outfits worn by those who provided the news directly to the masses and on whose looks and delivery rested the elements of the all-important ratings. She'd already earned her stripes with two International Emmy Awards, one Peabody, and the Courage in Journalism Award.

A true blonde with bright blue eyes that reflected her Scandinavian heritage, her tall, slim body was built for the screen. Her viewers would revel in this transition from the field, moving from a short-cropped haircut that would fit under a cap to long glowing tresses that would frame her perfect face.

Prancing the runway as a model didn't offer the excitement of journalism but certainly appealed now that she'd reached her thirties. Pounding the halls of the Kremlin was a poor substitute. She could certainly deliver the news, and the swagger she'd developed in the field would give her show a poignant, edgy yet natural tone. Her guests would include Presidents and Prime Ministers, Ambassadors, Statesmen, and officials from the Foreign Office.

She successfully used all her womanly wiles to get the access, including an unplanned office tryst with Urodov. She had caught him on one of his days of not showering. The smell of his body mixed with his overpowering cologne and the heat generated by his frantic movements repulsed her. When she thought back to the time, it made her gag with revulsion. But if nothing else, she was focused on the bigger prize, the brass ring almost in her grasp. She deserved it.

Weeks in the planning, her interview was abruptly canceled without explanation. Determined to find out the reason why, she marched from office to office inside the Kremlin becoming more suspicious as the day continued. No answers. She returned to her one-room flat and tried to drown her frustration with a bottle of cold vodka. After the second glass, she began to connect the dots from all the conversations she'd had during the trial and what she had heard in the hallways and offices that day. She tried to convince herself that the wild conclusion she reached was not plausible. Impossible might be a better word. No one would believe that the State had lost its prisoner and that no one knew where he was. But that's the story which emerged from her anesthetized brain.

She'd found an even more compelling story with the General missing, which brought a scintillating array of scenarios into play. People would gobble up the revelations like the Buckingham Palace rumors that usually filled much of the newspaper's column inches. Refilling her glass, she opened her laptop and began writing in automatic, the words coming onto the screen as if dictated directly from her relaxed and now creative brain. She concluded her report with a series of tantalizing hypotheticals which would leave her readers with an appetite for more and perhaps force some answers from the Russians. She visualized her on-camera report the following morning.

"We think the man put on trial in such a public way is now behind bars in Moscow's central prison. But if that's the case, why was this journalist denied a routine interview with him? That question has not yet been answered, but it leads to some bizarre speculation. Has the general who committed these treasonous acts for self-aggrandizement been dispatched and taken out with the trash with no ceremony? Or perhaps more likely, has the General been given a new identity or is he being prepared for some sort of clandestine mission? Or has the general escaped the maximum-security facility where he is supposedly incarcerated. We'll continue to dig for answers. Stay tuned. Reporting from Moscow, I'm Emma Bolden."

There could be no clearer evidence of her genius than to be handed such a situation and make a great story from it. Lesser journalists would have drunk the same vodka and accepted defeat, whimpering and paralyzed by the setback. No, she would not fall into that trap. Her mind worked with great clarity as she completed the story and added some vignettes from her hushed conversations in the Kremlin. An advanced copy of the story was transmitted to a colleague at the *Washington Post*, opening up another front in her career-building effort. She couldn't believe her good fortune in being at the right place at the right time with what would surely become a page-one story with her byline.

After sending the story, she washed her underclothes in the tiny kitchen sink and hung them to dry on a flimsy wooden rack at the foot of the bed. This too will change, she said to herself. She pulled a worn one-piece nightshirt over her body and crawled into the single bed, falling into a deep and satisfying, alcohol-induced sleep. Tomorrow, she would awaken as a new person.

CHAPTER THIRTY

Washington, DC

"Let's see if I've got this right," the Secretary of State summarized, pausing to look down both sides of a long conference table where his principal deputies had gathered. "We believe that a Russian General recently brought to trial for a series of military crimes and for fencing a truckload of artifacts thought to be from Czar Alexander's reign escapes from a high security prison in the heart of Moscow after his very public sentencing. And the same General has vanished into thin air along with an unknown quantity of nuclear tipped projectile shells that were thought to be long since destroyed as part of some arms control deal, as well as some quantity of chemical warfare agents. We don't know how he got to wherever he is, and we have no clue as to what his plans might be. And this is based on reporting by a British journalist who is also a sometime stringer for *The Washington Post*. What's her reporting track record? The byline says Moscow but is she really there?"

"Yes, sir. She is fluent in Russian and several other languages and has been assigned to Moscow for the past three years. She's the one who reported on the Russian incursion in Ukraine and won an International Emmy Award for journalism. She's got a reputation for digging up details other journalists can't find, and her writing has been held up as a standard for international reporting."

With his questions answered, the Secretary continued. "The Pentagon and all of our allies have been silent on this issue. We are hearing crickets. All of you believe the reporting and recommend that I take this matter to the President's National Security Advisor. How am I doing so far?" The head nods from the table confirmed the accuracy of the three hours he'd spent with the team trying to analyze the speculation that fueled the meeting. The Secretary of State adjusted his necktie before continuing.

"We've heard nothing from the Rooskies about this escape or the missing munitions, and our Administration's response might include a military operation to recover this material wherever it might be." The Secretary paused. "I've got to tell you folks, I'm a bit skeptical of the news reports and the lack of communication from Moscow. Other than reporting a potential embarrassment for the White House and the impact on the bilateral talks scheduled for later in the summer, I don't see any clear path to action on this matter at the present time. Hell, we don't even know there was an escape. I've got more questions than I have answers. At this point, let's include what we know in the daily report and not get everyone's hair on fire. Does anyone disagree? I'd like to see a file on this General. See if our friends over at Langley have anything they would be willing to share." The Secretary took a drink of cold coffee before wrapping up the meeting with specific actions.

"Tom, please work up a cable for Embassy Moscow to see if we can draw out some additional information. I'll call Defense and see if they can pulse some of their contacts. This sounds like a story someone sent into "That's Incredible." We got through April Fool's Day without any of you reeling me in like you did last year, but this story is so bizarre it must be real. Who knows, maybe our friends in the Kremlin will admit that they have a problem and tell us how they will handle it. I hope so. Tom will take point on this. Feed him any updates. Let's start a rhythm around this subject and keep it front and center. I'll make sure the President is sensitized to the report and hope that the press doesn't start a feeding frenzy when the news breaks. Thanks everyone."

The Secretary returned to his office and sat down heavily in his chair, exhaling after his dismissive performance in front of his staff. His objective was to question the event so the responsible individuals would dig harder and faster, but sometimes his bedside manner was too direct and rough around the edges. Why couldn't he learn to be more diplomatic with his own inner circle?

If true, this incident would drive a major impact on the United States' foreign policy and would complicate some of the informal alliances that seemed to be working in the Middle East to throw up a bulwark against Iran. There were lots of eggs to scramble, and the Secretary did not want to get any egg on his face or the President's.

CHAPTER THIRTY-ONE

The idea of a waterway connecting the Red Sea to the north-flowing Nile River or directly with the Mediterranean itself had sparked the imagination of regional potentates throughout history. The best efforts from early Egypt were only able to produce a narrow channel connecting the Red Sea with the Nile. Over time, interest in such projects ebbed and flowed like the tide itself with little or no progress being made.

Even Napoléon sent a team of archaeologists and engineers to find the ancient canal built by the pharaohs and to explore the feasibility of building a new one. He reportedly thought that the project would prove too complicated and costly because of the differential between water levels in the Red Sea and Nile. Subsequent surveys proved the information he was given to be in error. Ironically, the French finally took the first modern step in building the canal when de Lesseps negotiated and bulldogged the design through all the wickets and began work on the Mediterranean end in 1859.

Once it opened ten years later, steam-propelled ships saved nearly two weeks of transit time by cutting through the man-made desert trough of the Suez Canal and the Great Bitter Lake and onward to the Red Sea. Even with the advent of fees and onerous requirements for pilotage imposed by the Canal authority, the alternative, transiting all the way around Africa, had become too costly and particularly dangerous during certain times of the year.

Recently, the price of crude oil had jumped dramatically after a bloodless coup in Saudi Arabia. The powerful Crown Prince deposed his enfeebled father, who seemed resigned to break the tradition of maintaining his grip on the Kingdom until death. The reformer taking the throne faced the house of cards that the royal family had been building for years, although he too had a reputation as a prolific spender, once buying a $500 million-dollar yacht and an old French castle in a single weekend in France.

The entire Kingdom was only a step away from returning to its desert roots, governed by a tribal system based on preservation of the royal family and the raw power it could wield. As Saudi Arabia teetered on the brink of downfall, all the ruling family needed to do was to open up the spigot or jack-up the price of crude for a few months to refill the royal coffers sufficiently to continue the charade for another year or two. That's exactly what the new ruler had done after demanding that all the OPEC countries fall in line.

The price of crude oil, much of which originated from wells in Saudi Arabia, was the metric most closely monitored by ship operators. Cargo hauling was negotiated on a number of known factors such as port of origin and destination as well as the number of containers and the weight of the load. These factors could be entered into a spread sheet and the cost calculated easily. However, the price of oil drove cost directly and weighted the calculations as a multiplier, not just another factor.

With the price of crude jumping up to north of $150 per barrel, today's calculus made the canal the most economical choice for most transits. Its recent expansion accommodated super carriers of greater dimensions in length, beam and navigational draft up to sixty-six feet and improved the scheduling of the transiting ships, reducing the transit time by another ten hours. Modern shipbuilders trumpeted the use of energy saving devices such as pre-swirl stators to channel the water into the propellers improving hydrodynamics and using bamboo flooring or composites for containers made of light-weight, high-tensile steel. The cost of fuel was the bottom line for any and all energy savings. Never was the phase 'time is money' more apt. The sooner the ship operators could turn off the engines, the higher the margins and profits accrued by the owners and shareholders.

The metrics all favored the concept that General Zlodeyev was counting on: the modernization of the ancient toll collection system for ships transiting the Red Sea.

CHAPTER THIRTY-TWO

Moscow, Russia

The full story broke just before the line-ups for the weekend news shows were finalized, and the networks were scrambling to find some pundits who could embellish the story that appeared on the front page of Thursday's edition. Emma Bolden's reporting was captured on virtually all the broadcast and cable news stations, and she was in great demand for follow-ups.

In London, her home news organization was preparing to capitalize on breaking the story and had agreed that she would return home the following week. Demands from the networks in the United States were flowing across the pond, and she would be scheduled for live appearances after some specials that would first air in Britain. Emma Bolden's dreams looked as if they might come true after all. Some broadcasters predicted that the cold war would turn measurably colder because of this incident. The fact that the General had not been located set off a series of speculative commentaries.

Standing with the forlorn façade of the Kremlin at her back, her close-cropped blonde hair had a subtle sweep to it, and the cameras were placed to accentuate her height and beauty. Gone were the workaday clothes, replaced by a fashionable, conservative suit and colorful scarf at her throat.

"General Nikolai Zlodeyev was a legend within the Russian Special Forces. He commanded an elite cadre of fighters from the Alpha Group, the Federation's secretive palace guard, which operated under the President's direct control. In the United States, a Defense Department official familiar with the Russian armed forces said that the Alpha Group was like Britain's SAS on steroids. Tried, convicted and sentenced to sixty years in prison just days ago, he was publicly stripped of his rank and sent to the general population in Moscow's central prison. Among the many crimes he stood trial for were the excessive use of deadly force and the rape and torture of citizens. The Ministry here says that such atrocities are expressly forbidden under the ethics code of the armed forces of the Federation. Still, the most fascinating of his offenses was finding a large trove of artifacts dating to the rule of Czar Alexander I and then possessing the unmitigated gall to offer them to the highest bidder. This treasure was loaded and transported to unknown locations and made available via the dark web to the international marketplace. A huge cache of palace treasures, numbering thousands of pieces, now lies spread across the globe, the property of wealthy collectors. I can confirm that the General is missing after what I've been told was a daring and ingenious escape. He is believed to be in another country after successfully avoiding the dragnet that closed on Moscow like a steel trap. No one admits to knowing his whereabouts. Complicating his escape is a missing quantity of nuclear weapons and chemical agents. I can report tonight that the Russian Federation is greatly embarrassed by the high-level defection, and the President himself plans to address the nation sometime this weekend. Though many questions remain unanswered, this story presents a troubling development for the entire free world. Reporting live from Moscow, this is Emma Bolden."

CHAPTER THIRTY-THREE

Washington, DC

Stories of a rogue Russian General who escaped from a high security prison and somehow managed to commandeer an aircraft to take him, a band of loyal fighters and an unknown number of special weapons to a tired old town that used to be the center of Yemen's coffee industry began to be told over cocktails in the center of the universe, Washington, D.C. The accounts were casually built from fragments originated in hundreds of offices across the town, all connected in some way to the vast federal bureaucracy.

A tall, thin, bird-like man with molting hair and Coke bottle glasses stood at the podium as the President entered the Situation Room. Because of the urgency of the matter, the President's office had carved out a full sixty minutes for this briefing by canceling other appointments. The President was pleased with the change as he looked forward to something different in his schedule, which nowadays seemed so mundane. Still glowing in his version of the election outcomes, that feeling of satisfaction soon was replaced with the challenge of getting legislation through a divided and bitterly partisan, clearly obstructionist Congress. Passive aggressiveness had won the hearts of the other party, and they would smile and play endless matches of rope-a-dope with their rivals until they got something tangible in return for their stingy support. Investigations were so numerous that they were difficult to track. The overlapping scope ensured that everyone could be subpoenaed for almost any infraction or hint of one. As soon as the birdman began lecturing the audience about the history of Yemen with a nasal delivery that was excruciating for the listeners, he was doomed. Within the space of a minute, the President's patience ran out as he cut the briefer off mid-sentence. Still it was the kindest of gentlemanly rebukes.

"I hate to interrupt your fascinating history of the country, but need to understand the impact of the crisis we are now facing. What does a great deal of money and a cache of weapons of mass destruction at a decrepit old seaport town in Yemen add up to? It just makes no sense to me that this General, stripped of his authority and rank, and some of his fighters are trying to re-vitalize the coffee industry," he said, looking at the Secretaries of State and Defense. "Why Yemen in the middle of a civil war? He could have settled in Monaco or Switzerland or walked across our porous southern border and found a nice place in San Diego. And why the nukes?"

The Secretary of State rose to the opportunity. He explained, "There are no targets that he can hold hostage from Yemen unless he makes a deal with Iran to hold the Kingdom at risk. He needs a delivery system to hit Riyadh or Mecca from Mocha, but I don't see the purpose."

"Mecca from Mocha — that sounds almost poetic," replied the President sarcastically.

"I don't want to overstate his options, but mounting a military operation from Yemen seems like a long shot to me. I don't know what he's up to and apparently, neither do the Russians. However, I will defer military speculation to my friend from the Pentagon."

"OK. So, my questions still remain, and I'd like answers to them. What's the assessment?"

The Secretary of Defense weighed in, "Much as I hate to agree with my esteemed colleague from State, I'd say we've got to take a wait and see approach on this one. I don't see the need for considering military action until some clear threats are made to our national security interests. Any sort of delivery system is months, if not years, away. I propose that we standup an interagency cell to track the situation and try to get a better handle on his short-term activities and long-term goals."

"I agree," said the President. "Let's keep an eye on the situation. Are our close friends dialed in to this mess?"

"Yes, Mr. President," whistled the man at the podium.

The President stood and walked past the outer row of chairs ringing the conference table and spotted Dan Steele. He stopped and extended his hand. Steele stood up to greet the President.

"Dan, how are you doing? I see you are walking on your own power now. That's good news."

"Thanks, Mr. President. I'm back in battery now and just returned to work."

"OK. Still working with the Admiral?"

"Yes, sir. It's good to be back."

"Any involvement with this Russian defector?"

"Nothing formal, but we're all monitoring what's happening."

"Good, I feel better already. Great to see you. Stay safe."

CHAPTER THIRTY-FOUR

Mocha, Yemen

Two weeks after the General's escape, a clearer picture began to emerge. Zlodeyev and his band of men were located in Yemen. A Tupelov transport plane was missing and believed lost returning from Sana'a. Nuclear-tipped artillery shells and drums of nerve agent were missing. At least thirty fighters accompanied him.

Real time intelligence flowed from the ground, and overhead sensors were streaming live video of a seaside compound in Mocha believed to be his new home. There were additional intelligence agents who were sent to Yemen where a post was established in the Russian Embassy in Sana'a, and field agents infiltrated Mocha.

While Zlodeyev could delegate cooking and cleaning tasks to locals, he would never consider hiring them for security. There was too much at stake. He looked forward to spending his fortune someplace where he did not have to look over his shoulder. Perimeter surveillance cameras were linked to a console in the operations center which was manned twenty-four hours a day. Additional precautions were taken in the vast no man's land surrounding the compound's walls with the seeding of land mines and trip wires, which were sometimes set off by the local population of baboons. No one left the compound during the first three weeks after arrival because of the defensive preparations which needed to be completed. Among those measures was the erection of tall timbers the size of telephone poles just inside the perimeter fence. A composite wire was strung from fixtures at the top of these poles across the compound like a thousand string sitar.

Evenings were relaxed with the majority of the crew eating in the dining room, enjoying a full range of meals prepared on site by a

Russian émigré who had spent the last twenty years in Yemen looking after the needs of the Russian Navy in Aden. The media room and gym proved to be the usual after-dinner hangouts for the fighters, who could be called to defend the compound at any time night or day. No communication with the outside world was permitted until Zlodeyev deemed it safe. There were few complaints as the men trained to repel an attack and fell into a comfortable existence in the field, not complaining about their restrictive environment or comparatively luxurious, though spartan living conditions. All had experienced far worse.

With the General's location confirmed, Urodov argued for a quick strike to take advantage of the limited time the fighters had to dig in and to defend themselves against a military assault. His plan was briefed, but the President's political advisers lobbied persuasively for additional time to study other options. Besides, they were already fully occupied preparing Russia's formal objection to the Korean Peninsula unification plan and a transition proposal to replace Assad in Syria.

Any plan had to address securing the weapons and ensuring they could not be detonated or dispersed. The ramifications of the loss of these weapons on an international scale were significant, and the Russians had not formally divulged the extent of the problem to any of the members of the United Nations Security Council. Nor had they owned up to the false certification of their destruction. That they had not been destroyed was considered a venial sin and would warrant the equivalent of a slap on the wrist. However, the theft of the weapons by one of their own was an unforgivable sin against the State.

The Federation's priorities were straight-forward: recovery of the weapons was overriding, and punishment of the offenders would be a secondary concern. Safeguarding the remaining artifacts and money generated as the result of their sale was a distant third objective. Many ministers wanted to use any residual funds to find and re-purchase the missing artifacts. Of Russia's multiple irons in the fire, the Zlodeyev situation was clearly a lower priority for the group of political scientists guiding the policies. Geopolitics had the final word.

Infuriated, Urodov stormed over to the President's military deputy's office and railed against the civilians voting to table his quick strike proposal, which laid out in great detail the means of neutralizing the threat of the special weapons and containing the fighters and Zlodeyev. There would be no escape this time. Urodov even proposed a name for the operation: "Iron Hand."

"You know every day we give Zlodeyev to make his little compound a fortress complicates a military option. More men will die trying to root him out and secure the weapons. And what kind of outcome will we have then?" Urodov asked rhetorically. "A strategic waterway closed for years to come, tens of thousands of dead at our hands? What are they thinking about?"

"Uri, I understand and share your frustration. Be patient, you'll get your chance to face Zlodeyev. Keep working on the military option, and I will begin working at the political level to sell your plan. Perhaps if some of the details were leaked to the right people, we might find some allies for your strike," he said in a soothing manner. "Both of us know that Nikolai will make it difficult for any plan to work as we'd like. He is a very clever fellow, but his days are numbered. Keep working, my friend. We will be revisiting your plan soon enough."

"Thank you, comrade. Those political bastards make my blood boil," he sputtered.

"I know." The Military Deputy position rotated among the services. The man currently assigned was a well-connected Army careerist. He walked to the sideboard and pulled a bottle of boutique vodka from a small refrigerator, pouring two glasses. Holding his glass up to salute Urodov, he remarked, "I only drink this on important occasions. Your visit and our talk today certainly qualify."

The two tinked their glasses together and drained them in a single gulp. Urodov wiped his uniformed sleeve against the side of his mouth to blot a drop of the clear liquid.

"Press on, Uri. I will work this plan with you. You will have your way, I promise."

CHAPTER THIRTY-FIVE

Mocha, Yemen

Since arriving in Mocha, the General and Sergei were constantly on the road, negotiating with their new neighbors as the compound was transformed into a desert citadel. During the hot summer months, they met with several groups of Houthi rebels, the current and exiled Yemeni government, officials from Somalia as well as the pirates that preyed on ships transiting their coasts.

Many viewed the General as an entrepreneur and business visionary. His philanthropy was well known in Mocha where he'd already established a following with the number of people employed at the compound as cooks, cleaners, landscapers, and gardeners. Yemenis did not religiously follow the news. In an isolated country so poor with the daily misery of life made more difficult by an ongoing civil war, what was the reason to further burden their souls with the awful daily events elsewhere? They were not directly affected nor was their plight improved. There was the expected jabber about the General, where he'd come from, how he'd earned his bottomless wealth and questions about his motives and long-term commitment to Yemen. But in the end, no one bothered to look past the obvious which was on display every day. Here was a generous man who made today a better day. That's all that counted.

The deal-making began in earnest. The value proposition was simple. While some people doubted the implementation, the lure of a steady flow of money appealed to everyone. The opportunity to line one's pockets with no risk was every investor's dream. The General's proposal would establish a virtual maritime toll booth at the southern end of the Red Sea, imposing a tax on ships transiting the international waterway that separated Yemen from Africa. Plenty of superhighways had multiple toll stations along the tarmac. Every armchair strategist in the world understood the concept of a maritime chokepoint. However, the world's classic choke points had never been controlled by a group backed up with weapons that could close it for years. The General knew that the few straits and narrow waterways around the globe used for maritime trade had never been really threatened in any credible way, until now. Assessing a modest toll collected through a simple electronic bank transfer seemed like a reasonable proposal.

All the locals signed up for a piece of the action. What was left to do was to implement the toll. Again, the people were curious, but no one really cared how the demand for a toll would be enforced by the small group of men living in the new compound just a short distance from Mocha. With the compound secure, the threat of a quick strike had passed, and the General turned his mind to building the capability to ensure that the money could be collected. He couldn't threaten every ship with nuclear or chemical weapons but would rely on conventional means that would bring the shippers to their knees. Sergei was still plugged into the intelligence network in Moscow, both electronically and via a small group of trusted colleagues that were well-paid for their information.

Implementing his vision for the toll took a giant step forward with the arrival of Richie Bouffard. The General found the ex-US Navy SEAL via some friends in the Russian mafia. Bouffard would coordinate the construction and operation of an undefined weapons system. The General was prepared to give him a large playing field if he had better ideas about the mechanics of giving their monetary demands some real backbone. Empty threats would not intimidate the masters, nor the owners and operators. Zlodeyev knew he was trying to impose a tax on a group historically resistant to any demands affecting their free use of waterways.

Hiring Richie Bouffard proved to be an unpopular decision within the group of Russian deserters. The idea of bringing on an American to join in the venture and the profit-sharing incentives seemed like an unnecessary expense. In the end, they were persuaded that the team needed an asset like Bouffard. The General promised to keep the American on a short leash. If he didn't deliver for the team, he would be sent packing.

The *World Maritime News* announcement of the toll beginning in October rocked the shipping industry and caused outrage among the major carriers.

Mocha Announces New Toll for Red Sea

> An organization based in Mocha, Yemen has announced that a toll would be levied on vessels transiting the Gulf of Aden northbound to the Red Sea and Suez Canal and those vessels transiting the Red Sea southbound and passing through the Gulf of Aden. The toll will be imposed on all vessels displacing more than 10,000 tons. This is an unprecedented step taken by the group claiming to represent the interests of the civil war wracked state of Yemen, both its elected government and the rebels that rule sections of the country as well as the pirates of Somalia. Vessels paying the tax will proceed at normal transit speeds and are guaranteed free passage along Somalia's coast which has seen a spike in piracy over the last several years despite the presence of warships in the vicinity. We are unable to confirm the veracity of this announcement or identify the parties behind it, so shippers should be prepared and exercise due caution when the tolls take effect in October.

For years, the shipping industry had followed the practice of registering vessels in a few countries where the taxes and fees were minimal, and the normally rigorous requirements for inspections, safety equipment and crew qualifications were lax or non-existent. The term flags of convenience was just that. Panama, the Marshall Islands and Liberia were among the top countries attracting ship owners seeking relaxed standards and tax havens. Complicit insurers merely raised rates to compensate for the lack of enforced requirements. Crews were cut to the bone, and the eyeballs looking out over the horizon to avoid collisions had been replaced with high tech warning devices and alarms that would warn of anything that lay along the ship's track. Of course, the law of gross tonnage was always in play, and the larger the vessel, the more important it became for smaller vessels to get out of the way, no matter what the International Rules of the Road required. Such was the lackadaisical situation that had replaced prudent seamanship and vigilant watch keeping.

Of course, those countries where the vessels were flagged were mute about the news. However, the shippers began predicting the financial impact on goods delivered to Europe, Asia and the United States. Countries that had fought tooth and nail over trade terms for the past decade and the negligible marginal costs provided good fodder for the politicians, free trade advocates, and international lawyers who quickly joined the fray.

How could an impoverished country like Yemen with no clear structure of control within the government make such demands and how could they impose the tariff? Yemen didn't even have a navy to enforce the charges. Who believed they possessed the authority to levy a toll on shippers using an international waterway?

CHAPTER THIRTY-SIX

Mocha, Yemen

Still a little jet lagged and hung over from a high-altitude buzz, Richie Bouffard arrived at the compound just before the gate closed for the day. He had landed in London too late to catch the connecting flight to Sana'a, and the long layover provided sufficient time for him to get sauced in the business class lounge. A car met him at the airport in Sana'a where he first felt the intense heat from a mid-day blast oven, choking on the ambient air temperature, which exceeded 110 degrees. He slept on and off during the drive to Mocha and downed several liters of bottled water during the journey. He hadn't had any real work since a short-term stint in Syria, as a weapons instructor training the Syrian Democratic Forces to use US-supplied weapons in their fight against the Assad regime. Getting checks written from the US Treasury was a rich contradiction that made him laugh every time he got paid.

He was recruited by someone spotting his credentials in the back of a magazine that offered the services of military tradesman on a per diem basis. Richie responded to the query with a demand for a three-month minimum assignment for $2,000 per day plus lodging and meal expenses. He was mad at himself for not asking for more. The terms sounded OK, but the thought of working in Yemen made him crazy. Muslim countries frowned upon the vices that made Richie happy. Women had to be limited in a small outpost like Mocha, and the food was always a little suspect. Proper refrigeration was tough with the high daily temperatures, and Richie didn't like to drink warm beer. After a night's sleep, a shower, solid food and a set of fresh clothing, Richie felt almost normal as he knocked on the General's office door for their first meeting.

Wearing a pair of rip-stop shorts and dime store flip flops, a garish Hawaiian shirt featuring a hooked swordfish breaking the water to shake the hook, and a faded ball cap with "Florida" silk-screened on its bill, he walked into the open office carrying a plastic water bottle in his hand, slumping heavily into one of the chairs in front of the large wooden desk. There was no first meeting sniffing as the General remained seated, getting right to the point.

"Well Mr. Bouffard, we formally announced a toll for ships transiting this waterway. You have less than two months to design, procure and install a system that will ensure we get paid. I assume that we will have to back up our demand at least once, perhaps twice in a visible way. Do you understand?" asked the General, chiding himself for hiring Richie without the usual vetting process and appalled by the crude, colorful tattoos that covered the visible parts of his spindly body. There was something about Richie that rubbed him the wrong way from the moment he stepped over the threshold.

"That's wild. To set up an electronic toll on an international waterway is a really interesting scheme." Richie took a thoughtful gulp from his water bottle and wiped his mouth with his forearm, exposing his last name inked in large old English letters on its underside to the General. He then paused to finger a large gold trident suspended by a thick gold chain around his neck.

"It'll be an interesting challenge," he continued. "I'm somewhat familiar with this part of the Red Sea. I'll need some detailed hydrography charts of the waters off Mocha to see if we can set up something near the channel which I can operate from a boat or from shore. There's no sense getting wet if you don't have to," he laughed. Richie Bouffard felt comfortable and leaned back in his chair. "I've met some of your crew, and they are certainly a capable group. It feels good to be back with a team."

The General ignored his attempt at gratuitous small talk and moved on. "So, get what you need to understand the underwater landscape. Munitions may be difficult to obtain so you will have to improvise. I'd like you to give me a plan before the end of the month. It doesn't have to be perfect, but the first test will be important for the world to see that we are not bluffing, OK?"

"Sure thing, General. I'll need several diving rigs, nothing fancy for this depth, just some SCUBA tanks and regulators, and an air compressor. We also need a dive boat."

"Fine," said the General.

"I'm also keeping my ear to the ground on the US side to see if anyone is thinking about sending in the cavalry to stop this operation and retrieve those munitions that you supposedly brought with you." Richie wanted to impress the General with the knowledge he'd gained before leaving the States for Yemen.

"Good. My contacts told me you would be a valuable asset and that you were particularly creative when it came to the use of weapons. I understand you are also very lucky with the ladies," the General said, confirming his ability to play the same game.

Richie threw his head back and laughed. "That's a real compliment. I did spot a few split-tails this morning here in the compound, but nothing that interests me. Maybe I'll get into town one of these days and see what I can find. A man must do what he has to do. By the way General, my friends call me Snake." The General rose behind his desk. Richie jumped to his feet and shook the General's outstretched hand, now realizing that his new boss was a man of massive physical size and strength. He left the office and walked confidently down the hallway. This will be a good gig he thought to himself. And I'll leave here a rich man.

CHAPTER THIRTY-SEVEN

Washington, DC

"The National Security Advisor asked our team to start planning an unconventional operation in Mocha where this Russian general is holed up with a cadre of his hand-picked fighters. As you know, he's got an unknown supply of tactical nukes and several drums of chemical agents that makes the stuff they've been using in Syria seem like an air freshener," said the Admiral to the team. "Dan, I think you should take point on this and try to find out what you can. I'm certain there are lots of different organizations trying to sort out this goat rope. I've got a call in to Captain Owens who will tell me which office has the lead for the Navy. I think the chances of us getting tied into something this big are remote, but those are the orders of the day."

"Sure, Admiral. I'll take this on. But if all this is true, I'd say that we've got one hell of a mess on our hands. This is a big deal. Countries from everywhere in the world use that waterway. I can see it now, special operations teams from three different countries trying to make a clandestine assault the same night while three other countries try to drop precision munitions to neutralize the people and secure the specials," said Steele. "It makes my head hurt. I'll start a folder on the shared drive where everyone can see what I collect on this situation."

After the meeting, Steele spent several hours studying the material couriered over from the Pentagon and made a list of the offices tasked to keep tabs on Yemen, calling several points of contact and identifying himself as a member of a contractor team hired to work special operations planning for the National Security Advisor. Such a company did exist, and the Pisces team wore company badges to validate their bona fides without revealing the existence of the small operational cell. He also sent an email to Colonel Bullard at the

USDAO in Sana'a to see if he could get some intelligence from someone on the ground.

Steele leaned back in his chair and tried to look at the situation from an objective point of view: a small group of Russian special operators, fugitives from the Federation, led by a disgraced General caught with his hand in the till, living in an isolated part of the world intent on setting up a toll on an international waterway and backed by weapons of terrible potential destruction. While it seemed like the goofy plot out of a dime novel, the scenario was playing out in real time. And what could the civilized nations, with all their high-tech weapons and trained forces, do about it? Absolutely nothing without the risk of killing lots of people and perhaps closing a waterway for years to come. It looked like a classic standoff.

CHAPTER THIRTY-EIGHT

Mocha, Yemen

Bouffard stood in front of a wall-sized chart of the lower part of the Red Sea.

"General, here is the navigational chart for the Bab el Mandeb Traffic Separation Scheme used by ships passing north and south through the strait. Think of it as a maritime superhighway with no lines or barriers to keep ships in their lanes and avoid collisions. And it works. The depth contours for the water on either side of the channel are important. You can see that the water is deep in the shipping channels. Some of the vessels transiting draw over sixty feet of water. The chart also shows the depth of water right off Mocha. I can tell you this place will need some serious dredging if we intend to bring vessels of any size into our little port."

"You are briefing a chart that I'm very familiar with. I'm interested in your plan to back-up our toll demand with something that will make the choice very simple. Either pay the toll or suffer dire consequences including loss of the cargo and perhaps the lives of the crew."

"Sergei told me you had a tendency to want to get to the last slide without all the buildup. OK, let's throw up slide ten." An enlarged section of the same chart filled the screen. He continued, "I simplified the plan after remembering that we didn't have the Pentagon's budget to play with." His attempt at humor didn't change the General's hard-faced look. Others in the room could see that Richie Bouffard's laid back style did not mesh very well with the General's expectations.

"On the edges of the north bound lane of the channel, the water depth shallows to less than 150-feet. Here is that depth curve,"

Richie said, as he traced the gradient with a laser pointer. "The 300-foot curve is almost on top of it so the drop-off is very steep." He clicked to the next slide, showing four locations on the east side numbered like buoys. "Here are the locations where we will place what the US Navy calls Quickstrike mines."

"What are these Quickstrike mines?"

"The Quickstrike is a shallow water mine used to destroy ships. They are simple iron bombs that have been repurposed for a naval mission. They are moored on the bottom."

"But they are for shallow water. Your other chart shows that the water is very deep where the ships will travel. And why would you only place them on the east side of the channel?" the General asked.

"Water depth, mainly. We can strike a target in either lane, but the water on the western side of the channel, the southbound lane, is much deeper and the gradient is more gradual, it doesn't shoal so rapidly. That would complicate the placement, if we are just using SCUBA which is what is available in this part of the world. Simple is preferred, and I didn't want to develop a complicated plan with too many moving parts. As I was saying, these are the mines used to stop a maritime force in its tracks, and that's why they were developed."

"Are you just going to put in a requisition for these mines to the US Navy or build them yourself here in Mocha?" The General's sarcastic question sparked a nervous laughter within the group listening to the briefing.

"No, General. The US Navy would not be willing to let any of these rascals go, especially to someone like me. But if you take a look at the larger chart, you'll see this tiny country of Djibouti just down the road. It's a garden spot just like Mocha. It's really nothing more than an outpost, but Djibouti hosts several thousand members of the US Armed Services at a facility called Camp Lemonnier. Among other things, the camp was established to house prepositioned stocks of munitions for wartime contingency purposes. You can see why these munitions would include Quickstrike mines. I won't bore you with all the details, but let's just say that the wartime stocks are now depleted by four rounds that are already stored here on the compound." He tapped a blow-up of the armaments on the screen.

"The mines are stored in molded plastic clamshell containers that are inventoried once a month. The dudes doing the inventory just check off the containers rather than inspecting the weapons themselves and accounting for them by individual serial number, so it's unlikely that the missing inventory will ever be discovered. If you approve my plan, these mines will be positioned this coming week by me and one of my Russian colleagues who has some diving experience."

"I don't understand. You put the mines in shallow water to sink a ship a mile away operating in deep water. Are the mines effective at that distance?"

"That's the magic, General. We will make these mines mobile and drive them to the target."

"How will they be controlled?" asked the General.

"Very simply," he replied. "Each of the charges will be tethered to the bottom and operate on a discrete radio frequency. A small buoy connected to the mine will enable me to release it and start its propulsion system which uses the same fuel source as older torpedoes. When exposed to specific compounds, a chemical reaction produces gas that turns a propeller. We'll be able to reach both the north and south bound traffic. The southbound traffic just requires more time for the weapon to transit."

"How will the mines damage the vessels? Are they designed to explode near the vessel or on its hull?"

"Well, General, these are actually iron bombs that have been modified as mines so they are really dumb. However, I have designed sleds that will maneuver the mines so they will detonate under the ship's hull and hopefully break the ship's back by tearing apart the keel, the main strength member of most ships. Basically, we'll moor the mines in about 120 feet of water just on the edge of the channel. They will be made neutrally buoyant by the addition of large flotation bags attached to offset their 600-pound weight. The mines will be cradled in a simple self-propelled sled made of welded angle iron which will enable us to steer the mine to its intended target with a simple joystick that I can control from here. Once released from its tether, the mine will deploy a GPS tracking wire which will allow us to watch its progress and control the intercept. I calculate that the sled can travel at about three knots. We'll refine that with a few practice runs using the transport rig with a similar load. But that's plenty of speed to intercept one of these cargo ships that should be doing about twelve knots through the Traffic Separation Scheme."

Richie took a pull from his water bottle and continued, confident with his command of the operational details.

"It's a matter of simple trigonometry to calculate the target lead angle for an intercept. These puppies come in at least three variants, and I think that the 500-pound model which I was able to get will be just right for our needs. You are talking about the equivalent of 400 pounds of high explosive being detonated under a ship's hull. There are no merchant ship hulls in the world able to withstand that type of blast. Hell, few military vessels would be mission capable after taking a hit like that. Ships are designed to resist the force of the water and the impact of waves. No ship is able to withstand the creation of a large air bubble pushing up against its hull."

"And what happens if the ship speeds up or slows down?"

"I don't expect that will happen, because I will order the ships to maintain speed through the Traffic Separation Scheme over VHF radio Channel Sixteen, by pretending that I'm part of the shipping control station in Aden. The proximity fusing of these weapons will take care of any variations in speed or any math errors I may have made in the fire control calculations. Do you have any other questions?" The General shook his head and looked around the room to see if there were any questions.

"I was told you were the best in the business. It can't be quite as easy as you suggest, but I'm ready to become a believer. Simple plans are the only ones that survive. I like this one. Keep me posted."

"General, if I may, what we do need are two RHIBs."

"RHIBs?" the General asked.

"Sorry, General, I tend to speak in acronyms. RHIBs are Rigid Hull Inflatable Boats. We need two of them powered by twin 150 horsepower outboard engines."

"And what is the purpose for these RHIBs?" asked the General.

"Well, they could be used for water skiing," he said, watching the General to see if his suggestion sparked a smile. It didn't so he moved on. "But in this case, if everything else fails, we'll use two boats to suspend a satchel charge on lines straddling the ship's track. Once the bow crosses the line connecting the two RHIBs, we'll keep tension on it, and it should slide back on the ship's hull. We'll time this process out and will energize an electromagnet using a capacitor bank in the RHIB when the charge is aft of the main machinery spaces where the propeller shafts pass through the ship's hull. The charge will attach itself to the steel hull and then go boom. Then, the ship starts flooding. It's the back-up plan to what I just briefed. It's part of my SEAL training where we learn that one is none and that two is one. Let's put it this way. It will get the master's undivided attention and stop any ship."

"OK, I'm sure you've already found a source for these boats. Get them."

"That's right, General. I don't see a problem getting things into place before your deadline."

"Very good. It seems like a workable plan," said the General as he looked left and right. "Any further comments from the team?"

There were none.

"OK. Proceed."

CHAPTER THIRTY-NINE

Moscow, Russia

"General Urodov, do you have a complete picture of conditions on the ground?"

"Yes, Mr. President, we've gotten weeks of dedicated satellite coverage of the area and worked through the entire electromagnetic spectrum searching for both active and passive defenses. Our assets on the ground have been able to give us a clear picture inside the compound, its surveillance capabilities, and the weapons carried by the fighters. The compound itself is surrounded by a thick twelve-foot-high baked clay wall that has both electronic detection and surveillance cameras.

Its main access is on the northern side where the road branches off the coast highway about a half mile from the compound gate where there is a checkpoint and guard shack manned during the day. We've seen some evidence of land mines seeded along the southern perimeter also. Inside the compound, the men routinely carry side-arms, and we believe they have the special weapons secured in a separate building on the northern part of the compound, here. That's why my team plans make an assault on the compound here, directly from the water side that is open. We've had local intelligence in place for several weeks and have employed a Somali cook who works at the compound every day to verify the details of the defense posture of the compound. The compound layout is presented in the next slide." Urodov used a laser pointer to point out and describe the stand of tall date palm trees that surrounded the compound as well as the location of its operations center and communications facility.

"Are you certain the nuclear munitions and chemicals are

stored in the outlying building at the northern part of the compound?"

"Not 100%, Mr. President. Their location is based on the process of elimination. We know where they are not located but cannot verify that they are in that building. It makes sense that Zlodeyev would segregate those weapons and probably wire them with a timer in a lock box. I'm certain there is a single key, and he personally controls it."

Urodov laid out the operational details of the plan in a high-level briefing that he'd given at least twenty times before as he worked his way up the chain of command. The President placed both hands palm down on the top of the table and looked at the people lining the table. Two of his aides looked at each other and smiled. They'd seen this pattern before and knew what was coming. After all, they wrote the moment's script.

"Ladies and gentlemen, we must take direct action to recover these weapons, long believed to have been destroyed, and repatriate the deserters from the Russian Federation Armed Forces for trials and punishment, particularly General Zlodeyev who is leading them. I also hope to recover the remainder of Czar Alexander's treasure which rightfully belongs here in Moscow. The Defense Committees have been briefed, and I'm told agree with the plan." The President looked at his senior civilian adviser and military chiefs for a head nod before continuing. "I am confident that this action is appropriate to the task at hand. However, before I formally approve this action by the Alpha Group, I would ask all of you at the table to voice your agreement with what General Urodov has outlined and raise any remaining concerns."

Those at the table readily gave their verbal approval of the plan. Consensus ruled. If this kind of raid could reverse the damage done by the Zlodeyev escape, the likely scapegoats might avoid their pending death sentences. The detailed military planning would continue. The weather guessers would drive the deployment timing. Everyone was hopeful that the plan could be executed quickly, before the first toll was collected, an event which would likely add another layer of diplomatic complication.

General Urodov and his team would be using a full-scale model of the compound constructed at Milos Air Base to fine-tune their tactics. They had an approved plan and just had to wait until the weather would optimally support a raid that would make them modern-day military heroes. Elated, Urodov displayed a confident smile, visualizing Zlodeyev's head in a large bell jar atop his display case. If the General were taken alive, he would ask the firing squad to kill him using shots to his body in order to preserve his face for Urodov to display.

CHAPTER FORTY

Washington, DC

Diplomacy worked quietly behind the scenes. It had been over four months since the first reports of Zlodeyev's defection. The situation in Yemen was placed under a giant microscope by Western countries trying to define a means of resolution acceptable to all with participation by any country which volunteered. Most important was how any initiative would be funded and which country would lead it. Plans were being worked on both unilateral and multilateral levels. Because countries would be dealing with a rogue Russian general and a small number of fighters, it was not a single nation state somehow misbehaving. Nor was the misbehavior being carried out in a place where the Western nations were able to influence the host country to intercede with a local solution.

The complexity of the situation required delicate tip-toeing rather than a frontal assault. It was a diplomatic stew where each country would add its own ingredients in its own amounts, thinking that the end result would be deemed delicious by everyone. These were the early days of crisis evaluation, a creative free-for-all where every idea was accepted and nothing discounted. Over time, the unconstrained activity of the early planning cycle would inevitably yield to a small basket of options that would be worked by the larger players who would also fund any effort, whether diplomatic or military.

Though the Russian Federation persisted in denying the reports of Zlodeyev's escape and the loss of weapons of mass destruction, details were emerging that told a different story. At the State Department, the standing thirty-minute meeting had been supplanted by a working group operating from a small war room where it had become the full time focus for a dozen crisis planners.

The daily briefing to the Secretary always seemed to spill over to a full hour or more. The Secretary entered the room with a steaming mug of coffee, sitting down at the table and seeing a weary group ready to update him. The crisis was taking its toll on the people trying to make sense out of the situation from a wide variety of information sources.

"Go," said the Secretary to the briefer patiently waiting for him to get settled at the end of the table.

"Mr. Secretary, there is little change to the situation since yesterday's briefing. We had a conference call with our colleagues in UK this morning, and they suggested that we send a cable to the Russians asking them to confirm the General's escape and the loss of weapons. We need to get some additional details on what he took so we can plan the proper action. There is no legitimacy to the group other than the fact that we believe they control a number of nuclear-tipped artillery shells and also a quantity of chemical or biological weapons that threaten the region. Thus far, the Russians have been non-responsive to our informal inquiries, but we believe they may be organizing a unilateral military action to secure the deserters and the weapons. We agree with that aim, but believe that diplomatic alternatives should be explored first."

"Tom, I agree. The Russians' failure to even acknowledge the situation is maddening. I sense that they are trying to buy time and, if they are successful with a quick military operation, they will never formally acknowledge what happened. If the operation is unsuccessful, then we've got a much larger problem. What do you suggest?"

"We've tried a series of cables at different levels and also engaged the Russian ambassador and his staff and they disavow any knowledge of the situation. They are stone-walling. My view is that the situation has reached the level of a Red Phone call from the President."

"Use the Red Phone? Forgive me if I sound a little sarcastic. I am trying to anticipate the President's reaction. What would you have him say?" the Secretary continued, "We have indications that one of your generals escaped and moved to Yemen and that he might have taken some weapons that could be very dangerous. What are you planning to do about it?"

"Something like that. We would prepare a script for the call."

"Sounds like we are proposing something which makes the President look weak. Somewhere in this vast enterprise, we must have some more information. Are we that desperate? Bring me some facts to show the President that this scenario could play out very badly for all of us if he doesn't take some action now."

"We'll apply some fresh thinking to this and see if we can come up with something more compelling for Thursday's meeting. I understand that you are tied up tomorrow."

"Yes, Tom, I'm out of pocket tomorrow. There's a September 11th memorial event in New York which a number of us will attend. It's hard to believe it happened eighteen years ago. Thanks everybody," he waved as he took his empty coffee cup and left the room.

After weeks of toiling together, the working group was exhausted and felt defeated after the Secretary's wire-brushing. Tom saw it differently.

"OK, team. We successfully planted the idea of a Presidential level communication with Moscow. That's a major accomplishment. Now, we must find some compelling evidence to support our recommendation. I know you are all whipped, and we obviously need a fresh approach. It's 2:30 p.m. If you leave now, you may beat the beltway traffic. Take the rest of the day off to re-charge. If you can, take tomorrow off and look at this problem from a different vantage point. Let's reconvene bright and early Thursday morning. Thank you."

CHAPTER FORTY-ONE

Over the Red Sea

Because of his consummate skills as an action officer observed during his first headquarters assignment, Urodov had been made a permanent fixture within the military bureaucracy. With years spent away from the operational forces, his fighting skills atrophied, and he developed some poor personal habits that enabled him to cope with the stresses of planning, budgeting, investigating and covering up.

The sedentary lifestyle compounded the effects of constant smoking, excessive drinking and the frequent use of amphetamines. Since he initially argued for a quick military strike four months ago, Urodov had ended his thirty-year love affair with nicotine and gave up alcohol and pills altogether. He added fifteen pounds of muscle to his frame by an intense conditioning program. No one trained as hard as he did, re-qualifying on every weapon the Alpha team carried and demonstrating a solid grasp of small unit tactics. The group selected for the mission was hand-picked by Urodov from a large number of volunteers. He had developed a broad following after Zlodeyev's fall from grace. Leading the operation had given him the opportunity to rejoin the operational side and to set a new course for his career. He was fit and ready.

After this mission, Urodov felt confident that people in the halls of the Kremlin would be eying him for bigger and better things. He'd already gotten a strong vote of confidence from the Council of Ministers. The President called him Uri and even sent him an encouraging hand-written note before the team's departure. He was ready to bring Zlodeyev back to face a military tribunal and the long rifles of a firing squad.

There were already whispers about his ascendancy in the military ranks and even heading the Intelligence Directorate. Though never tested with an operation of this magnitude, Urodov made it clear that it was his solemn duty to lead this mission. Zlodeyev would wish that he'd never toyed with his boss and elected to thumb his nose at the Court that was prepared to forgive him for his sins against the State with the requisite level of contrition. Urodov himself would cast the final stone.

Urodov had worked for weeks trying to build consensus for a military response to the situation on the ground. He had to pull out all the stops to finally wrangle an agreement through a series of State Secretaries and the President. After delivering this final briefing honed during what seemed like a thousand other opportunities, he felt very confident and expected to see a thumbs-up from everyone at the table.

***

The loudspeaker blared the words:

"Drop Zone 15."

The men completed equipment and weapons checks inside the unmarked transport aircraft. It would be a High-Altitude Low Opening approach from 25,000 feet, a technique invented by the US Air Force and first used in Laos to insert a special operations unit directly into enemy held territory. Urodov expected a fire-fight once they got on the ground, so the element of surprise was critical. The simple plan was to attack the compound while the deserters slept, overwhelming their defenses with a coordinated assault which would likely be interpreted as a larger force which had successfully surrounded the compound and against which there was no defensible position. The element of surprise and the perception of a superior force would blanket the compound in a fog of war that would lead to a quick surrender.

The special weapons would be secured, and General Zlodeyev would return in chains to face swift justice. It reminded Urodov of the old movie where King Kong was captured and brought back to civilization in shackles. Except in this case, there would be no escape from captivity. The story on everyone's lips throughout the Federation would have a positive outcome and a happy ending for those respecting and supporting the government and its institutions. There would still be a visible purge of those who had failed to control a single prisoner and to permit this embarrassing escape to occur.

It was show time: the green light flashed, and the thirty-one-man team double-timed out of the plane, falling into the black night.

The trip down from 25,000 feet was an uneventful two and one-half minutes, helped in part by the moonless night over the Arabian Peninsula and the cold, dry desert air pushed from the interior out over the Red Sea.

Urodov listened to the clipped reports at 2,000 feet when the chutes opened. Guided by an electronic beacon dropped on the roof of the compound days before by a small drone that looked like a desert bird in flight, the team focused on the landing zone, a narrow strip of sand between the compound and the harbor shallowed by the silt carried by the flow of the Red Sea. Now hanging from a thousand strands of nylon and vulnerable to small arms fire, the team concentrated on readying their weapons during the last seconds of their descent.

Helmet-mounted cameras would record the final descent and action on the ground, and Urodov would transform the footage into a heroic movie recording the event to further Russian nationalism and create the kind of emotional upwelling within the population to support the rebuilding of the former Soviet Union. One of Alpha Group would be armed only with a camera carried to shadow Urodov during the operation to give his face to the mission. The capture of bin Laden would pale in comparison to this capture. Urodov would capitalize on this operation for the glory of the Motherland first and his own self-serving notoriety a close second. He was about to enter the pages of history as part of the glorious quest to rebuild the USSR.

What was missing from the intelligence reports and the scale model of the compound on which Urodov and his team trained were the strands of one quarter inch clear monofilament razor wire, almost invisible, strung tightly across the compound at three-foot intervals on vertical timbers cabled together and buried in the ground twelve feet apart and projecting sixteen feet above, extending all the way to the water's edge.

CHAPTER FORTY-TWO

Mocha, Yemen

Aroused by the pulsing shriek of a 105-decibel general alarm and huge stadium lights which turned the compound into daylight, the General and his armed fighters responded automatically as they had trained to do. Moving to predetermined positions around the compound to permit a clear field of fire while minimizing friendly crossfire, the fighters were in position within 10 seconds of the alarm's call to arms.

Within another minute, they were walking upright, each man armed with a pistol and several with shotguns, intently inspecting the battlefield for signs of life, stepping around the bodies sprawled on the ground in contorted positions. The razor wire strung above the compound had done its job. The helmets and black silk balaclavas were pulled off the heads of the dead soldiers revealing friends and colleagues the compound team had fought with, trained with and eaten supper within their homes. It was like a family where all the cousins and in-laws were now dead. Many of the men were brought to tears after seeing their friends' separated bodies spread across the compound's parched ground, thirsty for the blood flowing from the severed parts.

Ten minutes had elapsed when the last single shot was fired into the head of a man clinging to life. Zlodeyev gathered the team together. Bottles of cold vodka and glasses appeared. It was an emotionally charged moment as they toasted their colleagues and paid their respects. Eyes reddened from where he'd wiped away the tears that he shared with the others, Zlodeyev addressed the team.

"I know this is very tough for many of us. The brave men killed tonight were comrades that we knew and loved. Many of us have lost good friends. So, it is a moment of sadness for all of us," Zlodeyev said in a solemn voice. "But I remind you, we are in a brutal knife fight with the world. Only the strongest will survive. These men were tough, capable and bent on taking us down. Be prepared and always ready as you were tonight. Don't forget, our brothers came to kill us or take us back home for a life in prison. They failed this time, but there will be other attempts. It's either us or them. Don't lose sight of that fact as you understandably grieve these terrible deaths. Now, we have another six hours of darkness ahead. I want our dead comrades to remain in their current positions until the overhead sensors have an opportunity to zoom in on the results of this military action. We will discuss a way to deal with the bodies by mid-day."

Zlodeyev stepped around the tangled body parts that littered the compound grounds. He found Urodov near another man's outstretched arms still holding a video camera. The arms had been neatly sliced above the man's elbows. Hearing the faint whir of a mechanical device, the general realized that the camera was still filming and turned it off. He looked at Urodov's face and quietly admired his former boss for his burning desire to settle the score with the man who had jeopardized his career. The wire had severed Urodov's torso just under his rib cage. His liver hung out of his torso as the blood emptied from organs violently guillotined by his own body weight.

The General marveled at the size of the human body's largest organ. He resisted the urge to kneel closer to Urodov, wondering if he had applied his signature cologne for the assault. Instead, the General raised his glass and paid a final tribute to the vanquished, enjoying the burn of the cold clean liquid down his throat. Grieving for those he recognized, he felt nothing but disdain for Urodov. Despite his courage to lead such a mission, he lived and now died as a bureaucratic weasel who didn't deserve a single tear.

CHAPTER FORTY-THREE

Mocha, Yemen

Local military communications nodes monitored the operation, and the discrete frequency selected for reporting. The rapid-fire automatic bursts associated with a raid against a well-armed adversary with the luxury of solid walls to protect them was what everyone expected to hear on the short-range VHF channels. Instead, nothing other than agonized screams of shock and an occasional single gunshot were heard

Operators shared puzzled looks with each other. There was no active firefight in progress. Linguists listened to communications between an organized team, but it became apparent that the men speaking in Russian were not the crew which dropped out of the moonless sky. They all had numbered call signs to permit clipped one-way transmissions and to avoid intercept, and the voices they were hearing spoke in the clear, obviously not concerned with who might be listening.

Still in the air, the transport plane that carried the paratroopers to Mocha traveled north towards Taiz International Airport located seventy miles away. Officially, the airport was closed, but the runway was clear and undamaged, and the transport's crew was accustomed to landing in less hospitable environments. The airport's 5,000-foot elevation would facilitate communications from the team on the ground and serve as a relay station for those monitoring the raid from Moscow. However, a defeat did not need to be monitored.

Satellites in geosynchronous orbit kept their antenna arrays tuned, constantly surveying the operations area. Other listening posts deployed along the coastline in Ethiopia and on boats patrolling the lower Red Sea also listened for the team waiting for them to declare that the compound was secure, so that other specialists, including nuclear weapons experts staged in Aden could move to the area to safe the munitions.

In minutes, the linguists were able to piece together that the talkers were the intended targets of the raid. They were discussing the dead and wounded visitors whose sudden drop from the skies awakened them in the middle of the night. The occasional gunshot was assessed to be a caring single shot to the head for the few remaining with little life and in tortuous pain. It would be a gesture of humanity which one soldier might do for a colleague knowing that survival was impossible. It seemed clear that there was no attempt to save any of the combatants, regardless of the extent of their injuries.

Several of the listening posts were shocked to hear an unexpected transmission on the frequency for the mission.

"This is two-seven."

"Yes, two-seven, this is Kingpin," replied one of the operators on the transport aircraft, still at 20,000 feet and beginning its descent to land at Taiz.

"Kingpin, my parachute had a broken steering line. I estimate I landed 1,000 yards north of the drop zone. I must have been knocked unconscious during the landing. I've heard nothing from the team, only sporadic gunfire. What are my instructions?"

"We believe the operation failed and those surviving the initial assault, even if wounded, have been killed by the compound fighters. Are you injured?"

"No."

"You may be the only one alive. This is the first transmission on this frequency since the raid. Stay at your current position. We have another five to six hours of darkness, so just be prepared to move out at first light, sooner if directed. More to follow. Kingpin out."

After the communication with what appeared to be the operation's sole survivor, the Alpha Group coordinator on the airplane said, "I'm going to make the first report to Central on the secure satellite phone and ask for further instructions."

Central was the call sign of an operations center inside the Kremlin which provided contingency support for out of area operations conducted by any branch of the Russian Federation Armed Forces. The President sat in an armchair staring at a wall-sized map of the objective area and listened for the sounds from the front, surrounded by high ranking military officers and a cadre of civilian advisers. There had been a one-way satellite feed showing the last minutes of the descent on the darkened compound and then some desperate screams followed by flashes of gunfire. The compound was illuminated like a stadium. A video feed from separate helmet-mounted cameras would project on a large four-paneled screen. Two parts of the screen remained blank. A third camera was motionless and pointed towards the dark sky, its lens overpowered by the brilliant lights of the compound.

The fourth camera clearly captured the results of the raid. It showed the corner of the compound's stuccoed building with a fixed image, a still shot. The President watched in anguish as a bare-chested man wearing brightly colored shorts and sneakers approached the camera. The end of a pistol came into view, enlarging as it got closer, followed by a single brilliant flash as a single bullet shattered the helmet-mounted camera. The screen went blank. After penetrating the camera's optics, the bullet continued into the frontal lobe of the operator barely clinging to life, killing him instantly.

Central had already queried the plane multiple times because there was no direct reporting from the scene, thinking that there was probably a communications glitch. Such was the state of modern communications that permitted those sitting in comfortable, secure offices to watch and to listen to the action as if they were there. Since Urodov and the cameraman were equipped with two-way satellite transceivers, Central expected these reports and wanted to believe that they had the option of directing the tactical movements of the force on the ground. The call would likely trigger a flood of questions from the chain of command that the team in the plane could not answer. Central never responded well to bad news.

Having heard the clipped radio transmission, Richie Bouffard became the hunter. He paralleled the beach north of the compound stalking his prey. He spotted two-seven lying in a prone position in a shallow wadi, his weapon aimed south along the shore. Two-seven was intently focused on the evident failure of the operation and trying to recall the maps of the area. He felt compelled to follow the orders he'd received but also thought about retreating further from the compound as a safety measure. What was the difference if he were 3,000 yards from the compound instead of the 1,000 yards he'd estimated? His mind shifted to survival mode. How would the compound fighters even know he was missing? His self-talk ran the gamut of feeling safe and secure to being near panic with vulnerability.

Bouffard detected that the man heard or sensed something as his eyes searched the darkness for the source of the sound. His eyes found Richie and the barrel of his gun swung in his direction. It was too late. A quick burst from Richie's machine gun disrupted his thought pattern in a violent way. Keeping his gun leveled at the man, Bouffard approached the wadi and rolled two-seven on his back, feeling the man's neck for a pulse.

The heart muscle was still beating in the man's chest, and he detected its weak, thready discharge. Suddenly the man's hand grabbed Richie's forearm in a tight grip. Startled, the hunter screamed and fell backwards as he shook off the desperate grip and sent another burst of lead into the man's chest. The man's heart stopped beating. The American did not shoot the man in the head in deference to his Russian colleagues that might want to see his unmarked face, identify him and pay their respects. He struggled to hoist the dead weight of the man's body onto his shoulder and started trudging along the beach towards the compound. Bringing the dead Russian back to the compound would erase any of the residual concern the other fighters felt about him. This act would change him from an outsider to one of the team.

CHAPTER FORTY-FOUR

Moscow, Russia

After witnessing the raid firsthand, a shaken President walked from the operations center, telling his aide to call a meeting of his inner circle in an hour. Though most of the invitees had watched the debacle with the President, there were others that would be awakened to join the President in his Kremlin conference room for a 03:00 a.m. meeting to discuss how to deal with a bungled Alpha Group raid on the compound in Mocha. The President couldn't quite pinpoint his emotional state but did feel better after several glasses of vodka. There had been no time to script the meeting, so the somber group which assembled was not sure what to expect.

"Gentlemen, I'm certain all of you are now aware of the disaster in Yemen. Many of you saw it unfold with me. Also, most of you reviewed the plans and some of you helped guide my decision on this course of action. So, make no mistake, we are in this together. We need to take the initiative now to control this situation and to override the criticism that will pour in from all sides. In a few hours, people will be asking some very pointed questions, and we chose not to discuss this operation with anyone outside the Federation. I'm sure many of you believed that comrade Urodov's plan would be flawlessly executed, and we would be basking in the glow of another victory delivered by our special operations forces. However, it did not happen. We need an integrated response with the proper notifications and material to feed the press." The President paused and took a gulp from the water glass on the table.

"Vladimir, I want you to coordinate this effort. Clear your desk of all other matters. We are going to be fighting for our collective lives here. The first order of business is to find some means of communicating with Zlodeyev. Our mission in Aden should be able to help, and we have scores of people already there. If we must enter the compound waving a white flag, so be it. What will it take to persuade Zlodeyev to abandon this folly and to return the weapons? Immunity? Re-locate him and his men in a third country? I am not suggesting any sort of amnesty, or am I? Frankly, I don't care what it takes. We must reverse this military failure with something tangible to show the world we are doing something constructive to resolve the situation. Maybe we can persuade him to give up the property he has stolen. Perhaps we could buy it back? I'm open to any suggestions on how to extricate ourselves from the mess without further damage. I would also like to arrange for the dignified return of our countrymen from that hell-hole. This is very ugly, gentlemen." The President was clearly shaken but quickly regained his composure as he articulated the final order of the day.

"Josef," he said, addressing his senior military strategist, "I want you to plan a strike that will level the compound and turn it back into desert. Perhaps we can avoid the special weapons altogether with our precision munitions, but we need a military option in our pocket, whether Vladimir is successful on the diplomatic side or not. I want that bastard Zlodeyev's head on a pike."

A political firestorm was raging, a crisis of massive proportion which would threaten the Russian Federation to its very core. The President knew the effort to save his position would be monumental. The international diplomacy required to reassure his friends and foes alike that he was still rational and in charge would become a diplomatic time-sink. He had to get multiple action lines working now and have them continue without his close personal oversight.

CHAPTER FORTY-FIVE

Washington, DC

"Mr. President, based on all-source reporting, we can confirm that the Russians assaulted the Mocha compound in Yemen from the air last night. We estimate that the military action failed as the forces were stopped in their tracks and believed dead. We'll know more with the daylight. This is based on radio intercepts and some HUMINT reports coming in from Moscow."

The Intelligence Community pulled together an array of data points, snippets of voice communications and reports from the field to confirm that the Russians had carried out what appeared to be a failed attack on the Mocha Compound. The remote location and the normal electronic fingerprint of the area made it easy to see that something different occurred in the compound. Connecting the dots to suggest exactly what happened was the hallmark of a coordinated intelligence effort. Cameras from overhead satellites zoomed in on the illuminated compound but were ineffective in seeing the action on the ground because lasers pointed directly upward over the compound dazzled the sensors, effectively blocking their view of the action. Even their infrared capability was hampered.

"What happened on the ground? I'm certain that the Russians sent in their best operators to deal with this group."

"It's difficult to say. Our analysts are all working to understand how the raid failed. We hope to get a better picture after sunup."

"Have we heard anything from the Russians?" the President asked.

"Nothing yet."

CHAPTER FORTY-SIX

Washington, DC

After a morning run around Capitol Hill, Steele returned to his rented house just a stone's throw from the office. The two-story homes were just a few years old, built as part of the effort to turn Southeast into a safe, family-oriented neighborhood where all the necessities and conveniences were within a short walk. After showering, he got dressed for work, wearing a pair of khaki pants with a blue button-down shirt and tie with colors matching the shirt. With a smile on his face, he remembered Jill's sage advice for wearing the proper tie. She had made life so simple. He missed her every minute of every day. Arriving at the M street office at 0645, Steele made his way to the cavern and found the bedrock suite of offices already open. A burned smell from a pot of coffee confirmed that it had been on the warmer for hours. His breakfast was ready. He guessed the Admiral had been rousted out of bed for some emergency.

Steele logged onto his desktop computer and saw an email from Colonel Bullard marked by a red symbol flagging its priority. Several attachments had been appended to his simple note that read "Looks like the Russians tried to storm the compound. FUBAR. What could the next move be?" Regards, Terry.

Steele clicked on the first of a half dozen attachments and looked in horror as he studied the grisly photos. Nausea swept over him as he viewed the violent end to so many lives. He retched stomach acid into the wastebasket and thought about the brothers he'd lost on similar missions.

The still unidentified composite strands that cut the paratroopers to shreds were strung above the roof line of the single-story building, with limbs and shredded uniforms hanging like laundry out to dry. Even though in the final seconds of the jump with their bodies in a vertical crouch preparing for the landing and ready to fight at the same time, it was impossible to slip through the overhead slicing machine unscathed.

Several of the Russian Alpha group missed their mark, landing outside the compound in the scrub desert surrounding it. They were either blown to bits by the protective minefield or were killed by one of the fighters rousted from their beds with the blare of a general alarm. It was sounded by the watch-stander in the operations center who watched the first paratroopers fall to the ground in large chunks, their nylon canopies still billowing.

As the point man for Pisces, Steele established a number of communications links to other agencies and the uniformed services. An early intelligence report suggested that over thirty men jumped the previous night, and there were no survivors. Steele wondered if he would ever meet the invincible General in combat. Pouring a second cup of breakfast, he began digesting the volumes of intelligence reports spewing forth from seemingly independent organizations. Steele had developed the ability to scan such reporting, rapidly wading through mountains of information to find the important nuggets efficiently. As he analyzed the sketchy details from Yemen, he concluded that another trip there would be a useful expenditure of time and effort to understand the lay of the land.

In the small office pantry for a glass of water, Steele met the Admiral filling his coffee cup.

"Morning Admiral, you are up early this morning," said Steele.

"Actually, it was late last night when I got a call. The Russians finally showed their hand and raided the compound in Yemen. It was a disaster.

"I know," said Steele, "The Defense Attaché in Sana'a sent me some photos from the landing zone that are hard to look at. The compound's defenses are very effective."

"I'm glad you are up to speed. We need to come up with a concept for a covert operation to secure the compound pronto. It will be full of holes, but we need to develop something that our boss can start socializing with the President."

"I have some ideas. Why don't I get them down on a couple of slides, discuss with Sandy and Cass, and we can review the concept later today. Will that work?" asked Steele.

"Great," said the Admiral.

"It seems to me that a trip over there might be useful. What do you think?"

"I had the same thought but felt reluctant to ask you. I'm still a little sensitive after the operation in Turkey. As you know, everyone in this town expects a zero defects operation with no collateral damage and no loose ends. It certainly stifles initiative. But, if you think it's time for a trip, I'll support it and run the idea past Hank Owens. I'm sure he'll agree, so give me a crisp list of objectives that I can use to sell Hank."

"I've already been working on it. I'll have something in your in-box in the next thirty minutes," said Steele. He returned to his office thinking that his next trip to Yemen would probably not be his last.

CHAPTER FORTY-SEVEN

Mocha, Yemen

Following the abortive aerial raid, General Zlodeyev tossed and turned most of the short night. Thinking about the fighters who died in the raid and the reaction of his crew, he ordered the compound gates to be closed and directed that the usual day workers be turned away, advising them they would be paid for the day's work and to return at the usual time the following morning. He also taped a hand-written note in the dining facility announcing a meeting in the arena at 11:00 a.m. to avoid disrupting established schedules.

Zlodeyev shook hands with the men as they joined him in the arena. He noticed that they exhibited the signs of little or no rest, too much alcohol and long bouts of crying over the brothers they lost the previous night.

"Good morning. I can see that many of you had the same type of night I did. You can bet the satellites have taken plenty of photos of our fallen comrades by now. I wanted to discuss my thoughts about how we should dispose of them. What I propose is a plan which honors them in a manner that recognizes their sacrifice for the same country we have left and the reality of our conditions here in Mocha. None of us wants these bodies to be used by Moscow to somehow explain their actions or cover up their mistakes, and it's not practical to store them until some group can travel to Mocha to collect them. We expose ourselves unnecessarily with such a plan. First, we'll collect any personal items the men may have carried on this mission and photographs of any unmarked faces to return to the wife, parents, or next of kin. Sergei will obtain all the addresses via his contacts. We will mail the packages to the survivors along with some money to help each family cope with their loss. I will contribute the money from my personal funds.

Weapons will be collected, cleaned and added to our armory. Here in the arena, the bodies and all body parts will be stripped and wrapped in plain white muslin sheeting. The bodies will be stacked on a barge to be constructed today here in the compound using empty oil drums for flotation. Firewood will be layered with local charcoal saturated with aviation fuel to cover the barge's deck onto which we will arrange the bodies. As a practical matter, the fire must burn very hot to cremate our brothers properly. After a sunset service here in the compound, the barge will be towed offshore and set on fire. Sergei and I have put together assignment lists, and the logistics efforts to carry out this plan are already underway. However, if someone has other ideas, I am ready to listen and decide on a course of action on which we can all agree. Sergei, call the roll."

Each of the fighters gave his affirmation verbally to the plan. There was no further discussion as the men received their assignments. It brought closure to the sadness so many of them felt. The funeral pyre would mark the end of their grieving.

As the sun set, the fighters gathered on the shoreline and shed their final tears, toasting their fallen comrades and wishing them good fortune on the way to their individual Valhalla. Seen for miles around, the barge anchored several hundred yards offshore burned brightly all night. By morning, the empty platform still smoldered, but its human cargo had been turned ino gravelly piles of gray bone fragments and ash.

CHAPTER FORTY-EIGHT

Washington, DC

After weeks of speculation, the Russians finally admitted the facts in a back-channel communiqué to the State Department: General Nikolai Zlodeyev had escaped from the Moscow central prison with 120 nuclear-tipped howitzer shells and six large drums of a chemical nerve agent described as experimental. Because their attempt at retrieving the weapons and returning the General to custody had failed, the Russians had cleverly made their problem everyone else's.

The US government reacted by internally labeling the Russian admission a crisis. Working groups formed quickly. Questions circulated and fanned the flames of the situation until it was like a California wildfire, stoked by the Santa Ana winds, jumping fire breaks and rushing up the dry canyon walls at a mile per minute. Washington loved a crisis. This was the time when reputations were established. No one was quite sure which agency would take the lead and which would come up with the winning strategy, so it was always a double-edged sword of sorts. Nimble talkers were needed. Those that could hold a press conference and appear to be fully engaged, delivering a prepared statement and answering a dozen questions without saying a thing. So much pablum.

The task of studying the options and coming up with recommendations usually fell to the deputies. They would gather the right people and drive the project with fourteen-hour days for weeks on end. This is the environment that sorted out the wheat from the chaff, the time when would-be administration secretaries, undersecretaries, and future agency heads would cut their teeth. The level of frenzied activity telegraphed to the press that something big was afoot inside the vast network of Washington's government-owned or leased buildings.

Bits and pieces of the story seeped out slowly at first, like little rivulets of water forcing their way to the surface of chiseled granite that line the roadways of New Hampshire. It took just hours for people in the press to begin to connect the dots. A leading question at the daily White House briefing. An off the record conversation at one of the watering holes within walking distance of the Capitol. Staffers were easy targets in this environment, and they too became part of the information flow that changed from a weeping seam into a raging torrent. Almost overnight, the whole world was waking up to the fragmented story of a rogue Russian General traveling to a remote, isolated part of the world with a cache of nuclear weapons and drums of chemical weapons in his carry-on luggage.

Newspaper headlines around the world blared the story from their front pages. A convicted Russian Mad Man was loose. An unearthed fortune in treasures from the reign of Alexander I. Nuclear and chemical weapons taken as easily as if they were penny candy within a child's reach. An ill-conceived attempt to secure the weapons complete with disturbing photos. News teams everywhere jumped in with all their resources to cover the next big story. How could he be stopped?

Though the specifics of what Zlodeyev took were considered classified, photos of similar shells found their way into newspapers along with articles about their capability. The question of the manner of detonation was broached to scientists, old weapons experts and even novelists who perhaps gave the most lucid insight into what the Russians might do. The naval strategists who had long used the term "strategic waterway" were now being hounded to define exactly what that meant. Economists joined the academic fray, forecasting a rise in consumer prices if cargo had to transit around Africa. The Saudis were nervous, calling an emergency meeting of OPEC to discuss the impact on oil exports.

Washington worshipped a crisis, and so did the rest of the world. However, Washington was where the next steps were always determined. From the viewpoint of the casual observer, it appeared like an intractable problem where no one had tried the right type of diplomacy, and no country seemed to have the ideal military component to ensure success without the higher than acceptable probability of incalculable damage. No country wanted to be the one to announce simultaneously the good and bad news. The good news would be Zlodeyev and his merry band of fighters are dead. The bad news is that our troops are also dead and the strait is now closed because of high radiation levels for the next seven to ten years.

Particularly telling was the collective lack of a clear strategy to resolve the issue without backing the rogue General into a corner and forcing him to detonate the equivalent of the blast that leveled Hiroshima and Nagasaki. The answer was not a brutal frontal assault with overwhelming force. No, a more measured approach needed to be taken to find the leverage points that might be exploited by influencers and others. This called for building a coalition and using all the tools in each nation's kit bag to determine a course of action that would restore order in a country ruled by mayhem and disorder. Was the fractured world order ready to step up to confront this crisis?

CHAPTER FORTY-NINE

Container Ship *Ernest H. Shackleton*

Ernest H. Shackleton joined the active fleet of one of the world's largest shipping companies in 2012. Nearly four football fields in length and capable of carrying the equivalent of 10,000 containers or 187,000 tons of cargo in her holds and topside, the ship was transiting west through the Indian Ocean after stops in several ports in China and a final stop in Malaysia.

Shackleton's cargo load on the westbound leg of the journey was larger than expected so the voyage could prove to be more profitable than originally forecast. Captain Ian MacGregor, a pure Scotsman who could trace his family's maritime genealogy back several hundred years fumed in his cabin while taking a satellite conference call from the ship's operators in Marseilles and its owners in London.

Now positioned 200 miles south of Colombo, Sri Lanka on the track he laid out in his sailing plan, *Shackleton* would be arriving at the Bab el Mandeb in five days, pushing along at an economical speed of twenty-two knots on the voyage's final leg, bound for several stops in Europe and then on to the United States. After the final containers were off-loaded in Newark, New Jersey, the ship was scheduled for a two-week maintenance period. MacGregor held the bulkhead-mounted radiotelephone handset as he sat at the small desk in his cabin located just aft of the ship's bridge.

"I don't know who this group thinks they are, but I've never paid a toll before reaching the canal and don't intend to this time. If you ask me, this is organized piracy. They've taken a page out of the Somali pirates' playbook and are trying to legitimize it."

"Ian, we don't like the scheme either but must decide on the risk — reward quotient. We don't know how they can impose a fee for using an international waterway, but we are not anxious to take the risk. Going around Africa and backtracking into the Med will add about two weeks to the voyage, but we think that's the safe bet. Our underwriters agree with that course of action too."

"Have they imposed the toll on any other vessels? We know they announced that it would take effect in October, but I've not heard anything from any of the other Masters confirming it. There's been nothing on the wire either. I don't even know how much they will demand, do any of you?"

The line was silent as the two groups assembled for the call exchanged head shakes and shoulder shrugs. MacGregor ran his hand through his red hair and stroked his beard, opening the conversation again on a different tack.

"Why can't I just play dumb and tell them I was not aware of the situation and apologize for my ignorance."

"Jesus, Ian, how could they think that we'd give command of one of the world's largest cargo ships to an imbecile? No one would buy that explanation."

"You've got my track, and I'd say that you need to make a decision in the next thirty-six hours if we are going to preserve the revenue from this trip. My vote is to call their bluff. But then again, I'm only the Captain. *Shackleton* out."

He left the cabin that adjoined the bridge of the ship, a T-shaped structure spanning the ship's beam and rising ten stories above the main deck. It seemed wedged between the stacked containers. Through the row of large double-paned bridge windows, he surveyed the cargo containers stacked on the long forward deck that made the ship look like a floating shoe box. No classic lines here. The ship's architects designed the vessel to hold nothing but standard containers to maximize the load. Even the bow had a boxy look. The ship was built with no allowance for graceful maritime curves which caught the eye and improved stability in heavy seas.

During the ship's construction, there were endless debates about the protrusion just below the waterline that set up a favorable flow over the ship's hull and provided the added benefit of a double-digit fuel efficiency. It had become a religious debate. Naval architects could argue for days about the design of the ship's nose, and each could prove that his design was more efficient. Some owners were even going back and giving their vessels nose jobs to remove the bulbous bow. It was one of those never-ending epic discussions that had no rational end.

MacGregor opened the watertight door on the starboard side and stood on the wing of the bridge staring down the ship's straight sides into the water 120 feet below. He'd been at this trade for forty-five years since he first signed on as an Able Seaman at age seventeen. His fiery red beard curled and twisted into his untamed hair, the same color, thick and coarse as a cocoa mat. The merchant fleet was run by accountants and business men who knew nothing of the sea. It was his life and only true companion. His starched khaki uniform bore the colors of his Clan on the shirt pocket flaps and points of his collar. Never married, there was no son to carry on the family's maritime tradition. A sad realization. He had long marveled at the strength of his family's lineage, but somehow forgot that he was responsible for extending it into the future.

Back on the bridge, he studied the electronic chart and looked at the track. The estimated time of arrival at the Bab el Mandeb where the southern end of the Red Sea narrows and joins the Gulf of Aden was in fifty-two hours. Nodding to the single man on watch, he returned to his cabin.

Donning steel-toed boots, a helmet and safety glasses, he started a daily tour of the ship that included inspecting the stacked containers on deck, those in the cavernous holds below and finally the engine room where the two story eleven-cylinder diesel engine spun the fixed pitch propeller. This daily at-sea ritual lasted nearly two hours. It was tiring, but MacGregor believed it was the only way to monitor the pulse of the ship's condition and the attentiveness of the crew. He varied his daily route just to keep everyone on his toes. The other advantage to the routine was that it kept him far from the TELEXES that deluged his desktop computer and occasional calls that he could answer later. Reminiscing about the old days before satellites changed the world, MacGregor had been the master of his fate for many years before electronics tied him and his ship on a short leash. The freedom and the uncomplicated life at sea made it so appealing. Of late, it had become far too complicated.

CHAPTER FIFTY

Container Ship *Ernest H. Shackleton*

After twenty-four hours, no decision had been reached, exactly the outcome that MacGregor had predicted. He listened to the talking head on the other end of the satellite call and visualized him sitting in the comfort of his London office, overlooking the hubbub of traffic and protected from the wretched exhaust by a high-tech air conditioner that featured an electrostatic filter that made the office space like an electronics manufacturing clean room.

"We are still working to see if the group in Mocha has imposed any tolls and what they might have to leverage any shipping line to pay. We queried the Foreign Office, but they seem to work on their own internal time schedule, not on anyone else's."

The Captain closed his eyes for relief. His bright blue eyes never failed to leave an impression. The orbs were so vivid and clear that they looked unnatural, like colored contact lenses. The talker had the annoying habit of pronouncing schedule as if it were spelled said-dule. He opened his eyes as the monotone continued.

"Right, we'll try to pull a few more strings and will send a TELEX by day's end. Regardless, I will call you at seven a.m. tomorrow morning. Anything else?"

"No, thanks for the call. *Shackleton* out."

MacGregor walked out to the bridge and looked at the electronic charting system console. He changed the view, blowing up the last 200 miles of the navigational track. The track ran straight to the Bab el Mandeb. The land masses on either side of the strait narrowed and the shoal water, depicted in a light blue, extended right to the edge of the shipping channel.

MacGregor felt a sudden unexplained claustrophobia studying the chart. He searched his mind for a rational reason for the response but found none. The colors of the chart blurred into the form of a terrifying maw, and he shuddered at the sight. Uneasy, he needed to clear his mind and physically challenge his body with an extended tour of the ship. If all went according to the ship's plan, *Shackleton* would be moving into congested waters tomorrow morning, requiring his presence and attention on the ship's bridge for the transit of the Strait.

CHAPTER FIFTY-ONE

Container Ship *Ernest H. Shackleton*

MacGregor heard the beep on the computer monitor mounted above his single, very firm bed. In the screen's right corner, a twenty-four-hour clock flashed the time in red numerals: 0220. He was accustomed to being awakened multiple times during the course of a single night and had the ability to take a verbal report, see an alarm or be called to the bridge while another ship would cross in the front of *Shackleton* or overtake it from astern. He trained himself to be fully alert when awakened and could return to sleep within seconds of putting his head back down on the pillow. By company regulations, the Master was always on the ship's bridge when another ship or shoal water fell within a five-mile electronic circle slaved to *Shackleton's* position.

Using the touch screen to scan a number of tabs, MacGregor looked at the flashing COMMUNICATIONS. He opened the tab and found a TELEX from London. He grinned as he thought about all the bureaucrats arguing into the night about his transit plans. They worked hard that day and many would take the following day off because of it. MacGregor would be the one to stand tall and transit into the maw of the Bab el Mandeb all by himself. The owners and operators took his recommendation after weighing countless facts and then sent him on his way with a simple message — they were more interested in marginal revenue than anything else. MacGregor clicked off the monitor and fell back to sleep before the dim red lights on the screen winked out.

CHAPTER FIFTY-TWO

Container Ship *Ernest H. Shackleton*

Twenty miles from the eastern entrance of the Bab el Mandeb Traffic Separation Scheme where the shoal waters pinched the open sea down to a narrow funnel, the VHF radio crackled on the ship's bridge.

"Cargo vessel *Ernest H. Shackleton*, this is Mocha Control, how do you read me?"

MacGregor ignored the radio call and maintained sixteen knots. He would have to slow the vessel soon to line up with any other vessels heading north to the Red Sea, and the ship took a long time to reduce its momentum. The ship could not turn on a dime either. *Shackleton's* maneuverability was limited. No one wanted any of the topside cargo to shift, and the flap rudder hanging aft of the single propeller nearly 1,000 feet from the bow had little immediate effect even when thrown over forty degrees from the ship's heading, particularly at speeds under sixteen knots. Stopping was another matter.

"Cargo vessel *Ernest H. Shackleton*, this is Mocha Control, come in please."

"This is *Shackleton*. You are loud and clear, Mocha Control. I am slowing to twelve knots and ready to enter the northbound channel."

"Roger, *Shackleton*. We sent you a TELEX regarding the toll charges for your vessel which go into effect today. We have not received payment. What are your intentions? Over."

"My intention is to proceed on my intended track. I received no TELEX regarding tolls," he lied. "The owners and operators of this line have given me no instructions, so I intend to proceed on my track adhering to the Traffic Separation Scheme and the International Rules of the Road."

"*Shackleton*, you must pay the toll prior to entering the Traffic Separation Scheme. Recommend you change course and anchor due east of Perim Island until you can arrange payment through your company."

"Mocha Control, I have a tight transit and delivery schedule that will not permit delays. Again, my intention is to transit through the Strait's northbound channel into the Red Sea. Over."

"This is Mocha Control. We understand your intentions and urge you to reconsider. The toll charges are not negotiable. Recommend that you proceed to a suitable anchorage for your ship and wait until the proper financial arrangements are made so you may continue your voyage. Proceed and your ship and crew will suffer terrible consequences."

"This is *Shackleton*. Bugger off. Out."

CHAPTER FIFTY-THREE

Mocha, Yemen

The General peered intently over Richie Bouffard's shoulder at the satellite-generated track of *Ernest H. Shackleton* that originated from a transponder located above the ship's bridge. *Shackleton* had transited the Bab el Mandeb Traffic Separation Scheme three hours ago and was now located in the northbound channel only twenty miles from the waters just off Mocha.

"Well, Mr. Snake, here's the test you have been waiting for. Is there a button for me to push to make it all happen?"

"No, General. It's not quite that automated, but we are ready to rock and roll. I plan to use the northern-most mine. Do you want the ship disabled or sunk?"

"I don't believe in half measures," answered the General. "Use two of your mines and sink the ship."

Shackleton turned precisely to enter the middle of the north-bound channel, the equivalent of a maritime superhighway where two ships could safely pass each other while heading in opposite directions with several hundred yards clearance. MacGregor glanced at the chart console where the radar sweep found the channel clear ahead on both sides. That gave him additional room in case these hooligans from Mocha Control tried something cute. MacGregor was a seaman's seaman who knew the ship from the keel to the uppermost mast and everything in between. He knew the engine inside out, the operation of the pumps and valves and how to load the cargo so the ship could sail on an even keel. Wondering how they could impede the progress of this mammoth steel beast he commanded, MacGregor was confident but also on guard. He had called Mocha Control's bluff and, based on the last four hours and the radar picture of the waters ahead, he was beginning to think that he was almost clear of their empty threat.

Bouffard's spindly body hunched over the small screen of the commercial radar repeater found most commonly on offshore fishing boats. He had built a makeshift plywood stand to house the radar electronics. The business end of the radar was a four-foot long antenna blade positioned on a tower at the end of the pier. Observing an expected blob of returned radar energy merge with the generated symbol of *Shackleton* moving in the channel, he consulted a piece of graph paper and calculated the ship's speed as thirteen knots. A digital timer was set to three minutes, as he carefully plotted *Shackleton's* track in the north-bound channel. The graph paper gauge laid out transit speeds from nine to sixteen knots and calculated intercepts based on the fixed speed of the sled-mounted Quickstrike mines.

Bouffard noted that many of his Russian colleagues crowded into the control room to watch the first test. Some were still skeptical, but to a man, they were impressed with the American's resourcefulness and confidence in designing and setting up the muscle to support the toll. Snake's puckish attitude was more serious at the console. Because of the unexpected raid on the compound, he had not been able to test the propulsion units as he planned.

MacGregor stood on the starboard bridge wing with his binoculars, wondering how Mocha Control could possibly disrupt this great ship's transit. All he could see of the shoreline nine miles away were some low-lying buildings and the remnants of an ancient wharf that had fallen into disrepair. He saw what appeared to be a modern concrete building facing the water, thinking it must be one of those subscription club resorts, but he saw no sign of flags, thatched bungalows or exotic swimming pools.

In his head, he re-played the recent radio exchange while scanning the coastline. The first radio contact sounded solicitous, the second a bit more demanding and the third exchange somewhat ominous, but still, he was making steady progress and saw nothing along the track ahead to give him concern. The uneasy feeling returned again and MacGregor tried unsuccessfully to answer why. He tried to just ignore it.

Snake stared at the digital timer on the console and announced, "It's show time."

There were four pushbuttons mounted neatly into the plywood for activating the four mines that he'd procured from US Navy stocks pre-positioned at Djibouti. He lifted a clear Plexiglas cover and depressed one of the buttons to release the tethered mine and to start its sled. It illuminated. Seconds later, a symbol came into view off the eastern side of the channel well ahead of *Shackleton's* position. The track of the sled appeared as a series of small dots. Exactly 45 seconds later, he pushed the second button with great fanfare and the second sled began its short underwater transit. The second sled's dots appeared to overlay the first but the time delay accounted for the transit speed of *Shackleton* in the channel, and he had calculated an aim point aft near the engine room. The die was cast. The ability to abort a mission once set in motion hadn't even been considered.

MacGregor spotted a steel tower with a rotating radar sitting on the end the pier and thought the entire threat of tolls must be an elaborate intimidation scam set up by some high-tech pirates. MacGregor thought of a phrase he'd heard years ago from another master. "I was born at night, but not last night." He ducked inside the air-conditioned bridge and studied the charts that depicted the area in the upper Red Sea where the ship would anchor while the next north-bound convoy was organized before entering the canal. In another twenty minutes, after a twenty-five-degree course adjustment where the transit lanes moved to a northwesterly direction, Mocha Control would fade away, a distant memory blotted out by the stacked containers aft.

Snake had a rapt audience and kept up a running commentary of the sled's progress to the intercept point, sounding like a broadcaster at a football game. He made routine movements elaborate and cited obscure facts that were irrelevant to the operation but secured his position as the irreplaceable man on the team. The puckish manner returned. "OK, we've got just over a minute until intercept, so I suggest all of you head down to the pier to have a better look at what effect high explosive has on the underwater hull of a large ship. It will be like one of those planned building demolitions in slo-mo." Most of the Russians did not understand what Richie had said but followed the General out of the control room and towards the pier.

On the bridge wing, MacGregor inhaled the warm salt air and let it expand his chest, exhaling slowly. The breathing helped. He was calm and steady, feeling a bead of sweat form and trickle into the small of his back. *Shackleton* was invincible, on track and nearing a turn to port in the channel when MacGregor felt an odd shudder as the first mine detonated near the starboard bow, nearly 800' forward from his position on the bridge, a geyser of water shooting as high as the second tier of containers above the deck edge. Rushing back through the open bridge wing door, he heard the alarms and then saw the blinking red bars pinpointing a fault in the forward part of the ship outlined on the screen of the centerline console that displayed the status of its main propulsion engine, electrical generators, tank levels and internal pumps.

"Bridge, Central Control, we have an indication of a problem in the forward ballast tank. I will send one of the engineers forward to check things out." A routine report to be handled in a routine manner. Everything was under control on the massive ship. Less than a minute later, MacGregor felt another tremor that seemed to gently lift the ship vertically when the second mine detonated aft between the cavernous engine room and the large bronze propeller. He saw the water along the hull boiling with gas released by the second explosion. More alarms sounded and red lights illuminated before the console screen went blank.

"Captain?" came the desperate question over the internal communications system, still operating because of a battery-fed power supply that would last for nearly an hour. A lighted button on the communications box identified the call as Central Control. "The hull has been breached. Both generators just tripped off line, and the engine room is flooding."

The voice trailed off as the line went dead. The Engineering control station was normally unmanned, except for times when the ship was entering port, operating in narrow waterways or transiting a congested part of the ocean, where an operator could override the computer controls and take action for a scenario that the computer could not recognize. Though many of the most critical functions could be controlled from the bridge itself, losing communication with the watch-stander monitoring the ship's major organs added to the emergency.

With all the health and sensory surveillance systems built into the ship's design, computers controlled most ship's operations. Cargo ships were not built to the same standards as warships, and the number of watertight bulkheads dividing the ship's hull was reduced to save construction costs. Similarly, watertight doors and hatches had been replaced with lightweight aluminum joiner doors that would not impede any sort of flooding in the engine room or cargo holds. There was no reason any ship of this size would face a situation that would threaten its stability at sea. *Shackleton* was a seagoing thoroughbred built to withstand anything that the sea could throw in her path. None of the ship architects had any reason to worry about the watertight integrity of the hull.

MacGregor reverted to his gut instincts, developed over his years at sea facing disasters that would occur at the worst possible times. He knew his ship and did not hesitate. He stepped to the helmsman's station and turned a one-inch knob all the way to the right, hoping that the steering motors would swing the giant rudder and that the water rushing past the hull would be enough to drive the ship to starboard out of the channel. The water at this part of the channel shoaled rapidly, with the 300-foot and 150-foot depth curves almost on top of each other. From there, the bottom shallowed to an underwater plateau, that ended at the shoreline.

MacGregor knew that the ship's bulbous nose, once out of the channel, would begin to plow a furrow in the bottom. He prided himself as a Captain who never had experienced a grounding, major fire or collision, laughing at the irony of his efforts to now deliberately park the large ship on the coral and sandy bottom outside the channel. The further irony lay exactly where he wanted to turn the ship, towards the old coffee port of Mocha.

The steering motors were designed to operate from a secondary power source as they were vital when propulsion was lost, but the secondary sources of power were also gone. MacGregor could see the ship's bow swing almost imperceptibly against the shoreline and checked the magnetic compass to verify the ship's bow was turning. Perhaps the explosion caused the rudder control circuitry to fail in the full starboard position or maybe it was torn from its post and hung in the water. Whatever the reason, the ship was turning. He raised his binoculars hanging by a strap around his neck and looked at the radar tower at the end of Mocha's pier, seeing men lined up on the sea wall watching the spectacle of a ship's end, and the Master's desperate attempt to save her.

Shackleton's crew stood out on deck watching the shoreline come into sharper view as the ship's hull began to scrape through the soft sandy bottom. It took twenty minutes for the ship to stop, after it plowed through the channel edge and moved closer to the shoreline. The water around the ship turned brown as the steel hull churned the sea bottom, raising great clouds of suspended mud, sand and coral.

The flooding of the after-engineering spaces quickened when the ship stopped. As the largest open space on the ship outside its hold, the engine room spanned the ship's full beam of 175 feet and housed the ship's vital organs. The bow was tightly wedged into the bottom while the after part of the ship hung over the steep natural walls of the channel and began filling with water, causing the ship's bow to rise. Cargo in the containers began to move ever so slightly aft, the effect being compounded within thousands of containers that were also straining the hardware securing them to others and to the main deck. The edge of the channel wall was formed of coral, its porous spongy structure hardened over time. *Shackleton* was now like a seesaw with the middle of the ship balanced on an unyielding natural fulcrum, its bow buried in a sandy bottom and its stern hanging out into water with a depth of 600 feet.

CHAPTER FIFTY-FOUR

Mocha, Yemen

The men standing along the seawall in Mocha couldn't believe their eyes. They watched the entire event unfold as the long hull topped with layers of containers change its aspect from the beam to bow on. Now there was a huge cargo ship parked on their doorstep. Elated, the men joked among themselves — they could be pirates too. To plunder and pillage a huge ship would be great sport. The General greeted Bouffard when he joined them on the sea wall.

"Snake," he cried, "Great work! Very impressive."

"Yep, that was fun. Those Quickstrike mines really pack a punch. I'd love to take a look at the damage to the hull, but I think it's probably covered by the bottom."

Sergei joined the conversation, "I don't think we'll have any problems with ships paying the toll now. This will be front page news all over the world by morning. There will also be intense pressure to do something, anything to address this disaster, and we will be the targets."

"Don't worry, Sergei, we have the strongest hand in the game, and there is no way any country will risk the consequences of provoking us to use the special weapons." Bottles of vodka were brought from the bar's walk-in refrigerator and poured into open glasses held by the fighters.

"Comrades, we are now operational. Money will soon be flowing into our coffers. I'd like to recognize Mr. Snake for his professional efforts in this achievement." The General and other fighters raised their glasses in his direction, toasting him and hearing the coins drop into the till with a deafening sound. Just like the General promised, they would all become very rich.

After several rounds of toasts, the men returned to the structure they called home. Dinner would begin in an hour. Some continued the celebration at the bar while others were ready to fall into their beds after such a momentous day.

The major news organizations had limited assets in Yemen to cover the plight of the people affected by the bombing and civil war and relied on the wire services for most of their reporting. International aid agencies were there in full force, and there was a high interest story to be told, but getting any well-known reporters to travel to Yemen was a tough sell. The unexpected crisis unfolding in the waters off the war-racked country complicated the information flow. Photos of *Shackleton* were in high demand. Reports of the dangers to maritime trade needed on-site coverage. One report revealed that a group of Somali pirates boarded the *Shackleton* as if it were abandoned and open for plunder. Within twenty-four hours of being a modern-day container ship ruling the maritime trade, *Shackleton* would become fresh carrion for the locals. It was a maritime free-for-all, and no invitation was required to join.

CHAPTER FIFTY-FIVE

Container Ship *Ernest H. Shackleton*

Ian MacGregor felt the change as the ship moved to the right side of the shipping channel and contacted the bottom. As the massive steel hull plates pushed into the bottom, he visualized her bulbous bow plowing a furrow ahead of the rest of the hull. There was nothing more he could do. He thought ahead to the immediate needs of the next few hours. Stabilize the ship. Account for the crew. Report the situation and GPS coordinates to the suits in London and Marseilles, even if relayed by handheld radio. Warn maritime traffic about the grounding and have them stand clear. An emergency TELEX would be sent to all ships in the region, advising them of *Shackleton's* position. The warning could not be transmitted by *Shackleton,* but any passing ship would recognize the situation, and sufficient data would soon be on the airways to issue an immediate alert to other mariners.

A broad range of notifications would be made automatically, and the plight of the great ship would be the talk of the entire maritime trade before sunset. The shipping line operatives would scour the region for floating cranes and all available lighterage to remove the cargo containers. Maritime insurers would begin assessing their potential liabilities. Lawyers for the companies that loaded *Shackleton's* deck with containers would be next.

The Captain pondered the idea of issuing a mayday but quickly put the thought to rest. There was no imminent danger to shipping or his cargo and crew nor did he see any signs that the breach in the underwater hull caused any of the fuel tanks to rupture. No ship under his command would issue the desperate plea for anyone's help, regardless of the cause. He would advise maritime authorities that his ship was safely aground, its location and impact on the shipping channels. The environmental hazards were another matter. Let the suits sort all of that out he told himself.

A dozen scenarios danced in his head, but one thing was for sure. This would be his final voyage and, after the inquiry, he'd be parked ashore just like *Shackleton*, put at a desk far from the sea doing what clerks do to keep everything straight. He could almost hear the whispers as the office passersby pointed in his direction and told the story of the great mariner who ran his ship aground. That was not the life for him. Some of the thoughts he conjured up were overwhelming. Without propulsion and electrical power and with the ship's hydrodynamic lines pushing against a soft bottom, the great ship's position was fixed. MacGregor stepped out onto the exposed wing of the bridge and looked straight down to the muddy cloud of water against the hull, inspecting pieces of flotsam on its surface and confirmed that the great ship was now an unnatural pinnacle, pushing up from the sea surrounding her. From the time the Captain turned the small knob on the helmsman's console until he verified that the forward part of the ship was at rest felt like an eternity, though only a few minutes had elapsed.

Things began to play out in slow motion. With the propeller suspended in the water 500 feet above the bottom, *Shackleton's* bow began to rise from the suction of the sticky mud encasing the smooth hull, pulled down by the sheer weight of the progressive flooding in the after part of the ship. The rate of change was not discernible to the naked eye. The trim of the ship began to change over the course of hours. Larger than four football fields, *Shackleton* was designed to operate in virtually any kind of weather and any sea condition. At sea, the length of the ship itself would remain level as the hull would be pushing through several swells simultaneously without pitching. Other vessels would be raised up on the crest of a swell which would drive the bow deep into the middle of the next one. That was warship stuff. The weight of *Shackleton's* hull and cargo and its deep draft guaranteed a stable deck without straining the containers stacked six high.

Startled and confused, the crew found their way to the bridge where they knew the Captain would be. The general announcing system was not operating so they climbed to the bridge to get answers from a man they all trusted. Speaking their native languages, the frantic din on the bridge became too much for MacGregor, a man who demanded that the bridge remain quiet and businesslike. Finally, MacGregor was asked by the First Mate to address the crew and try to reduce their anxiety.

"The ship sustained at least two underwater explosions, one forward near the bow and one aft under the engine room that tripped the main engine, generators, and auxiliaries offline. *Shackleton* is aground on the right side of the transit channel. I'd say that the after third or perhaps half of the ship is hanging over deep water. Because I don't know how well supported the ship is on the bottom, I think it's time to get the lifeboat lowered. There is no immediate danger, but there is the possibility that the ship could slip stern first into deeper water and sink. We are about eight miles from the nearest shore that way." The Captain pointed in the direction of Mocha and several crew members looked out the bridge windows for signs of civilization. Few of the crew could swim, and many carried inflatable life jacket pouches. All of them knew how to wear and inflate the life jackets. Under the direction of the First Mate, the crew departed the bridge, and MacGregor continued to assess the situation. Any seasoned mariners would describe *Shackleton's* grounded condition as "in extremis", one step away from another disaster.

Once *Shackleton* was aground, pushing on the mud and sand and crushing the delicate coral structures, the contents of containers began to shift. As the containers were all painted steel boxes with no means of observing the contents from the exterior, the unseen cargo shifts were also taking place in slow motion. Sound was the only indication that the cargo was shifting. As the tension on the steel cables changed, the strain on the exterior lashings created a sound like the strumming of a guitar punctuated by the percussive bangs of loads shifting within individual containers. Contents slid on the container's floor, tensioning straps and chains holding heavy loads in place. It had the effect of a thousand blackboards emitting the awful sound of screeching chalk that never stopped.

Each container's bill of lading described the contents packed inside in varying levels of detail. Some containers were filled with dry goods such as fabric and bolts of upholstery material. Other containers were jammed with machinery and tooling such as high-speed steel bars destined for manufacturing facilities in Europe and the United States. The interior of containers was rarely inspected for the adequacy of the internal dunnage to prevent damage from chafing or cargo movement. Additionally, bills of lading often disguised the actual contents of containers to avoid destination port duties.

Each fraction of a degree change in the angle of *Shackleton's* deck had a domino effect with thousands of containers straining against the ratcheted hold downs that were designed to secure racks of containers placed on top of each other to the main deck. Shifting cargo caused containers to edge aft towards the stern a millimeter at a time as the heavy propulsion and machinery spaces, now with the added weight of hundreds of tons of seawater naturally tried to pull the forward half of the hull into the channel abyss. Beginning as almost imperceptible scrapes accompanied by the hum of straining cables, one container would shift to find a resting place against an adjacent one held down in a similar manner.

Containers started to move aft as cables snapped trying to hold the additional weight of the shifting contents. Shrill, the sound level increased until it reminded MacGregor of a banshee's scream that his mother had told him about as a young boy. The mighty ship was in great peril, and nothing could stop the horrific chain reaction that could crush then sweep away the after part of the towering deck house into the deep sea below.

Thousands of containers were "lost" every year because of fires or groundings or improper lashing. Pushing off the proper seamanship in one port compounded the problem over a series of port calls. No loading supervisor wanted to spend his crew's time fixing others' negligence. In reality, the progression from port to port just made the situation worse. *Shackleton's* master was known as a stickler for detail, including all the elements of proper seamanship. Once he had disrupted a carefully orchestrated port loading and unloading scheme because of missing twist locks between container tiers and improper tension of turnbuckles on the crisscrossed lashings that secured containers to each other vertically by means of heavy cables or straps. This voyage had been no different, and *Shackleton's* cargo was properly secured for a routine transit between ports.

MacGregor could see the change in the ship's trim by looking at the dark ring on the inside of his coffee mug. On the bow side of the cup it was visible, the cold dark liquid below exposing it. The ship was inexorably moving from a straight and level trim to being down by the stern. He glanced at the magnetic compass on the ship's centerline and saw the annoying bubble in the oil filled sphere that never moved from the center of the compass. Now the bubble had moved forward towards the bow a fraction of an inch.

It took hours for the first containers to break free of the lashings and fall into the sea. Tons of additional strain were put on the threaded rods and turnbuckles securing the uppermost containers. Some of those failed where the cables were joined together with metal couplings to form hard eyes that violently separated. In others, the threads simply stripped and the fittings fractured under the additional weight. Twist locks either shattered or were pulled free of the oval fittings at the corners of the containers where they had been installed. The sound of the cargo tearing away was deafening.

Some of the steel boxes cascaded into the sea and floated away from the hull. Others slowly filled with water, bobbing on the surface before disappearing under it. Containers holding machinery and equipment simply fell into the water and continued to the bottom. Within hours, there were watercraft of every description around *Shackleton*. An emergency Notice to Mariners had been issued advising ships to use extreme caution when traveling the Traffic Separation Scheme whose north-bound lane was completely blocked. The route was clogged with bobbing containers, some of which were floating just under the surface. These presented a true hazard to navigation, as the steel boxes could punch a hole in a ship's hull. Few conscientious mariners would risk transiting through waters trashed with containers.

A damaged propeller might require weeks in a drydock and a long period out of service. On the open sea, it was easy to avoid an area where containers had been lost. But here in a narrow strait, there was no maneuvering room to avoid them.

Before nightfall, the story went viral on social media. The first photos of the stranded *Shackleton* looking like a beached whale on Cape Cod would be on the front pages of most of the world's daily papers. Hundreds of containers littered the surface, surrounded *Shackleton* and began to drift away as night fell on the stranded vessel. The deck was now canted as more seawater filled the engine room and hold. Scores of small craft were on the scene, tugs that had been called in from Aden by the suits in London, fishing boats and even some long narrow Somali boats looking for some goods they might re-sell. The unflappable Captain seemed paralyzed on the bridge. Nothing like this had ever happened to him or to any of his proud maritime forebears. He was startled when he saw the First Mate's lips moving but heard no sound.

"Captain, the lifeboat is loaded. I'd like permission to cast off and stand clear of the hull." the man said.

"Of course," he said knowing that the boat had been lowered using its own weight to work the motor driven cables and sheaves. "Is the crew OK?" he asked.

"All accounted for. One of the Filipino oilers is dead. Looks like he died of blunt force trauma when the force of the underwater explosion blew him against the metal catwalk around the main propulsion electric motor. His neck was broken. We put him in a reefer box in the hold. What are your intentions, Captain?"

"I'm not sure. The way the ship is positioned makes me wonder if the stress on the double bottom and torsion box may break the ship's back. I just don't know how we'll end up. I thought about dropping the hook to prevent the ship from sliding into deep water but taking that weight off the forward part of the ship could accelerate the flooding aft and cause the stern to sink. It's a trade-off. What do you think?"

"I think it's time to get off the ship for your own safety. The ship is in a precarious position, and it will certainly get worse ahead."

MacGregor looked at the man, his bright blue eyes drilling twin holes right through his body and said, "I'll stay with the ship. Cast off and stand-by." The mate turned to leave the bridge and MacGregor spoke again. "George, you are a very capable Mate who deserves to command one of these ships. I've made that clear in a number of reports to the company. Fair winds."

"Thank you, Captain."

The bow was up at perhaps a 30-degree angle from the plane of the water and seemed to be balanced on a fulcrum at the edge of the channel. The deepest part of the channel would swallow the after part of the ship. *Ernest H. Shackleton* seemed destined to remain in an upright position as a very expensive channel marker. There was nothing any human could do to save the ship now. The bulbous bow looked like some fickle finger pointed directly at Mocha. The sea would win. It always did.

CHAPTER FIFTY-SIX

Washington, DC

Steele felt divorced from the real action and out of the loop in terms of the contingency planning he knew was being done within other parts of the government. Pisces was not in the forefront of military planning, and Steele had to live with the facts. However, the cell could plug into any of the intelligence streams as a listen only, passive player. Various operational commands monitored all the VHF channel 16 traffic via a small local fishing boat from the port of Assab in Eritrea, the country due west of Mocha, and a shore-based receiver cleverly disguised as a scrub plant that managed to grow along the coast north of the compound.

Both posts converted the scratchy VHF transmissions to a highly packed data stream pushed through a small dish that automatically tracked a communications satellite and relayed the transmission with a delay of less than two seconds. The Pentagon controlled both sensors as a means of keeping a pulse on a potentially threatening situation that might involve the military services. The Kingdom's intelligence services were working the area as well, worried about the impact of cash infusions somehow distributed to the Houthi rebels. The Saudi-led bombing campaign was on another of its pauses while negotiators tried to reason with the various factions all claiming to be in charge of the shaky remnants of Yemen's central government.

Steele could listen to the conversations as if he were within the frequency range of about twenty-five miles, hearing the usual back and forth from maritime commerce transiting the strait and the guarded questions about the new toll charges. The casual conversations between ships often began in English, but after the identifications were exchanged, it reverted back to the native language of the masters, sometimes coming back to English if the ships could not find a shared basis for communication.

Though not a trained linguist, Steele could pick up the thread of the conversation and make sense of the exchange based on a few snippets of the languages he'd heard around the world. Chinese proved to be the most difficult, but still the threads were hanging there in space for the careful listener. Ships continued to pass without any sign that the date announced by the Mocha group meant a thing. No tolls were being collected, no challenges issued, and no change to transit plans were made.

What he heard when he logged on to his computer on the first day of October changed all that. Tapping into the live audio feed being relayed from thousands of miles away, he heard the still frantic transmissions of the maritime disaster that had just occurred. The voice circuit was clobbered with undisciplined chatter involving what sounded like hundreds of participants speaking in unrecognizable regional dialects. What was unmistakable was the edge to the conversations that signaled a maritime emergency of some type occurring in the narrow waters separating the Arabian Peninsula from the northern coast of East Africa.

As he tried to piece together the dialog, several news sites popped onto his screen with the first reports of the *Ernest H. Shackleton* grounding at the edge of the shipping channel. Initial news reports were sketchy. He searched an on-line database of merchant ships and found *Shackleton*, a modern vessel which incorporated all the latest technology available to the maritime trade: a super cargo vessel larger than an aircraft carrier, mind-blowing cargo capacity, operated by a small crew of twenty-two, optimized hull form to reduce drag, reduced carbon dioxide emissions, and an electronically controlled engine. This large poster-child of modern maritime technology seemed to have somehow broken down in the channel and now squatted on the shoals with its stern hanging perilously over deep water. He heard a clear transmission in English between the First Mate and Master regarding the condition of the ship and the unstable conditions aboard.

Yemen was eight hours ahead of Eastern Standard Time. It was 3:00 p.m. when Steele heard the transmission between the First Mate and Master. The fact that the two were communicating via handheld radio confirmed that something serious was underway. For the First Mate and crew to depart the ship in a lifeboat was extraordinary in today's world. Steele had once been on a US Navy ship which had lost propulsion and electrical power. He recalled that momentary feeling of hopelessness before the emergency diesel generators started and picked up the ship's electrical load. *Shackleton* was aground and flooding with no means of combating the inexorable combination of physics and the sea.

Steele wondered how such a ship could be disabled. An act of God? He had a sickening feeling in his stomach, thinking about the havoc wreaked on this monster ship and how Mocha Control might have delivered it. He kept the speaker on in the background, wondering what might happen so many thousand miles away in the hours ahead.

CHAPTER FIFTY-SEVEN

Container Ship *Ernest H. Shackleton*

The First Mate and crew remained in the lifeboat bobbing among the hundreds of containers breaking free of their lashings and falling into the water. A graduate of the Massachusetts Maritime Academy located in Bourne, Massachusetts, George Bauer was a very capable operator who had a bright future ahead, until today. As the Master of a smaller container ship working for the same line, he'd demonstrated all the traits owners look for in a rising maritime star. The assignment as First Mate of *Shackleton* was more of a finishing school. How much his future would be damaged by the day's events was uncertain, but career-wise, he was probably mortally wounded. Even though there was no causal connection between "acts of God" and the ship's Captain, the responsibility for the disaster would be MacGregor's. Those near the Captain would often be tarred with the same brush.

A waning gibbous moon illuminated the box-filled surface of the water while the terrible shifting and sliding screech still echoed across its surface. The First Mate reported that the bulbous nose of the ship was just visible above the waterline and the water at the stern was covering the ship's name painted across the flat steel plates in ten-foot letters. He once again pleaded with the Master to abandon his post on the bridge and join the crew in the lifeboat. That old unwritten rule about masters going down with their ships was passé in today's world.

Captain Ian MacGregor watched the unfolding of the maritime tragedy as if he were some external observer with a full view of the ship and its surroundings. He saw his career and family's proud maritime heritage swirling down the vortex of a low point drain. Exhausted mentally and physically, he took the easy way out. Using his flashlight to retreat down the dark, canted deck into his cabin behind the ship's bridge, he spun the black dial of a small safe bolted to the bulkhead above his desk and pulled out a .45 caliber pistol. The porthole in his cabin let in the moon's bright light, but he needed the flashlight to inspect the magazine, full of the short heavy slugs. He rammed the magazine home into the gun's grip with a clean metallic click and chambered a single round.

Opening the joiner door to his small bathroom, he stood in front of the narrow mirror above the sink, shining the light between the mirror and his face which took on a frightening look. He could still see the bristling beard, the dull color of rust, that nearly covered the collar points of his clan's colors. His blue eyes looked tired and somehow had lost their brilliant hue. After a long look at his determined face in the mirror, Ian MacGregor carefully placed the muzzle of the heavy pistol under his chin where it disappeared into his thick beard. Without any hesitation, he squeezed the trigger and blew off the top of his head.

By morning, *Shackleton's* stern was resting under the water, wedged into the bottom at a depth of 600' with just under half the ship exposed above the water with the bow pointing skyward at a steep angle. Captain McGregor was crumpled against the bulkhead of his cabin's small bathroom with his blood coagulated in the vee formed by the bulkhead and pitched deck, with bits of his frenzied red hair splattered all over the white ceiling.

CHAPTER FIFTY-EIGHT

London, UK

Met curbside and escorted into the large news building in Central London, Emma Bolden enjoyed being treated like royalty. She'd prepared for this moment virtually her entire life but specifically in the weeks that followed her front-page reporting on the escape of General Zlodeyev. That story transformed her into a fresh celebrity among journalists, and she'd made the rounds of talk shows, invited back to London to receive an award for investigative reporting. No other story reported on during the year could top what she broke, and there was little on the horizon as far as news other than the continuing tragedy in Yemen's civil war and the on again off again bombing raids by the Saudi-led coalition. Iran had stepped up its military assistance to the Houthis, including delivery of air defense systems that had successfully shot down a number of the Kingdom's foreign-built combat aircraft.

She was the talk of the town and savored the attention. Today's meeting would be a perfect time for the organization to offer her a new role. Wearing a stylish new suit, her hair had been coiffed into a style that accentuated her Scandinavian features. Confident, she exuded a stage presence and anticipated a plan would be laid out for her transition back to the home office and offer of her own weekly show. With high expectations, she was swept into the avant-garde office suite of Terry Ayers, an executive news producer who had asked to have a sit-down with the woman. They had never met. He floated high up in the organization's ether, and she was one of those in the trenches who'd had an opportunity to finally crawl out of them. The timing could not have been better.

His greeting was too warm. Too personal. The first sign of

trouble was when he offered her a drink at 10:00 a.m. in the morning. He feasted on her with his eyes. Rather than extol her reporting and congratulate her on the praise she'd received from her peers and the industry, he jumped right to the point.

"My Emma, you do look delicious." She was counting on a professional discussion about her future with the news. He was anticipating another easy conquest as the boss who held the keys to her future. In a thinly disguised attempt at negotiation, Terry Ayers invited Emma to have a closer look at some erotic etchings that he had mounted in the adjoining room to stimulate their conversation. She declined. Sure, she'd bedded Urodov to get an exclusive but would not offer herself to a man only interested in his own self-satisfaction. Neither got what they wanted. Instead, after expressing the gratitude of the media giant almost as an afterthought, Emma was asked to follow the story to Yemen and see if she could be the face of the emerging story about the General, now thought to be behind the sinking of a modern-day cargo vessel just off its shores. She was better than that.

Piqued, she left with her dignity intact, but the proposal of flying to another war zone to cover the story was a slap in the face. She asked for a few days off to think over the assignment Ayers offered her. He reluctantly granted her request.

"Would you like to get together later today for a relaxing dinner?"

"Thank you but I've already made plans for this evening," she replied, trying to maintain her composure as he leered at her.

She needed to take a hard look at other options. She compared the hostility of this work environment with the war zones she'd covered, and there was no comparison. There were other news organizations. The only thing she knew for sure was that her relationship with this one would soon end. She relished the idea of taking Ayers down but was also aware that such a move would make her radioactive within the industry. Women making public accusations often found future career options very limited. She was a known commodity, confident and capable of taking her current level of fame and building it into something closer to the position she sought. She felt relieved when reaching the curb and finding the waiting car.

CHAPTER FIFTY-NINE

Washington, DC

The weekend news was unsettling. *The Washington Post* covered the *Shackleton* disaster, presenting the few known facts along with details about the ship, an update on the piracy situation off Somalia, and some relevant graphics regarding the waterway stretching between the Mediterranean and Arabian Seas and its vital trade statistics. Its investigative reporters dug up the announcement of the toll being imposed by Mocha Control and raised the question of how such a toll might be enforced.

After a restless night, Steele went into the office early on Monday morning, feeling like one of hundreds of thousands of faceless bureaucrats hired to keep the bloated US government functioning for another week. The low clouds and light rain added to the depressing situation.

A second crisis had now beset Yemen as Steele watched the scene recorded from space. The ship was aground, and containers were still falling from its slanted decks. He thought back to the idea of traveling to Yemen that had been approved by Hank Owens weeks before. He'd taken his eye off the ball. A meeting of the inter-agency working group, and the fact that Sandy Matthews had a scheduling conflict postponed the trip. Steele questioned his own judgment in putting off the trip because of a meeting. Washington ran on meetings, mostly of little or no consequence. Steele was certain that each of the agencies was staffed with professional meeting attendees, people who dutifully signed the 'I was there' attendance sheet and wrote brief reports to their bosses who'd been invited in the first place. Now the opportunity was lost, and Yemen would be filling with negotiators, maritime insurers, news reporters and others. Or was the opportunity actually lost he questioned with an internal two-sided debate?

Now it was critically important to get to Yemen and maybe the influx of people would provide additional cover for Steele, who wanted to remain an anonymous face in the crowd. He surveyed available flights and found one leaving later in the day. After booking it, he figured-out his timeline, notifications and what he would need for the trip, starting to mentally pack. A brief email to Colonel Bullard in Sana'a outlined his plans and proposed a late afternoon visit to the Embassy the following day after his arrival to get things rolling. Steele felt better when he was doing something, even if he were headed in the wrong direction.

Impetuous was a term that appeared in a Report of Fitness from Steele's early days as a US Navy SEAL. His Commanding Officer tried to explain it away as a compliment which reflected Steele's aggressiveness. Jill was horrified with the description of his behavior and knew its use was pejorative. Certain the word would have a negative impact on his promotion opportunities in the future, she urged him to have another discussion with the CO, but it never happened. Dan was busy, the CO was traveling, we're into the next evaluation cycle, et cetera. They had endless discussions about the matter. It was like a splinter of wood left under the skin. It gradually walled off, but it was a sore point in their marriage that neither of them ever forgot.

The Admiral was in the Pentagon for a string of meetings that would keep him on the Virginia side of the Potomac the entire day, so Steele sent him a text message that began with the acronym UNODIR, Navy talk for Unless Otherwise Directed. That gave the Admiral the final vote on Steele's plans, and he knew the Admiral would not be reluctant to reel him in if he thought Steele was embarking on some foolhardy quest. The Admiral sent him a simple acknowledgment of his travel plans: "K, b safe."

As the plane lifted off the runway from Dulles, Steele thought about his last trip to Yemen and wrestled with his doubts and the little voices in his head that warned him that he was volunteering to once again expose himself to certain danger.

He brushed aside the voices and tried to concentrate on how *Shackleton* was sunk. There was no evidence of an attack topside. Steele reasoned if an explosives-filled container were loaded in the right cell below decks in the hold, that might cause the rupture in the hull. But what about the timing? How could such a device be triggered from ashore? There were no visible signs of damage above the waterline. Something tethered to the bottom? Steele had studied the charts and knew the depth of water in the northbound channel where the great ship was sunk was 600 feet. If mines were moored in the channel, how were they sown? How would they be released? Contact detonators? How would they obtain the buoyancy necessary to rise to a shallow depth? What about timing? Hundreds of questions swirled in his head.

A dive to 600 feet would require specialized diving equipment and mixed gas, probably impossible to find in Yemen. A mini-submarine? Charges placed against the ship's hull by a man-operated underwater sled? Impossible because of the ship's speed and the force of the water rushing along the hull. Perhaps explosive charges placed by divers in *Shackleton's* last port stop. Plausible but a little far-fetched.

Steele concluded that the attack came from underwater, but he couldn't put together the right combination of explosives, placement, delivery and communications. Someone with a knowledge of explosives and an understanding of the underwater fire control problem must be involved. Maybe someone from the General's Alpha Group had underwater demolition experience. To think that such a plan could be executed in one of the world's major waterways was troubling. There would be several dive teams going to look at the ship's underwater hull to determine whether the ship could be raised or just sold as is to the highest bidder for salvage and scrap. A first-hand look at the underwater damage would give Steele some insight into the capability of Mocha Control and perhaps the people involved. Steele added this to his mental list of actions, determined to join a dive team and see things for himself.

After another hour of concentration, he concluded the insurance and salvage experts would put together a detailed report of the underwater hull damage and perform the forensic tests of interest to determine the cause. Those would be easy to get through government channels. Instead, Steele would focus on locating the remnants of any explosive devices away from the hull. He would be searching for the delivery scheme, how the explosives may have been controlled and from where.

Steele's mind again reviewed the many factors in play: a modern cargo ship disabled after an underwater attack by Mocha Control using what appeared to be conventional explosives. A country at war, fighting external forces as well as a gut-wrenching civil war which had caused a major humanitarian crisis and was tearing Yemen apart. The previous trip to Sana'a where he was attacked twice in a matter of minutes. A diabolical Russian General holding a trump card that would win any hand. And here he was, voluntarily traveling to make sense of it all. What was wrong with this picture? Steele laughed to himself and tried to position his body to fall asleep.

PART III

CHAPTER SIXTY

The news from Yemen took everyone by surprise — a British flagged cargo ship aground in international waters while transiting north of the Bab el Mandeb. With the loss of propulsion and electrical power, the ship somehow managed to steer to the right side of the channel and park on the bottom as the after part of the ship continued to sink.

As the former ruler of the maritime trade over much of the globe as well as the ship's owners, the British were outraged. Endlessly debating the details of the never-ending saga of Brexit was replaced by the story of the large ship flying the Union Jack now sitting in the middle of a busy waterway off the coast of Yemen. The stage was set for a series of comical Parliamentary debates on what the Brits might do about it. A confidence vote was looming for the new Prime Minister, already battered by a bitterly divided government.

Underwater obstacles not found on the chart? An act of piracy? Terrorism? Pundits on every cable news channel speculated about the cause of the incident. Some blamed a Houthi-backed terror cell operating in Yemen and manned by Somali pirates who upped their game by using explosives. School children got a geography lesson as maps were displayed to educate them on the location of the poor country on everyone's mind. A rogue Russian submarine was implicated. One theory suggested the use of a microwave system emanating from three different points on the globe causing catastrophic failure of all the vessel's electric and electronic systems. Most of the talking heads were not even aware of the true situation in Mocha and the toll previously announced in maritime shipping notices. Environmentalists were already describing the incalculable impact on the ecology of the waterway with the combination of containers on the bottom and the certainty of ruptured fuel tanks.

The news anchors were flustered, the armchair strategists guarded. There were no seasoned reporters in Yemen. The local stringers were incapable of translating what happened for consumption by the general public. Crews readied for the opportunity to report directly from Yemen, forgetting a civil war was tearing the country apart. The smartest news channels interviewed maritime experts who sailed the waters and understood what it would take to disable a modern cargo carrier like *Ernest H. Shackleton*. Most of them concentrated on the usual causes for groundings which were loss of steering control, sloppy piloting, and poor seamanship.

In the United States, the Defense Committees from both chambers of Congress were inundated with calls, and the Pentagon dialed up the wartime footing in the region. A query was sent from the White House requesting a range of options to signal that the United States would not idly stand by and have international waters treated as if they were someone's back yard pond. The President's response to the recent Iranian attacks on merchant ships in the Gulf of Oman was viewed as a dangerous political misstep. A different course of action would be required. Alerts were transmitted by virtually every level of government, and relief agencies readied their beleaguered response teams.

Members of Congress who took safe positions on the Seapower and Projection Forces Subcommittee were now asked to step forward and comment on the situation. Those committee positions were not the assignments which catapulted members to leadership positions within the plum committees or made them possible contenders for higher office. They were quiet harbors for those members nearing the end of their final terms or life, whichever came first.

The Pentagon released a transcript of the VHF Channel sixteen radio exchange between Mocha Control and *Ernest H. Shackleton* which connected the dots of cause and effect but did not the means. A British tabloid captured the world reaction in a single word on its front page in the largest font available: **SUNK???**

CHAPTER SIXTY-ONE

The Russian Federation's attempt to recover the bodies of Urodov and his Alpha Group commandos seemed an appropriate overture to the group of expatriates in Mocha and an easy way to begin a dialog. After all, they had once been loyal sons of the Federation and defended the nation's interests on far flung battlefields. The President had given the Minister of Foreign Affairs a free hand to open a communications link with the group and recover the bodies of the fallen immediately. However, before the well-greased gears of diplomacy even started to turn, Zlodeyev had given Urodov and his team a fiery Viking sendoff less than twelve hours after the devastating raid.

There were frustrating brain-storming sessions in Moscow as well as many of the world's capitals trying to identify the leverage points that might be used to begin communicating, the acknowledged first step in conflict resolution. Moscow delivered a tactical, satellite-based communications set to the deserters, but it remained unopened outside the compound's gate.

The British diverted one of the boats used to support the diving operation on *Shackleton*, and it tied up to the small pier in front of the compound under a large British flag. Violently rebuffed, the boat limped away from the pier with bullet holes near its waterline and its navigation lights shattered. Other methods, both direct and indirect, were tried without success. It was a particularly knotty problem in a country with a fluid central government, warring factions, the constant threat of external attacks and the absence of the rule of law and common courtesy that characterized most of the other countries' dialogs. Raw diplomacy without all the civilized trappings was very hard work, and there were no easy answers.

Steele had seen diplomacy work all over the world. Countless military missions were scrubbed at the eleventh hour because the diplomats finally found some common ground that permitted a collective push towards resolution. Steele and the teams were put "on hold" like calling a credit card company to question charges made on your account. They would hear the telephone music for days, weeks and sometimes months before they were called back into the action or the mission was shelved indefinitely. The diplomatic path out of the woods was always preferred to create the conditions where differences could be discussed around a large conference table in some capital city at a leisurely pace. Communications over an extended period of time usually resulted in resolution of some kind, where both sides would save face, regardless of what the terms of any agreement might be.

Everyone expected that all the diplomatic efforts to resolve the crisis would have to be exhausted before the military got involved. Time itself was well known to resolve conflict, and there was little appetite around to world to use force of any kind to compel a solution. The working groups were beat. Daily meetings were now held three times each week, and the teams stopped working on weekends. In Yemen, the crisis found a shaky equilibrium. Ships were paying the tolls and transiting the waterway unscathed. A new normal had replaced the old.

Shackleton's remaining topside containers were removed using a jury-rigged crane leveled on the ship's canted deck. While *Shackleton's* insurance portfolio included the usual coverage for the hull, machinery, and cargo, and Protection and Indemnity for third party claims, there were other risks facing the owners. The media attention attracted environmentalists including Greenpeace. While *Shackleton's* ultimate fate was still being analyzed by marine surveyors, ship builders, and salvage specialists, others were actively patrolling the waters surrounding the hull looking for the rainbowed sheen on the surface that would confirm that the ship's fuel tanks were leaking.

The ship's position complicated any thought of patching and refloating the giant because the afterpart of the ship had been filled with corrosive salt water and the depth of water posed challenges to any plan to refloat the ship and to set it free of the underwater landscape for repair. The British took charge of the salvage operation and were moving ahead at what seemed to be a snail's pace. Small underwater cameras, self-propelled and driven from the surface pinpointed the damage to the ship's hull. It didn't take long for the forensic investigators to conclude that *Shackleton's* hull had been torn open by two massive underwater explosions. At the same time, the US Government admitted that the missing CAPTOR mines were the likely source of the explosions. Of course, the ship's owners were thrilled with the news. So were the insurance carriers. Not only would the US Government be forced to make restitution but also would shoulder the cost of other claims arising from lost cargo or environmental impact. The condition of the ship's backbone, the box girder forming the keel, was not yet certain, but no one really cared. With Uncle Sam involved, minimal financial impact on the owners was all but guaranteed.

CHAPTER SIXTY-TWO

Mocha, Yemen

There was no particular daily routine inside the compound, and the fighters had ample time to pursue any activities of interest. All were expected to maintain a high level of fitness, and the mornings were generally devoted to individual physical activities. The large, well-equipped gym attracted many and offered a necessary adjunct to yoga, swimming, and running around the periphery of the compound. Zlodeyev himself spent at least two hours in the weight room daily, which featured both stationary machines and a wide selection of weights. As a weightlifter, he was in a class by himself and no one came close to matching his strength.

Zlodeyev established a strict curfew with the compound's gate locked and monitored after midnight. Fighters wishing to spend the night away from the compound could do so with an overnight pass that would require them to return not later than 10:00 a.m. the following morning. While most adults would bristle at the thought of a curfew, it made little difference to the fighters who had endured restrictions far worse.

The new compound had a positive impact on the local economy both for the people employed there during the day and the other services that catered to men living on its isolated coastline. Several watering holes served food and siddiqi, a locally distilled spirit whose name is a variation of the phrase "my friend" in Arabic. Several local women turned tricks in response to the needs of the Russians who came to town looking for amusement. People everywhere understood street economics, and supply would always respond to demand.

Every three months, the compound took on a carnival-like atmosphere when the arena came alive with a wide range of entertainment, which always included blood sport. Like an elaborate tail-gate event, there was a charcoal grill set up with a wide variety of meats, including organ meats for the more adventurous. Large ice-filled coolers chilled bottles of vodka and beer, though several of the Russian fighters preferred the buzz from chewing Qat, the leaf of a local flowering evergreen shrub. With its combination of stimulant and narcotic properties, it was sold in small bundles and used like leaf chewing tobacco. Qat sometimes led to a euphoric glow and other times to manic and delusional behavior and violent hallucinations. It seemed like the perfect tonic of choice for the fighters living in the compound.

Pairings were made between the men who had a beef to settle or just wanted to have a good fight. Sergei's resourcefulness was often on display as he procured animals, mostly from the continent across the water, to serve as opponents. At thirty feet in diameter, a four-foot wall defined the arena's perimeter. Its larger size offered more space to maneuver for the contestants. A thick duck canvas covered the ground, providing sure footing and keeping the dust down. Sited at the north end of the main building, Zlodeyev constructed the arena to let the fighters blow off some steam and to promote cohesiveness within the group. Though it had only been used for two separate compound events, blood stains spotted the canvas.

On this night, two Russians tired of sharing the same girl in town would settle their dispute in a man to man bare-knuckled contest, two fighters would engage in a local iron man competition with several challenges, and Richie Bouffard would go up against a crazy baboon captured in the mountains in Asir national park in Abha, Saudi Arabia. Though playing before a very small crowd, the arena contests provided a night of male-only revelry, which ended with the participants bleeding and the audience drunk or stoned or both, except for three watch-standers monitoring the compound's security system and walking its lighted perimeter.

Seated in what many of his fighters called the emperor's section of the bleachers, Zlodeyev presided over the contests and carried a weighted red flag similar to the challenge flag in professional football where a coach formally questions a referee's call. He would use the flag to end a match where there was a clear victor and to avoid permanent injury or death. Animals were usually fought until they were dead.

Traveling from Sana'a, Colonel Bullard visited the town more frequently and installed a number of cameras in town to capture the images of the Russians who would bring laundry, shop for clothing or other sundries locally which they could not procure via the internet. Though no vendor would offer two-day guaranteed delivery to Mocha, the relaxed atmosphere in the compound would tolerate a short wait for ordered goods. To date, Bullard had collected photos of twenty individual Russians coming into town and provided the photos to the State Department and Defense Intelligence Service.

CHAPTER SIXTY-THREE

Washington, DC

Officials from Sandia National Laboratories, Los Alamos, Lawrence Livermore, Johns Hopkins, and Massachusetts Institute of Technology's Lincoln Laboratories sat at the table in front of the intelligence committees of both chambers for a rare joint session. Today's closed-door hearing was highly classified. The nation's Federally Funded Research and Development Centers were civilian institutions given Federal funding for scientific research and to prepare assessments on adversary capability and potential innovations by looking at changes in operational patterns and clues from material procurements. The focus of today's hearing was the impact of the weapons lifted from Russian inventories and now sitting next to an international waterway of strategic importance.

Much of the work of these national labs relied on assumptions made to fill in the major information gaps. That enabled the lab to reach a range of conclusions.

"We divided the task into multiple pieces to facilitate the analysis," said the youngish looking man identified as the Director of MIT Lincoln Labs. "First, based on intelligence estimates, we addressed the question of arming and detonating the projectiles and did the same for the ability to disperse the chemical weapons. Second, we addressed a series of scenarios about the effect of the use of nuclear material and chemicals and then the two taken together using modeling and simulation." The man paused and acknowledged his colleagues to the right and left.

"While today's nuclear weapons pack a punch thousands of times more powerful than Little Boy and Fat Man combined, the

Russian 155-millimeter nuclear artillery shells could create a blast equivalent to 120,000 pounds of TNT. An explosion of this magnitude on the ground would produce significant kinetic damage and long-term radiation effects. Perhaps a minor conflagration by modern standards, but nonetheless, an explosion of epic proportion if all the economic, political, and human costs are factored into the calculation. How the nuclear material is packaged and how it might be triggered is a question we wrestled with. We looked at both cases, whether detonated by a plutonium core or configurated as a dirty bomb. The radiation dose curves and blast effects would be limited if fission were not achieved. In either case, there is sufficient material to cause catastrophic regional consequences.

Our collective estimation of the worst-case scenario would be the death of 200,000 people over an area of 2,000 square miles. Areas along the Red Sea and all the way to the Suez would be affected. The population centers in Yemen, Eritrea, Ethiopia, Somalia, Sudan, Egypt, and Saudi Arabia bordering the Red Sea would be decimated by the fallout. The effect on the center of Islam in Mecca would be less severe, but the annual pilgrimage could not be safely conducted. This waterway would take about ten years for natural remediation without active intervention to neutralize the effects of the radiation. None of us can assess exactly what it would take to return the waterway to service. I should note that the error bars on this analysis suggest an uncertainty of perhaps eighty per cent."

"Thank you, gentlemen, for that sobering assessment. The committee will recess now and will ask you to return for further discussions and some questions. We will reconvene in one hour." He banged the gavel on its sound block, ending the session.

The Committee chairman leaned back in his chair and engaged the minority chair from the other party on his left.

"Well, Melanie, I think we can agree on the fact that we've got a real mess in Yemen, and I can't see an easy path to resolution."

"No question about it. We just need to keep the cowboy over there in the large white house on Pennsylvania Avenue in check, so we can deal with this situation without the kind of collateral damage the labs are predicting. This is not a race to see how we can screw this up, but Lord knows we need a plan to resolve it. Every outcome sounds like a worst case scenario to me."

"I agree with that. Have these guys briefed the Armed Services Committees yet?"

"Not that I know of, but they certainly should. I think your friend over there in the White House should hear this too, though he's probably getting something similar from Defense. This is frightening stuff."

CHAPTER SIXTY-FOUR

Mocha, Yemen

An expediter hustled Steele through the diplomatic line of Customs and Immigration at the Sana'a International Airport, and he was delivered to Colonel Bullard just outside its porous perimeter.

"You just can't get enough of paradise, can you?" Bullard joked as he shook Steele's hand and escorted him to the SUV Steele recognized from his previous trip. "If you are ready to travel, I'd like to just head down to Mocha directly. I can brief you on the way. It's a long trip, and I've got both good news and bad. The good news is that I found a hotel room in town for tonight. The bad news is we'll have to share it." He lifted the tailgate and Steele threw his small duffel bag inside.

"That's OK as long as there are two beds. It's better than sleeping under the stars."

"Yep, two beds. Well, I figure we'll get there about midnight and can get an early start in the morning."

"Sounds good," said Steele.

After traveling sixteen hours to get to Yemen, the last thing Steele wanted to do was to drive to Mocha, but under the circumstances, the trip would help him reset his internal clock to the local time. He planned a three-day trip to Yemen, and his focus was on its southern coast. Small talk dominated the conversation until they were outside the airport and headed south. The *Shackleton* disaster had shifted the attention of the international news away from the humanitarian crisis to the apparent control of an international waterway by a rebel group operating for themselves.

"There's a pistol in the glove box in case we need it. I don't expect any trouble, but the bandits have been active in the last few months and know the number of foreigners traveling south will increase with the *Shackleton* disaster. They are on the lookout for fresh meat."

"OK," said Steele, reaching in and coming out with a Glock nine-millimeter in his hand. He saw several more loaded clips. Bullard had packed for the trip. Being armed made him more relaxed than he was during his last trip to the country with the UN, but also nervous. Yemen stood at the very edge of civilization, teetering on the brink of oblivion.

Bullard began a long situational briefing that lasted for the first half of the trip, providing details and the in-country perspective absent from the updates Steele had gotten through the Navy working group. Much of the information was repetitive which meant simply that no one in Washington had been given an opportunity to spin the data one way or another for personal or organizational reasons.

"We've gotten some better info on the compound, and the latest photos of the Russians are behind you on the back seat."

Steele paged through the three-ring binder, scanning the details from land surveys carried out years before. The old coffee processing facility had been abandoned, and there were no recent data on anything inside its boundaries. One survey dated in late 1893 depicted a hand dug, deep water well on the property that must have been part of the coffee enterprise. A series of buildings supported processing of the beans including washing, drying, sorting and bagging for ships that would tie up at the finger pier.

"Can you imagine how long it took to dig a well by hand?" asked Steele.

"Must have taken months. The satellite views indicate that it's still there, probably dried up and abandoned like the rest of the place. How Zlodeyev found this parcel of land and bought it is still a mystery. We just know that an international real estate agent from the UAE handled the transaction. Everything appears in order according to the Embassy's counselor who studied the documents recording the sale."

Steele thumbed through the photos of the hard men who called the compound home. He reacted to a picture of Richie Bouffard, wearing his gold trident necklace and drinking beer at a bar which also featured female entertainment.

"This guy is Richie Bouffard, a former SEAL who got kicked off the team and court-martialed out of the Navy. I was the investigating officer. He is one bad hombre. I wonder how he ended up here?"

"Hard to say. We did trace a job search for an underwater explosives expert listed in one of those international job websites to the team in Mocha but don't know if anything came of it. By the way, there's a US Navy diver coming over from Bahrain to dive with you tomorrow. He's got all the gear coming up on a boat from the base in Djibouti. As you can imagine, boats and diving equipment are in short supply since *Shackleton* sunk, but requests from the Embassy usually get priority."

After a short night on a lumpy bed, Steele felt he'd been tossed into a burlap bag and kicked all over the playing field by two opposing soccer teams. Awakened by the sunrise call to prayer, he was stiff and sore. He needed more sleep or a shot of caffeine. Bullard was already up and in the bathroom, so Steele pulled on his wrinkled travel clothes and headed downstairs to relieve himself in the lobby's men's room and to find some coffee. The dining area was small and busy, and first impressions signaled both a lack of waiters and a low standard of cleanliness. Still feeling dazed, Steele took a warm seat just vacated by an armed uniformed fighter dressed and ready for work, another day of combat. Since the city had been liberated in 2015 from Houthi control, Mocha had become a base camp for the pro-government forces.

The city of 15,000 people had seen a recent influx of westerners because of the *Shackleton* grounding and anticipated many more. Insurers, lawyers, and salvage experts were being drawn from the region and all over Europe. Both hotels in town were overbooked. Steele wondered if the murky tepid coffee served in a cup with brown drips on its sides was brewed from local beans. It didn't really matter. He left the table after gulping the cup's contents and walked to the bar where he bought a fresh cup that was spicy and hot served in a single-use paper cup. Drinking it black while slowly returning to the real world, his body aches began anew after they too were awakened by the liquid stimulant.

After breakfast, more coffee and an infusion of mixed fruit juices, Steele felt human again. Bullard expertly navigated the streets to a commercial pier where they spotted a boat flying a small US flag at its stern. The dive boat turned out to be a new 11-meter Special Forces RHIB fitted with twin Caterpillar six-cylinder diesel engines that pushed the boat through virtually any type of seas. In calm water, it could travel at speeds above forty knots. A short, uniformed fireplug introduced himself as Boatswain's Mate Second Class Rick Stoeppler. He was wearing a short sleeve khaki jumpsuit with his last name stenciled over the left breast pocket and a faded chambray ball cap labeled with an undecipherable acronym and the word Djibouti. His light hair was buzzed to the scalp and framed a face that looked like it had been exposed to the elements for centuries. Stoeppler even sported old school navy tattoos — hinges connected his muscled lower and upper arms in the front and spiderwebs grew from the point of his elbows on the back. The boat reflected his professionalism. It was spotless, and its brightwork gleamed in the hot morning sun.

The three were joined by the Navy diver from Bahrain, dressed in jeans and a tee-shirt. A tall and lanky Irishman, Kevin O'Connor was Stoeppler's opposite. Minutes later, Stoeppler stood at the center console, steering the boat out of the harbor and heading towards the dive site eleven miles away. They reached their destination just after 10:00 a.m. observing boat traffic that included the usual fishermen and others attracted to the containers still floating around *Shackleton* two miles to the north.

Steele and the US Navy diver studied the chart and agreed on a starting point and the area to be searched, planning a dive along the 150-foot curve. *Shackleton's* momentum propelled the ship close to two miles further along its general track while slowing as it contacted the bottom with its hull. That complicated their rough calculations which could be off as much as a mile, but it was a starting point. Using GPS, they anchored an end point buoy 500 yards northwest from the starting point that emitted a homing signal. Attired in thin nylon shorty wetsuits reflecting the water temperature of seventy-five degrees, the two strapped on standard ninety cubic foot aluminum air tanks and a full-face mask that featured a built-in communications microphone serving as an underwater walkie talkie, linking them to each other and to the base station on the RHIB. The plan was recapped to Bullard and Stoeppler who would remain topside. Rolling backwards off the gunwales, both divers headed towards the bottom through the warm, gin clear water.

Once the bottom, covered with an abundance of live coral with spectacular color came into view, they leveled off and swam about thirty feet apart moving steadily on a compass bearing viewed on a "heads up" display inside their face masks. There was little tidal effect in this part of the Red Sea. Because of the unlimited visibility, their search swath covered nearly ninety feet in width. They planned for a twenty-minute dive at 120 feet with a twenty-minute decompression stop at fifteen feet to permit the nitrogen absorbed into their blood streams at that depth to become tiny bubbles that could be safely carried in their tissues. Without the stop, they might suffer decompression sickness, or the bends, which usually results in prolonged joint pain but can lead to permanent paralysis.

While not precisely following the conservative calculations prescribed in the Navy dive tables, both divers felt comfortable with the planned parameters. There were two additional ninety cubic foot tanks charged and ready to go on the boat. The schools of small fish moving in and out of the coral fronds were mesmerizing, and the bright colors overloaded the senses. Along the dive route were containers from *Shackleton* lying on the bottom. Steele noted one container standing vertically on a patch of hard coral and two others that were stacked. Reaching the end point line, both divers started a slow ascent to a depth of fifteen feet for a brief period of decompression, talking as they hung motionless on the line.

"These containers on the bottom make me wonder if we'll be able to find anything. The sites where the weapons were fixed to the bottom could be buried under tons of debris," said Steele.

"Yeah, I agree. We'll be lucky to find anything on the bottom. This is a real change in scenery for me. Other than the containers, this is beautiful undisturbed coral. It's much more vivid than the stuff we see in the Gulf," said the US Navy diver. "Plus, there are no sea snakes here. I hate those critters."

At the end of the decompression stop, their tanks were yanked up and over the side by Stoeppler and secured. Both divers climbed up the short ladder hung over the gunwale and hauled themselves over the side of the RHIB and stood dripping saltwater. After removing the rest of their gear and toweling off, they reviewed a GPS trace of their dive and agreed to begin the next leg after a surface interval which approximated the dive table guidelines.

After relaxing on the surface for an hour and drinking several liters of bottled water, both divers strapped on fresh tanks and descended to their new starting point. They were swimming in formation at about 120 feet when Steele felt something press against his mask. It felt like fishing line. He pulled it away. At first glance, it appeared to be a heavy monofilament that seemed to lead towards the surface, with the other end snagged on something deeper. There were no fishermen in sight when the two divers entered the water. He held the line in front of his mask and saw a thread-like braided copper wire shielded in translucent plastic. He had seen similar wire used to set off underwater charges.

"Kevin," he said into the mask, "This looks like the det cord I've seen the EOD use. Looks like it's secured to something topside and leads down over the shelf. I'm going to follow it down. I'll make it quick and will spend another twenty minutes at our decompression stop, OK?"

O'Connor joined Steele and looked at the line he held in his hand. "Yeah, this is different than any fishing line I've seen before. No problem. I'll hang out here. I won't worry if you're back in no more than five minutes."

Steele circled the line with his thumb and forefinger and headed into the depths. The water was clear as a bell and ambient light penetrated the water column so that his visibility remained excellent. As the depth increased, the only thing he could hear was his own breathing, and he could sense the change in atmospheric pressure which doubled with each additional thirty-three feet of depth.

He was still fifty feet from the end of the line when he spotted it. It looked like the head of a giant moray eel peeking out from under the edge of a sunken container looking for its next meal. His depth gauge indicated 196 feet. A dark green Quickstrike mine was visible with its long cylindrical body crushed on an angle iron frame. Torn remnants of a rubberized nylon lift bag waved in the water like fronds of soft coral. The container must have dislodged the mine and pushed it down the slope until it came to rest against a calcified coral head that looked like an oversized bollard on the underwater ridge. Steele got close enough to read the white serial number stenciled on the weapon's nose and then followed the wire back to the 120-foot depth where he joined the other diver. He gave the OK sign and said "bingo" into the microphone. Steele signaled for both divers to start the ascent. A Quickstrike mine made mobile with a simple sled. Ingenious. A rig that Richie Bouffard probably put together. Steele immediately knew how *Shackleton* was sunk. But how would Mocha Control get a Quickstrike mine?

"We've may have trouble; a Somali longboat is coming in for a closer look." Stoeppler's voice from the surface more than 100 feet away sounded ominous. As the divers started their ascent, Steele heard him trying to raise the base in Djibouti on the external radio and then the confused sounds of background voices yelling. Stoeppler wedged the topside microphone of the underwater communications system between two seat cushions, keeping it keyed to let the divers know what was happening, while Steele and O'Connor continued to follow their bubbles towards the surface. They saw a long narrow underwater hull alongside the RHIB with an outboard engine hanging off the stern. They could hear bits and pieces of the conversation above. The men in the smaller boat were Somalis operating out of Assab. With their home waters being patrolled by warships of several nations, the opportunities for piracy had dried up like the wadis after a hard rain.

"This area is closed to boats," the oldest of the men said in halting English.

Bullard responded in Arabic. "This is a US government boat. We are in international waters and have divers in the water. After they surface, we will depart the area."

"We like your boat very much," said the leader. Steele interpreted the compliment as a thinly disguised statement of intent. The pirates planned to steal the RHIB. Two Somalis jumped into the boat with rifles at the ready while the two others kept their weapons leveled at Bullard and Stoeppler. One of them yanked the spiraled microphone cord out of the communications box and cast it on the deck. The only question was whether Stoeppler and Bullard would wind up dead or face a long swim to the beach. All four of the pirates were now on the RHIB.

Steele and O'Connor communicated via hand signals. There was a manual kill switch on the boat's transom required by the Navy as a safety precaution. The switch interrupted the starting circuitry to protect divers from the spinning propellers. After flipping the switch to the OFF position, Steele slipped out of his tank banded to an inflatable buoyancy compensator and let his weight belt drop into the depths. Both divers hung their tanks from the RHIB's propellers and continued to breathe compressed air from their regulators as they monitored events topside.

"Adil, start the boat."

A younger man slung his rifle and walked behind the centerline steering console where he found the button labeled START and depressed it. A small screen illuminated and indicated that the starting circuitry was disabled. His father repeated the process without success.

"What does this mean?" the man asked leveling his gun at Stoeppler.

"It's a kill switch designed to prevent the engines from starting when there are divers in the water."

"Where is the switch?"

"It's underwater on the hull just aft of the propellers on the centerline."

The man spoke to one of the other men standing in what amounted to a wraparound dress that he dropped on the deck of the RHIB, stripping down to his shorts and picking up a diving mask. The leader spoke to the man in Arabic, making sure that he knew the location of the switch.

The man climbed down the ladder and stepped off into the water. He adjusted his mask, took a deep breath and swam right into Steele's waiting arms. He held the man underwater until he'd taken a few panicked gulps of saltwater and then pushed him up alongside his entry point where he took in air in a screaming frenzy. Startled, the leader and one of the accomplices jumped to the gunwale pointing their gun barrels over the side and down towards the water.

The shimmering images were distorted, but there was no mistaking the gun barrels held in the pirates' hands. Steele and the Navy diver kicked their fins hard, their bodies coming up out of the water in a synchronized move, swinging their arms to grab the gun barrels with one hand and a fist full of whatever they could reach with the other, pulling the two pirates into the water. Holding the flailing men underwater separated them from their rifles. Taking advantage of the confusion, Stoeppler swung into action and took down the final pirate with a vicious tackle that left the man unconscious.

Not knowing the situation topside, Steele hoisted himself over the gunwale, ready for another fight on deck. There was none. Stoeppler threw a life ring to the three men gulping air and treading water while O'Connor climbed the ladder and fell over the gunwale, dropping to the deck exhausted. This dive was certainly different from his normal routine of underwater hull inspections and fitting an occasional cofferdam for waterborne repairs.

Stoeppler produced large plastic tie wraps from his toolbox and secured the unconscious pirate's hands behind him and bound his feet in a similar manner. He then retrieved the radio microphone and stripped the wires to make a temporary repair. Within minutes, he was communicating with the base at Djibouti. Steele kept an eye on the three Somalis hugging the life ring tied off to a cleat near the transom and enjoyed some fresh water from a large plastic liter bottle.

Bullard saw a hand-held radio in the stern of the pirates' boat and saw some paper taped to the hull protected by a plastic sandwich wrapper. He dropped down into the fiberglass long boat and pulled the paper off the hull. Written in Arabic, Bullard saw the call sign Mocha Control and two radio frequencies. One by one, the three pirates were brought back into their boat and their hands bound behind them. Bullard began an informal interrogation in Arabic. The leader said that they were hired by a Mr. Richie and described the viper tattooed on his face. They were paid to keep boats out of an area near the channel and radio Mocha Control if they had any problems. They were paid like waitresses, earning a small weekly salary but able to confiscate anything they wanted from their enforcement as bonuses.

O'Connor collected the diving gear left under the boat while the team waited for instructions on what to do with the pirates. Stoeppler contacted the EOD team at the base and provided the serial number and coordinates of the Quickstrike mine. He also got through to the base Executive Officer and suggested that an inventory by weapon serial number be ordered ASAP. A Yemeni Coast Guard patrol boat was released from its coastal patrol to take the pirates and their long boat into custody. By the time the Coast Guard boat arrived, the sun was moving towards the horizon, and Steele felt the impact of the day compounded by his long travel tighten his extremities. He was physically whipped and actually looked forward to another night on the lumpy bed.

Finally pier side, Steele and Bullard thanked the two men who'd lived through a harrowing day with a frightening find on the bottom. Stoeppler and O'Connor would refuel the boat and return to the base in Djibouti. The base Executive Officer confirmed that four Quickstrike mines were missing from the secure weapons warehouse.

Steele and Bullard had an early supper in the crowded hotel, a mezze platter with fresh pita bread, olives, white cheese and the usual eggplant puree and hummus followed by a stack of skewered grilled meat on a bed of rice that Bullard ordered well done to kill any lingering *e coli* that may have started to grow. Steele was satisfied that he'd gotten more than he bargained for from this trip and was already planning against the backdrop that had been so painfully painted over the last twenty-four hours.

In mid-sentence, Steele pushed his chair back and mumbled "head call" to Bullard and took the long way around past the small lobby bar, protected by a standing wall of thirsty patrons. Steele returned and explained his sudden action.

"There's a guy at the bar wearing one of those Aussie bush hats and a desert work outfit cut from that peculiar green cloth that defies description. He has a scar on the back of his head that I needed to look at to confirm he is the guy I recognized. Last time I saw him he worked for Langley. Now what do you suppose the Agency is doing here in Mocha?"

"Maybe he signed up for an African wildlife safari and got on the wrong plane," Bullard deadpanned.

Laughing, Steele said, "He worked in the Russian directorate a couple of years ago. It's definitely the same guy. I think I'll ask him to join us for a drink."

Steele took a polite minute to reach the bar and wedged his body next to the bush-hatted man with a dark, iceless drink in front of him.

"I hope you are not going to put that on your expense report," said Steele, peering intently at the man's face from 18 inches away.

"What do you want, Yank?" he replied with an authentic down under drawl.

"Just wanted to see if you might be interested in comparing notes. Perhaps your business and ours might have some helpful overlap."

"What are you talking about? Why don't you just buy a drink and piss-off?"

"Our table is over there in the corner if you'd like to join us. By the way, I'm impressed with the rig and your accent. The old scar on the back of your neck was the giveaway."

Steele returned to the table by himself.

"Wrong guy?" asked Bullard.

"No. Right guy. Let's give him ten minutes to join us. If he doesn't, we'll let it drop. I don't want to blow anybody's cover."

The Aussie walked past the table and gave Steele a slight head nod as he walked out into hotel's open courtyard, a remnant of Ottoman times. Steele and Bullard waited to see if anyone was following the man and then walked out together, finding him sitting on a bench. The three huddled and Steele summarized the discovery of the Quickstrike mines and the encounter with the Somalis. The Aussie just listened. Steele baited his hook with a fresh morsel and threw it out to the man who appeared to be bored and ready to leave.

"So, I think that you are here with a team planning to snatch one of the Russian fighters for a conversation," said Steele to the man. "A better idea might be to grab Richie Bouffard, still a US citizen, and extradite him on a string of charges including murder, theft of US government weapons, and piracy. Since the Quickstrike mines were controlled by foreigners, you might be able to get an espionage charge to stick. I'm not sure he'll talk, but he's known to be living in the compound, and the handiwork we saw on the Quickstrike mines has his fingerprints all over it. What do you think?"

"Perhaps we can talk further, mate, but first I'd like to get a fix on your current role. Who can I contact?"

"Captain Hank Owens in the National Security Advisor's office."

"Good. I'm going up to my room to practice playing my didgeridoo and will be in touch." The Aussie left the bench with a wide smile.

"314," said Steele.

Back in his room, the Aussie pulled a plastic fan from his bag and unfolded it on the desk where it was transformed into a clear hemisphere which he placed over his head. He dialed a cell phone on the desk which was wired into the plastic bonnet. His voice was encrypted and then transmitted via a small button at the top of the clear parasol in small bursts to a satellite tracking the source from a geosynchronous orbit 25,000 miles in space.

The Aussie spoke after hearing a number of tones signaling that his call was synchronized. "I was assigned as an Agency rep to this team called 'Stormy Weather' that Steele led. It was stood up after the Veteran's Day attacks in 2016. He's an ex-Navy SEAL whose family drowned in the Chesapeake Bay Bridge Tunnel collapse. He survived. Ran a very good team. He was like a dog on a meat wagon. I'm told they successfully thwarted an attack on the President during last year's Independence Day celebration in Boston. Focused, determined and energized. I'm not compromised so we can continue as planned, but I think there may be some value in further discussion. I just wanted to make sure that we vetted Steele before I talk with him again."

"Got it. Stand-by."

The harsh metallic jangle of the phone was loud enough to wake the dead, Steele thought as he lifted the receiver.

"Just wanted to let you know that we have selected your candidate for the job opening. I look forward to talking with you again soon."

The one-way conversation answered a number of questions. Steele arranged a return trip to the United States from Sana'a the following night. He and Bullard briefly planned the next day and decided on a mid-morning start for the return trip to the capital. Settling back on the lumpy bed, wondering about the origin of the mattress and what made it so uncomfortable, Steele fell asleep thinking about what cards the small troubled country of Yemen would deal him next.

CHAPTER SIXTY-FIVE

Washington, DC

The Operations directorate of the Joint Staff baselined all the attendees to the situation in Yemen and the recent explosions that crippled a cargo vessel now parked precipitously on the edge of a natural underwater canyon that formed the shipping channel. Overhead lights brightened, and the Vice Chairman took the floor from his seat in the tank, a small conference room inside a large operations center from which the next war would be planned and fought. The Vice Chairman of the Joint Chiefs of Staff was a highly decorated Army General raised in a military family, following his father and grandfather through West Point and into a distinguished career. His son was a senior cadet at West Point and had just been selected as First Captain of the Corps of Cadets.

"We've got one hell of a situation down in Yemen," he said with a smooth, molasses-like southern drawl. "After last week's attack on *Shackleton*, we all know that this is going to be one of those messes we will be asked to clean up. This Russian group is few in numbers, we estimate under forty men, but they are trained, well-armed and possess a joker no one wants them to play. Based on what's happened to date, I don't expect this crisis will end at the negotiation table, and we have to be ready to move when called. I know all the special operators are itching for a chance to go in and shut down this party, but it's more complicated than that. We've got lots of people interested that the waterway stays open and with a civil war still raging in Yemen, we are dealing with a real hairball. That said, the planning must begin yesterday, and we need to look at the full range of options using military force. Because it's water, I'm giving the lead to the Navy to start the planning and coordination with State's working group."

"Sir, if I could push back on that decision," said an Army General representing his service at the meeting, "the Army is accustomed to how these special operators think and any assault on the compound would likely come from the ground given the failure of the recent Russian operation. We already have teams in East Africa reining in the Somalis, so we are in a better position than the Navy to lead the planning."

"George, thank you for pointing out the Army's expertise of which I'm fully aware. And just to make this meeting more efficient, I made the decision to go with the Navy as the lead service for this crisis and don't need to hear from the Air Force, Marines, Coast Guard or Special Operations Command the reasons why their organization should take charge. The Chairman met with all the Service Chiefs on this issue, and we are unanimous in this decision. There will be opportunities for broad participation by all the services in any military operation, and I'm certain the Navy will make appropriate use of the capabilities across all of our joint warfighting organizations."

The Vice knew that each of the services had been coached to volunteer to lead the effort despite the unanimity of the service chiefs. In Washington, leading such an operation would enhance the service's position in the budgeting process and enable them to push forward their programs by pointing to ongoing operations. Every new crisis had the effect of pouring a bucket of blood into a wading pool of sharks representing each of the military services. With blood in the water, there was always a battle to see which service would come out on top.

CHAPTER SIXTY-SIX

Washington, DC

The Navy Working Group charged with planning for a military operation ramped up the intelligence posture dramatically. They had a white board of essential information identified as information gaps or needs and were diligently working down the list to get a better fix on the compound layout, the individual fighters, the watch organization, the armory, and as the top priority, the location of the special weapons on the compound.

A number of local sources had been developed, a few with regular access to the compound, including suppliers of propane and foodstuffs and the postal service. Communications intercept capability was stepped up. Apparently, the compound was being run as an independent organization with no pattern of regular reporting to a chain of command. Most of the external communications were streaming internet movies or personal orders to European and US companies for specialty goods. Communication between the compound and Russia was limited to a single IP address.

Following the money had emerged as a time-tested means of gaining insight into any terrorist's operations. A team of forensic financial analysts untangled the account structure set up in Madagascar and understood how the money flowed into individual accounts. The balances were already staggering. Arrangements could be made to freeze those accounts if and when required. Of course, there were other accounts they would never discover.

Steele preferred to work on the periphery of the group, attending their periodic briefings when he could. He had no interest in getting mired down in the endless data calls, action items and the administration of such a team. However, it clearly had value that he could use for his own purposes, and he could feed areas for further research to the team a variety of ways. The Navy Working Group found a recent Russian retiree who had worked in the Alpha Group, and he had been helpful in identifying the Russians deserters who fled with Zlodeyev.

As the briefer reviewed the intelligence updates to the small group, a new unidentified photo of one of the fighters flashed on the screen. Steele stood up at his chair.

"That's Richie Bouffard," he said. "He's a former SEAL who was thrown out of the Navy after a court-martial with a bad conduct discharge. Among other things, he is an expert in blowing things up. There's no doubt in my mind that he was the one who designed the explosive packages that crippled *Shackleton*."

"How well do you know him?" asked one of the people at the table searching for a potential leverage point.

"Very well. I investigated the incident that got him court-martialed. He hates me."

CHAPTER SIXTY-SEVEN

Washington, DC

In the cavern, Steele spread nautical charts over two folding tables pushed together in a small conference room with the compound area depicted on a clear acetate overlay. Sandy and Cass met with him at least three times a week to keep abreast of developments and to review the clandestine approaches Steele bubbled up for their review. Admiral Wright scheduled a session weekly to review plans and put a cold objective eyeball on the work of the team.

"A submerged assault seems like a good alternative, but that too will be high risk as any team would be waltzing ashore through a mine field into an open kill zone in front of a well-defended compound," explained Steele to his office colleagues.

"Is there any way to clear the overhead razor wire?" asked Sandy.

"Possible, I suppose. If the wire could be cleared, entering the compound might be more feasible with a fast rope insertion, but that would eliminate the advantage of surprise," said Steele.

"What's a fast rope?" asked Sandy

"It's a technique to bring troops to an area using a helo that has no place to land. The troops slide down ropes to the ground. But I can't think of how to remove the razor wire."

"Is there any way to tunnel in?" asked Cass.

"I've looked at this abandoned well on the compound that served the community as well as the coffee farmers bringing their beans to market in the old days, but I just don't know what condition it's in or how we would get there without some heavy equipment that would obviously raise an alarm. I've seen a footnote on one of the surveys labeling it a garbage pit."

"What about that high tech Swiss boring machine used in the Chesapeake Bay Bridge and Tunnel terrorist attack?" Cass regretted the words that came out of her mouth as she was concentrating on the task at hand and momentarily forgot that the explosive charges which breached the shell of the tunnel killed Steele's family.

Cass blurted out, "Sorry, Dan. I didn't want to bring that up."

"It's OK, Cass. That's why we have these sessions. We are trying to come up with a workable approach and you are right, that boring capability might be useful in this case. Thanks. Let me work on that idea. That's all I had for today. I'll get the briefing shell posted first thing tomorrow morning so you can look at it before we meet with the Admiral."

CHAPTER SIXTY-EIGHT

Mocha, Yemen

It was the equivalent of a Saturday night in Yemen and Richie Bouffard was looking forward to drinking a few glasses of sid and spending the evening with his favorite girl.

At midnight, the control room watchstander called the General.

"General, Mr. Snake has not returned to the Compound."

"OK, this is the second time this month. When he returns, let me know, and I'll bring him in for a serious discussion." With *Shackleton* grounded and the toll system in automatic, the General had been evaluating the continued usefulness of Bouffard. He had no real friends among the Russians except for the diver who helped him anchor the Quickstrike mines on the bottom. That friendship was driven by the success of their venture more than a personal liking between the two men. If this were a television show, Richie would be the first person voted off the island.

Later that afternoon, the General took aside two of his fighters and asked them to make a sweep of the town and locate Richie. The next morning, neither had returned. The General called a meeting.

"Men, as you know, Mr. Snake went missing two days ago and yesterday, Uri and Fyodor failed to return to the compound. I suspect that one or more of the European countries or perhaps the United States is trying to decimate our numbers by peeling off members of our team when they are in town. They know how many people we have here in the compound. So, we will limit the number of people leaving the compound and have them guarded by the Yemeni army. We will not tolerate any further losses."

CHAPTER SIXTY-NINE

Washington, DC

A brown internal routing folder landed in Steele's desktop inbox overnight. Its last stop was the National Security Advisor's office in the Pentagon. Unwrapping the red string figure-eighted around two plastic buttons, Steele pulled out a plain white business envelope with his name printed on the front which bore no franking or return address. The envelope contained a single sheet of paper with a black and white photo of Richie Bouffard's trident necklace.

Steele smiled to himself. Snatched by the Agency, Bouffard was now a guest at some unknown rendition center where they would extract information and pass it on to a select number of people having a need-to-know. As he pinned the photo on the cork board above his desk, Steele hoped that he would be on that list. What Richie might provide would be critical to the plan that Steele was developing in the cavern. Without it, the probability of success might shrink to single digits.

CHAPTER SEVENTY

Mediterranean Sea

Only 38 years old, Navy Commander Sydney Garrison had moved through her naval career with lightning speed. After a string of accelerated promotions, she took command of USS *Newport*, a missile-carrying Los Angeles class attack submarine, discovering both the exhilaration of command and at the same time its weighty responsibility. She shouldered that burden with professionalism and grace and was universally admired for her leadership in making *Newport* the acknowledged best boat in the squadron.

Being admired by your seniors is one thing, but what set Sydney apart was her natural ability to lead under any circumstances. For that, her peers recommended her for the Vice Admiral James B. Stockdale Award for Inspirational Leadership, one of the most prestigious peer-nominated Navy awards named for the highly decorated combat fighter pilot who spent eight years as the senior officer imprisoned by the North Vietnamese. His personal heroic conduct there led to the award of the Congressional Medal of Honor.

There was something else about Sydney. A classic beauty, she caught everyone's eye. Her hard body caused an animal reaction in most men who saw her. Still single, she had put the Navy first and seemed in no hurry to tie herself to a sea anchor that might slow her down. She was on course to become the first woman Chief of Naval Operations, and she could achieve that goal all on her own. With strawberry blonde hair and bright sea green eyes, she wore no makeup and was more attractive in a starched khaki uniform than any other naval officer Steele had ever seen.

A nuclear physicist, her father was a well-known US Navy civilian who never grew tired of his work with nuclear-powered submarines. Her mother was a painter who experimented with watercolors and oils trying to capture the subtle nuance of the shorelines where they'd always lived. From an early age, Sydney had developed a fascination with submarines and had models of each class strewn around her bedroom like dolls. Her father took her on every dependent's cruise that he could, and the nuclear engineers were always happy to have him aboard. Sure, he noted things and suggested material improvements in the engineering spaces but only to be helpful. He was not an inspector to find fault. That was common enough in the silent service. Early in her teenage years, Sydney set a goal for herself that countered Navy policy. She wanted to become a submarine Commanding Officer, knowing that overcoming the years of hide-bound reluctance within the Navy to achieve her dreams would be next to impossible.

While her academic standing and strong sports ability gave her a choice of colleges, she earned an appointment to the Naval Academy and left the family home in Mystic, Connecticut for Annapolis, Maryland. A standout there, she led the brigade of midshipmen in her senior year, captained the basketball team and maintained a 4.0 grade point average. Since submarine duty was still closed to women, she joined the surface navy as an Anti-Submarine Warfare officer where she contributed to doctrinal changes still in effect on destroyers. At the Naval Postgraduate School in Monterey, California, she received a Master's Degree in Physics while spending her free time SCUBA-diving and sailing. While in Department Head school awaiting orders, she met with the Lieutenant detailer, an officer who monitors the career progress of a group of individual officers and makes decisions about follow-on assignments.

"What I really want to do is join the submarine force."

Taken aback, the detailer responded, "The nuclear submarine programs are closed to women, so why don't you consider an aircraft carrier."

"No thanks," she said firmly, "I want to serve on a submarine, so I guess I'll have to wait on surface combatants until the Navy opens things up."

The detailer made some notes about the headstrong woman she just met and talked to the Captain running the school. He couldn't have been more supportive, saying that Sydney Garrison would be an excellent choice if the Navy decided to move away from its restrictive personnel policies. So, she became a guinea pig of sorts, sent to Nuclear Power School and assigned to an attack submarine as Chief Engineer. After back-to-back Department Head tours in two different submarines, she joined the Submarine Group Staff in Groton, Connecticut before getting her orders to command USS *Newport*. There, she was a standout by any measure. She worked hard, took care of her crew and made *Newport* the envy of the submarine force. Both her parents were thrilled with the difficult path she had taken to live a lifelong dream.

Operating in the Mediterranean Sea on routine patrol when the message was received, Commander Garrison found the ship's Operations Officer in the Control Room refilling a ceramic coffee cup decorated with the ship's crest on one side and the common three letter OPS abbreviation on the other. It had never been washed. The inside was almost black from the never-ending cups of coffee that seemed to be his major source of sustenance.

She slid the message across the plotting table within his narrow field of view. He recognized her long thin fingers and manicured nails trimmed for her job and straightened up as he read the message sent from the Joint Chiefs of Staff.

> Heads-up! You will receive an official schedule change via regular communications. *Newport* is to proceed to Port Said and join the Southbound convoy soonest. From there you will take station off the coast of Saudi Arabia near Jeddah to monitor a political situation in Yemen. Smooth sailing, Ramses

"Who's Ramses?" asked the Operations Officer, peering over his glasses.

"Just a friend on the Joint Staff. What do you make of this?"

"I don't know. It could have something to do with that Russian General who escaped the country with a couple of dozen fighters and some special weapons. He's announced a toll on vessels transiting the Red Sea or coming through the Indian Ocean headed for the Suez. I've seen some traffic that links the grounding of the containership *Ernest H. Shackleton* to the new toll. It's not clear to me how he might have been involved, but he's holding the big cards. I'll get a new track laid out with the Navigator. I recommend we start heading that way ASAP."

"I agree. Thanks, Tom."

Off the southern coast of Crete, *Newport* was stationed in the maritime equivalent of a large playing field marked by corner posts which corresponded to specific navigation points on a chart. The box was a comfortable twenty miles square. Her depth was a safe 250 feet. As the boat turned on a southeasterly heading, Garrison thought about the schedule change and what role an attack submarine might play. The ship carried a mix of torpedoes and mines, Harpoon anti-ship missiles as well as Tomahawk cruise missiles used for long range attacks on targets ashore. In addition, the ship was outfitted with a sophisticated electronic warfare suite which enabled the boat to function like a forward deployed National Security Agency node. However, with no linguists aboard, there would be little gained from intercepting communications except to pinpoint locations from which the signals emanated.

Garrison returned to her cabin and debated whether or not to advise the crew of the change of plans. She decided against it, until the ship received the official notification. Rumors spread like a wildfire aboard ships, whether they were floating majestically on the surface or operating at depth below it. Sailors loved to hear the rumors, and then each would seek out those who were in the right place to confirm or deny or modify the story and get it closer to the truth. The trusted insiders knew that violating confidences would have a long-term impact on their careers. They would usually avoid the truth-seekers until they enjoined their bosses to quell the rumors with a verbal message to the crew over the general announcing system or something official in the Plan of the Day.

Newport had departed her home port of Gaeta, Italy ten days before for a routine forty-five-day patrol. Strapped with requirements all over the globe, *Newport* had been reassigned to the Mediterranean to begin what the Navy termed a rotational deployment from a permanent overseas base. The brass had argued for more ships to be positioned overseas to avoid the transit times for an Atlantic-based ship to arrive in its designated operating area. That translated into a longer time on station but reduced the number of operational days in a standard deployment. The US Navy's Chief of Naval Operations was a Surface Warfare Officer who had worked as a Cruiser Destroyer Group scheduler early in his career, keeping tabs on forty-three ships, so he was familiar with the challenges of managing finite resources against expanding operational requirements. He also knew that the number of hulls would remain about the same, so he had to get more out of each one in a creative way. Thus, the rotational deployment scheme was born.

Garrison knew the next few days would be demanding as the submarine would join a bevy of other ships in Port Said, anchored and awaiting instructions about their position in the southbound convoy and when they would begin lining up, a process where tens of ships were hoisting their anchors and guessing how the procession would be formed. The Southbound convoys began their transit late at night. Close quarters with multiple ships, a constant chatter on the radios, confusing navigation lights and no way to identify the ships waiting raised the pucker factor on every ship's bridge. Warships were generally assigned positions very near the front of the convoy by the Canal authority so that was an advantage. Getting to the head of the line safely was the challenge. A mandatory pilot would be embarked who would keep up a constant yammer in Arabic on the radio. The pilot's voices always sounded argumentative, as if someone else was claiming a birthright or first-born child. Wildly emotional, the pilots constantly gesticulated with their hands, acting as if an ordinary transaction were something like a life or death situation. *Newport* would transit the Suez Canal on the surface, a submarine's most vulnerable position.

She had signed the night orders and could make another round of the ship's operating spaces, watch a movie or continue reading the novel closed above her narrow, fold-down berth. Knowing that she would be on the exposed bridge for the canal transit, a long, sleepless, boring, nighttime march of ships threading their way through the waterway cut into the desert floor, she decided to take a combat nap while awaiting the official orders. She kicked off her black shoes and lay down on her bed. On her back with her hands laced behind her head between the pillow and her hair, she closed her eyes and visualized what she might face over the next thirty-six hours. Her body was relaxed. She had once read that taking this position was equivalent to ninety per cent of deep sleep. While the number might be disputed, she knew a combat nap would refresh and recharge her for the next challenge. Her mind recalled the transfer of the SEAL team months before and wondered if the events were in any way connected as she quickly drifted off to sleep.

CHAPTER SEVENTY-ONE

Mocha, Yemen

Each week, Sergei posted the tally of tolls collected and projected revenue for the following week based on the number of ships declaring intent to transit the Suez Canal. Since the *Shackleton* incident, the transactions had become routine, and none of the ships passing through the waterway had tried to stiff the Mocha Group. Most ship owners merely thought of the toll as another expense that would be passed on to the shippers and, at the end of the supply chain, the hapless consumers whose goods would increase a few cents.

The toll proceeds were staggering. Most weeks recorded twenty-five to thirty million dollars in revenues with an average toll of $100,000 for each vessel. More than 300 ships passed through the canal each week and the charges levied were calculated on a number of variables including the size of the vessel, gross weight of the cargo, the reported cargo value and the type of goods carried. Sergei developed a simple algorithm and maintained a database of ship transits and assessments. To date, the only unpaid toll was *Shackleton's*.

Sergei calculated the tolls in advance and had an efficient means of tracking electronic payments that were routinely being made a day or more before each ship began its transit. The tolls were set to have a modest impact on the operating margin, without being so excessive that ships would take the longer route around the Cape of Good Hope. Within a month, the individual ships and shipping companies had become accustomed to the charges, and they had become as routine as paying for harbor services such as dock fees and garbage collection. One of the major lines had already tried to negotiate lower rates based on the number of vessels and frequency of passage on the same route. The international outcry had died down as well. It seemed that there was little to be done about the financial annoyance imposed, and every mariner who passed the hulk of the *Ernest H. Shackleton* knew full well the penalty for non-payment.

Zlodeyev made payments in cash to the Houthi rebels, the exiled government of Yemen, the Somali pirates and others whose support was necessary to continue operations. Everyone seemed pleased with the financial arrangements. A donation was made every month to local charities and relief organizations trying to stabilize the living conditions in Yemen and caring for orphaned children. Though rarely seen in the town, Zlodeyev became something of a modern-day Robin Hood, taking money from the rich shipping lines and sharing it with the country's poor and needy.

The fighters' share of the revenue was secured in individual business accounts registered in Madagascar. Each of them also had an untraceable account in Switzerland and received a generous wad of cash to spend on local shopping, booze and whatever type of companionship interested them. The local economy felt blessed to host a business venture like this one.

CHAPTER SEVENTY-TWO

Washington, DC

Steele had been working for weeks on a concept to secure the weapons. Sandy Matthews, Cass Thomas, Nate Jones and Admiral Wright all reviewed the plan, and it had been briefed up to the National Security Advisor. She had asked that the briefing be given to select offices in Washington including the Pentagon. Steele assumed that the plan would be considered for some DOD component's execution and never believed that he might be involved in implementing it. This morning's session was scheduled in an E-Ring conference room in the Pentagon.

"Thank you, General. The compound is well-fortified with a minefield around the perimeter and the Yemeni Army guarding the entrance via the road here." Steele steered the laser pointer on a large-scale diagram of the compound being projected onto a rear-projection screen. There were a dozen people at the table, and the gallery chairs were empty.

"The plan consists of two independent actions. First, an insertion of a small team of five SEALs through an abandoned well located here."

A Navy officer interrupted Steele. "Are you just going to get beamed into the well?"

"No sir. We will be inserted through a carbon nanotube fabric pipe deployed from a torpedo fired from a Los Angeles class submarine."

"Is this capability in our inventory? I'm not even aware of it."

"The boring technology developed by the Swiss is mature, used by the terrorist group that planted the explosives on the Chesapeake Bay Bridge and Tunnel in 2016. Our underwater weapons geniuses at NUWC Newport will marry the drilling machine to a 21" torpedo with a sabot shroud which enables a boring machine to begin working after the torpedo's momentum ends."

"Is it wire-guided?"

"Yes. The torpedo will be guided for the first 3,000 yards, which will establish the path for the subsequent boring. Once the torpedo hits the slope of the bottom and stops, the boring machine is activated and an operator will guide it manually using the boring head itself."

"I'm not following. How will you communicate with the torpedo that's fifty feet under the ground?"

"There is no communication." Steele advanced the slides to a schematic of a modified MK 48 torpedo. Its nineteen-foot length was divided into its major component sections. The boring machine would replace the sonar and guidance control in the torpedo's nose, followed by a section to transport the horizontal operator. The carbon nanotube fabricator took up the next six feet, followed by the fuel and propulsion modules.

"Are you telling me this torpedo is guided by a man inside?" asked one of the attendees, wincing with incredulity.

"Yes, sir. That is correct. Think of the torpedo as a SEAL Delivery Vehicle for one. The boring machine replaces the torpedo's sonar package on the front end, and the high explosive is removed so that a man can fit into the compartment here and steer the torpedo during the final underground portion of the trip. The propulsion plant will be jettisoned once the torpedo impacts the bottom at a depth of twenty-five feet. The torpedo will be programmed to run ten feet below the water surface and then make a terminal maneuver to dive to twenty-five feet before leveling off at a slight angle upwards towards the well. We've analyzed the geological composition of the soil on either side of the compound and expect the torpedo will excavate the first fifty feet or so with its momentum before the boring machine takes over. The total tunnel length will be 220 feet. The nanotube fabricator is capable of deploying 300 feet of material so we've got a margin of fifty feet."

"I apologize, Mr. Steele. A little tough for this old West Pointer to follow. I'd like you to start over and deliver your briefing from the top without interruptions from any of my colleagues at the table. Just take it slow and explain the approach so a dumb major can follow you. Right now, this plan looks to me like the one where the mad scientist calls for a miracle as step number three."

Steele reviewed the plan without interruption, answering numerous potential questions by addressing the same hard spots that he and the Pisces team wrestled with during the months of refinement. The silent nods around the table confirmed that some of the skepticism had been reduced. He also addressed the special operations insertion as the initial action and the timed Tomahawk strike from naval assets as the second. The actions were sequential but independent.

"What about our allies? Are they unilaterally planning actions too?"

"I am not aware of any such plans, but estimate that the Brits are likely contemplating a special operations action."

"Who is the guinea pig serving as the pilot for this torpedo?"

A tentative response about someone being trained as the operator would undercut the plan, so Steele stepped into the breach to bring more credibility to the plan.

"I am."

"No disrespect Mr. Steele, but why would the US government with all its special forces components choose to have a civilian carry out this mission?"

"First, deniability if the plan runs off the tracks, and we have an accidental detonation of the nuclear material or if a chemical cloud moves up the Red Sea. Second, I'm familiar with the technology. Third, I'm a volunteer."

"OK," said the man at the head of the table. "I've got it. Thank you for the briefing. We've got four additional briefings today and tomorrow and will make a recommendation. Yours is the second briefing of the day. I can tell you that I still don't like the odds of success, but I'm confident it has a better chance of working than the plan we listened to this morning."

CHAPTER SEVENTY-THREE

Washington, DC

Thanksgiving week led up to Jill's favorite holiday. Steele recalled the few Thanksgivings they had shared together with their twin boys, who were too young to appreciate all the joyous effort their mother put into the holiday. The table would be filled with friends, wives whose husbands were operating in faraway places and a few veterans that would enjoy the military setting and loving banquet set before them. The memories of those days always transported Steele into a momentary depression from which he could escape only through his own strong will.

The decision briefing for President Bowles drove a myriad of pre-briefings with all the services and the Joint Staff. Of course, the opportunity to tinker with the plan appealed to many of these military officers and civilians in the chain of command. By the time Steele briefed a service chief, he had already collected a mountain of critiques, suggestions, and recommended variations. The "death by a thousand cuts" gauntlet that had to be run by someone preparing to brief the President could only be completed by the strong, seasoned, confident players.

"Thank you, Dan, for the detailed briefing of the intended operation. I appreciate the time and effort the chain of command has put into formulating a plan to secure the WMDs and neutralize those who control them. However, the number of "firsts" in this operation troubles me. Steering a manned torpedo, no pun intended, to a target using technology never actually tested using a torpedo is a red flag in my view. Giving a specific window of time to a small team of special operators before launching a coordinated Tomahawk strike seems like high risk too. Have we really wrung out all the risks thoroughly? Do we really understand the likelihood of this band of criminals having the know-how to detonate the nukes? How could they use the chemical weapons without some delivery system?"

"All good questions, Mr. President," answered the Chairman. "I wish I had the answers to them but don't. This operation is certainly high risk, but it seems more likely to succeed and exposes fewer people as opposed to the aerial assault the Russians tried. None of the options we have studied are good ones. This plan moved to the top because it bounds the uncertainty. It's high risk but also high payoff. I think it's unlikely that General Zlodeyev would detonate the nuclear warheads or release the chemical weapons based on a small operation that is not going to make him feel like he's backed into a corner. A larger force might cause that. There is a small window of time when the follow-on Tomahawk strike can be turned off if we are successful."

The President looked at the Chairman of the Joint Chiefs of Staff with an icy stare.

"And what does successful mean? We are spending almost $700 billion dollars on defense every year, and this is the best plan we can come up with?"

"No, sir. It's the only plan that we've come up with that has a chance of success. I would assess the probability of success of this operation to be no more than twenty-five percent. This plus the Tomahawk strike brings us to eighty percent. Even with the low probability of success, we avoid exposing our forces to a well-trained force fighting from a defensible fortress surrounded by layered active and passive protective measures. Getting past those is a major obstacle, and this creative assault just might save a lot of lives and keep a strategic waterway open. It also allows us to keep faith with our coalition, which will participate in the Tomahawk strike but not the Special Operations insertion."

"The strongest military on the planet plus our allies' capable military forces, and we are talking about sending in a handful of men to stop this madman? I'm more than a bit surprised. I understand the logic and the options but just don't like the calculus. If the Special Ops probability of success is twenty-five percent and the cumulative probability of success is eighty percent with the Tomahawks, is the high-risk torpedo shot worth the effort?"

"Yes, for two reasons," replied the Chairman of the Joint Chiefs of Staff. "First, if we could avoid the Tomahawk strike, that reduces the potential of high impact collateral damage, and second, the probability of success of a Tomahawk strike by itself is sixty percent. The Tomahawks would fly to a known point and detonate, but there's no substitute for having human eyes on the target. If the special ops team can destroy the trigger to prevent a full-on nuclear blast, the residual problem will be manageable and the impact maybe five percent of what it could be."

"OK, I've got it. When will this option be ready for execution?"

"Once we get the green light, Mr. President, we can be ready to go within thirty days' time."

"OK, please proceed. I'd like to turn up the heat on the negotiations front to see if we can find a diplomatic way to resolve this crisis before we send our people on such a mission. The most powerful military in the free world seems impotent to deal with this dangerous entrepreneur. He won't talk to anybody. The press has labeled this crisis a standoff, and I guess that's an accurate description. It seems like a lopsided proposition, and I know that we are not making this lunatic ten feet tall.

But the fact we know that he is armed and very dangerous cannot be discounted. If there's anything I can do or if I need to talk to any of my counterparts, I'm ready to do that night or day. We are in deep weeds here, but, again, I want to fully explore all options on the diplomatic front first. General, you have my undivided attention. Dan, you've gotten us out of a very bad spot before, and I personally appreciate your dedication. But you are not superman or a magician, and this operation makes me very nervous. Please continue to refine the plan and do whatever you can to reduce the risk and increase the probability of success, OK?"

"Yes, Mr. President."

CHAPTER SEVENTY-FOUR

Washington, DC

Within an hour of the meeting with the President, Steele called all the men on his hand-picked team. Having a specific individual ripped out of any military organization on short notice was difficult. A by name call trampled the Commanding Officer's prerogative, and the expected response would be to nominate a substitute. That would be the first offer and start the negotiating. The National Security Advisor understood the issues and gave Steele the power to pick his team. Steele wanted to start with a cadre of seven additional souls to accommodate potential drops.

Training for this mission would be the biggest challenge. The MK 48 torpedo sat on a stand at the Navy Undersea Warfare Center in Newport, RI. The water conditions and underwater topography of Newport were completely different from that of Mocha, Yemen. There was no submarine available to carry out the practice run, which was not feasible anyway since only a single MK 48 torpedo was available to be modified. That was the war shot. There would be only one bite at the apple.

Steele started to work at the white board and soon had an options matrix covering the white board as well as a dozen pieces of poster-sized butcher paper. It finally hit him over the head that he was trying too hard to replicate the conditions expected in Yemen. What training was really required? He would be shot from a submarine and the others would follow the nanotube pipe to the abandoned well. The team would crawl out of the well and fan out within the compound, secure the weapons and then skedaddle before the Tomahawks began raining in. What was apparent from this exercise was the importance of additional intelligence about the compound, the layout and perhaps some specialized sensors to locate the specials. Richie Bouffard was the best source of the kind of information Steele needed.

CHAPTER SEVENTY-FIVE

Newport, Rhode Island

All seven of the SEALS selected by Steele showed up a week later at the Naval Undersea Warfare Center, NUWC for short, in Newport, Rhode Island. They were ushered into a laboratory and met by the Commanding Officer and three civilians. Cradled on a long torpedo stand in front of them lay the prototype delivery vehicle that had been cobbled together to fit into a standard torpedo tube. It looked like a Rube Goldberg design instead of the fully assembled unitary package they'd expected. The sections were not yet mated together and the custom mounting rings needed to join the sections were not in sight. The CO was the first to speak.

"We've been working some technical issues on the concept that you sent up here last month, Mr. Steele, and I can tell you it hasn't been as straightforward as you might have imagined. The innards of an active torpedo are crammed with lots of stuff mounted on machined blocks and in some cases, shock mounted to withstand the acceleration of the fish. This particular torpedo, a MK 48 Advanced Capability service round, was in the queue for re-work because it was accidentally dropped from a crane lowering it into the hull of a submarine. We understand this is a priority, but we'll need more time to ensure that none of the components we intend to re-use were damaged before moving forward with modifications."

"Captain, you were sent explicit instructions outlining the needs and the required availability date. I'm not aware that you have reported any hard spots that would impact the delivery date, or did I miss something?"

"No, Mr. Steele, you missed nothing. Here at the lab we are used to a little different pace, and I guess we just didn't fully understand the urgency of your need."

"Captain, I'd like to have a word with you in private if I may."

"Whatever you want to say, Mr. Steele, you can say it right here. We are just like a family in this command."

"Fine. You are 18 days behind the schedule laid out in the letter sent from the Pentagon's Director of Defense Research and Engineering (Advanced Capabilities). If you want to remain the head of this happy family tomorrow, I recommend that you get the best team on this project right now. Do I make myself clear, Captain? If you'd prefer to hear the same message from the Under Secretary himself, I can arrange that."

"No, Mr. Steele. I understand completely. You'll have a revised schedule first thing tomorrow morning, OK?"

"That will be fine. Thank you, Captain."

The team gathered around the torpedo and said nothing.

"Who's the lead on this project?" Steele asked.

"Well, he's off this afternoon, but I'm the lead when he's not here."

Steele felt his heart skip a beat. He was shocked with the attitude displayed by the project's leaders.

"OK, perhaps you could walk us through the state of the preparation and acquaint the team with the major building blocks of this machine."

Hours later, Steele and the team piled into a rented van and drove down to the Newport waterfront, stopping at the first sign advertising seafood and cold beer. The group found a large table and had several pitchers of beer before ordering a selection of fresh seafood.

After dinner, the team returned to the base where they were billeted at the Bachelor Officers Quarters. They would meet the following morning a few hundred yards away in a SCIF, a facility designed and certified for highly classified discussions, located at the Wargaming Center at the Naval War College.

As Steele sat alone at the desk in his room, he felt nauseous. He had drunk too much beer and ate too much fried seafood. There would be a price to pay for the excesses in the morning. However, the root cause of his nausea was not the rich food and swilling draft beer, but the number of moving parts in the operation and the lack of a completed delivery vehicle. Everything depended on a clandestine insertion, and the countdown clock was already ticking in his head. He felt trapped with little maneuvering room. A fleeting thought crossed his mind. It might be better to pull the plug on the operation early and cut the losses rather than swim against the tide to continue. Who was he kidding? He needed to get real and also needed some sleep. Maybe this was all a bad dream?

CHAPTER SEVENTY-SIX

Newport, Rhode Island

After checking-in at the secure facility at the Wargaming Center, Steele briefed the tactical plan to the team. After answering hours of questions, the group discussed how to train for the mission now that the machine was not even close to delivery. They quickly agreed that there were too many constraints and too little time to even dry run the operation. The usual training process of repetition and practice would never work with this insertion. There were too many variables. The known unknowns covered several large sheets of paper. Instead, their concentration shifted to the compound once they had reached their point of departure in the abandoned well. How would they secure the weapons, disarm the triggering mechanism, and neutralize the chemical weapons before the strike? And what would happen if one of the vaunted Tomahawks dropped a 1 or 0 in its guidance system that caused an error of a few hundred feet?

The attitude at NUWC changed overnight. When Steele and the team paid an afternoon visit to the facility just north of the piers that used to be the bustling home of the US Navy's Atlantic Fleet, there was a beehive of activity in the bay where the torpedo was supported by a series of stands to place the separate but unmated parts of the torpedo in their order of assembly. A sense of urgency was apparent from the moment the team was met at the front desk and escorted to the lab that was yesterday's sleepy hollow. The Commanding Officer was involved and animated with technicians scurrying around taking measurements with calipers and discussing hydrodynamic impacts of various design changes such as bolt circles for mating rings.

Approaching the team with high energy and fully engaged, the Captain shook hands with all of the visitors and moved them to the side of the torpedo as technicians streamed back and forth.

"Good afternoon. I apologize for the confusion yesterday. We are getting back on track and have our best engineers on the project today." He waved over a heavy-set man with classic male pattern baldness whose hair fell over his ears and whose heavy beard gave him the look of an aging biker who'd already lived a very full life.

"I'd like to introduce Charlie Scott, one of our top torpedo designers who is the new lead for the project."

"Pleased to meet you," he said in a no-nonsense voice that signaled his knowledge and confidence at the same time. "We'll be able to put this thing together by your need date with maybe a day of margin. I thought that weight distribution would be the biggest challenge after I saw this heavy boring machine. Just look at the carbide cutters on this thing. Turns out that the warhead and this machine weigh almost the same so the counterweighting problem goes away. We've got the design for the sacrificial sabot on which the machine will cut its teeth, and the machine shop is cutting the mating rings to put everything together." The man moved to the other side of the torpedo to make sure that the team had a clear view and continued.

"We were planning to run the fuel lines forward to the boring machine on the outside of the torpedo shell but will keep them inside so there's no chance they'll get pinched and starve the engine. Back here, the carbon nanotube fabricator will fit just fine and will construct the tube when the torpedo hits the land and the propeller is jettisoned. The only issue there is that the fabricator may not be able to keep up with the speed of the torpedo as the first thirty to fifty feet of the tunnel will be bored by momentum. I'm no geologist but expect those areas may be prone to cave in. We don't have a fix for that yet. Which one of you fellas is going to steer this thing home?"

"That would be me," answered Steele.

"Well, I've dealt with a fairly broad range of technology over the years, but this is a first. I've researched the Kaiten manned suicide torpedoes the Imperial Japanese Navy used in World War II. Without a warhead, I assume this fish will be a means of getting into a place that's not accessible any other way. I also assume that you are not on some sort of suicide mission. We don't hear much from the field after we put together something like this, so I would appreciate knowing how it worked."

"I hope to be able to deliver that report myself," said Steele. "Are there any other hard spots we need to know about?"

"Not really. The CO called me yesterday afternoon to take over this project so I haven't had time to read all the working papers. The previous lead was headed in the right direction but way over his head in terms of driving the concept into real engineering. Let's just call it a stretch assignment gone wrong. We've got the right talent on the job and have everything we need. The CO told me to let him know if we run into any problems and gave me a blank check in terms of people and equipment, so I think we are all set."

"Good," said Steele. He walked up to the CO. "Looks like things are on track, Captain. I appreciate all the effort and your personal involvement. I feel much more confident than I did twenty-four hours ago."

"No problem. I feel better too with Charlie on the job. I don't know what the mission is but certainly understand that it's a top priority."

The team left the building elated. Steele had seen this type of firefighting in the past where a project was saved by bringing in the ace just before it went off the rails. Charlie seemed like the right person to lead the effort, but they were up against a complicated schedule with no room for error. Pulling a rabbit out of the hat might appear to be a solution, but Steele worried about all the unintended consequences of a sudden change of leadership within a project team.

CHAPTER SEVENTY-SEVEN

Red Sea

Jeddah, Saudi Arabia was home to the Royal Saudi Naval Forces Western Fleet. The old port city and modern-day port of entry was accustomed to visitors, whether by the hundreds of thousands coming for the pilgrimage to Mecca or warships making a port call. Without the normal amusements sought after by sailors, Jeddah was not considered a liberty port, and the Captain decided to restrict the crew from going ashore. The submarine would remain in port for just a few hours. Ten civilians would embark on *Newport* in Jeddah. A single odd-looking MK 48 torpedo was loaded earlier in the day.

Carrying a green parachute bag with his gear, Steele almost stumbled over it when he encountered *Newport's* Captain on the quarterdeck. She was aware of the effect she had on men, but Steele seemed different right from the start. The message she'd gotten earlier in the week identified the team embarking on her submarine and identified him as the team lead. He would be calling the shots and using *Newport* as a delivery vehicle. She felt a slight electrical impulse move from her brain down through her extremities as he came aboard and gave her a broad smile. The electric jolt shocked her system in more ways than one. It surprised and scared her too.

"Good afternoon, Captain, I'm Dan Steele, and this is the team." He stood aside and introduced each of the men to the Captain.

"Welcome aboard to all of you. We will get underway in two hours." She turned to a ramrod straight khaki uniform to her right and said, "COB, please take these men below and show them to their berthing areas. They also will need to be issued dosimeters and get a safety briefing. Thanks."

"Yes, ma'am. Gentlemen, please follow me." The COB or Chief of the Boat took charge of the visitors. As the Senior Enlisted Advisor to the Commanding Officer, he served in a critical position aboard a submarine and enjoyed an incredible span of both responsibility and influence.

Steele first noted how clean the ship was. He'd been on many ships during his time as an active duty SEAL, and a handful of submarines. The narrow passageways gleamed as if they were an operating theater. Piping systems, valves and cableways were neatly laid out and clearly labeled. Only the air seemed different. It was the smell of air held in a container that had absorbed all the odors of hot steam, machinery oil, food, the toilets and showers, and humans in close quarters. Distinct, the air was clean, but even the CO2 scrubbers were unable to strip off the smells that clung to every molecule. Those living aboard were not even aware of it. When returning after a mission, whether six days or six months, the families waiting on the pier were greeted with the bizarre odor that was part of the fabric of working on a submarine.

Steele's team was berthed in several compartments and hoped they wouldn't be subjected to hot-bunking during the operation. There were 140 berths available to bed down the full crew of 134 plus the newly arrived riders so sharing a bed was not uncommon, even in the world's most modern submarine.

"Mr. Steele, your presence is requested in the wardroom," blared the ship's internal announcing system.

Steele knew the diminutive compartment where the officers ate their meals in shifts. The small dining table could accommodate six officers at the same time and the lounge chairs maybe two or three others using lap trays. The wardroom doubled as a meeting location, as all *Newport's* interior space was at a premium. Steele re-traced his steps through the narrow passageways and found the wardroom minutes later. He walked through the door and found the Captain waiting for him, a cup of coffee in front of her on the small laminate table. She gestured towards an open seat across the table, and he slid into it.

"First, Mr. Steele," she said, "we will be getting underway soon. If you or any of your team need anything else for the mission, now would be the only time to get it."

"Well, Captain, we know that the torpedo is loaded, and there should have been a diplomatic pouch from the Embassy delivered that has some additional hardware. If that's aboard, we have everything we need."

"Yes, that arrived and has been stowed in our armory. I know that you have some experience with submarines but just wanted to review the ground rules. We've displaced some of our Chief Petty Officers so that you and your tactical team can be berthed together. You'll join the crew in the General Mess for meals. I expect you to control your team. They will be treated just like any other crewmember during their time aboard and observe the ship's routine. Is that clear?"

"Yes," responded Steele, somewhat put off by the formality and serious tone of her voice.

"Now, how should I address you? Lieutenant? Mr. Steele?"

"Dan would be fine, Captain."

"OK, Dan it is. I've read the details of the plan you briefed up the chain and think it's bold and innovative but also high risk. I will do everything I can to support you and your team and would like nothing better than to stop this General from using the weapons he brought with him. As you know, we monitor the radiation absorbed by the crew and keep track of it, but obviously, it's a non-lethal amount. If my math is correct, what he is reported to possess is several times the force of Hiroshima and Nagasaki combined."

"Correct. The labs have done all the analysis and if detonated properly, the blast would have a large area effect and the residual radiation would cause the strait to shut down for years."

"Right. What else do I need to know about you, Dan?"

***

Newport maneuvered smartly from the pier and headed out past the breakwater into the open sea. It was a short sea detail with the water depth dropping off quickly. Once in open water, the boat submerged and Sydney Garrison ordered the watch team to begin fifteen minutes of angles and dangles, a routine to ensure that the ship was properly secured for sea. The boat would dive at a steep down angle and then reverse itself with a steep up angle maneuver. Some Commanding Officers added another layer of complexity by banking the submarine through a series of thirty degree turns where the boat really demonstrated the mastery of its domain. It wasn't quite the same as aviators going through sharp turns, flying straight up or rolling an aircraft, but it was certainly an easy way to get the crew and any passengers ready for sea.

Though *Newport* was not necessarily concerned about radiated noise during this operation, the boat needed to be prepared to operate in a near silent condition at sea. Stecle had been through the exercises before on another submarine and marveled at the technology that went into the design of these undersea killers. He also was impressed that the angles and dangles performed by *Newport* were far and away the most thorough testing he'd witnessed. Sydney Garrison expected a high level of professionalism in everything *Newport* did.

CHAPTER SEVENTY-EIGHT

Red Sea

During the transit to the location where *Newport* would gingerly approach the shoal waters and fire the torpedo, Steele spent hours with the sub's Captain, reviewing the plan and contingencies. Most of the time, Steele's deputy was present as well as *Newport's* Operations Officer and Weapons Officer. Steele felt a pleasant tension grow between himself and Sydney Garrison and worried about the impact on the mission.

"Hey, Dan," said his number two after an afternoon briefing, "Is the CO just really interested in the mission or is she just trying to get closer to you? I mean, she is smart as hell and easy on the eyes, but I hope all the attention doesn't distract you too much."

"You are imagining things, Mike. There's nothing there. She is probably just worried about her career."

"Seriously? I know I've got a dull normal IQ, but what I see is as obvious as a two-by-four upside the head."

"You are dreaming." Steele would quickly change the subject. The truth was that he'd seen the same looks, the casual brush of the hand and the intentional invasion of his personal space which he hadn't resisted. He felt conflicted and confused. Frequently, he reminded himself to keep his head in the game and to concentrate on the mission at hand. He also was honest enough with himself to recognize the reality of the situation.

With *Newport* at depth in the narrow shipping channel, the execute order finally came. Maneuvering a mile north of *Shackleton's* position on the edge of the channel, the submarine navigated precisely through a natural chasm in the sea bed with clearance of no more than twenty yards on either side of her hull. Of course, the charts did not account for sunken containers that may have reduced the clearance ever further. The Captain raised the periscope up from the tower and peered with a night vision sight at the target area. A sub would usually fire its torpedoes using its deadly accurate periscope linked to gyroscopes spinning at a high number of revolutions to deliver precision accuracy to the fire-control system. In this case, the firing bearing would be calculated by a directional radio receiver mounted on the same mast. The target: the abandoned deep well not visible from the sub's position but marked with an electronic beacon deposited by a drone days before.

Steele lost any connection with time and space but felt that the minutes since he'd been placed in the round coffin had been an eternity. Just before climbing into the tube, wearing just cotton shorts and a T-shirt, he heard one of the sailors loudly announce that the Captain had entered the space. Garrison nodded to the torpedo handlers and the civilian who declared the boring machine ready. Steele lay inside the tube with his arms extended and shivered with the thought of being fired into a hostile compound through the water and digging his way to the well. What would happen if the torpedo hit an old hulk left on the bottom? He would simply die with no way to escape and little chance of rescue by the other divers who would enter the bored hole with no means to extricate the torpedo. Second thoughts streamed through his mind. Had he honestly addressed all the risks to the operation or given short shrift to those that involved his personal well-being?

Steele calculated that the re-breather would generate quality air with a twenty-minute margin until the scrubbers would lose their ability to provide sufficient oxygen to sustain life. He quickly reviewed the probabilities for mission success and realized that he had used optimistic multipliers for the combined probability of all the moving parts performing as he confidently predicted. He was accustomed to working with odds stacked against him, but he knew this was a very long shot. He wondered how the odds makers in Los Vegas would call it.

"Dan, are you ready for this?" asked Sydney Garrison in a soft voice standing at the side of the torpedo with her back to the team that would position and fire it.

"As ready as I'll ever be, Captain," he replied.

"Good luck, Dan, and please remember that I'm thinking about you," she said tenderly. She bent down and found his mouth with hers and gave him a warm, soft kiss that signaled far more than good luck. Sydney Garrison believed that she'd found her Mr. Right in Dan Steele and was not going to lose him by being timid. If she could have yanked him from the tube and had one of the others take his place, she would have done so. During the short time they'd been together on the boat, she had gotten to know him, though he'd been closed-mouthed and reticent to talk about his past. She respected that. Her friend Ramses got a copy of his unclassified service record and sent it to her, so she had a clearer picture of the man she had in her sights.

Twelve precision-made fasteners were spun into the watertight shell. Steele had never experienced claustrophobia, until now. Being confined in the narrow torpedo body with a simple joy stick to control the boring head, illumination from several tiny LEDs and no climate control made the coffin unbearable. Steele fought to maintain control against his mounting fear, trying to pinpoint its source. The crew smoothly repositioned the torpedo from the loading tray on a short lateral trip before being inserted into an armored tube built into the bow section of the submarine. Steele visualized Jill and his two young sons, hoping it would calm his jangled nerves. It didn't help. Flashing images of Jill and the boys, teammates that had never returned from missions, and even Sydney Garrison's smile flooded his mind like some tachistoscope connected directly to his brain, flashing the images too quickly for comprehension.

According to the weaponeers, no one had ever been shot from a submarine in a MK 48 torpedo. The inner door of the torpedo tube opened and the warshot was silently maneuvered into place. As the heavy inner door closed, Steele felt the panic spread through his body like wildfire, sending so many messages over his sensory neurons that his internal body temperature rose. He wondered if the cold sea water that would enter the tube when the outer tube cap opened would reduce his core body temperature.

His body's communications system reached the danger level and was on the verge of shutdown because of synaptic overload. Normally steady, his breathing rate increased dramatically, and he couldn't seem to control it. There was no way he could call off the mission, and he felt he was on the edge of blacking out. No communications existed beyond the coffin-like shell of the torpedo. No one heard him bang his fists on its walls.

He felt the torpedo move. Then the crew began backing out the fasteners that held him in the steel tomb. He couldn't understand why, but his breathing ratcheted up to a panic state. The shell was removed, and Steele pulled the re-breather's mouthpiece from his lips, gasping for air in the torpedo room like a fish flopping on the deck of a boat, barely recognizing the sub's weapons officer standing over the tube.

"The operation has been scrubbed."

"Why?" asked Steele, his rapid breathing matching his elevated heartbeat.

"Not sure. It wasn't from this end."

Steele climbed out of the tube, his face white from the unknown fear he experienced in the tube. His legs felt like jelly, barely able to support his body upright. He steadied himself on the loading tray. Drained physically and emotionally, Steele knew that the odds of mission success had probably just been halved by this unnerving experience. Could he even get back in the tube? For the first time in his life, he needed an injection of something to calm down.

As embarked civilians with no military rank, Steele and his team ate their meals in the crew's mess. Just as he was wolfing down a late supper after his ordeal in the torpedo, Steele saw the Commanding Officer walk through the tiny dining area and approach the table.

"Mr. Steele," she said, "I'd like to discuss the shot with you. I'll be in my cabin in twenty minutes." Her direct, business-like tone surprised him. Was she reading his mind?

Steele knocked on the door and entered the cabin. Sydney Garrison stood in front of him, her open arms beckoning him to embrace her. He stopped.

"Come in, Dan, and have a seat," she said, "We need to talk."

Garrison's stateroom was a generous eight feet square with a small table big enough to accommodate two people. A small desk, illuminated status board and an internal phone handset were all built in.

Steele took a seat at the table with Sydney Garrison directly across from him. They both started to talk at the same time. Steele stopped first.

"Dan, I wanted to talk about three things. First, the mission was scrubbed this morning after the Chief of Naval Operations got a report from NUWC regarding the machining on the mating rings of the first two sections of the torpedo. They wanted to ensure that the groove for the O-ring and the O-ring itself were matched in size. It sounds like a checklist oversight. The NUWC tech who accompanied the torpedo will disassemble the first two sections and take measurements to make sure that your compartment stays watertight at depth. That's fine with me, Dan. I'm anxious that you complete this op in one piece and breathing air, not seawater, even though I'm told your nickname is Gills."

"Where did you hear that?"

"I can't recall. Maybe from one of your team," Garrison replied, trying to cover up the fact that she learned the nickname only by reading his personnel file.

"I never told any of these guys. Anyway, that was a nickname that I had on the team a long time ago."

"OK. Second, and most important, I heard from the guys in the handling room that you were shaken when you came out of the torpedo this morning."

"Shaken? That's an understatement. No, I felt claustrophobic. My breathing was out of control. I was on the verge of a panic attack," Steele responded. Sydney Garrison slid her hands across the narrow table and took Steele's hands in hers. Soft and warm, her hands soothed Steele's jangled nerves.

"Dan, this mission depends on your steering the torpedo into the bottom of that well. What's going to happen when we get the order to execute? I won't knowingly put you and your team in harm's way if you are not ready."

"No, Captain. I am fully ready. After I climbed out of the torpedo this morning, one of the techs found a loose fitting on the rebreather that was the root cause of the problem. Having a logical explanation for my reaction is important. I saw the ship's doc, and he confirmed that my response to the lack of oxygen seemed consistent. We have re-checked all the internal fittings so now I'm confident."

"OK." said Garrison, making a mental note to follow-up with the ship's physician. Her hands were gently exploring the surface of Steele's hands and the base of his fingers.

"Now, Dan, the other thing I want to..." The knock at the Captain's door interrupted the conversation.

"Come in," said Garrison, pulling her hands away as she turned towards the cabin door.

"Captain, we just received an immediate Top-Secret message. The Operations Officer asks that you come to the radio room immediately."

Garrison slid out from her side of the table and Steele followed suit.

"I'll catch up with you later," she said as the three of them left the small cabin.

CHAPTER SEVENTY-NINE

Red Sea

A technical one-day stand-down was ordered by the Pentagon. This enabled Steele to review the plan with the team and have them recheck all the hardware and systems on which the mission would rely. Sydney Garrison directed a similar effort on *Newport* as a means of reducing the uncertainty of executing the shot. She reviewed the plans with minute attention and asked a thousand new questions, knowing that her commitment to mission success would flow naturally down the chain of command so everyone had the same level of interest as she did. That was the magic that a good Commanding Officer would bring to a ship or submarine without constantly barking orders or looking over everyone's shoulder. It was what leadership at sea was all about.

The two kept bumping into each other during the day. These unplanned meetings were friendly and good-natured. Sydney learned that Steele had a wry sense of humor which she frequently tested. He enjoyed the back and forth with her but suppressed the unfamiliar feelings in his body when he was with her. Often laughing, she had an easy smile that crinkled the skin around the iridescent green eyes. When they were together, her eyes pierced his, as if she were examining his soul, not to cause him pain or uncover secrets, but to understand what really made his core being tick. Comfortable in her own skin, she exuded confidence, well-founded on her technical knowledge and a caring command climate where everyone shared her commitment to operational excellence.

Still guarded, he had shared some of his past with her but was reluctant to reveal his vulnerability. She was an attractive and desirable woman. So was Jill, and it felt like yesterday that he had put his arms around her for the final time. While his mind told Steele to slow down, his heart felt a lightness and a definite attraction for Sydney Garrison. He had to resist the urge to respond to her less than subtle overtures as best he could.

On any US Navy ship, particularly a submarine, there is nothing that happens which the crew does know or find out, even if the activity takes place behind closed doors. There are no secrets aboard ships. At one point during the stand-down, they met in the wardroom while getting refueled with coffee. No one else was in the space. Garrison had been touring the ship. Steele noticed a dark ring of sweat around the collar of her blue jumpsuit and tiny beads of sweat clinging to microscopic hairs on her upper lip. She was the epitome of a hard-working, driven professional but was also kind, generous, and empathetic. As the Commanding Officer, she consciously tried to make an emotional connection with each member of the crew, often spending time getting to know them better and understanding their personal motivations. She made everyone feel important and valued. And this was not for show. Sydney Garrison believed it.

"Hi, Dan. How are you doing?"

Steele was immediately on guard. The question wasn't about the torpedo or the mechanical things that had to work correctly for the mission to succeed. The question was about him. Was he so sensitive that he was parsing everything that the CO said?

"Fine, Captain. We have checked and re-checked everything, and we are ready to go."

"Aside from the equipment, are you ready, Dan?" She looked into his dark eyes intently, studying them for any sign of emotion, of fear or love.

"Yes, I am completely ready and confident. I appreciate all your personal interest in the mission and the team."

"Thanks. Yes, I want to support the team and accomplish the mission. And I'm also very interested in you, Dan. It's hard for me to tell you what I'm feeling these days, but I think we share a lot of the same interests and perhaps some feelings towards each other. I hope so. I'll see you again before the shoot."

She brushed his lips lightly with hers and left the wardroom.

CHAPTER EIGHTY

Red Sea

It took twenty-four hours for the torpedo case to be disassembled and inspected. The milled groove and O-ring met all the design specifications so the mating surfaces were cleaned and a ribbon of silicone applied outside the O-ring which was lubricated and re-installed. Numbered body-bound bolts were torqued flush with the torpedo's skin to ensure a watertight seal. Steele's plan was back on for a shot the following evening. A dark night with the full moon shrouded in a thick layer of clouds was predicted. Based on intelligence reporting, it was also the night for the quarterly arena contests that would distract most of the fighters. The few participating would be exhausted, the spectators would be inebriated, and Steele and his team could overpower the watch organization. At least that was the assumption that finally set the mission in motion.

CHAPTER EIGHTY-ONE

Moscow, Russia

"We know the Americans are preparing to attack the Compound. Based on some of our sources and analysis of previous military operations, our assessment is that they will launch a cruise missile strike in the next forty-eight to seventy-two hours. Our long-range modernized Bear aircraft have been secretly deployed to Tehran and are prepared to strike when ordered. The Americans will think that we will use them in Syria as we did a few years ago."

"Good," said the President. "I want this option executed as soon as possible, before the Americans launch their strike. If we are successful in bombing the compound, we'll take credit for neutralizing the threat and saving the world. Our image on the geopolitical stage will be enhanced and once again, the US and their allies will be seen as a feckless group without the conviction to eliminate the threat. Nothing could be better for us. If the bombing detonates a nuclear blast, we'll blame the Americans for the reckless decision to attack a compound where nuclear weapons as well as chemical agents were known to be located."

"Yes, Mr. President. Our aircraft will be dropping American precision-guided bombs so it will be very difficult for the Americans to deny their involvement. We know that their stealth bombers are still grounded because of software errors, but no one else is aware of that degradation to their readiness so this provides a better cover for our bombing. We will call for a United Nations team to perform the forensics after the attack."

"Josep, this is a brilliant plan and accomplishes multiple objectives at once. I can't see a scenario where we lose anything. Well done, comrade."

CHAPTER EIGHTY-TWO

Red Sea

The citizens of Iowa had lobbied hard for another ship to be named for the corn state. The last commissioned USS *Iowa (BB-61)*, the lead ship of a class of four battleships, had been decommissioned in 1990. For years, it had been shuffled around the Navy Inactive Ships Facility anchorages where the dreadnought joined rows of gray hulls the Navy had decommissioned but could not strike for readiness reasons.

It looked certain that *Iowa* would become a floating museum in San Francisco, and the US Navy even towed the ship from Philadelphia through the Panama Canal to a facility outside San Francisco to speed the process. At the eleventh hour, a councilman halted the plan to make the dreadnought an attraction on the waterfront arguing that having a warship down on the piers would not be consistent with the city's ambiance and, more importantly, its core values.

Fortunately, the city of San Pedro was happy to find some pier space for the battlewagon, and the ship became one of the top attractions for people visiting the Los Angeles area. An army of volunteers descended on the ship to maintain it as the museum plans expanded.

Eventually, the State's lobbying paid off and the latest Arleigh Burke Class destroyer was christened USS *Iowa*. This was a new flight of the destroyer that had become the workhorse of the fleet.

As its first Commanding Officer, Bill Wilson ran a tight ship. His number one priority was readiness, defined as the ability of the ship to respond to whatever came their way in a timely and professional manner. He would not tolerate lackadaisical performance from anyone in the crew and demanded that any operation be approached as if it were the same as going to war. Constantly in motion throughout the ship, there was not a single space on the ship that he had not inspected. When he entered a space, he would develop an overall impression and then look for the posted compartment check-off list which listed the valves and fittings located inside which were critical to maintaining watertight integrity during combat, fire or flooding. Armed with a flashlight carried in his back pocket, Wilson would spot-check maintenance actions several times every day.

Iowa had been detached from an exercise in the South China Sea to the Gulf of Aden, in support of a special operations mission that would be followed by a Tomahawk strike. Though most of the plan was boiler plate, Wilson studied it in minute detail. He wanted to make sure that the destroyer could respond to this tasking or any other with 100% effectiveness. Fair-minded, the crew understood what drove him to seek excellence in everything the ship did. There was no question in anyone's mind that *Iowa* would survive an encounter with the enemy and could dole out punishment from its weapons systems with speed and accuracy. *Iowa* carried an inventory of 60 Tomahawk cruise missiles that could be ripple-fired from vertical launchers.

Iowa was assigned an operating box off the port of Assab, Eritrea which gave the ship a clear shot across the narrow waterway to Mocha, the small city with the undivided attention of the sea-going countries of the world. Its mission was maritime surveillance. The short distance to Mocha preempted participation in the strike US and Allied ships and submarines would launch as a flurry of Tomahawk cruise missiles would converge on the compound. Every sweep of the surface search radar painted *Shackleton* whose position seemed very secure on the edge of the deep-water channel. Wilson would have preferred additional maneuvering room. Operating his ship in congested and narrow waters deepened the lines on his brow. He wore a perpetual frown on his face. Spending every hour of every day honing the ship and the crew to an unmatched state of readiness, he found the weight of command crushing and enjoyed none of its exhilaration.

CHAPTER EIGHTY-THREE

Red Sea

Steele began taking long deep breaths on the rebreather to stem the fear gripping him. Unable to move in a thick-walled twenty-one-inch tube inserted into another tube in the sub's hull with no communication, his world was closing in. Sure, he'd been there before, but this time in the confined space gave him another paralyzing taste of claustrophobia. He tried to think of other things, and nothing seemed to work so he knew that controlling his breathing was the only thing he could do to keep the instinct to fight his way out of the tube at bay. Much of his torment had spilled over from the aborted first mission.

He thought back to the goodbye from the Captain. He felt the attraction between them, but, until the first kiss, wondered if it was just a game for her. No one could deny her attractiveness, but she had not achieved her position commanding one of the deadliest fighting machines in the US Navy inventory by being a seductress tempting men and then pulling the rug out from under them just for the pleasure of watching them fall. There was more to Sydney Garrison than that.

The previous evening, Steele had knocked and entered her cabin, standing in the doorway until she waved him in from the tiny desk.

"Excuse me, Captain. I have an outgoing message for your approval."

"This looks fine, Dan," she said as she initialed the top of the single typed page. She did not pencil-whip the document or edit the text. Steele knew his job, and she knew hers. She handed the message back to Steele who was drawing in the scent of her space on the ship.

It certainly smelled better than the berthing area where he and the team bedded down.

"How is the team?" she asked.

"We are ready. I think there's a better than even chance we can pull this off before the Tomahawks destroy the compound. We are anxious to start moving. It's the waiting that is hard to take."

"Not to put any more pressure on you, Dan, but the Russians have raised the stakes a little higher. We just got an intell report that they have staged a couple of modernized Bears in Iran that may be trying to get involved. It could be Syria again with a cruise missile strike, but at least some the analysts believe they may fly to Mocha to solve the problem on their own."

"All the more reason for us to carry out our plan ASAP," said Steele, a hard determination coming through in his voice.

The Captain stood up and faced him. "You are a brave man, Dan Steele. I like that." At five feet ten inches, Captain Garrison pushed up on her toes and vigorously kissed Steele. Then she backed away, her bright green eyes still locked to his. The silence was broken when the ship's navigator knocked on the door and entered the cabin.

"Excuse me, Captain, I've got the night orders prepared for your signature."

"Come in, George, Dan and I just finished."

"Thank you, Captain," said Steele as he squeezed around the navigator and continued into the passageway outside the cabin. He dropped the message off at the radio room and headed back to the berthing compartment. What Steele really needed was the open space for a long run to clear his head.

Steele heard the torpedo tube bow caps open and the slosh of water against the metal coffin that entombed him. Ready to shoot, he thought. Soon, he would be traveling underwater at a speed of fifty knots before hitting the soft mud. The regular dust storms deposited a fine particulate that was constantly added to the bottom. But Steele wasn't concerned about the fine sand that fell to the bottom. What were the chances the torpedo would miss the inevitable debris that collected in a harbor over the years? In the past, ships often broke free of their moorings, swept away before sinking. The bottom of a harbor was a fascinating place. Steele's life had been saved by a large I-beam standing upright in Boston Harbor eighteen months ago.

The remainder of the team would follow the torpedo on a SEAL Delivery Vehicle, waiting on the bottom after the torpedo was fired. The geometry of the mission called for Steele to signal before the rest of the team would begin crawling through the tube. They would all meet up in the abandoned well.

He didn't feel another thing for what seemed a very long time, just lying in a twenty-one-inch diameter tube, listening and wondering what the shot would feel like as he suddenly accelerated from zero to over fifty knots in just seconds. Here he was, in a long tube about to be fired into a muddy wall aiming for an abandoned well where he would be joined by the rest of the team to secure specials in the middle of the night. So bizarre that it had to be fantasy!

Steele's breathing steadied during the long wait. He set the soles of his feet firmly against a cold metal baffle plate separating him from the fuel tank of the torpedo. The allocation of interior space was based on the size of the boring machine, the carbon nanotube fabric module and the fuel tank and propulsion sections. Fuel needed to run the boring machine and spin out the tunnel liner was a precious commodity so Steele's compartment had shrunk to sixty-nine inches, six inches shorter than his body's height.

He felt the instantaneous acceleration buckling his legs, his knees being painfully pressed against the cold metal shell, the force trying to puddle his body into a gelatinous mass against the baffle plate. It was a painful beginning. Steele straightened his body and regained the position needed to steer the boring machine to its destination.

CHAPTER EIGHTY-FOUR

Mocha Compound

The short ride in the torpedo through the water was over in a flash. After the terminal maneuver which ended with the fish slamming into the soft sloping bottom where the firing's reverse occurred, Steele felt the propulsion unit separate as he was flung forward with the rapid deceleration of impacting solid ground. He braced his body for the impact trying to avoid his skull becoming a shock absorber. The calculations presented during his final briefing projected that the torpedo's momentum would drive it between twenty and fifty feet into the muck before the boring machine would begin excavating at a rate of five feet per minute. The underwater shot would cover the 4,000 yards in just under three minutes with the remaining distance excavated by advancing the boring machine. Total elapsed time from the torpedo being fired to entering the abandoned well would be about forty minutes.

Steele thought back to the option where the team would deploy directly from the submarine in a swimmer delivery vehicle and manhandle the boring machine to drill the tunnel. They assumed that the drilling machine could begin the job closer to the sea wall and the overall distance would be reduced to 120 feet. This option was discounted because of the difficulty of getting the hole aligned in all three dimensions. There would be nothing clandestine about breaking ground within the compound in the open area short of the well. Using a programmed, guided torpedo to start the tunnel would almost ensure a bore at the proper angle. Additionally, the underwater lights needed to set up the equipment could be seen at a shallow depth. But that option seemed preferable to the one Steele was executing now.

The boring machine started without a hitch, chewing through

the sabot like a famished dog. Keeping the boring machine pointed at the beacon in the well, Steele's dark eyes were crossing as he stared at the electronic bullseye mounted on the forward baffle plate and moved a small joystick to keep the machine centered on target. He had no ability to gauge the progress underground except the steady sound of the rotating head gnawing the soil and pressing it around the perimeter of the hole with hydraulic paddles fitted just behind the cutting head.

The steady hum of the boring suddenly turned into a deafening shriek inside the tube, and the torpedo shell began to vibrate violently as the hardened cutter plates began chewing something metallic. Perhaps an iron anchor that had been lost centuries ago. Inside the torpedo, the sound became a high-pitched piercing squeal, and the vibration made Steele feel like an ice cube being energetically shaken in a cocktail glass. His teeth chattered in his jaw, even though separated by the rebreather's mouthpiece. Minutes of raw fear surged through his cramped body as the temperature inside his narrow module increased with the hot, shearing metal to metal contact. He wondered how much abuse the carbide cutter heads could take before becoming so dull that they could not continue the forward progress. The vibration ended as suddenly as it began, and the renewed sound of excavating solid ground was ironically comforting. Steele kept the boring machine centered in the bullseye and tried to calm his rattled nerves.

The hum of the drilling machine changed again, signaling that it was boring the air instead of solid ground. Steele turned off the rotating heads and listened. The only thing he could hear were the beads of sweat steadily dripping off his body onto the metal interior. Turning the interior cam locks to open the torpedo shell hatch, he carefully pushed it from the watertight gasket.

Something solid was preventing it from opening more than six inches. Steele pushed harder and felt a slight movement. Perhaps the torpedo entered the well under two feet of discarded building materials. Pushing harder from his position, which offered very little leverage, the obstacle moved, and he drew in a fresh breath of dank air having the old smell and taste of rotting vegetation. In the darkness, he exited the tube and stretched his limbs, trying to orient to his surroundings.

He retrieved the tool bag taped to the metal baffle plate and unfolded a small entrenching tool, clearing the soil around the torpedo shell to remove it from the tunnel opening. The sandy soil was compacted but loose. The nanotube fabric cured immediately and was exceptionally strong. Was it strong enough to prevent the weight of thirty feet of loose soil from flattening the pipe with a cave-in? Steele pulled the torpedo shell and the tube fabricator from the bored hole, cutting the fabric which felt like a piece of flexible plastic drain pipe. Studying the luminous hands on his watch, he pressed the button on a pocket-sized pager to signal the team to begin the crawl through the narrow pipe to the well.

The condition of the first thirty feet of the tunnel stood out as a worry bead because the tube fabricator could not keep up with the speed of the torpedo. That part of the tunnel would be the shakiest part of the ingress and escape route. Steele pushed the thought to the back of his mind. He'd been in dark places before, but this one was the darkest. They had planned on having no visibility at the bottom of the well so reality met expectation. Steele pulled on a black one-piece leotard fitted with a Kevlar chest plate and a hood with face mask. He slid an Ipe throwing knife under the fabric covering each of his forearms.

Minutes later, he pulled the first of the team into the well. The second man squeezed Steele's arm once to signal that all was OK. Soon, there were five of them at the bottom of the well. They removed the narrow re-breathers and staged them in the curved hatch that Steele removed. The remaining member of the team was moving alone in the shallow waters. His job was to kill the power system.

With the team in the well ready to move, Steele pressed the button on the pager a second time. This signal would start the strike clock. The team had one hour to secure the weapons before the first Tomahawk hit the ground. A ship operating in the Eastern Mediterranean Sea would fire the first missile. Unless the team could declare their mission achieved in thirty minutes and communicate with the command center aboard the Task Force commander's flag ship, the launch would be executed as planned in the formal strike order. The signal also set a timer for the last SEAL now hiding in shallow water under the finger pier to cut the generator power seven minutes before the Tomahawks arrived.

"Captain, they're in," said the Tactical Action Officer in a loud voice. The twenty-four-hour clock showed the time in dull red numerals where local time was displayed in days, hours, minutes and seconds: 16:20:55:22. Right on schedule.

"OK, thanks Tom," said Captain Garrison from eight feet away as she stared at the chart on the plotting table showing the position of *Newport* and an enlarged collage of photos of the compound overlaying the land mass of Yemen. "Let's see if we can get back into deeper water without scraping anything."

Newport was in a very tight location selected for firing, requiring that the boat back out of its position into deeper water accommodating the sub's length. There was no back-up camera on *Newport's* stern that would make this job easier. Garrison knew the submarine's maneuvering characteristics and could drive it as skillfully as the Corvette garaged in the basement of her second floor flat in downtown Gaeta, Italy. She felt she was leaving Dan Steele behind when all she wanted to do was to get closer to the man she'd fallen in love with in the few days they'd known each other.

At the bottom of the debris covered well, the distance to the top of the waist high wall surrounding it was only eight feet which was scaled from the shoulders of one of the SEALs. The men crouched alongside the well, dressed in black, their weapons ready. Located at the southern end of the compound, the team would have to make its way along the main building and past the arena to the northern end of the compound, about a hundred yards from the main building. Three of them would form a wide defensive perimeter while the other two would head straight for the compound's northernmost building.

They were just moving out from behind the well when an armed man walked down the road and stopped to light up a cigarette. He wore a shoulder-mounted radio that emitted a constant audible background hum. Walking in the shadows towards the well, the guard unzipped his pants to relieve himself against the well's exterior. In a single fluid motion, Steele stood and buried one of his Ipe knives in the man's chest. Two of the team dragged the dead man to the shadowed side of the well.

The team fanned out and headed north using the palm trees for cover. They reached the end of the main building and were about to skirt the arena when they heard the metallic movement of a weapons slide and a loud voice.

"Halt! You will put your weapons down slowly in front of you. Now." Steele could hear the crackle of a radio and the sound of footsteps on the concrete walkway surrounding the main building. The other security rover armed with a machine pistol was now backing up the first man. They'd been busted and had barely begun the mission. The team was traveling light, carrying only their MP5s and some spare clips of ammunition. It seemed that the Russian fighters were somehow expecting them.

Relieved of their weapons and with their hands on their heads, the five men were marched into the arena. They were presented to the General.

"I found them near the south wall of the main complex. All of them were armed with machine guns and one had a knife, nothing else."

The General left his seat and stepped down to the ground where he towered above the black clad men who stood before him. He approached Steele as the man closest to his height.

"What brings you to the compound? I don't recall inviting any other guests for tonight's festivities. Perhaps we will have a change to the fight bill."

Steele responded. "We are here to secure the special weapons that you brought with you from Russia."

"Where are you from?"

"The United States."

"I am not surprised that the United States is involved in such a mission, but to send five lightly armed commandos into this fortress is an amateur move. That does surprise me. Are you just a scouting party? Are there more troops on the way?"

Steele did not respond quickly enough for the General and, in a flash, he drove a fist into Steele's mid-section, lifting his body off the ground. He fell heavily to the arena floor before getting up and returning to his place in front of the General.

"Not tonight," he said evenly, "But you can be assured that troops will come at some point and take you and your fighters out of Mocha in chains."

The General threw his head back and roared with laughter. "You've been watching too many movies my boy. That may happen in Hollywood but not in the real world." He turned to one of the guards. "Lock them in the animal cage by the grill so they can watch some real men test their fighting skills. Take this one," the General pointed to one of the team, "and get him out of that silly suit and into some shorts. We'll see what kind of men the United States sent in to capture us. And find out where they penetrated the compound's defenses and destroy it." Zlodeyev returned to his seat and spoke to the assembled crowd. "We will take ten minutes to find where our uninvited guests entered the compound and will make some adjustments to the evening's activities."

Minutes later, the fighters returned carrying one of their own, the knife still in his chest.

"They killed Anton. Looks like they came in through the abandoned well which is now a firepit."

"I see," said General, walking over to the dead man and pulling the knife from his chest and wiping the blood on the man's shirt. He inspected the knife and felt it weight.

"Impressive weapon. Certainly not military issue. It's got good balance and weight." Still holding the knife, the General returned to his seat to re-start the entertainment.

Steele's mind was working in overdrive. The team was captured, without weapons or communications, and a Tomahawk strike would be launched in fifty minutes. And one of his team had been selected to go one-on-one with a Russian fighter. He knew the operation was high risk, but he hadn't put himself in front of four other brave Americans to die in an allied strike.

CHAPTER EIGHTY-FIVE

The White House Situation Room

President Bowles paced around the conference table with his hands thrust into his pockets and his head concentrating on the carpeted path he followed. A dozen of his closest civilian and military advisors sat at the large conference table listening to the reports from the scene. They were surrounded by large screen monitors that gave the place the look of a very exclusive sports bar offering live betting on any number of contests in progress all over the world. Hearing real time commentary from his military chiefs and political updates from the Secretary of State raised the level of tension in the room. All the briefings and preparations that led to today's action were history. It was showtime, and those gathered in the Situation Room had a seat on what could be an historic moment for the world, whether successful or not. A large countdown clock displayed the inexorable march towards the release of precision weapons with five-inch red numerals. The results of the strike could go either way, and the communications spin doctors were keeping tabs and updating several press releases in real time.

"Mr. President," exclaimed the Chairman of the Joint Chiefs of Staff. "We've got two unidentified aircraft at 45,000 feet at 500 knots over Iran about to go feet wet in the Gulf. Their electronic profile is consistent with the latest variant of the Bear bombers last known to be in Tehran."

The President stopped his nervous march and took his seat at the end of the polished mahogany table, its smooth surface blemished with access ports for power and data terminals driving multiple laptop computers lined up on its surface.

"Where are they headed?" asked the President, knowing that multiple radars tracked the two aircraft and that regional flight plans, overflight requests, and notifications were being checked by hundreds of uniformed and civilian personnel monitoring the operation now scrambling for the answer.

"We should know based on how they maneuver over Saudi Arabia. They are being tracked by multiple sensors."

"What are our options?" continued the President, who had resumed pacing around the table. An uncomfortable pause quieted the room.

"Yes, options," the President snapped, repeating his question. "I don't want those aircraft mucking up the operation in Yemen. We need more time. Can't we somehow warn them away? Intercept and escort them out of the region?"

"Mr. President, we've got no assets to intercept them," responded the Joint Chiefs of Staff Chairman, a four-star Navy Admiral charged with directing all US military forces as the President's most senior military adviser.

A Marine General wearing a set of headphones suddenly announced, "Central Command reports that Aegis Destroyers in the Persian Gulf are locked on the Bears. Neither aircraft has responded to radio challenges. The ships are preparing to defend themselves under the Rules of Engagement."

"What? Take out a Russian strategic bomber? You're not serious? I don't care what the Rules of Engagement allow. Shut them down! Get the Russian President on the Red Phone, now!" The President barked the command, glaring at those around the table. Despite all its moving parts, President Bowles assessed the event with disarming clarity, understanding that the situation left him very little maneuvering room. His advisers seemed stunned and incapable of focusing like the President could. A misstep here, 1500 miles away from the limited operation in Mocha, might lead to a string of events that would threaten the United States itself.

CHAPTER EIGHTY-SIX

Mocha, Yemen

Arena night seemed to provide a perfect backdrop for a clandestine raid on the compound. Steele had hoped it would cover the actions of his team and certainly didn't expect to become a participant in the festivities. The fighters filled the bleachers, except for the single guard in the operations office and the two men assigned roving patrol duties. No one in the compound would miss this night. Fixed halogen lights attracted swarms of flying bugs and brightly illuminated the fighting field. The contestants limbered up for the ring.

Jack Smith was the youngest member of the Steele's assault team. Selected to be the first combatant, Smith would face an older, well-proportioned Russian fighter whose tattoos were frightening with their dark images of death and destruction. Several of the figures had severed limbs, and the entire black portraiture was grim. Random Cyrillic symbols were added to the areas of skin not covered with scenes of man's endless struggles.

The rules of the fight were not known, but intelligence reports based on the statements of locals who cleaned up the compound after the previous arena nights revealed pools of blood and compound fighters swathed in bandages. Occasionally, there had been a limb broken, but no one was aware that any of the fights had gone to the death, except those against animals. Steele hoped the pattern would be continued.

Except for Smith, the team was sitting, caged in a sturdy wire mesh box about four feet square by eight feet long, located at one of the entrances to the arena, in clear view of the participants and observers, making an escape nearly impossible. None of the cage's support posts budged a millimeter when Steele tested them with his full body weight. The four SEALs just sat on the ground, helpless to carry out their assigned mission and dreading the upcoming bout.

Smith was nervous and ill-prepared for a no-holds-barred fight. He had learned all his fighting skills during SEAL training, conducted with padded pugil sticks and twenty-four-ounce boxing gloves. Tonight, he was paired against a seasoned fighter, rightfully angry with anyone trying to disrupt the sweet deal the Russian outcasts had created in Mocha. While the height and weight of the two fighters was about equal, the experience gap was huge. Smith had no illusions about his ability as he stepped into the ring and faced his opponent. The grim look on his face belied the fear he felt. He was squaring off against an experienced fighter in a bare-knuckled fight that could end his life.

The two fighters sized each other up as they paced in an ever-decreasing circle, closing quickly within an arm's length of each other. The barefooted Russian drew first blood with a vicious kick to Smith's head which sent him to one knee. He followed up with another kick aimed at the young man's head which Smith successfully blocked. He regained his stance and was learning quickly.

Having wrestled in high school, he remembered the low take downs that he would use on a mat, wondering how they might work in this arena. The Russian charged, trying to get close to begin pummeling the SEAL's body. Smith was ready this time and used the Russian's momentum to trip him and take him to the ground. Holding one of his arms at the wrist and with his other arm circling his waist, Smith had the Russian down, using a classic wrestling riding position. But that was the civilized version of the sport. This was brutal combat, and no points were awarded for takedowns or escapes. No one kept a tally. The Russian quickly rolled out of the hold, and both men were back on their feet facing each other.

The compound fighters were cheering their man on, yelling for blood. The Russian charged a second time and caught Smith flat-footed. With a high tackle, he drove him into the ground, sat on his chest and began using his fists on Smith's face as if it were a speed punching bag. Smith covered up and finally got his hands on the man's neck, pushing his chin skyward. His leg snaked around the man's head and pulled him backwards. Both fighters again got to their feet. Smith's face was bleeding heavily, and there was no corner man to stem the flow.

The Russian came in again, this time from the side. Smith slipped his arms around the fighter's neck and applied a traditional headlock, resisting his kidney punches until the man took a sizable bite out of his chest wall that broke the hold. Smith's strength was flagging, but he would never give up.

Unexpectedly, Zlodeyev threw the weighted red flag into the arena and admonished both fighters in a stern voice.

"You are both boring me. I've seen babushkas fight more capably than either of you. Josep, give them each a combat knife."

Smith had never fought with a knife but was certain the Russian was an expert. He'd been fascinated by videos he'd watched on the internet of hand-to-hand combat training of the Alpha group fighters. The knife reminded Smith of the old full tang K-Bar with a thick, hardened carbon steel blade that the SEALs had carried in training.

Smith recalled one of the training sessions where the instructor emphasized the triangle made up of the combatant's two feet and the extended weapon. In a session covering edged weapons, they were taught camming techniques to avoid the stab, slash or thrust using wooden knives. But this was far from a training session, and these were blades designed to incapacitate an opponent.

They warily circled each other, with the Russian making several thrusts to test Smith's defenses and his speed. The Russian found out easily that this type of combat was new to the young man. Smith looked for an opening and found none. He improvised, feeling the weight of the knife and trying to find its balance point. He held the knife by the blade and waited for his opponent to charge. As he did, Smith brought the knife to his shoulder and threw it at the Russian, who raised his arm to block the knife. The knife penetrated the forearm just above the wrist and broke both the radius and ulna as it traveled perpendicularly between the two bones. The Russian fell to his knees, and the red flag landed next to him signaling the end of the fight. Zlodeyev walked into the ring, pulling the knife from the man's broken forearm as he screamed in pain.

"Uri, you fight like a girl. Fight like that again and I'll remove your male parts and use them for fishing." Zlodeyev punctuated his threat by throwing the combat knife into the ground between the man's legs, close to the parts he intended to use for bait. One of the other fighters was a trained medic who stepped into the arena and rendered first aid to the wounded combatant before walking him out.

The victor of the fight, Smith, stood stunned and bleeding several yards from Zlodeyev. The General strode three deliberate paces away from Smith, then stopped and whirled like an overhand major lead fastballer pushing off the rubber to deliver a hundred miles per hour strike. Instead of a baseball, the General held Steele's Ipe knife in his right hand. The knife flashed through the air with blinding speed before entering Smith's neck just below his Adam's apple. The distance and speed of the weapon's travel didn't give Smith's brain a chance to process and to react to the attack. The knife was thrown with such force that it penetrated Smith's neck and severed his spinal cord. He fell backwards and rolled on his side, blood pumping through his neck and pooling on the canvas cover of the arena. The wooden blade could be seen protruding from the back of his neck. The SEAL was dead.

"Take him away and lay him next to Anton. Now we are even for the night."

Steele seethed inside the wire cage, his fingers curled around the wire boxes bending them with pure rage-driven strength. One of his team had been murdered, the mission was close to failure, and there was nothing he could do about it.

Zlodeyev strode to the center of the arena and announced the next match between one of the SEALS and a Russian named Petr, a heavily muscled fighter whose distinguishing physical feature was the matted black hair that covered his body and earned him the nickname 'gorilla man' from his colleagues.

Petr was in excellent physical condition, and he tested his muscles in the weight room every day, stolidly going through an extended routine to keep all his muscle groups tuned up and ready for fighting. While his body hair gave him an animal-like appearance, Gorilla Man ate no red meat and didn't drink or smoke.

Zlodeyev selected Steele as the next fighter. He had been intently studying Gorilla man from the cage. The hirsute vegan's muscle fibers were short, compacted from lifting weights. His flexibility was limited and his limbs did not function over the entire range of natural movement. Steele parried Gorilla man's short powerful punches to his body, moving quickly to get the man off balance and maneuver him to the ground where he applied a submission hold cutting off Petr's air supply. The match was short and decisive. Steele's legs felt as if he were trying to squeeze an iron pipe, and the Gorilla man stubbornly resisted until he blacked out. The red flag hit the canvas at the same time the lights in the stadium and the rest of the compound were extinguished.

CHAPTER EIGHTY-SEVEN

Mocha, Yemen

With the power cut, pandemonium ensued. This was one scenario the Russian fighters had not envisioned. Most were feeling the effects of whatever they were drinking, chewing, smoking or snorting and stumbled out of the arena to arm themselves in the main building. Everyone was on the move.

Steele stole a brief look at the General, who bolted from his seat and headed to one of the entryways spoking off the small amphitheater. Steele made a beeline for the large dog cage where his three teammates were held and slid the door bolt back to free them.

"OK, guys. Head to the well and get the hell out of here. I'm going to follow the General. I'll see you at the rendezvous point. Move."

Steele turned and ran through the darkened arena after the General. The location of the nuclear weapons had been determined by tiny drones flying over the compound and collecting multiple air samples. After several sniffer missions, the scientists pinpointed the low slung, modern stuccoed building matching the exterior of the main facility as the magazine. Steele knew the way without light but was thankful for the full moon that, despite the clouds, lit the compound like it was a late afternoon day.

Certain that the General knew that the arrival of his team and killing the power were preparatory actions prior to a likely assault, Steele wondered whether the General was heading to the building to initiate a regional Armageddon or to escape or maybe both. Perhaps he had his own tunnel leading back into the sea.

Steele was running, the General was walking. He unlocked the door and entered the building. Steele got to the entrance just after the sturdy steel door closed and clicked shut. Steele thought: the General is preparing the weapons for a major blast and the Tomahawk strike is minutes away. Those cruise missiles will land on a target already destroyed and a waterway made unusable for years to come. This mission had stupid written all over it. Despite the voices in his head repeating the word futile, Steele pressed on and needed to go through what appeared to be a reinforced metal door with a very strong lock.

The concrete on the door jamb bulged slightly from the plane of the exterior wall and may have been weakened over time as the chloride in the sand used in the aggregate mixture caused the steel frame to corrode and to expand. Steele found part of a broken concrete stepping stone on the ground and used it as a sledge hammer. After a series of sharp blows, a section of concrete fell out of the door jamb adjacent to the lock. Steele pried open the door and entered the brightly lit bunker not knowing what to expect but ready to disrupt whatever plans the General was setting into motion. He stood in the entryway and listened, hearing the low hum of a generator which provided a separate source of power for the bunker. There were other industrial sounds in the background like pumps whirring to push hydraulic fluid into a heavy ram. Did the generator have the capacity to carry significant electrical loads and detonate the weapons simultaneously?

Steele saw the General at the far end of the room getting into what looked like a space suit. He turned and spotted Steele.

"It appears that I underestimated the boy from the United States."

"Yes, you did. Are you getting dressed for the dance?" Steele's eyes scanned the room looking for how the nuclear-tipped shells were connected to the power source that would initiate the instantaneous chain reaction as they were detonated. How they were able to convert the velocity-based arming mechanism to one that would operate with an electrical charge puzzled the nuclear scientists who had studied the blast and radiation effects of a simultaneous detonation.

"No. I'm getting dressed to leave you and the others and to dodge the Tomahawks that must already be in flight."

Steele glanced away from the General and saw the short snouts of the projectiles standing upright in metal wire racks like soldiers at attention, ready to fight at their master's command.

"When do you plan to detonate the nukes or is the timer already counting down?" Steele asked.

The General laughed. "The nuclear-tipped projectile shells may be detonated and dispersed by your cruise missiles and will carry the gas as far as the wind will take it, all the way up the Red Sea to Mecca where the faithful will take a different trip around the Kaaba. For the first time in my life, I really do understand the meaning of the word deterrent. These weapons have not been wired or set for detonation. But everyone assumes that they have. Now, I need to finish my preparations for departure. Goodbye." He leveled a pistol at Steele as Sergei burst through the doorway and into the room, also carrying a pistol in his hand.

"Sergei. You are just in time," the General roared, "Please put a bullet in our guest's head while I finish preparing."

"Where are you going?" asked Sergei.

"I have a small rocket that will transport me into space, and I will parachute back to the desert far from here."

"Are you taking me with you?" asked Sergei in a trembling voice.

"No, Sergei. I'm sorry but this rocket carries a single person, and I only have one G-suit and oxygen supply.

Sergei took a position at the apex of a small triangle with the General and Steele at the other two points.

"You promised to take me with you."

"I know, I know. You are a great friend and brilliant planner, my son, but options were very limited and your body would not be able to take the punishment of going into space. Now, kill this man so we can discuss your escape."

Sergei took a step forward and pointed the gun at the General. "You promised," he said as he pulled the trigger and the shot reverberated with a sharp bang. The General grasped his side where the bullet impacted his torso with the slug hitting his rib mushrooming into a sharp cutting wheel, following the bone's curve and plowing through the flesh. With the General momentarily distracted, Steele moved towards Sergei and took his gun, taking a bead on the General's head with his arm extended. Only ten feet away, he had a clear shot but so did the General. Dumbstruck, Sergei backed away, watching in silence.

Two men, both looking down the other's gun barrel. The lights shone brightly.

The General held a nine-millimeter parabellum pistol carrying fifteen rounds, and Steele held a small pistol designed to fit into a lady's purse for self-defense. Its heft pointed to a small caliber with a six-shot magazine. But at this range, any well-placed shot would likely be fatal. Steele spoke first, in Russian.

"It could end this way, but wouldn't you prefer to kill me hand to hand? Or perhaps you don't have time. The missiles are already in the air and, if the clock on the wall is accurate, you have about four minutes before they will arrive. Do you have the balls for just one more encounter before leaving? What do you say, General Zlodeyev?

"Your pronunciation is very good. I commend you. You have caused me a great deal of trouble, so it would give me great pleasure to fight you," the General replied. Sergei whimpered on the floor curled into a fetal position, oblivious to the inbound strike that would level the compound and everything in it. The General had broken a promise to the young man. Now he spoke to him directly in the gentle voice of a father addressing his son.

"Sergei, I am very sorry. I do love you like a son, but this is now a man's game and you are not up to the task." He shot Sergei between the eyes and turned back to Steele.

"What is your name, boy?"

"Steele, Dan Steele."

"OK, Mr. Dan Steele, let's put down our weapons, so I can kill you with my bare hands."

CHAPTER EIGHTY-EIGHT

Mocha, Yemen

The two men studied each other before getting close enough to strike. Clearly mismatched, the General outweighed Steele by almost 150 pounds, stood six inches taller and his torso was cut, displaying individual muscle groups seen only in body-building magazines. Naked from his waist up and wearing a girdle-like one-piece G-suit over his legs, the upper part of the suit hung down behind him. The gunshot wound in his side was bleeding profusely. The General seemed to ignore it.

The General's body moved fluidly and, unlike Gorilla man, he had preserved the full range of motion. His sharply defined torso, arms and muscled neck revealed he was in top fighting form, a gladiator with one last fight standing between him and freedom. Veins lay on top of the smooth muscles, pushed to the surface of the skin by their bulk. Connective tissues stood out from the base of his neck like thick ropes holding his head in place. The man lived for violence and combat. The need to defeat his enemies at close quarters was his life's tonic, the center of his satisfaction. Steele needed to keep his invincible opponent fighting until the inbound Tomahawks might make his escape impossible.

For the second time in an hour's time, the General struck first with an organ-crushing punch to the side of Steele's midsection designed to incapacitate him with a single deadly body blow. It too lifted him in the air and propelled him backwards before he landed hard on the concrete floor. Steele got up, searching to find any physical weaknesses in the General's body that might give him an opening. He found none, thinking about a take down and discouraged when viewing the granite pillars swathed in the snug fitting nylon material of the G-suit.

The General pursued and delivered a second blow with Steele backed into a metal shelving unit with particle board shelves. The General's fist missed Steele and slammed into one of its angle iron uprights, bending its frame and shattering the particle board it supported into wood chips, sending splinters in an exploding circle. This fight could not be won by dodging blows. Steele needed to physically weaken the General to buy more time.

Steele swept his leg in a roundhouse kick that landed on the side of the General's knee. It felt as if he'd kicked a granite fence post. There was no reaction. A second punch from the General almost connected as Steele rolled to his left. The General's knuckles clipped him on the side of his head, opening up a gash. He saw stars. Steele needed to prolong the beating as long as he could. The General readied for the kill.

There would be no more dodging. The General calmly walked up to Steele, wrapped his massive arms around his chest and began to squeeze the life out of him. Steele sputtered, expelling the last of the air in his lungs as he felt his back and ribs being compressed. The General's grip tightened as if his arms were an oil-filled hydraulic vise. Two desperate head butts just bloodied the General's nose and chin. Bending his arm that was pinned to his side, Steele strained to grasp the General's exposed rib. It felt like a piece of steel reinforcement bar wet with warm, sticky blood. He pushed his fingertips further into the General's thorax and held the rib, trying to twist it to release the death hold. Steele was losing consciousness, not able to breathe or oxygenate his muscles. There were no pressure points within Steele's reach to incapacitate the General. Nor would his protective muscle sheath permit the access Steele needed to stimulate those nerve junctions.

On the verge of blacking out, Steele entered a state of mind where he could barely feel the crushing grip any longer. The General took a few steps across the floor and slammed Steele on the open wire box holding a dozen artillery shells. The projectile tips were blunt, but Steele felt areas of intense pressure as the General pressed his body into the points. He then pulled another stacked wire box of a dozen shells weighing more than 700 pounds on top of Steele's limp frame, pinning him to the cage between projectile tips like some Hindu worshiper demonstrating his devotion by lying on a bed of nails. Able to breathe again despite the weight on his chest, Steele expected to see the tips of the projectiles peeking through the top of his chest as others were pushing downward through his body.

Satisfied that Steele was pinned in place and going nowhere, Zlodeyev pulled the G-suit over his upper body. The closely woven nylon stemmed the flow of blood from his side, but it still seeped out through the fabric in a widening blotch of bright red. With his remaining strength, Steele struggled to free himself, trying to push the rack of projectiles off his body and move the metal tips that felt like they were gradually piercing his back and chest.

The General's escape craft was an early prototype of the Chinese Dong Feng missile developed by military research scientists as a carrier killer, part of their strategy to control the South China Sea. Only the US Navy's aircraft carriers presented a potential impediment to Chinese domination of that sea's vast expanse. In response, the Chinese military embarked on two specific long-term actions: first, to develop a missile capable of disabling a carrier and neutralizing the devastating power of its air wing and second, to seize the disputed islands and, by dredging and filling, expand the specks of land into fixed forward air bases to reduce reaction time and to permit a multi-front attack force. It had taken years of research and development, aggressive ambition, and diplomatic maneuvering, but both objectives had been accomplished.

Just over thirty feet long and a yard in diameter, the two-stage prototype had been built in the mid-1980s as part of the development and testing period which ended when the rocket entered service in 1991. The sophisticated control system had been replaced by a single board computer programmed to fly 850 miles on a ballistic trajectory before the nose section would separate to reenter the atmosphere, deploying drogue parachutes at 100,000 feet.

Though the current variant of the missile flew a mind-boggling

Mach ten, this version was slower at half the speed. With the flight path programmed and preset to northeast, the only instrument in the craft was an altimeter. As a prototype, everything else had been stripped for reuse in subsequent testing models. The General purchased the prototype for a song from the Chinese. He had the solid fuel remixed and a custom chair installed to accommodate his body. Beyond that, the rocket was less complex than a self-driving car. Open the fuel valves, push the ignition switches, sit back and enjoy the flight.

Steele saw the General climb a short set of metal stairs leading to an access panel near the building's ceiling and duck into the compartment of the rocket, strapping himself into a chair just aft of the nose and closing the access scuttle.

Steele mustered enough residual strength to push the cage off the top of his body, sending the heavy shells scattering across the floor. He rolled off the bed of nails, grabbing the General's gun and blindly emptying the clip into the rocket shell without any apparent effect. There were several sharp clicks as the fuel valves opened. The ignition process began as the room filled with noxious gas.

Acrid superheated exhaust filled the room as Steele stumbled through the open door and fell to the ground. He heard the thunderous roar of the booster and was blinded by the fire lifting the General into space. The fireball created by the liftoff swept through the building and licked at Steele's body as he lay helplessly outside the doorway of the bunker.

Glancing at his watch, Steele knew that there were 90 seconds until the Tomahawks rained down and obliterated the compound. He was cutting things too close. Summoning energy from somewhere deep in his body, Steele stood. Less than two hundred yards separated him from the well. If not injured, he estimated that he'd be in the tunnel before the first Tomahawks slammed into the compound. In his current condition, that estimate seemed way off. Unlike Zlodeyev's bunker, the abandoned well was in the Tomahawk target area. He just hoped that the first missile would not collapse the tunnel and bury him alive. Steele was confident that his teammates were safely floating in the water near the entry point.

Steele moved as quickly as his broken body would allow. The rocket's lift off illuminated the dark compound like a bright sun in a cloudless sky. He ran as fast as he could across the back of the main building. With fifty feet to go, he heard the high-pitched whir of bullets flying past his body. There was no time to jink to complicate someone's aimpoint. He could only push his broken body to hobble unsteadily in a straight line.

CHAPTER EIGHTY-NINE

Mocha, Yemen

A former cosmonaut had told the General that nothing could prepare someone for the raw power of a rocket thrusting into space. Truck-mounted, this variant of the Chinese prototype was built to carry chemical weapons that would be widely dispersed over a battlefield to incapacitate a holding or advancing force within a range of 1,000 miles. The gas container would fall from miles above the target area, and the contents would be released when commanded or at a pre-set altitude that could be programmed based on weather conditions. The Chinese modified the chemical tank to carry a single passenger. The rocket was programmed to propel the General on a ballistic course with a trajectory apogee of 300 miles, followed by a re-entry slowed by two drogue parachutes deployed near the edge of space. At 80,000 feet, Zlodeyev would open the hatch and free fall until opening his own parachute at 3,000 feet.

With no light coming from the ground in Saudi Arabia's Empty Quarter, Zlodeyev would not be able to see his landing zone during the descent, but counted on a soft landing in the miles of sandy hills that were uninhabited and where his return to earth might be witnessed by only the wild camels that traversed its emptiness. His target was where the vast desert joined the unmarked narrow coastal strip of land known as the United Arab Emirates and its larger neighbor, Oman.

Zlodeyev's mind was already concentrating on his future and the persona he would adopt living in the UAE, oblivious to the fact that his small rocket was hurtling into space at almost 3,800 miles per hour. The cosmonaut was correct, the intense power of riding a rocket into space was like nothing the General had ever experienced.

CHAPTER NINETY

Gulf of Aden

"Continue a sector search of the area and stand ready to engage anything that emerges from the shoreline," ordered the Tactical Action Officer on an Aegis Destroyer positioned south in the Gulf of Aden. Pacing behind two console operators glued to their consoles, his watch team was ready. The Captain had already given the TAO the authority to shoot anything that looked like a threat. An Airborne Early Warning aircraft was monitoring a no-fly zone over the area. Intelligence didn't know what conventional weapons might be positioned in the compound to complicate the tactical situation for the carrier operating in the Indian Ocean or the pair of Aegis destroyers teaming up with *Newport* and *Iowa* to keep tabs on the progress of the operation ashore. Other Tomahawk-equipped ships in the Mediterranean Sea and Persian Gulf had just contributed their own cruise missiles to the massive strike that would obliterate the compound. Precision strike was critical to avoid the hell that could be unintentionally unleashed if one of the missiles were to stray from its intended flight path.

Anticipating that the standoff in Yemen might end with an attack on the compound, complete with naval forces that had the capability to shoot down a missile, the General had purchased several self-propelled directional flares that would confuse the radar operators as well as any heat seeking surface-to-air missiles that might be launched to bring down his escape craft. Within seconds of launch, once sufficient thrust was developed by the rocket, Zlodeyev's flight should have enough velocity to evade most surface-to-air weapons. That was the theory. But those first few seconds were critical to his survival. He was alone and headed skyward, being pushed by a massive first stage booster.

Suddenly, something separated from the land mass painted by the surface radar's constant pulses. Whatever it was, it was moving up very fast. The watch team on the ship's bridge saw the sky brighten and what appeared to be a missile and its plume a second before it was detected and already in track by the phased array Aegis Weapons system, a system developed to counter the barrage of deadly cruise missiles that the Soviet Union had deployed while the US Navy seemed fixated on the pipe dream of a 600 ship Navy and introducing new uniform styles. Jolted out of its reverie in the late 1970s, the Navy had been playing catch-up until the US defense spending buried the USSR and ended the Cold War. The Aegis system was a major outgrowth of that defense rebuilding effort and one of its most successful achievements.

The TAO did not hesitate. "Take track B01."

Armored hatches opened on the ship's deck as a pair of Standard Missiles emerged from the vertical launch tubes, engulfing the bridge in a cloud of smoke from the launcher and the white-hot flames from the two-stage, solid-fuel rocket booster, enabling an intercept speed of 2,600 miles per hour.

Milliseconds later the operator reported, "Birds away."

The nimble missiles were on their way to a deadly intercept, closing the lateral distance of twenty-five miles between the ship and shoreline launch point while moving skyward to meet the rocket on its flight path. Zlodeyev's rocket was headed straight up from its launch point, putting the interceptors in a tail chase. The missiles needed to be very close to activate the proximity fuse for its fragmentation warhead to disable the control surfaces, making it impossible for an enemy missile to continue along the intended flight path. Zlodeyev's rocket reached its maximum thrust in seconds, screaming toward space at five times the speed of sound.

Today's Standard Missile performed its surface-to-air mission with great effectiveness against closing targets at any speed, less capably with crossing targets, and poorly in a tail chase. Zlodeyev's rocket shot straight up at a speed of 3,800 miles per hour, giving it a speed advantage over the closing interceptors of over 1,200 miles per hour. The geometry just wouldn't work. The radar operator reported that the distance to target intercept was increasing, not decreasing. Likewise, the time to intercept was also increasing. The engagement was over in seconds. The ships carrying the missiles capable of engaging Zlodeyev's craft were stationed in the Persian Gulf as part of a layered regional defense.

The TAO had no idea where the rocket was heading or what its payload might be. It could be an anti-ship cruise missile or something else. Within seconds, the ship's Combat Direction Center confirmed that firing a third missile would prove futile. Aegis continued to track the missile and to feed the information into the systems that monitor launches all over the world. Satellites detected the missile launch immediately with infrared sensors and automatically sent missile warning alerts through the elaborate command and control network designed to protect the United States from a ballistic missile attack originating from anywhere on the planet.

Multiple ideas flooded through the TAO's mind at once. As the cross section diminished with altitude, other operators were alerted, including Patriot units in Saudi Arabia and THAAD batteries in the UAE. The Russian Federation was also alerted. Zlodeyev's rocket was tracked by several sensors during its brief flight of less than twelve minutes. The radars and other sensors following Zlodeyev reported that the rocket simply disappeared over the vast void of the Empty Quarter.

CHAPTER NINETY-ONE

Mocha, Yemen

When the team's path into the compound had been discovered, two five-gallon cans of gasoline were emptied on the rubble at the bottom of the well and ignited as a short-term fix until the entry point could be permanently destroyed. Just ten feet from the well, one of the fighter's bullets found its mark and shattered Steele's left elbow. He never broke stride, launching himself head first over the exterior wall into the well. Its open mouth was pitch black and still filled with smoke, and he could see the glow of charred debris covering its bottom on his flight downward. He heard other rounds hit the wall's side and knew that the fighters would be making the inside of the well a killing zone in seconds. He was out of time, but hoped he had a little residual luck left.

After the hard landing at the juncture of the well's interior wall and the edge of something with the hot dull red look of charcoal, Steele could hear the whine of Tomahawks screaming towards the compound. He felt the jarring impact and heard the deafening explosion as the first Tomahawk hit the ground. The Tomahawks would fly various paths and profiles. Strike planners would schedule a near simultaneous time on target to overwhelm any unknown defenses the compound might have such as short-range surface-to-air missiles. The latest intelligence estimates assessed the probability as very low so the Tomahawks were expected to reach their targets unscathed. Of course, this was the same intelligence apparatus that missed the minor detail of a large rocket and its erector-launcher buried on the compound for the General's escape.

Steele found the tunnel's mouth and pulled himself along the narrow passage with his arms and legs as the earth began to shake from the impact and detonations of the high explosive payloads hitting the compound. The inside of the tunnel was dry, its diameter restricting the full use of Steele's arms and legs, and reducing his progress to advance only a foot or so at a time. The going would be tough for one hundred and forty feet until he reached the underwater section of the tunnel.

Steele soon had his arms in the water. His left arm throbbed with excruciating pain from the gunshot wound. There was no time to take a personal inventory of his condition. Without thinking, he inhaled a series of long painful breaths to oxygenate his lungs, though the life-sustaining oxygen in the tunnel had been mostly depleted. His lungs felt like they were only partially filling with air. Second thoughts. Maybe they should have considered moving out across the beach. There was intelligence that sections of the beach had been mined, and any attempt to cross them might have proved fatal. But this escape route was far from optimum. Each Tomahawk hitting the compound shook the ground inside the tunnel and Steele wondered how much abuse the thin nanotube fabric could take while supporting the weight of the shifting ground above. How long an underwater swim could he make? Would he enter that warm black water with the same conviction that he could emerge on the other side?

The tunnel's diameter did not permit him to take long strokes to efficiently cover distance. Kicking and using his hands to scoop the water past his body in short pulls, he tried to remember exactly how far a swim this would be and recalled it was eighty feet. And then another thirty-five feet to the surface. Not a problem in a controlled training situation, but with the injuries racking his body, and the possibility that one of Zlodeyev's fighters might follow him, maybe more difficult.

SEALs knew what drowning was like. None of them wanted to die that way. They'd all been trained to do everything they could to prevent it. Steele hoped that he could pull his damaged body out the other end. It would be the longest swim of his life.

After perhaps a minute of slow progress in the water-filled tunnel, Steele felt a large part of the top of the tunnel cave-in. It felt like a large scoop of loam from a front-end loader had been dropped on his back, almost expelling the air from his lungs. With the additional weight, he pulled himself through the muddy sediment in total darkness, uncertain if he were making any forward progress or not. He thought there might be a breath of air left against the top of the tunnel where the earth was loosened by the explosions and pressed his lips upwards. He felt the soil, but it was saturated with water and he resisted the urge to try to pull in some air. The cavity had already filled with seawater so there was no relief.

He felt a film of the muddy ooze on his lips, trying to find the air-filled cavity of his mouth and lungs. Pulling himself through the thickening mud in the tunnel, he hoped that another cave in would not occur. Scraping his back along the top of the fabric tunnel enabled him to move along more efficiently. In his tortured mind, the total darkness in the narrow water-filled tunnel that seemed to be narrowing was terrifying. The only upside to his inability to orient himself was that he could not turn around.

Steele continued on with his lungs ready to burst with the time he'd held his breath. With no illusions about his chances for survival, he controlled his body as he could but knew he would be very lucky to make it through the rest of the tunnel and into open water. What about the first part of the tunnel prone to cave-in? Maybe his escape route had already been closed. The muddy water thickened into a viscous molasses. Pulling himself forward automatically, Steele had no idea how far he'd traveled or how far he had to go. Now oblivious to his injuries, and with his brain dying from lack of oxygen, his arms and legs moved instinctively, spurred on by the strong will to survive.

When he finally reached open water, it didn't register immediately. He continued swimming in the pipe but now realized that the constraints on his body were no longer there. He kicked hard, pulling his freed arms with full strokes towards the surface. A breath of fresh air was the only thought on his mind.

CHAPTER NINETY-TWO

Arabian Peninsula

After liftoff, the General's body was pushed with inconceivable force into the padded chair. Before that moment, he thought of gravitational forces as largely theoretical musings of mechanical engineers. He felt like a barbell weighing several tons had been dropped onto his chest, and he couldn't move it. Except this barbell was different. It pressed down on every part of his body at once. The G-suit fit like a protective girdle, compressing the veins in his arms and legs to stop his blood from pooling in his extremities so that he would not black out.

There was no viewing port for the General to see the rubbled compound burning or the rapidly disappearing landmass behind him. Filling his lungs and smiling with self-satisfaction, he breathed the gas mixture slowly, confident that he'd outsmarted his pursuers once again. He felt god-like, powerful and free.

The Chinese rocket had been modified to his simple specifications and delivered months before to their new naval base in Djibouti. Transported to the compound, it was placed in a concrete silo poured on site to house the missile's erector that had been removed from its truck mounts and anchored to large concrete pads in a trench alongside the bunker. The missile was elevated to its firing position by hydraulic erectors whose motors were connected to the bunker's generator-powered distribution system.

The General had been surprised at how easily the entire system had been to install, connect, and test. Just plug and play, including all the diagnostics. It worked the first time, right out of the box. There was no doubt that the Chinese would become the dominant power on earth in the future, he thought. It was just a matter of time. Zlodeyev had considered a large balloon for the escape but ruled it out because of the time it would take to inflate and the ease at which it could become a target for the ships that he expected to be patrolling the Red Sea and the Gulf of Aden.

The trip to the rocket's apogee of 300 miles above the Earth's surface would take just under seven minutes. From there, the rocket would continue along the trajectory until the payload separated and deployed large drogue parachutes to slow the craft in the thin air. Once below 80,000 feet, Zlodeyev would open the hatch and begin his descent, free falling through the icy atmosphere for several minutes at nearly the speed of sound before deploying a parachute for the final drop to the desert floor, landing on the windswept sand hills from which he would continue the journey to the sparsely inhabited inland towns of the UAE. His travel kit included a hand-held GPS receiver, a sleeve of gold coins, a first aid kit, and enough high protein energy bars and fluids for four days. He looked forward to a new life of luxury beyond the reach of those who wanted him dead.

The G-suit's thermal layer was designed to protect Zlodeyev from the frigid temperatures, and he was also plugged into a high-pressure miniature breathing flask. Unlike the recent record-setting sky dives from nearly 150,000 feet, the General did not have the luxury of a controlled ascent by a balloon nor a ground team to monitor his flight. This was a barebones operation, the initial phase of an escape that would test his ability and will to survive.

Zlodeyev had no intention of losing his freedom. He expected to relocate in a place where he could live richly and quietly, until another venture landed on his doorstep.

CHAPTER NINETY-THREE

Mocha, Yemen

Floating on their backs in the warm water with a front row seat as the last of the Tomahawks impacted the target area, the three remaining members of the team saw the explosions rock the compound. The blasts generated mini-tsunamis on the still water by vibrating the porous soil and shaking the shoreline. The SEAL assigned to cut off the generator set had not returned. Neither had Dan Steele. None of them talked. There was nothing they could do. Trying to dive down into the inky black water to find the tunnel entrance would be next to impossible. As the minutes ticked by, their worst fears mounted. It would be another gut-wrenching duty to bury their own. Suddenly, a small geyser erupted nearby as something broke the surface of the water. The team quickly swam to their teammate's side, helping him tread water. He was hyperventilating, taking in air in uncontrollable spasms. Every inhalation left him wincing in pain, but he was happy to still be feeling it.

"Did everyone make it?" he asked.

"We haven't seen Goody yet," replied one of the men.

"Dammit," said Steele, "He should have been the first one here."

Iowa proceeded slowly from its operating position to recover the SEALs. Nothing had been heard from the team since the signal confirming that they were inside the compound. The ship launched both RHIBs and its helicopter to search the water near the tunnel entry point. Other teams were getting ready to move ashore after mine clearance that would begin at dawn. Once the weapons experts deemed it safe, a larger group of Explosive Ordnance Disposal technicians, forensic investigators and medical personnel would be landed to start the grim work of collecting whatever was left of the fighters that had been scattered in a thousand pieces. Drones were already sampling the air above the compound to determine if anything other than high explosive residue was present. Marines in full exposure suits blocked the roadway to prevent the curious from getting close to the compound.

The helicopter found the team with its searchlight and directed the closest RHIB to recover them. Once aboard the RHIB, Steele insisted that the search continue for the missing SEAL. Both RHIBs and the helicopter searched the waters offshore without finding any sign of the missing SEAL. He could not be located. Finally, Steele's physical condition forced the team to return to *Iowa*. A rigid basket stretcher was lowered to the boat, and Steele was hoisted aboard while the other RHIB and helicopter continued the search. Steele was unconscious when the stretcher landed on the ship's deck.

Iowa's Commanding Officer sent a message to the naval task force participating in the strike confirming that what was left of the SEAL team had been recovered. One of them was dead and one still missing. When Sydney Garrison saw the message, her heart stopped. *Newport* had safely retreated from the torpedo firing point into deeper water and was operating at a depth of 250 feet, well away from the launch point, standing by to assist if required.

Based on Steele's life-threatening injuries, *Iowa* was detached from the naval task force immediately. The ship recovered both RHIBs and the helicopter, cranked up her four gas-turbine engines to full power and screamed past the hulk of *Shackleton* towards Jeddah, Saudi Arabia.

At dawn, most of the combatant elements of the strike group were ordered to proceed on duty assigned which in *Newport's* case meant to begin the transit through the Red Sea and the Suez Canal and across the Mediterranean Sea to the submarine's home port of Gaeta, Italy, sixty miles north of Naples. A large amphibious ship with helicopters, embarked Marines and an Explosive Ordnance Disposal detachment would assume duties as the on-scene commander. A cadre of nuclear weapons experts was ready to move ashore to make an assessment after a safe path to the bunker was marked.

Garrison waited for what seemed to her like an eternity before sending a private message to *Iowa's* Commanding Officer asking him to identify which of the SEALS was dead and who was still missing. Hours later, his response identified the missing SEAL as Michael Goodman. The dead SEAL was named Smith. Her heart mourned the death and likely loss of two of the SEALs she had transported to Mocha but, at the same time, lifted knowing that Dan Steele was still alive.

CHAPTER NINETY-FOUR

Red Sea

It was nearly midnight when Steele was carried into the ship's cramped sickbay. Steele awoke feeling dizzy and had lost track of time. The Corpsman on USS *Iowa* — a boyish looking petty officer with a shaved head and shirt sleeve tattoos found that three of the artillery shells had punctured his back, two others his chest wall, crushing the tissue and opening up his body to infection. Internal and external stitches were needed to close the wounds. His shattered left elbow was cleaned and his arm splinted. After being administered a heavy dose of antibiotics, the ship's helicopter flew Steele to Jeddah where a C-141 transport aircraft outfitted as a field hospital was parked to evacuate those wounded in the operation.

The medical team aboard the aircraft came well-equipped and fully staffed. With a dangerously elevated white count, Steele was flown straight to the US military hospital in Frankfurt, Germany, equipped with CAT scan equipment. Steele slipped in and out of consciousness during the five-hour flight, and the physicians were concerned about unseen internal injuries which made his condition beyond critical.

In Germany, he was rushed across the airfield into the base hospital where the field hospital physicians' suspicions were confirmed. X-rays showed three broken ribs and a likely hemorrhaging vertebral vein. CAT scans were done on every part of his broken body which revealed punctures to the peritoneum.

The runaway infection did not immediately respond to the big gun antibiotics the doctors administered with an intravenous drip. He also had blood in his urine which signaled internal injuries that might require some specialized surgery. For the time being, he was kept sedated and constantly pumped with IV fluids with a range of infection-killing antibiotics. Surgery on his left elbow would have to wait. The risk of losing Steele on the operating table was too high. Monitors tracked his vitals in an isolated ward designed to prevent the spread of any biologic contagion. Steele was fighting for his life.

He emerged from his coma after 24 hours in the intensive care unit. Surrounded by a bevy of white-coated physicians curious to see the patient, the attending doctor rattled off a lengthy laundry list of Steele's injuries. His description elicited a reaction as if the group were medical school students observing their first autopsy. Steele was conscious and aware of the doctor's voice but could not compute the physical danger he was in. Stubbornly clinging to life, it would be some time before he got out of the woods, if at all. It was still touch and go. Otherwise, he felt great.

CHAPTER NINETY-FIVE

Bethesda, Maryland

Seventy-two hours blurred by. Steele found himself back in familiar surroundings at the Walter Reed National Military Medical Center in Bethesda, Maryland. There he'd been greeted by his Pisces colleagues and even visited by the doctor who'd treated his wounds eighteen months ago. During the day, he was able to see visitors for an hour but remained in a medical trance which caused him to drift off in the middle of conversations. His prognosis was upgraded to guarded.

After several more days, the tide finally turned. Steele's condition improved and the fog lifted from his brain. His body's vital signs indicated a strong immune system that could take over for the medication that had kept him alive. Most important, his brain returned to normal. Able to walk the floors of the facility on his own, he was looking forward to his discharge and some real food. Cass brought him a tablet computer, and he finally got around to opening his email. He quickly scanned an overflowing mailbox jammed with several hundred messages. Two messages caught his eye. The older one was from Terry Bullard in Sana'a.

Heard you took an awful beating and hope you recover quickly. Target destroyed and conventional cleanup continues. Missing items successfully recovered. Look forward to connecting with you soon. When is your next trip to the garden spot of the Arabian Peninsula? I'll be here for a few more months before leaving for the last time. Take care. All the best, Terry

The second message was from USS *Newport* written days before.

Dan, arrived home just in time for Christmas. I'm told you are out of the woods and recovering. Good news! I plan to take a week off in the New Year. Why don't you meet me in Rome so we can do some sightseeing and continue the conversation we never finished? With love, S.G.

Steele responded with stone fingers on the small keyboard:

Sydney, I am on the road to recovery and would like that. Expect to be discharged later this week and will try to get medically cleared for an overseas flight. That will be the long pole. I look forward to continuing our conversation and exploring some other areas of mutual interest. This will be a long, slow journey. Looking forward to seeing you in Roma. Dan

CHAPTER NINETY-SIX

The civilized world had dodged the bullet just in time for the Holidays. Interest in the clean-up waned quickly from the news, and people gradually forgot about the powder keg that had been brought to Yemen with the power to change the course of world events in such an ugly way. Following mine clearance operations which discovered and cleared numerous areas seeded with mines which were also liberated from Russian stocks, an allied team wearing exposure suits and respirators began the process of collecting the special weapons from the General's lair.

Sergei was discovered on the floor, his dark hair singed off by the blast when the General lifted off into space but otherwise untouched by the Tomahawks that destroyed the compound. Exposed to the superheated exhaust gases of the rocket's plume, the shells remained intact, though several rounds were found scattered across the floor. The stability of the propellant was questionable and made handling more dangerous. They would be transported back to the United States to a specialized plant in Texas for disassembly in a deep underground bunker. Any nuclear material would be burned and then recycled and sold to nuclear power plants.

After several small samples were secured for further analysis, the chemical weapons were transformed into an inert jelly. The drums would also be transported to a secure site in Europe for further disposal. All the clean-up was conducted in a painstakingly methodical manner to minimize the risk of exposing the local population. Forensic work was a secondary effort which proceeded in parallel, but the destruction was so complete that little was left of the former seaside resort or its inhabitants. The perpetually paranoid Russians volunteered to help with the clean-up and disposal operation but were politely refused. They were in no position to make a scene over the reaction to their offer of help.

The Western powers took credit for securing the terrible weapons that had held the world hostage. All the military services were involved in the raid and clean-up and were pleased that their contributions were evenly divided to ensure a level playing field when the budget battles would begin.

Shipping lines were once again plying the waters with nothing more to worry about than the weather and uncertainty of labor in the ports of call on either side of the Suez. The fate of the container ship *Ernest H. Shackleton* was still being debated and would likely be settled in the courts. The fuel tanks had been hot-tapped using a submersible, and the environmental threat had been neutralized. Questions still remained about what to do with the hull. One proposal suggested cutting away the first 600 feet of the ship to be re-used on another hull. The other half of the ship lay deep underwater and probably would be scrapped. The northbound transit lane had been shifted to the west allowing mariners to safely navigate around the ship. Thousands of containers carried by *Shackleton* covered the bottom of the deep channel.

Forlorn Yemen returned to its continued state of internal civil war and the threat of further bombing led by their Saudi-allied neighbors in the Middle East. Life remained at its short, brutish level in the poor country with the humanitarian situation a true crisis by anyone's standard. A recent invasion of locusts postponed the death of many children benefitting from the uptick in their protein intake.

Newspapers were dissecting the events in Yemen in colorful timelines designed to keep their graphic artists on Staff and justifying more correspondents reporting from the field.

The regime in Moscow faltered but regained its former strength after a purge of its military and execution of a number of high-ranking officials responsible for safeguarding the weapons of mass destruction. The Red Phone exchange between President Bowles and his Russian counterpart changed the relationship between the two and led to an unprecedented level of respect and trust. Over his own advisers' objections, the Russian President recalled the Bear bombers over Saudi Arabia before they reached the Red Sea, averting another crisis.

The question on everyone's mind was Zlodeyev's whereabouts. Numerous stories danced on the pages of the tabloids revealing Zlodeyev alone had survived the attack by escaping on a rocket last seen going straight up to the heavens. One reporter suggested that he'd rendezvoused with an alien spaceship and had relocated to another galaxy. Most people assumed that his escape had failed and that he'd died in the rocket or in the vast desert of Saudi Arabia, aptly called the Empty Quarter. With help from the Saudi regime, Federation teams were sent into the desert to look for anything that would point to a safe landing and escape but if anything remained, it was quickly covered by the tons of windblown sand that changed the landscape daily. The 250,000 square miles of desert could hide a needle very well. There had been reports of a large white man walking out of the desert now living in a small border town in the UAE that the government was trying to populate.

Though the details of the SEAL raid were never publicly revealed, the story seeped out slowly within the teams, pieced together from comments made by the participants themselves or the people supporting the operation. *Newport's* crew kept their mouths shut for the most part, and no one asked where they'd been. But gradually, the story of the high-risk torpedo insertion, the bizarre fights in the arena and the daring attempt to secure the weapons, were woven together to become the conversation of the special operations community.

The same special operations family also mourned the loss of two of their own. The SEAL cutting the compound's power became the hero of the operation because of his selfless sacrifice. Michael Goodman's body was never found. He was carried on the rolls as missing in action, presumed dead. Jack Smith, killed by Zlodeyev's own hand, was memorialized with a change to the SEAL's training regimen which now allocated additional instruction in hand-to-hand combat including fighting with edged weapons.

After providing critical intelligence details about the compound's defenses and the operation and control of the stolen Quickstrike mines, Richie Bouffard offered little further value to the CIA. There had been a concerted effort to study the feasibility of re-purposing Richie for other Agency business, but his unpredictability proved to be too much of a liability for independent work in the field. He was convicted on a number of charges and incarcerated in a Federal prison while awaiting sentencing.

Emma Bolden's place in the sun was short-lived, but her consistent, reasoned reporting over the long term, including breaking the Zlodeyev trial and escape story, earned her a Sunday morning international news hour show for an American network. This was just what she wanted and provided some of the perquisites she'd worked so hard to attain.

Steele's wife, Jill, and the couple's two young sons were unaffected by the turmoil of the events in Yemen. All three lay peacefully in the ground not far from her parents' home in the Point section of Newport, Rhode Island. Jill's parents visited the grave site each Sunday, remembering their daughter who had brightened the earth for too few years, and the two boys, full of laughter and mischief, whose lives were cut short by a crazy man to whom the loss of innocent life meant nothing. It was merely collateral damage. Jill's father and mother had no idea where Dan Steele was or when he would come visit again, but they knew his daily labors were tied to those three bodies in the ground doing whatever he could to prevent the spread of evil to the United States.

CHAPTER NINETY-SEVEN

Dulles International Airport, Virginia

Steele sat by himself on a blue seat in a row of eight in the waiting area watching people flowing by the gate. While still uncertain about the path he was taking by flying to Italy to see Sydney Garrison, it was something he had to do for his own mental health. He had found peace with the decision and was ready for whatever might happen. At thirty years of age, he was still several years younger than she was. But, during his SEAL days and certainly for the past three years, he had repeatedly been put through the wringer and did not have the same level of energy. He felt perpetually tired.

Without a timetable, milestones and with no need to throw caution to the wind, he would just let it play out slowly, letting Sydney know he needed time. This was different than his relationship with Jill, so natural and uncomplicated. All he could do was face each day honestly, treat Sydney with respect and see if something good could materialize for both of them. When you boiled it all down, wasn't that simply what everyone wanted?

He smiled, slung his bag over his shoulder and walked confidently to the gate, ready to board the plane and fly into his future.

ABOUT THE AUTHOR

John P. Morse's novels are set in the near future, drawing heavily on his Navy career as a surface warfare officer serving on six combatant ships, two afloat staffs, and ashore in the Middle East. He deployed in all oceans of the world and commanded two combatant ships. Parts of his military service record still remain classified. After retiring from the US Navy, he worked for a large defense contractor for 16 years developing both domestic and international business. His widely acclaimed first novel, *Half Staff 2018*, introduced his principal protagonist, Dan Steele. He has written multiple articles and book reviews for professional journals, newspapers, and literary magazines. An accomplished diver, his world-wide diving experiences are reflected in Steele's underwater adventures. He and his wife, Carole, divide their time between southern New Jersey and southeastern Massachusetts.

www.johnpmorse.com

71833137R00217

Made in the
USA
Middletown, DE